# Montana Gold

Wings Press, Inc.

**Charles McRaven**

# Montana Gold

**Charles McRaven**

**A Wings ePress, Inc.**
Adventure, Mystery, Romance Novel

# Wings ePress, Inc.

Edited by: Jeanne Smith
Copy Edited by: Brian Hatfield
Executive Editor: Jeanne Smith
Cover Artist: Trisha FitzGerald-Jung
Images: Pixabay and Author



Wings ePress Books
www.wingsepress.com

Copyright © 2024 by: Charles McRaven
ISBN 979-8-89197-987-1

Published In the United States Of America

Wings ePress, Inc.
3000 N. Rock Road
Newton, KS 67114

# *Dedication*

For the Western contingent of our family: Chelsea, Dennis, Saoirse, Cormac

# One

The rumble of the diesel in the old Land Rover pickup ceased with its customary last-compression shudder, and I felt my shoulders relax. It had been a long, winding journey across a lot of America in the slow-moving vehicle, on secondary highways. Lots of camping, lots of looking at potential places to settle.

Too many miles.

But I was here, now: Missoula, Montana, the town that'd maybe been in my subconscious all along. And it was 1974 and everything was possible. Town maybe turn out to be less than it'd been cracked up to be, but this country so far had pretty much blown me away. After the sameness of prairie finally gave way to the mountains.

I'd managed to fish the north fork of the storied Blackfoot River on the way yesterday—had caught nothing—and slipped off the highway up yet another overgrown road to sleep in the truck camper cap I'd built. After the endless miles of North Dakota and eastern Montana, this place looked a lot like heaven should.

That camp-out had been a little weird. I'd awakened there in my pine grove hideaway to the sound of voices in the distance, seen a light. This place was empty, had a 'for sale' sign on it, which was why I'd chosen it: privacy. But somebody was out there doing something, middle of the night. At least two somebodies.

So, being naturally curious, I threw on clothes, boots, and slipped closer to see what this was all about. Saw two guys digging by flashlight. *Digging? Now, just whatthehell...* Then one of them filled a glass jar with soil, stuck a label on it. Then they filled the hole, which was a deep one, moved off a hundred yards, dug again.

Okay, getting soil samples: mystery solved. But why now? Couldn't wait for daylight? Or maybe didn't want anybody to know they were there. Strange.

But not my business: I'd gone back to the Rover, back to sleep.

~ * ~

I was close to broke. The job I'd landed those weeks after graduation from the little work-for-tuition college in southwest Missouri had been short duration. Stonework, and I had the basic tools with me. And yeah, I'd worked in the carpentry shop there the four years, had a Skilsaw, drill and toolbelt-full. I should survive.

I didn't fool myself my liberal arts degree in history would open any doors to the fabled good life, and that was just the half of it: I'd vowed never to let myself become a time-clock puncher for anybody's corporation if I could avoid it. Be my own boss.

Uncle who'd taught me masonry had pretty well nailed it:

"Work for th' other man, Harlan, he's payin' you less so he c'n make his off yer back. Work for y'self, y'get it all." Wasn't that simple, of course, but that was the way young Harlan Kemp would go.

Same uncle had left me the Rover, with some more advice:

"Thing'll be worth more th' older it gets, so try t'hang onto it long's y'can. Don't push it, 'twon't hardly ever wear out."

I hadn't pushed it. And yeah, a lotta guys had eyed the rig as I chugged by them. More so since that outfit in England had stopped exporting them to the U.S. just that year. The '59 Series II was already almost an antique, or at least rare. And it wouldn't pass the emission standards newly imposed on imports.

Actually, it was more the U.S. powers-that-be slamming restrictions on foreign stuff to protect our Detroit iron. The System: same setup I was out to dodge, best I could.

So I got coffee and pie and picked up a copy of the Missoula newspaper to get a feel for the place. Already'd seen all the bicycles and cute little specialty shops, and yeah, this *was* a college town. A real one.

Late June, so long-legged girls in shorts, hairy guys in tee shirts, lotsa young people. Like me. Place didn't look like a Western town, but of course that's just a stereotype.

Paper full of ads: psychics, self-help, yoga studios. Nothing much in the employment columns, but I knew most jobs don't get listed there. Or even at the employment office. Hey, I'd been preparing for this.

So I'd start cold, maybe cruise around the edges of town, see what was building. All these people, it had to be happening.

I was a bit surprised to see so many little houses. Poor folks? Surely not—university had to be paying a lotta people. I drove north up Rattlesnake Creek and things got more upscale. Bad stonework, though, of the round creek stones that mean too much mortar and the idea somebody threw them at a wall and they stuck.

I'd passed a hillside quarry not far upstream along the Blackfoot from where it joins the Clark Fork River. There was no excuse for not using that good ledge quartzite stone around here.

Except incompetence. But I hadn't seen much stonework back in town, either. No demand then?

So carpentry, it looked like, and probably a dozen guys trying for every job. But Uncle John had also told me that every foreman wishes for one more good hand, even if he can't get the owner to hire him. "That lets him fire th' slowest dude," he'd pointed out.

Maybe.

Third day of burning fuel and camping out, this gangly girl who worked at a grocery store back the way I'd come told me I might score a helper job with a big company putting up apartment buildings toward town. Grunt job, but maybe something'd break and I could move up, get it later. Didn't pay much, and I'd seen what rent was, this town people liked to come to. *Okay, stay at the campground a little longer, ask around, see if maybe out one of the highways places to live are better.*

I *had* seen a few big new hilltop houses out a few miles, so somebody was putting them up. I'd also heard the best time to get a job was when you already had one. Maybe less air of desperation evident or something.

But I didn't wanta work for anybody else, soon's I got a lead on something, preferably stonework. Had to keep reminding myself of that goal.

Got the job, probably because nobody else could afford to live on the wage. Lotta wheelbarrow work, moving things for other guys. *But just be patient, Kemp, it'll happen.*

Boss subcontracted out this thin, stick-on stone veneer on parts of these buildings, to a one-man masonry company. Guy named Tony, told me he hated this postage-stamp work, but it paid well and there was lots of it.

"Know of anything real, by any chance?"

"Well, there's this guy down close to Stevensville, building a timberframe for himself. Wants stone, but he's cheap. Got some fair stone collected, but I just can't gear down to what he can pay, or wait around till he's ready. You do rocks, then?"

"Some. Wouldn't wanta shoot you down on it, but I'd like to check that out, okay?"

"Sure, but like I told you, he's stretched thin, been on that job a couple years already, weekends mostly, and when he can scrape the bucks. But yeah, you got no family, overhead, you could prob'ly hit it a few days at a time, maybe find somethin' else along." He was slamming the random shapes on, covering square feet like a machine.

'Lick-'em-and-stick-'em,' Uncle John had called this work, and he'd refused to do it for anyone, no matter it was quick and easy. "No way that's stonework, boy," he'd spat. Independent cuss, and of course, growing up he'd been my idea of a real man.

My own father hadn't made it back from Vietnam, and Mom had eventually married a—get this—*librarian*. Guy had this city job, stayed indoors all the time, clung to that low-pay cog in the world's wheel, afraid to let go. Guess Mom needed stability. No brothers or sisters, and no, Lester and I didn't get along. That's why I'd stayed and worked with Uncle John a couple years before going to college. Took me a long time to close the hole Dad left in me, and I sorta dropped out.

And face it, I guess I never got along that well with anyone, looking back. Usually odd-man-out, and rarely dated in college. Mostly dumpy girls not quite able to conceal the desperation in their eyes. You hadda be poor to get into that school, and there was an air of 'loser' about the place. The professors seemed the kind couldn't get into top faculties, and most of the grads ended up coaching backwoods high school sports, teaching other non-achievers, or just finding mates. Like themselves.

But not to criticize. Here I was, loner, nobody's idea of a success, and not giving a healthy damn what people thought. Liked to think I had choices, though, even at the bottom of the stack.

~ * ~

Kay stacked groceries on their respective shelves when she wasn't at the check-out counter. Small place, and Mrs. Hall needed her, arthritic as she'd gotten. But this was definitely still just a baby step to whatever was supposed to come next.

This thing with Ron wasn't going anywhere, apparently. He was the least motivated creature taking up space on the planet, and lately it seemed they got together only at the gates of screaming boredom.

And then bored each other.

Kay wasn't the first girl the boys asked to the prom. Or even the one they settled for after the homecoming queen'd turned them down. Hell, she'd never even gone to a prom, and still told herself she hadn't missed a thing.

She'd earned a good degree here at U.M. in biology, was waiting for hits on her submitted **résumé**, marking time. Problem was, nobody in this end of the world seemed to want to hire biologists.

So, a year out of college, here she was still at Hall's Grocery, out on the highway that followed the Clark Fork River down from the high country. Living in an oversized closet-room in her boss's house next door for the fourth year now.

Kay was 5'11" and had grown lean and hard on her parents' ranch out of Ovando, 50 miles up Hwy 200. And they wanted her back, now the boys had married and moved away. But that'd mean going back to where she'd started; it'd mean these years, this study, this learning to be her own woman all would amount to zilch.

And—shudder—it might even mean reverting to the old conviction that ugly Kay McBryde didn't deserve better. That she'd be lucky to trap Ron into marriage, shoehorn him into the family's life, where he'd just vegetate, a bewildered blob, with his perpetually surprised eyes really astonished.

No.

Graduate work in medicine was a possibility, but she'd just paid off the student loans. And really, no taste for more insulated-from-the-world classrooms. There was a life out there, had to be. Not Disney ending/beginning with bluebirds and ribbons and smiles, but at least some sense of...*place,* maybe? Worth?

Oh, it'd happen. Law of averages said some sleazy little shoestring company with a smattering of research contracts would call. Sometime. Which would mean stifling herself in someplace like Iowa. Or Detroit or Mississippi.

Well, you went where the work was. And she guessed it'd be in Little Sky Country, not here where you could breathe. That realization had actually kept her from following up two barely-promising leads just after graduation. She'd foolishly believed she could hold out for something good. *Yeah, a year of reality sure changes your outlook.*

She hurried to the counter as old Zach Caperton plunked his daily six-pack of Bud on it, his white-whiskered grin showing the last two teeth that hit.

"Mornin', Mr. Caperton. You okay?"

"Shore, darlin'. When you gonna let me take you 'way f'm all this?"

"When 1940 pickup lines come around again, I guess. This all for you?"

"Oh, guess I need a coupla cans Vienna sausage an' s'm crackers. Man's gotta keep f'm starvin', I reckon."

"Okay, and you stay outta trouble, now. Guess Ethel's not back yet?" It was an in-joke: his wife'd been gone fifteen years.

"Might just, she gits tard of that truck driver. Wal, you stay sweet now, Kay," and he headed unsteadily out the door. Kay often wondered how just that ration of beer could so disable the man. *Psychological drunk, I guess.*

The wholesale truck was due, and she hadn't finished the list. Quick perusal of the shelves, scribble. The sound of the diesel, and big Ed Matthews letting off the air brakes outside.

"Hey, girl, whatcha need t'day? Got ever'thing but th' kitchen sink, an' it's here someplace. You been b'havin' now, Kay?" Big grin. Bigger gut.

"Naw, Ed. I spit on the sidewalk a while ago. You?"

"Oh, th' wife, she's got me walkin' th' chalk line, Kay. Git outta line in Great Falls at noon, she knows about it in Helena by two. This th' list?"

"So far. I'll check the storeroom while you fill this, okay? Been busy."

"That's good. This r'cession, things slowin' down all over." He went out, humming off-key.

*Routines. Ruts. Predictable days, people, events. What life's made up of while you plan bigger things. But Hall's store forever? Oh, here comes that construction bunch. Prepare to be teased, girl. Wonder what'd happen if I took one of 'em up on his joke proposition? Probably keel over.*

"Hey, Jimmy. How's Beth?"

"Bigger'n a house. Any day now. Y'got Heinekens?"

"Just in. Here y'go. You're not letting Beth drink, are you? Baby be uglier'n you."

"I'm crushed. But no, that woman's toein' th' line, afraid th' young un'll have two heads, she even looks at a beer."

A round, red-faced electrician named Simon came in behind the slope-shouldered Jimmy, eyes lost somewhere in all the beef. Kay knew he was shy, and the others teased him about it.

"Hey, Simon. How's my man?"

"Oh...well...ugh, I'm okay, I guess. How're you?" He was inspecting his shoes. Word was, this self-effacing dude was the best at wiring houses in the country. Maybe that made up for missing social skills. He bought his usual mini-donut snack and a big root beer.

"Oh, by the way, Simon, did that fellow I sent out get hired?" She hadn't caught his name, just that he was this stocky guy with big hands and forearms. No movie star.

"Harlan, th' one with th' Brit Jeep pickup? One with th' big ears?" Jimmy answered. "Yeah, boss took him on: helper. Think he sleeps in that truck. Hope he ain't beatin' my time with you, Kay," he teased. "C'mon, Simon, we gotta roll. See you, Kay." They left as three others came in, laughing, unwinding after another day pounding nails, butchering wood.

It was only a few minutes later I rolled up to thank the girl in the store for heading me toward my barely-job. She probably knew a lotta guys who stopped here, knew who was working, who needed a grunt or whatever. Yeah, regular central intelligence post, this little store.

"Hi. Heard you got hired by McClure."

"Did, and my belated thanks for the tip. By the way, I'm Harlan Kemp." I shoved a hand out.

"Kay McBryde, and glad to know you. Yeah, I know like I said, that job's not much, but I saw your Missouri license and guessed you needed to grab something."

"Right. I try to look cool, but I was really scrapin' it. Well, I need a few things, get me through the weekend." I browsed the shelves, needed substantial food, not snacks. That'd been my MO all along: stretch the bucks till they screamed, even if it meant cooking on the Coleman, trading convenience to save the hoarded green stuff. So, potatoes, rice, cornmeal, few cans. Some mono fishing line I use for cheap fly-line leader. They had ice at the campground that'd keep cheese, meat, but I aimed to be on the road looking for real work till Monday. The Bitterroot thing. Still ice in the chest, anyway.

"Need any help there? Camping out?" the girl asked, being helpful since the place was now about empty.

"Yeah, camping, and sure, if you know what'll keep me alive the cheapest." I looked at her maybe for the first time, really. Tall as me, looked strong. Wiry. Face what you'd hafta call plain, if you were being nice, and it flashed on me that good individual features don't always add up to pretty. Like bad ones sometimes do. Kay wasn't either.

"Well, you've got the basics there, but don't get scurvy; veggies won't kill you, or fruit. I've never believed the bacon-and-beans cowboy stories. Oh, supposedly turnips have most've what the body needs to survive."

"Okay, turnips it is. You major in nutrition?"

"Biology. You can see I'm using my degree to the fullest."

She was okay, friendly. I don't do friendly much, but I can stand it. All right, this'd get me stocked, so I piled it all on the counter.

"Like your truck," as she rang it up on an old-fashioned cash register. "Pretty rare, a diesel Rover."

"You know Land Rovers?"

"Not really. Dad bought one to chase cows on the ranch, but it kept breaking axles. He went back to a Jeep, but we still use horses mostly."

"Weak point, all right. I don't abuse mine, and it seems to like me. Plus, it goes a long way on a gallon. Well, Kay, be seein' you. Thanks again." I was headed outta there. Might've hung around a prettier woman, but I wanted on the road. *Pig.*

"Sure. Know you're gonna be hunting a better job. Good luck."

"It shows? Yeah, I'm really a stonemason."

"So no way you're just helper material. Oh, hello, Mrs. Wilson." She fluttered a hand at me. Not a manicured hand.

I decided it didn't make sense to head south on this Friday night—plenty time tomorrow—so I cooked, did laundry, avoided the expensive revelry I knew would be all over town, even with classes out for the summer at the university. *Ranch, huh? Yeah, horsey. That's the word. Girls I've known who're into horses like 'em better'n people.*

Well, enough idle curiosity. I'd get an early start, hit this lead before the guy down there wandered off for the weekend, then see what else might be happening, that far from town.

# Two

"No, Ron, I don't think that's a good idea." She could envision the proposed party as degenerating into a beer-sloshed gathering of others with nothing better to do, and it didn't attract her. "Besides, I've got a pile of responses to go through." *I wish.*

"You getting a real job? Where?"

"Of course I'm getting a job. Someday. Law of averages, you know. But I've gotta stay on top of this. Rain check, okay?"

"I guess. But the guys wanta go up to Flathead, lake cabin somebody's uncle's got. You really oughta come." He was almost pleading. Why did she get the impression he'd asked someone else first?

"Some other time. 'Bye, now." She punched off. *Now why'd I do that? Only man anywhere near my life, and I just blew him off.* Well, she knew why: *Harlan Kemp and his shiny Land Rover. Outdoors guy for sure. Calluses. Big ears?* She hadn't noticed his ears. *Maybe just got a haircut. No, his hair was long.*

*Wasn't it?* She couldn't remember. But no, the guy wasn't any prize, for sure.

*Like I'm one? I mean, to look at. Sure, I'm unclaimed treasure Dad always said, but who'd notice?*

There was one response, a lukewarm one at best, to her submitted **résumé**. Moscow, Idaho, about five hours away. She'd been there once, to a biology thing at that university. Rounded hills, lotsa farms, quiet town.

This was the stereotype company she'd dreaded: start-up, not much pay at first till business grew. Still, it was a maybe. Yeah, she'd follow up. *More than a year...*

Mrs. Hall had invited her to watch TV.

~ * ~

"Okay, we'll move on it," Bruce Calloway announced to the two other men seated in his Helena office. They'd just taken turns examining the glass jars of soil samples taken from above the north fork of the Blackfoot River area east of Ovando. "Just waiting for these, and they confirm the old rumors. We'll buy that place, and try for others next to it."

"It's a thousand acres. Can we afford it?" Si Selleck set the jeweler's loupe aside with his stubby fingers. Unlike Calloway, who was lean and quick in his movements, Selleck had an air of deliberation about him, a reluctance to disturb his bulk unless necessary.

"Hellyes, we can. Got to. These samples tell us we're looking at maybe hundreds of millions, Si. Not gold nuggets, but enough dust just in that strip on up from the river to make us rich. And I've no doubt there's a concentration near, where this trace originates. But just what we can wash out of that thousand makes it more than worth it. And we gotta move quick, before some Hollywood type buys it for a show ranch."

"I think we should wait for the assayer's report," the third man, who'd been in on the actual digging, opined. "We covered a lot of the ground, and yes, it's there, but let's be sure." Selleck nodded in approval at the younger man, Jack Samuels, who looked like a Boy Scout—the resemblance ended there--but possessed a degree in geology. Calloway, against his instincts, knew they were right, so he compromised.

"Okay then, I'll make an offer on the place enough lower the family won't take it, but we'll have our foot in the door. We can have the report when, Jack?"

"Give it a week. I'm told some fool or other is taking samples in every day, excited over one speck of color. Backlog there, but I've got a connection. Yeah, a week'll do it. So I agree: tie the land up. And did you contact the other neighbors?"

"Did. Old guy has five hundred acres down along the river, but it's been in that family like forever. Do know his sons have left the country, got careers somewhere, and only one daughter, just finished college. She'll prob'ly marry some Easterner, so think he'll realize he isn't gonna pass it down to the next generation."

"You talk to him?" from Selleck, "or are you guessing?"

"Did go by, which is how I know the situation. He said no, guessed he'd hang onto what he'd inherited, but I could see he wasn't blowing the idea off. Friendly enough dude, the way those old ones usually are, so I think give him some time to mull it over, he'd be open to an offer."

"Yeah," Selleck affirmed. "Work our way into it a bit at a time, probably get that place too. How about upstream?"

"Land doesn't stay on the river, which bends around a mountain. And trace peters out the further you get away," Samuels pointed out. "We did go down to the river, worked our way back onto that next place, and those samples look even better," indicating a separate set of labeled glass jars.

"So we tie up the Bujold thousand and go to work on McBryde, okay?" Calloway was eager to get the operation moving. After a brief exchange of silent eye contact, the others agreed. "And we should let at least the top investors know we're close, right?" Nods from both.

~ * ~

I liked the drive down the Bitterroot Valley. Up, actually, since the river flowed north. Peaks still snow-topped, this late. Someday I'd go up to Lolo Pass, and maybe over to fish those Idaho ravine-deep creeks I was hearing about. Nothing there, though, resembling jobs, I'd also heard. All National Forest.

The house under construction was a timberframe, old hand-hewn barn beams fitted tightly, next to a garage with an apartment over it. A small pile of quartzite stone humped up near some pathetic veneer over a concrete foundation. Somebody'd tried, but looked like he'd given up.

A man maybe fifty was wheelbarrowing dirt away from a cut in the upslope in front of the house, maybe to put in a retaining wall. *Yes!*

"Hi. You'd be Mr. Ridley, right?"

"That's right. Who're you?" Not unfriendly, but...wary?"

"I'm Harlan Kemp. I'm a stonemason and carpenter, and I like what you're doing here." I'd glimpsed a woman in a fenced garden with an irrigation sprayer going. Nice tall flowers, tomatoes, beans. That creek sound over it all.

"Thanks. Trying to do most of it myself, but it's slow going. Guess you're looking for a job?"

"I am, but I hear from the grapevine that you're not in a position to hire anybody full time."

"That's right. I spent a bunch getting help on this timberframe. Fellow up in the Sapphires. Have to ration the bucks."

"Well, I'm new here, and wanta get... established, I guess you'd say. So I'm willing to work cheaper, and maybe even part-time, if we could come to some arrangement." He saw me eyeing the bad veneer.

"Could maybe happen. But tell me, how do you like that work on the wall?" Test, of course. I didn't hesitate.

"It needs to be torn out and done right. No offense, if you did it."

"I did, and my wife agrees with you. I tried following directions in a book, but it isn't working. You have any pictures of your work with you?"

"A few." Uncle John had insisted I do just that. I had them loose in a folder, not professional, I knew. I don't do slick. Free-standing drystack, couple retaining walls, stone steps, veneer. One landscape pool with waterfall.

"Hey, this is nice. Where is it?"

"Afraid it's in Missouri and north Arkansas. Mostly sandstone, but you can see it's not that different from the quartzite you've got."

"Okay, so just saying I could afford you, what's your rate?"

"Depends. I don't charge by the hour, because that's not fair to you if I'm slow. Square foot of surface. And I pick the stone. Where'd this come from?" Indicating the pile.

"Permit from the National Forest. They let you pick up a few tons for a yearly fee. You probably know that."

"I do. For your own use. Okay, what you have here is most of the problem. Need better stone. If I supply it, permit stuff or bought cheap, say ten bucks a pickup load, I can work for seven a square foot. You supply the sand, cement."

"That's steep. I was thinking maybe just going with stucco over this plywood."

"Maybe. But on this site, you really want stone. Good stone."

"I do, but I've gotta be able to afford it. Let me show these pictures to my wife, see what she says."

"Sure." He took them, went toward the garden. I realized that this'd be just a stop-gap thing, if it happened at all. Trying to build your own house without financing it was a bear. Maybe this guy'd borrowed to buy the land and had to do it piecemeal. Not my problem, if he could pay me enough to get a start.

"Nancy says she likes your work, Harlan, but we want to see some of it, with this kind of stone. Think you could show us some, say one day's worth, maybe a little on this retaining wall and some veneer? Pay you like you said, seven a face foot for it. Okay?"

"Fair enough. Tell me where to find the stone, and it's a deal. When do you want me to start?"

"Up to you, since it's just a day."

"Well, if it won't offend you, I could find stone today, and work tomorrow, Sunday. And of course, the next question is, how steady could the work be?"

"We're in the process of refinancing, so by next week we should be able to offer you a couple months' work. More so if you can help me with the carpentry. You said you do that too."

"Sounds good. I get five an hour for that, so yeah, we could mix it up. And I'd need to know by tomorrow so I can give notice where I'm working now." Five was okay in the mid '70s, if I could get it. Uncle John always charged the max, believing that if you priced low, people would expect second-rate. He didn't do second-rate, and neither did I.

I could almost hear the wheels turning in Ridley's head as he calculated. *Oboy, here it comes: he's gonna chisel me.*

"Where you working now?"

"Missoula."

"Long drive, every day. Living there?"

"Campground. I go where the work is."

"Okay, you'd spend bucks driving, so how about four dollars for the carpentry, and I let you camp on down the creek." The wife, Nancy, had come up, smiling. Late 40s, sun-crinkled eyes, small woman, where her husband was tall, and sorta leaned forward, following his beak nose. "That okay, Nancy?"

"Sure. I'm Nancy." Hard hand. "We go a couple hundred yards down, beyond that grove, and there's actually a half-bathroom in that shed. Former owner wanted to build too, but he gave up on the project. He actually stayed in there while he built this garage and apartment. Primitive, but if you're used to camping..."

"I am. Just me and my truck. And flyrod."

"My kinda man." Ridley put a hand on my shoulder. We shook. Of course he could stiff me on this sample work, but I sensed these were honest people. Turned out the wife taught school, and he did something with investments: other people's money, so I guessed those people trusted him.

This would work, even if it didn't last long. And I'd stay outta their hair, keep it all business, do the job. Guy was apparently a good carpenter from what I could see, so maybe I wouldn't hafta undo anything else he screwed up.

I put the stuff from my truck into the cab and in the shed, lifted the camper cap off with my block-and-tackle, under a pair of ponderosas I strung a rope across between. Laid some scrap plywood on the aluminum truck bed to protect it, and headed out. Fifteen miles, Ridley'd said, and I had his permit in case a forest ranger came by.

*Okay, I'm in, if the rock's good, and we'll know that soon.* The Rover rumbled along, content to ferry me, or rocks, or anything else I could throw at it. No dealership closer than Helena, so I'd baby it along, like my livelihood depended on it. Which it did.

You get somebody else's stone, you pay for it, and then throw most of it out. I could haul nearly a ton without damaging my truck, and all of it would be usable. I'd be picky, remembering the mason's admonition: "Don't get bad stuff. Rocks are like women you pick up in a bar: no better-looking when you get them home." Or hell, men either, if you're a woman.

The stuff was up this forest fire-road, a rockslide above another clear, fast-flowing creek. Weathered, layered blocks and some good thin pieces. Lichens, which I love. When I hafta cut a stone, I put the fresh face outta sight, so my work looks like it's been there a century or so.

These stones were darker, and I wanted to mix in some lighter browns and grays. I remembered the little quarry on the Blackfoot. Maybe I could buy a load next week, or find more somewhere.

I picked around, maybe choosing one about every ten feet, the way you have to if you're not gonna have to cut too much. It takes about as much time to hunt for the right rock as it does to cut a mediocre one, and the natural one always looks better.

Most stonework is about appearance. You can side a house a lot cheaper with clapboard, board-and-batten, even stucco or that awful aluminum or plastic imitation. But even with its cost, good stonework will increase the value of that house many times over. And there's no upkeep, for a couple hundred years anyway, when the mortar finally erodes.

And not even then, if the stones are laid properly. That means setting each one so it'll stay in place even without mortar. Ideally, that's just fill, not glue.

I had all I dared load on the truck by midafternoon, and headed back down toward the Bitterroot, taking it easy. When I crossed the river bridge at Stevensville, two girls in bikinis were paddling a red canoe downstream. I hadda slow down to check them out, naturally, being normal.

They both waved, and so did I. *Damn, it'd be nice to have myself a pretty woman.* These were probably college girls from U.M. on a break from summer classes. Or not, maybe local, or a couple of those others who like me, had gravitated here. Fine looking, no matter their origins. And sure, probably both hooked up with cowboy studs already.

Only, where were those guys? Missing out, that's where. I drove on, mentally stroking smooth, tanned skin. *Okay, okay, get a grip on yourself, boy. Got work to do.* And anyway, behind those sunglasses, those two might've been bone ugly.

No, they weren't.

I unloaded at Ridley's place, the veneer stuff next to the house wall and the bigger retaining wall stones where he'd dug dirt and left a two-foot cut. He eyed the veneer stones.

"Looks like you're planning to lay them in like ledges, instead of flat to the wall. Nancy wants that."

"Yeah, rock doesn't occur in nature stood up on edge. Veneer should look like solid stone, and besides, laid horizontal it'll never get water behind it and freeze in winter, pop off the wall."

"I wanta watch, tomorrow; maybe I can learn."

*Yeah, and do me outta my job. But okay, it's harder than it looks, believe me. Besides, you've got a whole lotta months' more work ahead of you on this house. I'm not worried.*

All my stuff was with me, so I accepted their invitation to sleep in the shed. Set the ice chest, bedroll, other things inside, and decided to cruise the three miles into Stevensville, see what Saturday night was like. I put a sandwich together, grabbed a Coke and munched on the way.

Town about folded up the sidewalks before dark, it looked like, but there were a couple bars. Fat-tire pickups and motorcycles in front. I don't do bars: too expensive, too many lies being told, too many fights. And only a few hard-eyed women.

"Hey, nice truck," a burly, tattooed dude complimented. "Diesel sounds mean." He gave me the okay sign.

"Thanks, man. I like your big Harley, too." Stereotype, guy might be tame as a kitten.

No, he wasn't.

Ice cream drive-in on the highway had teenagers all around it, car radios blaring. I like ice cream, so parked, waded up to the window. Girl about twenty inside, big smile. Freckles, red hair.

"Teenagers driving you crazy?"

"For sure, but they're what keeps the place going. C'n I getcha?"

"Root beer float. You from around here?" Not a pickup line; I was just getting to know the place, people.

"Born an' raised. You?" I was sure she'd scored my Missouri accent, but hey, this was an old game.

"Missouri. I'm a stonemason. Working up Kootenai Creek."

"Great. Here y'go. Like your truck. Not a Jeep." Now my Rover is candy-apple red, Uncle John's work, and no, it's not in any way a Jeep. Skinny axles, for one thing.

"No, English. Land Rover. Takes me places I shouldn't go."

"I'll bet. Well, see you," as three post-adolescent girls in shorts and straining tee shirts came to the window. I waved, moved off. She threw me that smile. *Lou, her name tag says. Well, Lou, you're friendly enough. I'd say you stuck, after high school; maybe your folks own the place. No ring, so you're waiting around for your knight on his Honda bike. Or not. Maybe married, got two kids, ran the cheatin' loser off. Maybe* Lou and Tattoo, a match.

Town was barely a blip on the map, but important, in this farming, ranching country. Ridley'd told me that just downriver north, there was a ten-thousand-acre spread, been in the same family since homestead, 150 years ago. They even had their own suspension bridge over the Bitterroot. Well, maybe they'd want stonework someday.

I aimed to become *the* resident mason here, not the brick-and-block grunt, the specialist. Big dream for a guy not even on his first day, small job. But, gotta start somewhere, right?

I did worry about winter, probably less than five months away. What'd an outdoors guy do, here? Go south? Didn't wanta do that; these mountains had me. Just hafta rack up enough to hole up, maybe go crazy like a mountain man.

No, get some place with workspace, I could maybe do woodwork, furniture, custom stuff. Sure, but hafta work ahead to that. Maybe garage with room over. Heard it got way below zero here, too many days at a time. Shop'd mean heat, bucks spent, though. But if I aimed—and I did—to call my own shots, I'd hafta stay busy every minute, make all of them count.

No time for leggy girls in bikinis, for sure. Or even local friendlies with nice smiles. Later. There'd maybe be the woman for old Harlan sometime, when he was settled. But no way did I want the routine story: wife, snotty kids, rat race. No, I was gonna be independent, work outside 'The System,' paddle my own—okay, canoe. Not be a cog in a big wheel. *Yeah, like I've been doing pushing that wheelbarrow for other guys up on the McClure job.*

That night I dreamed of a red canoe, bikinis, my red Rover with a girl in it. Couldn't see her face under that cowboy hat. The girl in the store? Kay? Nah. But probably a great girl, really. Yeah, for some other cowboy.

I'd go for the bikinis.

~ * ~

Kay heard from a girlfriend who'd gone to Ron's party that it'd been a waste. He'd gotten drunk, gone to sleep with couples falling all over him, and they'd almost set the Flathead cabin on fire. The TV with Mrs. Hall had been bad, but forgettable as it was, maybe it'd saved her from disaster.

Ron had been her lab partner back when she'd been a sophomore, a lackluster student who'd barely passed. Seemed he lived for the frat parties on campus, but was usually odd-man out, which apparently didn't bother him much.

He'd asked Kay out when there was something that required a date, and those events pretty much comprised her social life. Once or twice he'd clumsily suggested sex, but talk about pointless! She was no Brigitte Bardot, but the big experience for her would have to wait for the man who'd give himself to her completely, and she to him. Certainly not to be wasted in a groping encounter with a somnolent wannabe playboy.

Saturday was busy at the store, as always. Mrs. Hall couldn't compete with the big chain stores, but had her regular local faithful—neighbors, folks who didn't want to buy high-priced gas to drive back into Missoula for the things they'd forgotten there.

So she'd unwind Sunday as usual, maybe run northeast to the ranch, see the folks. Or just see if any of her friends wanted to picnic down by the river. Or maybe she'd hike somewhere, if she was alone. The day would deserve more than a good book at home.

And well, she might start it off by going to church, something she'd neglected a lot during college and since. Couldn't hurt. Yes, she'd do that. First.

But it turned out to be something of a letdown. Same older people politely asking about her, same long sermon, same hymns she'd sung all her life. But she did feel strangely refreshed afterward, there on the building's steps, viewing the June day. Almost as if this day would be the start of something good. Just what, remained to be seen.

No one had wanted to join her, so she changed into jeans and her hiking boots, took her cowboy hat, and headed up into the mountains in her fourteen-year-old Ford Falcon. It hiccupped a little, but had always gotten her there, no matter where 'there' was.

She found herself wondering where the stonemason Harlan was, searching for work. Or maybe he was taking a break, stretched out on a river bank, beer in hand. No, he hadn't bought beer. Surely like he said, nursing his money. More likely fishing somewhere, that mono line he bought. She pictured the anglers who fished the creeks on her dad's ranch, the long looping lines glistening in the sun, the minute flies plopping the glassy surface. She liked to fish, but had let that go too, lately.

*But Harlan, now. Don't know of any other stonemasons around. Hard work surely, and I guess my generation's not into that so much. Is that why I don't want to go back home? Talk about work: feeding alfalfa at 20 below, horsing irrigation rigs in July. Dad needs me, but it's time to move on. Lotta hands need work, and he can pay, now he's not helping us in school.* A brief picture of Harlan Kemp on a horse, with a big hat. That almost made her laugh.

An overlook showed the Clark Fork valley spread out below, with the snow peaks of the Bitterroots off to the west that almost never lost those white caps. This was why she'd hate to leave this part of Montana, leave a part of her behind. Could she even do that?

She'd sent the reply to Moscow. Maybe something would come of that, maybe not. At least it'd change the equation, the status quo, one way or another. *Like a chess game: one minor move determines the whole direction of the game. Maybe it'll do that for me.*

Kay did not move from that sweeping overlook. Gradually the sun did move and gradually her conviction faded that this day would hold a new beginning. *But not an ending, either. Just more sameness.*

# *Three*

Sunday was a fine day. Hot, but there was shade under the big Ponderosas, and a breeze came up alongside the Bitterroots and some of it spilled across the rushing creek and onto me. Dry air, so I drank a lotta water, slammed stone. Set base rocks for the retaining wall, explaining to Ridley, whose front name was Tom, that what he'd read about deep stones at the bottom tapering to shallow at the top was all wrong.

"You've seen retaining walls that've failed?" I asked him.

"A few. Not that much stonework around here."

"If you look, you'll see the rocks come loose at the top, where there's freeze-and-thaw, cows step on them, they just get dislodged. Now, this is drystack, but it'll hold. Soil isn't liquid, that'd push more at the bottom. So we start just a foot back into the cut, then shelve back as we go up. Wall leans into the cut, soil pushes back, and it stays put. These capstones are wide, to hold everything solid."

"Nice stones, great lichen. Look like they grew here."

"My plan exactly. Okay, now I'll hit the veneer. One paramount principle: no vertical running joints. You use one stone to span each joint, like bricks. Which came later, of course."

"What about that big one you just laid? Won't there be a joint with the two you stacked next to it?"

"Not when I span it with this next one. Big one was to break up the horizontal line visually. Stronger if it's all even-height rows like bricks, but boring, amateurish."

I was nailing masonry ties to fit the joints in every other stone, grabbing rocks, spreading mortar. Couple of hours, I had two courses up, eight feet long, with very little shaping. I pushed mortar in where the joints were too deep, then raked them. Sponged off smears.

"Tomorrow morning early, you come out, wire-brush these joints. Mud'll be crumbly, and the stones will stand out. Joints recessed like this, they're in shadow and don't call attention to them."

Nancy Ridley had been watching, gardening trowel in hand. I'd picked up on her viewpoint: she wanted this beautiful, and to hell with the cost. I also knew Tom was thinking he could do this himself, once he'd seen me work. Wasn't gonna happen; I'd let him try this next week, and he'd be so frustrated, he'd give me the job.

I hoped.

"Now," I said, wrapping up late, "one of you wet this down after you brush the joints, about every two hours tomorrow. Mortar won't run by then, and it needs to be kept wet at least that long to cure. I've left these spaces for lighter-colored rocks, to break up the look. Use these dark ones all over, it'll all blur into non-stone, which I know you don't want." I pointed to two of the lighter ones that'd happened to be in Tom's pile I'd set. Nancy approved.

"So, this look okay?" I'd sponged water on the lichens and they'd greened up the way they do. *What's not to like, people?* I also realized I'd used every rock I'd gathered, plus.

"Well, I count sixteen face feet, including the top... capstones, on the retaining wall; you're fast, Harlan, but that's gonna cost me $112 for one day's work. Not sure I can afford you."

"Your call. I'm not asking to be paid for my time, but what I know and can do for you. And like I said earlier, I can space the work out, find other things to do, let you stretch it out..."

"But Tom," his wife pointed out, "I like this. I want this. And how do we know Harlan can get away to come back when we're ready?" She was on board.

"Okay then, we can just keep it flexible," he compromised. "Let's say you come back Saturday, work that day at least. I'm not ready to commit to the whole job; it's just too much money we need for plumbing, electrical, finishing. That okay? Then we can map it out better." And he gave me a check for $112.

"Thanks. Only problem would be if I get a big job they'd wanta keep me on, but I'll check with you first. Deal?"

"Deal." We shook. I loaded my gear in the Rover, lowered the cap onto it, secured it and chugged away. Could see them arguing in the rearview mirror. I grinned.

"I can do this, Nancy. I watched that boy place every stone, and yeah, I like his work, but we just won't have the bucks..."

"Take another look at what you tried, Tom. He knows his stuff."

"That was before. Okay, I can work from home Wednesday. I'll borrow that truck again, get only good stone this time, and duplicate his work. You'll see." He believed it.

"You promised him Saturday."

"Hedging my bets. If I blow it, we'll find a way to keep him on, at least part-time. Can you live with that?"

"Just don't let him get away. This's the best stonework I've seen."

~ * ~

It was almost dark by the time I got back to Missoula. A tattered Falcon turned onto the highway ahead of me as I neared town, and even at my pace, I caught up with it. Two turtles. Young woman driving it was tall—all I could see—but she wasn't in a hurry. *Okay, I'm not either, girl.*

She took the same turns I was about to, clear on to the little grocery store beyond town. Turned in. Got out as I cruised by.

Kay. I beeped my little English horn, waved. She waved back, big smile. *Whatthehell.* I stopped, backed, parked.

"Hey, girl. Wasn't stalking you."

"Oh, shucks." She came over. "Job-hunt go okay?"

"Did. Got rocks. Laid rocks. Got paid. Maybe more or less long-term." *Now what?* "You have a good Sunday?"

"Spent it daydreaming in the mountains after church. Where's your job?" She was tracing fingers over my truck, face in shadow.

"Outta Stevensville. Mason on the McClure job told me about it. Maybe sporadic, but nice house, landscaping. It's a start."

"Good. Hey, you look dry. Want something to drink?"

"Store's closed."

"I got the key. And I live right there, with Mrs. Hall." Who happened to be on her porch swing, watching. "C'mon and meet her. Known her since I was a kid."

"Sure. Hi, Mrs. Hall, I'm Harlan." I reached, took her hand.

"Well, hi yourself. Saw your shiny truck the other day. So you know my girl? Brash, calls me Hall. No respect."

"Barely. She put me onto a construction job, about saved me from starvation." She patted the swing next to her. I sat, gratefully.

"You look tired. Working on a Sunday?" Eyes keen, but not unkind.

"Guilty. Sort of a trial thing, stonework down off the Bitterroot. Promise I won't do it again." She waved it away. I liked her.

"Get the job?"

"I think so. Going back to work Saturday. Know for sure then."

Kay came out the store back door with cold Cokes, handed them around. Sat opposite us.

"Tell us about your truck," Mrs. Hall said. "Rare around here."

"Oh. Well, I had an uncle back in Missouri who liked to tinker with unusual vehicles. Lived here for a while and got to appreciating good workmanship: Studebakers, Mercedes, Packards. He got this Rover from somewhere, restored it. He died when I was in college, left it to me. They use them in Africa, all over the world in deserts, jungles. You've probably seen them in safari movies."

"Oh, yes, the great white hunters. You hunt?"

"Not much. Fishing's my vice."

"Get a license, then. Warden's all over anybody out of state. We sell 'em."

"Tomorrow after work. Saw some good holes on creeks and on the Bitterroot. Afraid I'm a dry-fly nut."

"So was my husband, Bert. Left me to run the store whenever a buddy said the water was right. Kay's an angler, too."

"Oh? Then you probably know where to stay away from. Won't ask you any secret places." She laughed. Nice voice, I noticed, sort of throaty.

"I'll say this: best place is a couple creeks on our ranch, big springs just boil up. Water so clear you have to sneak up on the trout. Dad actually charges fisherman a fee."

"Great, but I'm gonna hafta put even fishing on hold for now, focus on building up a stonework business, every spare minute. Don't see much of that—the real stuff—around here." Maybe these women knew of something, although Kay surely would've mentioned it before.

"Can't do it in the winter, I'm sure," Mrs. Hall pointed out. "Or do you make enough to go south then?" Laugh. She knew better.

"Try that, but I will need a fallback skill. Imagine carpentry dries up then, too."

"University jobs all year, but you can guess how many folks line up for those."

I enjoyed this. In the half-light from the store sign, we were indistinct, mostly friendly voices. I felt welcome, and had noted before the open, sometimes almost eager reception from these westerners.

I felt Kay's eyes on me.

*Doesn't have big ears at all. Jimmy's a jerk, probably sees other guys as competition, looking for a way to cheat on Beth. Like most dudes. Funny, running into Harlan like this. Mrs. Hall likes him. Matchmaker.*

"Well," I rose, stretched. "Gotta be ready to hit the Sheetrock and plywood tomorrow. Thanks for the drink, both of you. Be by for that fishing license after work. Oh, where's the nearest place to cash a paycheck?"

"I can do that," Mrs. Hall assured me. "Unless you're a millionaire." Chuckle. I thanked them again, aware of Kay's faint scent which sort of followed me to my truck. *Friends. Good to have 'em, new place. Sort of an anchor.*

I got through the next day, hoping Ridley had remembered to brush the joints in the veneer stone. There are otherwise good masons who neglect this simple step, and their mistakes are there forever. *No, Nancy'll see to that. My ally.*

~ * ~

Ron Gillespie hadn't believed Kay was too busy to go with him to that party. What? She have another date? Another guy? Nah, unfortunately for her, she was too easy to overlook. Had always been grateful when he'd asked her out.

Couldn't believe it'd been that almost-relationship all through college—and here he hadn't graduated yet—and a year since. But she'd always been there, helping him with studies, being his sure date when the fun girls had turned him down. She was solid, predictable.

Of course she *would* eventually find a decent job—too good at her specialty—and yeah, move away. Well, he would too, sooner or later. For now, though, he needed Kay. Maybe just the familiar, the comfortable, but real.

*Better be sure to hang onto what I've got, while I can.*

That young lady found herself looking forward to Harlan's promised stop by the store. She could imagine him at a wheelbarrow, moving things for the other carpenters, plumbers, painters. *He's no helper.* Surely wanting to be back on that creek, caressing stones. *Funny word, but I bet that's how he sees it— feels it. Those callused hands, muscled forearms. Putting stones in their destined places after their millions of years, waiting for just those hands...*

"Eggs. Yes, Mr. Caldwell, fresh from a farm up the Blackfoot. Free-range chickens, yes. How's Bertha? Arthritis still acting up, I guess. Yessir, we'll have green beans before Friday, up from south. Thanks, sir." She watched the white-fringed head bob its way to the aging Oldsmobile.

*Rare vehicles. Craftsmanship.* Maybe she should grab herself a semi-classic before they got hard to find and too expensive. She liked the jaunty Mustangs, the first ones, ten years old now, maybe cheap enough. Have to get some mechanic to check one out, though, not get a lemon...

*Okay!* But not right away. Maybe in a week or so... Oh, he'd probably be gone, then. *Stevensville. Have to find how to reach him.*

*Am I scheming, here? What makes me think Harlan Kemp will find me attractive? They all go for the cheerleaders, the trophies. Well...*

~ * ~

I did stop in, needed groceries and didn't want to drive into town and back to save a buck or two. Got the license, cashed Ridley's check. Thought about maybe finding a cheap place to live, but if I could stay free down on the Bitterroot...

"Oh," Kay seemed to remember, "I hear a lot about what's being built, you know. If I do hear of a stone job, how do I reach you?" *Innocent enough.*

"Good question. Not sure how long I'll be at Ridley's place—they've got a shed I can stay in—but yeah, I'd appreciate that a lot. Hmm. Tell you what: I'll get a P.O. box in Stevensville, and another in Missoula, let you know, okay? And thanks. For now, I'll be camping, one way or another. No telling where the next job will be."

"Yes. The way I see it, people will have to see your work before they'll want stone. Sort of a chipboard mentality here."

"Not everybody," Mrs. Hall said as she joined us. "Got any pictures of your stonework to show, Harlan?"

"I do. Yeah, let me..." I went to the Rover, got them. She spread them out on the counter, and both women examined them. Liked them. Eyes lit up. I felt a little embarrassed, for some reason. No need: I'm good.

"Okay now," the store owner announced, "you've gotta get this stuff where people can see it..."

"Like to, but can't afford to advertise. Journalism professor at my college said you have to repeat an ad forty times or so before it registers with the public."

"Really? No wonder my specials don't bring me any business. But okay, try this: what if you could do some work like this in a place everybody passes? I bet they'd start wanting it." Her red face was alight.

"Sure," Kay jumped in. "Say something like this terrific pool and waterfall. Oh, but I guess that'd be a big deal, expensive." Her earnest face showed confusion. *Girl's really shy, not used to talking to guys. About serious stuff, anyway.*

"Maybe not, if I could do it over time; it's all mostly labor. Rather spend that than ad money I don't have."

"We're onto something here, kids! Just suppose I wanted, say a retaining wall like this one, alongside the store, level more parking space. And plant vines, flowers like these. You give me a break on the cost; I get you the best advertising. Whattya think?" She looked for all the world like the cat that'd got the yellow bird.

"You'd do that?"

"Depends on the price. What's a good mason get?"

"Square face foot, so a two-foot-high wall, say twenty feet long, two more parking spaces, with the top capstones eighteen inches like in this picture, normally seven dollars a foot. That'd be four-ninety, without the digging. How about half?"

"$245." She seemed to be considering this, looking at the pictures. "Could we dig it with our old tractor bucket? Bert used to use it to plow the snow off. Kay does it now."

"Sure, if we don't hit solid rock. Never know what's under there."

"Nothing I know of. Say, couldn't my girl do the digging, leveling?"

"Don't see why not. We'd pile it up behind, then later backfill, level out what's left. Leave you more usable ground up there, too." I was liking this. Few pickup loads of stone...

"You up for this, Kay?" her boss asked.

"Sure. I've dug my share of dirt, manure, snow out at the ranch. Do it between customers." She liked the idea, I could see. Strong-looking woman—I said that—probably make a good stonemason, too.

"Let's do it, then." Mrs. Hall grabbed my hand, shook. "How soon?"

"Well, I gave notice at McClure today, and I'm promised for Saturday. Next week okay?"

"Done. How long'll it take?" She wanted this.

"Maybe three, four days, if Kay has it cut and leveled. I'll need to find rock. There's that little quarry up the Blackfoot, or you can get a permit from the Forest Service, cost twenty bucks. They say five tons a year, which is more'n we'll need for this. Has to be non-profit, but if you get it..."

"Check the quarry first. Old man Hawser owns it, and he's cheap, if it's for me. But yeah, I'll get that permit, too. Might just go for this waterfall, later." Her grin was as wide as the front door. Which just then opened to some of the guys from McClure.

"Leavin' us, Kemp," Jimmy accused. "Don't like us eh, Simon? I heard th' boss was gonna give you my job." Silly grin.

"Got rocks in my head, Jimmy. Your wife had that baby yet?"

"Nah, and I'm about to take out after Kay here, if you don't shoot me down. How 'bout it, girl?"

"You're all talk, Jimmy. Tell Beth to call me if I can help when the baby comes."

"Yes, me too," Mrs. Hall offered. "And if I even *suspect* you of mistreatin' that girl of yours, I'm gonna brain you." She probably would, too.

"Just kiddin'. Need my Heinekens, an' a steak t'celebrate when th' little 'un gits here." To me: "You live in that rig, Kemp?"

"Sometimes. Got a place t'stay on my new job up Bitterroot, though. I travel light."

"Good woman gits ahold've you she'd settle you down. Right, Kay?"

"Put a sock in it, Jimmy." But she'd colored. Made her sort of cute, for a minute. Sort of. Maybe good to work with, outdoor girl like that. *Nah, women are complications, even plain ones.*

Simon asked me, on our way out, checking my truck:

"What kinda fuel mileage you git with that thing, Harlan?"

"'Bout three times what you get with that big hoss of yours. Close to forty." That was stretching it, but if you included coasting down hills...

"No shit? An' it's four-wheel drive. With that winch, you don't never git stuck, do you?"

"Not for long. And if I don't try anything too stupid. Well, see you men in the morning."

I was grateful for those two women looking out for me, all over again. And yeah, I'd do Mrs. Hall a helluva job on that wall. Maybe she'd let me put up a sign. Needed a magnetic one on the truck door, too. No, it was aluminum. Well... I had the feeling I was on my way in this place.

# *Four*

Friday after my last half-day at McClure, I was rolling down to Ridleys' to get an early start on that job, with a load from the quarry, Fifteen bucks worth. I started to pass the store, but saw Kay's Falcon hood up. Well, I owed her, and yeah, I needed groceries...

"Trouble?" I indicated the car, noticing also the leveled ground, the cut just waiting for me.

"About worn out's the trouble. I've nursed this thing for five years, but afraid it's terminal. Tires worn out, battery's going, rust everywhere. Not worth putting more into. Got the charger on the battery now."

"Gonna get something else then?" Of course she was. I went into the store, started collecting basic edibles. She left me alone, busied herself somewhere, then came back.

"Your mentioning classic cars the other night got me thinking. Maybe a sort of investment, y'know? Maybe a

Studebaker Hawk? Mustang? Can't afford a Mark Two Lincoln or Thunderbird." *Wow, she knew cars.*

"Good idea. Seen anything you like?"

"A couple. Problem is, I don't know what's about to quit on one. Used car dealers scare me."

"Well, you didn't ask me, but do *not* buy from a dealer. Sharks... and you can find an individual who needs a mortgage payment or has to make bail or something, and save a bundle. Then sell yours for whatever you can get. Never trade: the other guy usually will up his price, try to get yours free.

"And gas is going up, you know. Probably hit a dollar a gallon, few years. Unless you want speed and power, stay away from big V8's."

"Specifics? I have no shame."

"Okay, you like the old Mustangs? I think they'll be collectors' items in the future. The little six has the same engine as your Falcon, good on gas. Stick-shift, not the automatic. Five or six hundred'll get you one in fair shape. High miles don't mean as much out here, lotsa highway driving. But try to stay under a hundred thousand miles. And the straight six engine is easy to rebuild: get another hundred thousand easy.

"All the sixties stuff rusts bad back East, and the unit bodies—no real frame under you—can't hold together if they're rusty. Avoid anything somebody's driven out here from back where they salt the roads."

"Wow, thanks. If I can remember all that. Yeah, I might get that dream job someday, and it'd be nice if I could get there to it."

"Sure. Well, see you Monday." I drove toward Highway 93 south, put Kay and her car project aside. *Mix these stones with a couple more loads from the forest, and be set.* If, as I suspected, Ridley'd tried to go ahead with the work, he'd be frustrated by now. And if he hired me, he'd just hafta wait till I got my ad wall up at the store.

Nobody was home at the Ridley place. Friday night out, I guessed. I unloaded this quarry rock right next to a sure-enough pile of the forest stuff he'd gathered during the week sometime. Some of it was good.

And saw the pathetic new attempt at veneer he'd managed. Well, our deal was still on, so I needed another good load for the work tomorrow. I decided to go on to the woods, use the remaining light and dawn to scrounge stone.

The rockslide area was a nice place to camp, even if it wasn't designated for that. I got maybe half a load in the twilight, then mindful of rattlesnakes, set up my tent by this creek.

I'd piled the necessities tightly in the truck cab with that other load, and hadn't taken time to rearrange at Ridleys'. Now, digging for something to cook, I came across a package wrapped in foil. *Now whatthehell?*

Two thick ham-on-ryes with the trimmings. *Now how'd that girl...?" Oh, while I was shopping. Damn, that was sweet.*

So, how should I handle this? No-pretty girl I'd never notice does something like this for me... I puzzled about this for a few minutes, then did the logical thing: I ate the sandwiches.

And wondered what I could do to return the favor. Took me all of a half-hour to come up with that one.

Now, after a week of pretty hard work, followed by horsing stone, load, unload, load, falling asleep by a whitewater creek was a no-brainer. Best night I could remember.

I made coffee at first light, chomped something left over, and topped out the load of stone. Was at the job setting retaining-wall rocks straight from the truck when Tom Ridley staggered up.

"Bad night?" I was chipper. Annoyingly so, I knew.

"You have no idea. Nancy likes to dance, and I don't even remember her driving us home." More than sore feet with this guy, easy to see.

"And please, *please* tear out that crap I did Wednesday. Dunno what I was thinking. And I swore I was gettin' rocks just like yours." Silly rueful grin. Bloodshot eyes.

"No problem. And here's a thermos of coffee; you need it more'n I do." He sure as hell did. Besides, Nancy, perky as ever, refilled it for me an hour later, with a conspiratorial grin. Tom stayed gone till after noon while she gardened.

I liked Nancy.

Asked Tom about the timber framer he'd mentioned. Learned he lived up an impossible non-road in the Sapphire Mountains across the Bitterroot, with an educated wife and a couple of home-schooled kids. Way, way off the grid. I figured the other people he built for would appreciate stonework, so I'd follow that up.

Day's end, I had another check in my pocket, the promise of ongoing work, maybe half-time, and Tom had a helluva retaining wall. I left his screwed-up veneer in place for now, to remind him how much he needed me. Hey, I studied some psychology in college.

Next morning, Sunday, I eased down the creek to Highway 93, and up (downriver) to the village of Florence. Followed the turns to a gravel road that looked as if it'd dead-end into a mountain. Every time a rutted driveway turned off to a rustic cabin, what was left of the road got rougher. Rocks almost a foot high you hadda dodge. Land Rover country for sure.

I climbed higher than high, at one time along the edge of a perilous ridge with nothing but space below my right-side wheels. In the distance were snow peaks that looked a week away.

Finally came to an open gate and a shaded sort of semi-plateau—nothing level up here—with a workshop hung out over the edge. Couple of trucks, tractor, even a portable sawmill, logs, beams all around. Beyond, up another carved-out road, I could see part of a log cabin. Take away the machinery, I could expect to see Jim Bridger or Jedediah Smith striding down, long rifle, buckskins and all. I parked well back in the only space I saw.

Instead, this bearded giant who'd stepped out of the shop held a Skilsaw, and had been reaching for a generator starter cord with his other hand. He set the saw down, came over with a grin that split whiskers with white teeth.

"You're the stonemason," he announced to my surprise, as he extended a hand that engulfed mine. "Saw Tom Ridley in Stevensville, told me a little 'bout you. Sorta figured y'might stop by." *Stop by? Yeah, right on my way.*

"You did?" was all I could manage. I realized my mouth had been open.

"Yeah, not a hard connection to make, timberframe and stone. I'm Rhys Carter, and you're Harlan Kemp, right?" He was appraising my Rover, of course. "Rig like that, everybody on the Bitterroot'll know you in a week. C'mon in an' see my shop."

Did that. And marveled. Every tool in its place on the walls, shavings swept, a complete woodworking shop, with top brand-name equipment. Up in the sky. A boy of about eleven was oiling a planer. He waved shyly.

"This's m'son, Cale. Daughter's up at the house with the wife." I thought I could hear a distant piano. *Up here?* "We're just straightenin' up t'day; I just finished a frame this week."

We talked shop a while, trucks, wood, stone, and how hard it was to get up here in winter. Very hard. Then Rhys invited me up to the cabin, and we climbed. A Jeep perched outside the door, and beyond it the world dropped away, to more and taller mountains out there. An attractive woman of mid-to-late thirties was hanging clothes on a line in the sun, with a slender girl maybe eight, helping.

"Moira, this's Harlan. He beats on rocks. Siobhan, come meet a man who drives a bright red truck." The wife came forward with a glad smile (visitors rare here, for sure), but the girl hung back, clinging to her mother's long skirt. Moira's hand was as rough as mine.

The talk never slowed. We found out all about where we were from, how they'd found this eagle's aerie (cheap), and how, impossibly, they had running water, LP gas fridge, gas mantle lights, gas cookstove, and even water heater.

About that water: seems a well driller had actually reached a lower spot on their land via an easier cutoff track, and found water. Rhys used a generator and submersible pump to fill a big tank on a surplus army 4x4, which he then hauled up to a bigger, buried tank (so it wouldn't freeze) for gravity feed to the house.

Wow.

They fed me. Showed me more of their modern-day pioneering. Moira even predictably made subtle mention of a single girl who raised goats and made cheese down near the river. *Thanks, but no thanks.* Or maybe later. I pictured a hippie, sunburned, impossibly long straight hair, maybe didn't shower often. *Now, that's chickenshit, Kemp. She might...*

But that subject had lightly passed as more things begged to be discussed.

Rhys did know of several prospects for my work, mostly in and around Missoula.

"That's where the money is. But some of these ranchers—the ones with big second homes and tax write-offs—like good work. I'll ask around."

It was a great visit, with his assurances that yes, he did need a hand with a frame now and then, and it paid better than straight carpentry. I left with the real idea that I could make it in my chosen field.

And winter? Just hafta wait and see. That's when Rhys and his son Cale hunted, holed up, hit the home-schooling with Moira and Siobhan. Also that lady was compiling a book on mountain wildflowers, and had a publisher for it.

Rough life, but they were still young enough to hack it, apparently. I could imagine cabin fever in spades, come January.

Rhys also made furniture, though, which he could do in the heated shop while snowed in.

~ * ~

After the stonemason left, the Carter family naturally talked about him.

"If he's as good as those pictures, he'll be in demand," Moira observed. "Hope you two can work together some."

"Yeah, seems like a good guy all right, knows carpentry, trucks, cars, got college. Might be okay in spite of that." A grin. "How'd you like Harlan, kids?"

"He's okay," Cale said. "Couldn't believe I shot that buck. Maybe he'll go hunting with us."

"He's got big ears," Siobhan said.

"Single." Moira's mind was working. "I'm sure he and Crescent would get along. She's locked herself in down there with nothing but those goats; I'd say they both need each other."

"Now, don't start matchmaking, Yenta," Rhys cautioned. "Folks gotta make their own beds, y'know, grown people, both of them."

"Oh, I know. It's just that..." and he knew his bride wouldn't let this go.

~ * ~

Okay, I'd asked this mountain man where I could catch fish, and he'd actually confided in me two of his favorite holes on the Bitterroot, and one on Kootenai Creek, down below the peaks from the Idaho line.

So as evening came on, I strung up and started dropping flies below riffles that swirled into deep river water below Florence. Had to climb a couple fences, but it was soon worth it. Insects buzzed above the current, and oftener than I'd have thought, a trout would grab one.

Now, like all fishermen, I was prepared to go home empty, with nothing but the experience, but my new streak of luck seemed to hold. As in, two sizeable brownies, and the thrill of playing them, landing them.

I put my gutted prizes in the ice chest and headed for Missoula at dark. Replenished the ice. Ate the last of the last day's cooking at the campground, then stretched out in the Rover's open bed under the stars. I'd left the camper cap at Ridley's place, and could take this arrangement, with a little insect repellent and a tarp, okay.

First thing in the morning after coffee and raisin bran, I drove to the store, which was already open. I off-loaded a few things behind it to make room for more stone, until I could see Kay had no customers. Mrs. Hall was there too, and I took the ice chest in.

"These are for both of you," I announced, "and Kay, I never had better sandwiches. Thanks." She blushed again, which again, made you forget what her face lacked. "Now I'm off to grab rocks. See you." I retreated before they could say anything embarrassing.

I reflected on the way to the quarry that folks—mostly women—were sure taking care of me, out this far from home. Warm feeling. But also a bit taken aback by Kay's obvious beyond-friendship interest. How to handle that? Not encourage it, for sure. No place for girls—any girls—in my plans. Just yet, anyway. Image of the bikini-clad pair in the canoe.

But not to hurt Kay's feelings, either. I remembered being so often the left-out hulking kid, the one chosen last for pickup ball games. The trying not to let it show.

She'd have been like that, the gawky girl the others left behind, overlooked or intentionally excluded from childhood adventures. And adolescent in-groups. Yeah, and high school cliques, the giggling dares and put-on sophistications. To endure the cuts, the cruelties. Probably took solace in horses on their ranch. But I'd noticed she wasn't gawky, now. No way: moved with a sort of grace, like a dancer.

And now she was being too nice to me, the guy with the driven determination to hack out his own corner of this West, and not give a hang, as Teddy Roosevelt had declared, for any man. Or woman. But it really did need dealing with, before any misunderstandings.

Didn't it?

I picked rocks. I loaded rocks. I hauled rocks. I set rocks with more care than ever in my life on this exhibit wall. I also soon saw that a two-foot height wouldn't handle all the dirt Kay had piled above. Or let enough of my work be seen well.

So, go at least another six inches high, on me. *This's already a win-win thing: won't hurt to give a little more.* But I needed more variety here. Mrs. Hall had her permit, so I worked a couple hours, then left for a closer section of National Forest designated on the map the service had provided. Before lunch, which as I said could turn out to be embarrassing. Hey, I was here to work, dammit.

Going hunting, mason-style. Good stone doesn't just jump out at you, it's coy, hidden. And one good rock out of a hundred in the woods is about the average, if you're lucky. So I spent precious hours on the spoor of stone, picking a few, carrying too many too far to the woods roads they make you stay on. Sometimes the permits specify no stones from streambeds, but a check of this one didn't state that. Good: just here along this brook were great flat capstones, their lichen green from splashed water. Heavy—no light rocks—but more than ideal. Some I could stand on edge and roll. *Reinvent the wheel, caveman.* I used the thick plank I'd borrowed from Tom Ridley to work the big ones up.

Late afternoon before I was satisfied with my load. Miles of downhill switchbacks, ridges, to a real road, then more to the site. Not much time for a good first-day showing. But I knew not to push my rig: wasn't really built for these loads.

~ * ~

"What was that about sandwiches, Kay? Harlan said..."

"It was nothing. I just fixed him a couple before he left Friday. He'd given me good advice about buying a car, which you know I've gotta do, and I just thought..." She trailed off.

"Kay, Kay. I've known you since you were in diapers. Don't give me that 'it's nothing' stuff. You like this guy. Hey, I like him too—no, don't interrupt. So, we girls have to put our heads together; this's new territory for you. Get him to go with you car hunting?"

She'd recovered. This friend/boss knew how her mind worked; she wasn't blind. So how much to reveal?

"Not yet, but you know of course, that was gonna be the next ploy."

"Good plan, but not to be obvious. Honey, I love you like a daughter, but you ain't gonna knock this boy's eyes out. So, play it a little slow. Let him think about what you've done for him so far, but don't embarrass him. He's gotta think he's calling the shots, making the choices."

"You're devious."

"Damn right. Plan's gotta be getting him used to you bein' around, helpful, but no way pushy. You're gonna let him know you've got a life, complete—well, not quite—without him or any other stud. Don't blush: every woman knows they're all just testosterone on two feet. So give it space."

"Hey, I'm no queen, but I'm not stupid. I just don't want him to wander off in three days. Which he will."

"Not for good. He likes it here. Obvious." She thought for a few minutes, stocking shelves. Then turned, beamed at Kay.

"Okay, you find a car for sale. Now. Take some time off from here; I can manage okay for a couple hours till the boys come after work. Bring it on a test drive, got it?"

"And make sure it's got problems, right? That Harlan the mechanic can spot. Oh, Hall, you are a schemer."

"How else could a poor widow survive? But then don't go for a good one till he's about through. Then he'll wanta check back, see that the car's okay after you've driven it more."

Kay hugged her.

# *Five*

I slammed rocks. Expected Kay to come out, watch, but she didn't. *Good, no distractions.* I had some great, long stones to span joints, and a few rough ones I could bury the ugly faces down in the dirt or back into the cut, leave good surfaces to build on and show to the world. I was using every secret I had on this job. Often stepped back, squinted to make sure it was right. *Take out that big face, little ones next to it too contrived. There, that's better. Don't get tunnel-vision here, Kemp.*

It was getting dark, store closed. The McClure boys had stopped by, joked, teased. I'd tuned them out, totally. Maybe even rudely. Then Mrs. Hall, not Kay, came out.

"You're gonna eat trout with me, Harlan, and don't try to get out of it. Kay's gone to town with friends, should be back soon, but we'll chow down anyway. Wash up there."

"Where do I surrender? That smells great." *So, not being a pest after all. Friends.* Just me and my co-conspirator, then. Or would Kay walk in, just on cue?

Phone rang. Mrs. Hall came back, shrugged.

"Girl won't be back till late. Know she wanted to eat fish with us. Well, her choice." We ate. Deep South hush-puppies, of all things, too. Well, I was from southern Missouri.

I went to the campground stuffed. German chocolate cake, ice cream. Could a man adopt a mother? I showered, dropped off under those incredible stars like one of my stones.

Morning. Up into the hills again. Hunt stones, haul stones. Lay drystack retaining wall stones. Damn, life was good. Kay came out once, gave me the okay sign, a smile. Just enough. I realized I'd actually wanted her with us last night. *Well, no big deal. And I'm really glad the girl's got friends. But Monday night?* Not my business.

Then it was Wednesday, and I'd turned in with a load from the quarry. No gearing down, no popping the clutch, but the Rover broke a rear axle, plain metal fatigue. Put it in 4wd and inched into position, unloaded, went to work, mentally calculating the time this repair would take.

Now, I'd heeded Uncle John's proactive advice, and picked up a pair of axles in Kansas City at the dealership there. Hadn't wanted to be stranded in Nowhere, Dakota (either one).

I worked on, finished the job. Went into the store to tell Mrs. Hall I had to operate on my truck, and could she leave the outside light on later for me to see by?

"Sure, hon. Need anything else?"

"Just some of that gear grease when I get the new axle in. And something to drain the old out."

"Take that old bucket. How long d'you think it'll take?"

"Couple, three hours. Oh, come see; I've finished the wall. Or do you need to stay inside?" Late customer?"

"It's okay, I see Kay's here. She can watch the store." I hadn't noticed the '66 Mustang that'd slipped in. Smelled it, though: oil smoke. I walked over.

"You buy this?"

"Maybe. Wow, wall looks great. Oh, there's Mrs. Stapleton. I'll go take care of her." And she vanished through the door.

My boss and I went over the retaining wall in detail. I pointed out where I'd left niches for rock plantings. But I couldn't get that beat-up Mustang somebody'd dumped on Kay out of my mind.

"Dunno much about growing things, but I know Hen-and-Chicks looks good, maybe some little flowers." I'd rolled the Rover out of the way so she could see. "And vines and stuff on top, to sort of drape down, break up the expanse of stone. Hafta water that, and moisture will work down, keep the rock stuff alive.

"I love it. Just what I wanted. It's great, Harlan!"

"Okay, thanks. Now watch this." I got the garden hose, sprayed water on the stone. Within 30 seconds, the lichen greened up, dust disappeared, and damn, that wall was perfection. *No modesty.*

"It's beautiful," Kay said from behind me. She'd closed the store, come out during my spiel. "But you'll need a way for customers to find you. Got business cards?"

"I'll get 'em. And I'll need an address soon. Get after that first." But this other thing needed doing. Now, before it could do more damage to my new friend. *Is she a friend? Well, sure.*

"But about this car…"

"What about it? No rust, not too many miles on it. I got a good price, if I take it." Little defensive.

"Don't. Please. Odometer's been run back. See the wear on the clutch pedal, brake? No way has this thing got just sixty thousand miles on it. And that wear on the front tires? Out of line. And the blue smoke…"

"Oh, the man said it might need valve seals. Said it was a cheap fix. And the price..."

"Not valve seals, or guides, engine's worn out. Start it."

She did. I beckoned her out to see under the hood, pulled the pcv hose. Oil blow-by clouded out.

"That's lost compression, blow-by from bad rings. It'll use lotsa oil, lose power, get bad mileage. Rebuild would fix this part, but that's money you don't have to spend. Shut it down." I moved around it. "Now there's Bondo here in the quarter panels, too. Rust been covered over." I tapped on the offending places, and they both heard the solid thumps instead of metal echo. Mrs. Hall frowned, shook her head. I spread my hands.

"I've been had, then." Kay was shamefaced.

"No way. Please tell me you're just test-driving it, right?"

"Yes, but I told him I'd probably buy it. Only four hundred dollars. Fooled by new paint, I guess."

"You put a deposit down?" I was indignant. *That jerk...*

"No..."

"Then take this piece of crap back. If I didn't hafta fix mine, I'd go with you. Guy sees a woman, he takes advantage. I..." Dammit, I was pissed: take advantage of a great girl like this...

"Leave yours till tomorrow," Mrs. Hall said. "I've got another bedroom. Don't let our girl get taken." She was pissed too.

*Our girl. Yeah, well...* But it was obvious Kay needed a hand, and she'd stayed outta my hair, fed me...

"Let's go. If it'll even start again."

We drove back across Missoula to this little shacky house with Kay's Falcon and a half-dozen automotive relics around it. Guy in a sweaty shirt came out, gave me the eye, worried.

"You like it?" He had me pegged as maybe the angry brother or something, and I guess could read my expression. Right then I felt real protective of Kay, and I wanted very much to splatter this dude's nose flat. We got out, she handed him the keys, turned to the Falcon without a word. I controlled it. Barely.

"Nice try, dude," and we drove away. Didn't say anything for a while. It was getting dark. Then:

"Thanks, Harlan. My fault. Thought you were gonna hit that guy."

"Should've. He'd never try that on a man. Guess I'm seeing a little of what this women's lib thing's all about." I shrugged. *Well, whythehell not?* "You wanta take some time off after I fix my rig tomorrow? Find you something decent?"

"Would you? Two sandwiches couldn't be worth that. And you brought trout."

"Which you didn't eat." Why did that annoy me?

"Oh... well, I... I mean..."

"'S okay, no strings. Hey, you've been great to me." I thought I'd better add "you and Mrs. Hall. Taking in a stranger."

"Aren't we all supposed to do that?"

"Oh sure, but most people..." *No, most people are out for whatever they can get.* But I remembered enduring compulsory chapel for four years at the college. Well, here was some of that, maybe some of living the faith we're supposed to have. "And I'm grateful, lady. Really am."

~ * ~

The Rover had a full-floating rear axle setup, which means the wheel runs free, doesn't have to be jacked up to replace the axle. I got on it early after a great breakfast courtesy of Mrs. Hall. Unbolted it, slid it out, catching the gear grease in the bucket. Cracks back from the break, which was right at the inside spline. Bits of metal in the housing.

Then I dropped the driveshaft, took the nuts off the differential studs, caught that grease, also filled with shiny metal fragments. I removed what was left of the axle pieces. Swabbed everything with a kerosene-soaked rag. Gears looked okay, mostly because I hadn't driven far. Even with the axle out, those chunks would've gotten to gear teeth: bad.

If necessary, I could've pulled the other axle too, and the driveshaft, so nothing vital would've turned as I front-wheel-drove home. Lucky this time.

The other axle showed a bit of a twist, so I replaced both, and resolved to order another set. I remembered a classic Jaguar sedan a friend had, that'd also broken an axle. Brits just dropped the ball there, I guess. Surely Rovers caught hell on those steep sheep farms in Yorkshire, Scotland, New Zealand. *Save a buck on steel, capitalist swine.*

I filled the differential with the 90-weight and was ready for the road by ten. On cue, Kay appeared with two root beers, cold.

It was a hot day, and she had on shorts and a halter. Her long legs were smooth and tanned, and I had to tear my eyes away from them. That started a sequence: I got up to her slim waist, and yes, firm breasts, moving just a little as she walked. *Damn. Stop this! Horny bastard!* But the eyes were smiling as she registered my checking her out, and for a moment my resolve to stay away from her turned to water. There was even this tingling...

I got it together finally, wiping hand cleaner, looking at the Rover, thinking gears, axles. Taking the cold bottle from her warm hand. Hoping she hadn't noticed anything embarrassing.

"Let's drive this rig, so nobody gets the idea you're thinking of trading. Cash, you get the best deal. And don't pay what they're asking."

"Figured that. And I've been saving the pennies for this."

Couple ads in the Missoula paper looked promising. One was a '50 Studebaker rocket-nose, not a classic, but in five, ten years, who knew? It had a stock-as-a-stove flat-head six, not that efficient a power plant.

Good enough car, but Kay didn't like the color, or the trashed interior. Neither did I: reminded me of a hog pen.

"Rode hard and put away wet."

"Horse talk. You a closet horse junkie?" That smile.

"Nah, but that fit just too well. And a '53 hardtop is a slicker Studebaker, if you can find one. Wanta see this other Mustang? Or the Firebird?"

"Both. Although I've got the feeling the Pontiac won't hold its value as well. The Mustang's got... well *attitude*."

"Yeah, that, for sure. But I found out in a college class the Ford CEO, Lee Iacocca, did the same polling and customer preference research for the Mustang as he did for the Edsel. Go figure."

"Wow. Oh, here's a P-1800 Volvo station wagon. Can't afford it, but let's look, okay?" She was like a kid. A kid with a nose for good cars.

"Sure, but if it means car payments, I wouldn't. All that interest."

"Yeah, like to stay debt-free. Just had one student loan, and sold my favorite horse to pay it off."

"Sorry to hear that. Shame we can't get around on horseback anymore. Tough though, dodging eighteen-wheelers."

"For sure. You read Edward Abbey's *The Brave Cowboy?*"

"No. Or not yet. Read *Desert Solitaire,* his signature piece."

"Well, I won't spoil it for you, then. Oh, there's the P-1800. I do like the looks of it. Must be nearly new, though."

It was a neat car. The P-1800 sportscar was also hot, but this had room for, well, saddles, camping stuff, whatever. We met the owner, a dark-haired divorcee who needed to sell. She was little; Kay was not.

"I can't get my knees under the steering wheel," she lamented, racking the seat all the way back.

"I'm desperate," the brunette almost wailed. "Make me an offer."

"Sorry, I can't drive it," Kay commiserated. "Good luck." We drove away regretfully.

The Mustang was a stick shift, six cylinder, blue, the rarer 4-speed, which might've been a replacement, and a hardtop.

"I'd really like a convertible, but I hear replacing tops isn't worth it."

"No," I told her, "and anything you leave inside is just a knife-slice from being stolen." I was checking the car over. College kid had gone abroad to study, and his mother needed to send him money.

"He never had any trouble with it," she insisted. All right, 85,000 miles, but on these long highways... Engine clean, no rust, interior still good. Tailpipe not blackened inside, which would mean burning oil, or too much gas. Kay slid the seat back, checked out the view. Started it up. I noticed the front tires were good, and not worn unevenly. Suspension a little light, but Ford used good steel. I'd read that's what inspired old Henry F. to build the light, cheap Model T instead of the heavier cars he couldn't sell, now almost seventy years ago.

We drove it. She out a few miles, I back. It was okay. I told her so. Now for the hard part.

"You're asking six hundred," Kay began. "That's pushing it for me. Can we deal a little?"

"Um. He needs the money. What'd you have in mind?"

Kay looked at me, but I turned palms up. This was her show: had to be worth it to her, not me.

"I can offer five." She'd seen this wasn't a cheap place. Kid studying abroad.

"Oh, I couldn't do that. Maybe five-seventy-five?"

"Five-fifty, cash. You think about it, ma'am." She turned, started for my truck. Game over.

"Okay, then. five-fifty. I'll get the title."

I thought about her Falcon. It had a few miles left in it, but the tires, battery, rust. Get $200, she'd be ahead. Take $150 in a pinch. Her choice.

Back at the store, Mrs. Hall inspected, approved. Thanked me. I waved it off. Hey, just a couple hours...

"I'll run an ad then," Kay decided, "or just put a sign on the old one, park it here. Okay, Hall?"

"Sure, save the ad money. What they see is what they get. You gone then, Harlan?"

"I guess. Go hunting for a cave somewhere south, since I'm expecting work that way." She handed me cash, actually hugged me. Nice woman.

"And I caught that about the extra wall height. So this's a bit more. And don't be a stranger. I'll send a note if anybody wants to shower you with money." There'd been several folks who'd admired the stonework, but so far no jobs from it.

Kay was suddenly shy. Then she took both my hands, looked me in the eye, thanked me. I noticed those eyes matched the car. And I did notice those legs again.

# Six

Paper listed a couple places for rent down the highway, and I cruised by. Didn't like any of them. Too close, road noise. Too claustrophobic. Then I realized I really didn't want to pay rent. What I wanted was to find a piece of ground a seller would let me pay on, camp until I could put up shelter. Long shot, but maybe Tom Ridley would know of something, or Rhys.

Time being, I knew I could stay in the Ridley shed, long's I kept them happy. Maybe help him some on the carpentry, free. The stone was where I wouldn't compromise. Work something out. *Girl sure was happy with that car. Well, wish her the best.* She'd surely get that good biology research job, go on with her life. Sad she wouldn't get the breaks good-looking people always got. Genes: couldn't control them. Good thing stonemasons didn't have to be movie stars.

~ * ~

I made the Ridley house, the stone part, look great. They'd gotten refinanced, and the job lasted till Rhys looked me up with a landscaping and timberframe shelter job on one of the big absentee-owned ranches.

Seemed Moira had scored the plantings, Rhys would do the shelter, and I could do the paths, stone steps, walls. It'd be a trial thing again, with a first-phase approval, but paid, the property manager said.

And there was a quarry on the property, no less. The stone was good quartzite, and big pieces. Big rock doesn't take much more time to lay than the right little one, and the job gets done quicker. And better looking.

I'd arranged to pay a pittance to the Ridleys to stay on after the stonework, and yeah, I'd helped Tom some. He was picky, though, so I stayed off the close work. Kinda odd, his being that good with wood and so clueless about stone. So I was a glorified helper, really. Been there; done that, no shame in it.

I'd meant to get back up to Missoula, check Kay's car over again, see her and Mrs. Hall, really the only people I knew there. Just got too busy, doing work I was good at, enjoying it, seeing the progress, knowing what I was doing would be there forever. And I was using my spare time place-hunting.

June had slipped through July, and now cool nights said it was halfway August. All the land listed for sale was overpriced, unless you had to climb up to it, like Rhys Carter's place. Soon everybody I met knew I was looking, and suggestions found their way to me.

Mrs. Hall sent a note about a job in Missoula I should look at. Maybe big, she wrote. *Well.* So I drove up, a day before the ranch job was to start. Big job I'd probably have to pull off, come winter. See about it though, naturally.

Kay's Mustang wasn't there, and I realized it'd been two months.

"She took that job in Idaho, Harlan. Said for me to tell you goodbye for her. Just left Tuesday. Was supposed to wait till the weekend. Got antsy, I guess. Miss that girl; known her family forever." *Damn. Should've at least called, checked in. Moscow, Idaho. About five hours by car. Seven by Rover.* I shook myself. *About this job...*

"The university. Some architect specifying stone on a new classroom building. Be bids, and a red-tape state job. Cattle call next week; got the date here somewhere. Imagine the big contractors will be all over it, but they've gotta use somebody to put those rocks up."

I looked at the specs. Had no idea how this lady had gotten onto this, but didn't ask. Hey, she knew everybody. And wow, thick veneer, eight inches; my kinda work. Local stone required. This could be good. Need a helper, maybe two. Scaffolding, mixer, which I could rent. Real truck, or I could hire hauling. But I'd want to choose every rock. *Well, cross that bridge...*

"I'll be there, ma'am, and thanks. Who you got helping here?" I looked around.

"Nobody yet. Kept putting it off. More people going in to the supermarkets, I can probably handle it myself. I just depended on Kay so much. She worked all since freshman year in college, stayed here, and this past year. Too far to her folks' place."

I was getting an idea. Whether I got the big job or not, I knew winter would shut me down. You can't even do drystack with the ground frozen; thaw, settling, will tear it apart later. And even if the university job could be tented and heated, I'd need a place to stay.

"You don't suppose, maybe come winter..." She jumped on it.

"Thought you'd never ask. You move into the spare room just's soon's you finish down there. Get the big one, okay. I can't pay much for store help, but you won't starve."

"You smooth-talking woman, you got the right redneck. And if I wasn't a green kid, I'd come courtin'."

"Bullshit. I know, when you're ready for it, you'll find the right girl. And by then, you'll be wise enough to recognize her." *Now, whatthehell's that supposed to mean? Kay? Nah, Kay's got a career. Meet herself a professor or something. Or anyway, that cowboy.*

So it was settled, place to spend the winter, place to work out of, address. Even phone. I promised to let her know the outcome of the bidding war, and left about a foot off the ground. Did miss seeing Kay though, somehow.

~ * ~

*Well, I've done it, got the job, made the move. Should've stayed to see Harlan; know Hall set that up. But he hasn't visited, written, called. Pretty clear he's not interested, and time to move on.* Or just maybe this was the space he needed, to think about her, realize how they could make a life together.

Anyway, she just couldn't have trusted herself around him just then, hoping, risking being put down. No, better a clean break, new life here. Challenging job, her field. She was only 23, plenty time ahead for... anything.

Finding a place to live, getting settled, learning the job filled her days, weeks. She sent Hall and her parents her address, phone number. Didn't send them to Harlan's P.O.boxes. If he should want to reach her, he could. If...

Her boss was a hungry, dedicated entrepreneur who worked sixty hours a week. She let him know she'd work hard, but with the low starting salary, she insisted on regular hours. He'd hoped to persuade her of the opportunity here, but she was firm about the hours. *Never want anything—job or whatever—more than the guy wants what you've got.* Her dad had hammered that into her, and she'd live by it.

Even with the absent Harlan Kemp.

~ * ~

The ranch job was a wet dream. Working with Rhys and Moira was great. We got to be best friends very soon, my kinda people. I hadn't cut the manager any slack on my price, and when the owner and his wife flew in from Seattle and saw my first work, I wished I'd upped it.

I'd set these big, lichened boulders at turnings of the path, and Moira had planted just the right bushes, vines, flowers around them. It all was to be a sort of outdoor retreat, with pools, waterfalls, stone seats and steps, almost a maze of hidden discoveries. *Yeah, what money and a good landscape architect can accomplish. Well, good people to carry it out really make it happen, read us.* Oh, and I'd used quiet little recirculating pumps, save water. Buried the electric wires, kept it pristine.

But the first snow hit, late September, and from then for six weeks there'd be rarer good days to work. We talked about our schedule, decided on just what we could get done in another month. By then Rhys had finished the 16-foot square shelter, to the owners' delight, and would cut and pre-assemble a second one in his shop over winter. Moira would continue to play Supermom till spring, including starting plants inside at windows.

And okay, after what good days we could grab, I'd be a storekeeper. The university job had gone to a big contractor as expected, who'd disdainfully declared he didn't want a 'backyard stonemason'. *Screw you too, dude.* He'd also wanted me to halve my price. *Your loss, loser.*

~ * ~

I could check out possible pieces of land even when the weather was only half bad, and I did. Learned that a falling-in shack on acreage actually lowered the price. And of course, the fact that location was all of it. No land on a river anywhere, which would've been nice. Up the creeks was great, like the Ridley place, but the almost-sheer mountains and the national forest slammed the gate on prospects before they were far enough out to be cheaper. Distance didn't seem to bother these people: go 80 miles to a specialty store or event, 150 miles to see friends.

I was realizing I'd come West a century too late; all the good places taken, the leftovers like anywhere, carved up into tiny lots with houses, nothing but the view of the mountains and rivers.

I could see I'd have to find that big place someone was willing to cut me a piece off. And for that I'd have to get close to that person, because it'd really be sort of a favor. Which would take time. Ingratiate myself, with absolutely no shame.

Or marry into a place? Chickenshit. And of course that would be the opposite of my determined independence. No, this wannabe mountain man would chart his own course, make his own way, succeed on his own.

With okay, a little help from his friends.

~ * ~

Late October came, and with it a halt to the ranch job. I said goodbye to Rhys and Moira, packed up my stuff at the Ridley place, told them I'd see them in the spring. Ahead lay nearly half a year of exile from my craft, a necessary hiatus I wasn't sure how well I'd handle. Probably go crazy, inside all the time, frustrated, dependent on Mrs. Hall for my very survival.

Well, at least I'd salted away a few bucks—no, quite a few bucks, with my low overhead—and now I'd learn firsthand what winter here could offer, if anything. And learn how to deal with it in the future. If it got too crazy, I guessed I could head south, but have to go a long way to escape it. And to what? Southern California zoo of people, high prices? Mexico and its poverty? No, Montana had me in its grip, and I was here, for better or worse.

So I moved my few possessions into the Hall house, began learning pricing, deliveries, stocking ...all the stuff. Country general store out of town, there was hardware, farm needs, motor oil, rope, and of course, groceries. No gas pumps, which would've been present a generation before.

Mrs. Hall didn't mother-hen me, which I couldn't have endured. She did suggest things, events I might like, but soon picked up on my preferred loner status. She'd drive her big old

Buick into town a couple times a week to see friends or just get away, but I was determined to hoard my dollars, read a lot at night, and stay put.

I got a library card, checked out a lot of books. Mix of favorite authors, Benet, Faulkner, poetry by T.S. Eliot and Yeats. I passed a bunch of Sundays reading, after attending church a couple times with Mrs. H.

She soon picked up that I wasn't getting much out of that. Oh, I was a believer, but I could see a sort of slide, a giving-in to what was politically correct, in the Protestant churches all over. Pressure groups pushing for more leniency, a new interpretation of Scripture. Didn't like that much.

I spent a few bucks to make my stonework portfolio more professional, had business cards printed, that sign on the truck with some special adhesive. And I whipped that store into painfully organized shape. Customer dropped an egg on the floor or kid smeared a glass case, I was all over it. You're gonna do something, do it right.

And I got bored as hell by December. Periodic snow, not nearly as bad as I'd expected, which I'd scrape off the parking lot with the blade on the old tractor. Dry air made being outside bearable, even with low temperatures, which was good. But could I last till April? Had to; simple as that. But by next winter, things'd have to change.

~ * ~

Kay McBryde's world revolved around water samples, pollution levels, reports, soil testing. Her boss wanted to expand their client base, broaden their services. He had a small staff, worked them hard. He'd explained to every new hire, including Kay, that all of them must give all they could to build the company that fed them.

She could do that, and did. But she'd also enrolled in the first of night classes at the university toward a combined master's and doctorate. It would take years, but as an employed resident, no out-of-state tuition. She could stand it, one course at a time. This explained, of course, her refusal to work additional hours.

Kay focused on water quality work. With her boss's encouragement. Her long-term plan was to earn the PhD, and keep tabs on openings back in Missoula. That area's streams were and would continue to be gold mines, worth saving. There'd be a good job there, in time. Like Harlan Kemp, she was determined to create her own choices, not have to settle for second-rate jobs and places she didn't want to live.

Moscow was a pleasant, friendly town, the kind of place, she soon saw, that you could suddenly realize you'd spent forty uneventful years in. That wasn't going to happen to Kay McBryde. The big sky of her home would never release its hold on her, as she'd realized that daydreaming day on the mountain back in June.

Harlan Kemp had been a brief possibility, seen in perspective, and she still liked to fantasize a little about him, those hard hands, powerful arms she'd wanted around her. But he was a memory now, a road not taken.

And what could she have done differently to bring them together? Not one thing. He had to pursue his own demons, chart and track his own course. And so did she, wherever that led.

She remembered vividly Hall's prediction that the two of them would find each other again, despite other lives they might live, other careers, other loves, even. Now she doubted it; the ugly duckling wasn't ever going to become a swan.

Ever since her early teenage, that awkward, embarrassed phase, she'd speculated on the fates of ugly girls. Too many had grabbed the first man who'd shown even a slight interest, and were living lives of diapers, dirty dishes, alcoholic husbands. Yes, who lusted after other women as if it were a right, their being chained to dowdy wives. She shuddered at the memory of Ron Gillespie.

There was also the stereotype missionary, serving in remote world-ends, rarely but not impossibly rendered more attractive by those usually-shy men's insulation from other women. She'd actually given that career a passing thought. But she believed one had to feel a call for that work, if she were honest.

There were the girls of all descriptions who blatantly set out to stalk their men, using the wiles honed for thousands of years of survival. And she guessed she'd lowered herself to just that with Harlan, with the gleeful conspiracy of dear Hall. *Lot of good that did,* and remembering still gave her a flush of shame.

Memories. That's all old people had, and she wasn't old. Yet. Maybe Harlan was just a... summer romance? Hardly that. A flirtation? She didn't know how to flirt. And with no response from him, she'd have felt foolish.

He hadn't wanted her.

*Oh, but the way his eyes devoured me that time, there in the hot morning sun. My legs, my crotch. My breasts. Then that staying on my eyes too long—not long enough—yes, just then he did want me.* And dammit, he'd enjoyed being next to her in his truck, car-hunting. And what had been in his mind, out there on that river, casting for trout to bring her? *Should've stayed that time, not played the hard-to-get game, despite Hall's advice.* Yeah, at least she'd have more memories now.

Kay knew she was giving in to a role she hated, that of the overlooked, even spurned woman. Dammit, there was so much more to life than a man. *A PhD. Maybe in five years. Six? I'll be under 30. I'll be on top, with choices. Prestige, even. Who expects a scientist to look like one of Charlie's Angels?*

*But he did want me, that time...*

# *Seven*

Third week in December, just before I was about to chuck it all and head out of this claustrophobic place, two things happened. The first was a package in the mail from Kay, which contained a heavy sheepskin winter cap, with fold-down ear flaps. No note. It was the warmest thing I'd ever worn, and well, this kindness just blew me away. Why'd she done that? I asked Mrs. Hall.

"Pretty clear to anybody but a blind man, Harlan. Girl likes you. And she's always been just about the sweetest thing on this earth. I about spanked her when she up and ran off early, didn't stay to see you."

"I'm sorry, too. Great girl. Shoulda made time to come see both of you."

So. I owed her something now. Well, I'd been combating the blahs with some wood carving when things were slow. Had done little birds, leaping trout, tiny horses. Yeah, horses: she'd sold hers. I packed one, sent it, no note either.

Then, second thing, I got a call at the store from Moira Carter, must've been down in town at a phone booth. They wanted me to come to their place for Christmas, stay a few days. I could imagine the non-road, the ice and snow. No, Rhys had plowed it with the Army 4x4 and they were getting in and out okay. Besides, I drove a Land Rover, didn't I?

"Won't hear of your refusing," she insisted. "Cale wants to go hunting with you, and Siobhan keeps talking about her rock star."

Could Mrs. Hall spare me? She could. Maybe she'd sensed my nearing the precipice, surely recognized cabin fever.

"Go. Stay a while. Business slow, people stocked up. I can handle this with one hand. Get outta here."

I went. Roads were clear, but I knew it'd be different up high. Not to worry: Rovers were made for this. Slid off, I could winch back on. And the worst weather would be next month or two. Or three.

Normal traffic on 93: these folks didn't all burrow in. I was overreacting. As I drove, I remembered a call from Kay weeks before. Mrs. Hall had talked, then handed the phone to me.

"Hey, girl. I apologize for not being here to see you off. Wanted to check your car over, too. Just got covered in work, but mostly it was just bad manners. You okay? Car running okay?" And car chatter kept the awkwardness down. Yeah, Mustang behaving. Yeah, working hard. Taking a course at the college. No vacation time till next summer, fall. Didn't know about Christmas. It fizzled, starting to be over.

"Well, you get downsized, we're holding your grocery career for you. Everybody misses you." A considered beat. "Me, too."

"Oh, well I miss... all of you, too. Hafta wrangle some time..."

"That'd be good. Stay sweet, girl. 'Bye, now." For sure, one thing Kay was, she was sweet.

Now, driving that non-road, I thought back to our times together, brief as they'd been. Really, being with her more wouldn't have cost me anything. And she was obviously not pining for me. *Surely got herself a grad student or some upwardly-mobile type there. So I wouldn't have been leading her on. Too Puritanical, I guess.* Hey, I wasn't a priest or anything. And the gifts? Well, Christmas and all...

And I would like to see her, really. She hadn't contacted Mrs. Hall about coming for a quick visit, so I wouldn't miss her, being at the Carters'. Speaking of, here came their mountain, and at first it wasn't bad, the light snows having melted on the south slopes.

But as the track wound into the dark ravines and sun-robbed steepness, the plowed verges rose white. Be there till spring, surely. Again I marveled at the way these friends were surviving, this far back, up, off and out of that system.

I wanted that.

Wanted the quiet, the stillness of the forest, the elk and the eagles and the bright streams of snow-melt. I wanted to become a part of this, needing little from the outside, subsisting maybe on just a few stone jobs a year, but here close to this magnificent earth.

It galled me to have to amass the cost of whatever niche I was to find, put in my time and muscle for people who could pay me, just to grab a sliver of this big country. For sure born that century too late. I could almost see myself back then, riding my trusty horse into these mountains, maybe trapping beaver, living by my wits, long rifle—no, they had lever-actions by then—handy for a stray deer. Pulling big trout out of the teeming streams, shooting fat geese out of the sky. Maybe making friends with whatever Indians were still around then.

Fantasy.

The kids swarmed me, seeming like a crowd. Moira hugged me, Rhys grabbed me like a lost brother. *Like to be that.* Cale flipped a switch, and battery-powered Christmas lights glowed. Siobhan clapped her eight-year-old hands in glee.

Plants crowded every window ledge, and the big woodstove Rhys had welded together crackled, warmed the place like summer. What an oasis, here on top of and beyond the struggling, ant-like rest of us on our flattened, inhabitable world.

Cale had to show me the deer quarters, hanging frozen in the smokehouse. And the big salted brown trout, halved and ready for the darker days of deep winter. He chattered on about our proposed hunt, places familiar to him but like Mars to me: this ridge, that swale. The other meadow, this gulch. We'd get our elk, for sure; he'd wish it into existence.

The place smelled great, with Moira's cooking, aromatic candle wax, leather and wool and joy. I was unwinding into a state of bliss, belonging here with these great people. *Hey, I might just not go back*, I thought, still fantasizing.

I gave Moira a miniature ring-neck pheasant I'd carved, and Siobhan a butterfly. Gave the others boxes of ammo I knew would fit the hunting rifles. They gave me warm gloves. Wow.

An engine outside, laboring up the last rise. An International Scout came into view, with a small muffled figure at the wheel. The kids rushed out, gave her—it was a her—the same welcome I'd gotten. She came inside, took off a fur cap to let a cascade of brown curls tumble down. Moira engulfed her in a prolonged hug, and silver laughter spilled out. I watched, wondering, but then not really, when this visitor presented the hostess with a big wrapped chunk of what had to be cheese.

The goat girl. The dyed-in-the-goat-hair hippie. She had this upturned nose in a bright, open face, wide-set eyes. And, coat off, a nice shape. Maybe a couple years older than me, but still a girl. And really tiny. Yeah, a self-sufficient, single, running-her-own-life girl. In spite of me, I felt my pulse quicken.

"This's Crescent," Moira turned her toward me. "Harlan Kemp, who does those terrific things with rocks you've seen." *Crescent*. Showed me a row of even, white teeth in a glad smile.

"Of course I've heard about you. Any of it true?" That laugh. "And I've seen your work, so it must be." *Okay, frank, but not mean.*

"And from the little I know of you, Crescent, you're living my dream." *Maybe a wet dream: damn, she's beautiful.*

"I wish. Daylight-to-dark goats. But hey, it's a living." She brushed those curls aside, clearly inspecting me. I felt like a lab specimen.

Moira had told me this girl had managed to keep hold of the cabin and 20 acres she and a now-departed husband had bought. She'd had a mortgage, but now finally a life, it seemed.

"Love your truck," she went on. "Diesel. You burn recycled veggie oil in it?" Well, Uncle John had, mostly as an experiment.

"Working on that. Restaurants dumping the stuff, paying people to haul it off. But I don't have a setup to filter it, haven't rigged a heater for it in the Rover yet."

"Wish I could find one. My hog eats gas, and it's going sky-high. International just chopped a big V8 in two for the Scout engine, and my half was the loser." *So, another woman who knows her wheels?*

"America needs to catch up with the world about diesel, all right. Our instant-gratification public just doesn't want to wait for glow plugs. Like ten, twenty seconds will ruin all they live for."

"Yeah, and the smell. Like gas is any better." Shift then, like gears. "What're you doing to survive this winter?"

"Staying with an older friend, helping her run her grocery store out of Missoula. Missing my rock fix."

"I guess. Moira tells me you're looking for land."

"Desperately. Paying rent burns me almost as much as punching a time clock. Gonna find a hole somewhere by summer or die."

"Know the feeling. Every morning, I go outside and just glory in my little spread. Mine, all mine. And finally, not the bank's." Smile, shrug. *Yeah, there'd be that for me, too, payments.* Prospect didn't thrill me. "We had help from the parents, but then I had to buy Glenn out."

Glenn. What kinda fool had he been? Well, not to judge: woman might really be hell to live with. No, she couldn't, the way these friends obviously loved her. Siobhan was sitting on her lap, playing with a curl. Moira had this secret smile on, and I knew I'd been set up.

I'd brought wine and a loaf of Mrs. Hall's homemade dark wheat bread, which she was teaching me to bake. We ate venison, stuffed on home-canned veggies, then had mincemeat pie, also venison. Never tasted better. Told Moira so.

"You're just tired of your own cooking. Rhys was eating out of cans too, when I met him. Crescent's the cook." *Way to be obvious, girl. And I'm with you.*

"Is she just being loyal, or do you enjoy cooking?"

"I survive." Shrug. "And now I make the time to try to do it right. Had too much of the grab-a-carb when we were in the system."

"And you make this terrific cheese." Which we were having with coffee or the wine. Some smoked thing, delicious.

"Yeah, and that's something of a hassle, or the goat milk is. Regulations. I've got a following for the raw milk, but now the food police are after me: not pasteurized, you know. Speaking of which, please sign my petition. I'm getting folks to back me, help me stand up for the right to be left alone." She dug in a tote bag and proffered a heavily-filled notebook. I signed. Gladly.

Before this sprite left, much later, she made sure I knew how to find her place, invited me down to see her operation.

"Ever milk a goat?"

"No. Milked cows growing up; guess I could manage." Semi-promise? I was sorry to see her green Scout trundling off down the mountain. *So this is how we're supposed to spend the winters.* Unless I'd read her wrong, Crescent was available, for one kind of a relationship or another. And Moira made sure to inform me that just then there was no significant other in the Crescent picture.

"But she's independent as a hog on ice. Her terms, all the way. We know you're that way too, and you might just butt heads, like her goats."

One thing for sure, any time I could spend with this woman this winter, wouldn't cut into serious stonework time. I was six days on at the store, but I'd be a fool if I didn't follow this up. That night, in the tiny loft room with Cale, I had trouble keeping this elf out of my dreams. Didn't try hard.

We set out in Rhys's 4wd pickup next morning for the ranch, down the mountain, across, up through the latched gate at least a mile on. Parked, followed Rhys off to a ridge above us.

"Good sight lines down this open draw, and two more on either side. Herd moves up into the open about a half-hour from now. We'll get set up, hidden." Cale was excited. He carried a 30-30 Winchester 94 lever-action, which I thought wasn't long-range enough. Rhys had loaned me a 30-06 like one Uncle John had taught me to use, and I was confident.

But no way would I take a shot Cale might get, and I knew Rhys was on board. He had a sporterized 303 Enfield, an antique English rifle I didn't know, but figured he did. Unless he'd given me his best gun. Probably had: nice scope.

We got situated near a bushed-around field Ponderosa, looking, we hoped, like thick bushes in our heavy coats and caps. Cale had two forked sticks he'd set up, crossing, supporting each other at his rifle barrel. I'd never seen that before, but yes, hold that sight steady.

An hour dragged by under a cold, overcast sky. I had my hands in pockets, not really ready for action, and I was getting chilled, from my seated bottom up. Then an elk cow showed, coming warily up out of a thicketed draw. She paused, pawed the thin snow, cropped grass that was mostly a memory. Slowly, others followed. Then I saw a bull, which had actually slipped up from somewhere, and was now leading his herd in a sneaky sort of way.

Others appeared, including a not-quite-grown bull, no match for Big Daddy, and some calves. The slightest breeze was toward us, and we stayed frozen. Not hard, just then.

Cale was squinting along the 30-30's open sights, following the young bull. I winked across at Rhys, who was watching his son. He grinned. But he also had his rifle ready, in case Cale missed. He held up a cautious finger, shook his head slightly at the boy to wait. He nodded.

The quarry moved like a glacier. *Slow and very cold.* I eased my gun around too, only to fire if both others missed. No great hunter, I still figured to carry my weight if it came to that.

150 yards: too far for the carbine. But the breeze shifted just enough that several of the elk lifted heads, sniffing. They looked around, *danger*. I saw Cale tense, readied my rifle. He'd miss, and how good was Rhys's old 303?

I knew the stock-still bull was seconds away from dashing away, the herd after him. I waited, not breathing.

The shot boomed beside me and the target jumped, ran a few steps as the others sped away, then fell. *Nice shot, kid.* I flashed a thumbs-up to Rhys. Cale was almost jumping up and down, but trying to look cool. We both slapped him on the back, congratulated the young Nimrod.

We field-dressed the bull, dragged him the steepest part of the open land down off the ridge, Rhys planning to come as high as he could with the truck. Which wasn't near enough, so we played tug-o-war with our prize another half-hour of sweating— yes—heaving, and blowing. Finally got it up two stout planks, like a big, yielding stone. Side-hilled down, drifting, tires biting, to the ranch road below.

With what I'd seen in their smokehouse, this meat should last the winter. Modern-day living off the land. The way a man was supposed to. *When I get my own place...*

~ * ~

I stayed another day as planned, helping skin, cut up, hang meat. Ate more of Moira's good cooking. Sang offkey along with Rhys's guitar and fiddle with the family. Felt the love here, the joy.

Tried not to think ahead to the time these home-schooled kids would want to drift away into the System, become part of it, break this warm circle, leave the parents to age, here. Not an old-folks lifestyle. Then Moira confided that she was newly-pregnant again. *Wow.* They'd lost the last one—cause unknown—and this would be the final; I learned she was late 30's.

So, new life here, the continuing of the family: great. But also the necessity of getting up and down the mountain for more years as they got the kids socialized, fitted them for the demands of life among us lowly.

Great visit. More than great. The warmth I felt as I chugged down the mountain wasn't all from the Rover's Spartan heater. Wonderful folks. Couldn't wait to be working with them again.

# *Eight*

Predictably, I headed for Crescent's place, with still enough daylight to appreciate it. Wasn't that far, and I wondered that I hadn't met her earlier. *Goats daylight to dark. Independent.* Okay, like me with rocks. She'd choose her people, blow the others off. Looked more and more like my kinda woman.

She was shutting the herd up for the night in a snug barn, picked up two milk buckets as I parked.

"Missed all the fun," was her greeting. *Oh, the milking.* Well, maybe later I could... "But you can help me feed. Just put these away." She disappeared into a stark concrete-block building for a moment, came out smiling. *Cute little thing. Like to put you in my pocket, take you home...*

We portioned out feed, hay, water. Wouldn't freeze till later, she explained, but in the really cold, she'd have to heat it first. Hassle. Smell of goat everywhere, in the air, on clothes, on me now. On her, which she must've scrubbed off before the Carter visit.

"Come inside now. I've cooked for two."

*Okay!* Expecting me, of course: woman knew the score. And turned out she could definitely cook. Spices, flavors, things I didn't know existed. I was sorry I hadn't brought something to share. Rude.

Then I saw handmade art all around. Hadn't noticed. Well, I had some more carvings with me. And I did have a tiny hummingbird on a thin leather string in the Rover. I went out, got it.

The light-blue eyes widened, and she put it around her neck with her thanks, shook out those curls. Then I got the smile of the year. Felt it to my toes. She poured us some spiced tea and we sat near the woodstove.

"Okay," she began. "I'm known for being blunt, but ground rules: I'm still recovering from a nasty divorce, and I'm sharp enough to know some time has to pass before I even think about another relationship. Which doesn't preclude being friends. So if you came here expecting a quick lay, sorry about that. I know this's the laid-back Seventies, but I don't buy into all the casual sex stuff.

"Moira tells me you're a good guy, and that you're set in stone—like that?—about being independent. That's why I said yes when she asked me up the mountain to meet you. She's a frustrated matchmaker, but I love her.

"I'm all about being my own boss too, and I'm mostly there. I can live cheap, now that the damn mortgage is gone. Just the necessary electric bill, the cheese thing.

"I think we could be friends. And wherever that might go in time, I'm okay with it. End of disclaimer." She put those eyes on me. Maybe a little too hard, but then went on.

"And if I've read you wrong, no offense intended. I don't want to come off as a Jewish princess here. Which I'm not; hoping the goat-shit disproves that."

"Hey, no expectations." *Liar*. "You've surely heard I'm nose-to-the-grindstone to find a place to live, not spending money, not making time for anything that could get in the way of that…"

"No women." Statement.

"Not so far, but I confess, with my craft shut down for the winter, I'm going hermit crazy."

"Horny." Another statement.

"Umm, in light of what you just said, let's not go there."

"Well, to put it all out there—oh, poor choice of words—I'm horny too. But sex has gotta be what it's supposed to be for me, total commitment. I thought that was what I was getting with Glenn, but turned out I wasn't. Learning from my mistakes. Anyway, my stance is meant to keep predator men away."

Okay, I wasn't about to become another mistake, then. And strangely, this clearing the air carried a little relief with it. Guess I hadn't had that four years of chapel for nothing. And come down to it, I believed the same way she did. Not that I'd have had the will power to resist if it'd turned out that way.

So, great evening. We talked about everything from goats to rocks to cars to interest rates. To our shared determination to be Moira's hogs on ice, outta the system and as far off the grid as we could get. A lot of our generation were trying to go back to nature: communes, yurts, growing organic food, living off the land. This girl was doing it. Rhys and Moira had cut expenses to the bone, but with kids, depended on outside work.

I hadn't crystallized my ideal setup yet, being open to whatever presented itself. Can't eat rocks, so I'd have to be able to find work. Didn't want to be as remote as they were. And of course the prospect of sharing this 20 acres with this delightful woman could be a possibility.

Sometime. On her terms.

If.

But yeah, definitely a friend, if I could actually keep my hands off that great body. And it looked like I had to. Never been just friends with a woman: guys were my friends; women were complications. Hell, I guess Kay and I were on the way to being friends till she left. And she wasn't pretty like Crescent. *Pig.* I hoped I was past the predator thing—hoped the male species was—and that I could get beyond seeing an attractive woman as a conquest.

But face it, all of us would rather wake up next morning to good-looking instead of ugly. And speaking of, it got late. Crescent hadn't seemed to want to end our talk-fest and neither had I. So now, ride off into the long-ago sunset? Or...

"You'll stay." Matter-of-factly. "And choice: you can milk goats in the morning or make breakfast. You must cook."

"Barely. Or we could both do both, which I like better. Okay?"

"Sure, if you don't just get in my way." *Did I say frank?* "So. Back room gets cold, so stoke the stove if you wake in the night. So'll I."

And with that she showed me the bathroom, we tidied up in the kitchen, then we parted. Of course I did a repeat of my fantasies with this provocative, delightful, forceful beauty, but did finally get some sleep.

The smell of coffee woke me, and I hurried to dress, make myself useful. Outside, the sun had chased away the threatened precipitation and was burning off a cold fog. Her place was near the river, and I guessed this was a daily occurrence. Lucky to find it, or spent a lot of bucks. Both, it turned out.

"We'll do food later. Grab a cup and come on, meet the beasts."

I did, we did, and I managed about a fourth of her milking skill. Later she showed me the milk/cheese operation in that temperature-controlled building. I was by now near starvation. There was apparently a lot more to be done, but she said later would do. *Good.*

I more or less stayed clear of her in the kitchen, but did whip up my biscuit specialty, big, solid ones you could build a wall with. None of that light, fluffy air-filled stuff for me.

"Mmm," Crescent approved. "Why'd I make anything else?" Then she served up omelets with a chef's dream in them. I'd also snared the ham skillet after she'd fried in it, and made my redneck gravy. Man could live on biscuits and gravy, and I had, many times. She had them first with the gravy, then honey. And ham. I zeroed in on the omelet, savoring the flavors, so we sort of honored each other's cooking.

Finally I tore myself away from this sweet lady, remembering I had a job, such as it was, and responsibilities. But I warned Crescent I'd be coming for future visits, so beware. She laughed, threw back that head, reached up and kissed me quick. Before I could get my arms around her, she pulled away, said goodbye. And kissed that little hummingbird as she waved.

My head was full of her on the way to Missoula, naturally: how we'd get used to each other, share, draw closer. How I'd become this woman's man, whatever it took. How our mutual contempt for the enslaving system would cement us together. How...

"Well, I see you're over the mopes," Mrs. Hall greeted. "Have a good visit?"

I told her yeah, it was great. Then she gave me this 'you-blew-it' look, and I wondered where I'd put my foot in the pie somewhere.

"You missed Kay again. She got a surprise couple days off, drove over from Moscow to see her folks. And us, of course. Apparently a last-minute thing. Really wanted to see you, Harlan."

Well, damn, here the brown bird had come to see me—no doubt there—and I was off with the nightingale. Or hummingbird? Anyway, fate, or whatever, was just telling me Kay was... yesterday, I guessed. Even if I *had* sort of missed her.

But Ms. H. waved it off, wanted to hear what was so great that'd lighted her boy up. So I told her all about the Carters, the Christmas, the hunt, the way they were so self-sufficient. I didn't mention Crescent, suspecting rightly that her loyalty to Kay would put a frown on that.

Kay. Kay was now in that very world I wanted out of. That Crescent was free of. Almost. Kay really belonged back on her parents' ranch. Long-legged Kay, cowgirl Kay. Generous, sweet Kay. Afraid for me she just didn't stack up well against Crescent.

So, although I'd had her in my thoughts a lot the past couple months, now I'd been to the mountain. In more ways than one. Guilty: run off to the first pretty face, never given Kay and me a chance. But no way had I ever seen her as—well—a *girl*, I guessed. What was the new term going around? Chauvinist? Well, maybe I wasn't that, exactly, but I was sure guilty of going for looks first.

No, Crescent might've attracted me first 'cause she was pretty, but there was so much more she had going for her. That refreshing frankness, that skill as a cook, that fierce independence. That same but different sweetness. That great little body... or didn't that count? Kay had a damn fine body too, and despite her height, she could move in a way that made you watch her. *Like to see her on a horse.*

Oh hell, I'd sworn to stay off women till I got set. What was I doing letting the hormones run me, just because I'd been bored, cooped up this way?

We got a freak January thaw, like I'd seen back East, and I got started on some raised, stone-terraced planting beds Mrs. Hall wanted. Dug way down to get below frost level so things'd stay put. Drove up to the forest, a closer part, and found good stone. Had to carry it farther, but so enjoyed being up in these creek canyons, with their sheltered drifts and steaming-in-the-sun south slopes, I was happy.

The ground thawed up the slope to the house, and I dug mud, set stones, contented as a fool. I'd overestimated winter.

Didn't last. Storm blew in, covered my stone pile, crowned the new wall like frosting. But that high lasted till well into February, when another meteorological lie said spring wasn't far off.

It was. But I got in some more hits, and did go check out possible land. And yes, my hands-off promise to myself eroded, and I sneaked off a couple Sundays to see Crescent. Hey, that was closer to where I'd decided to settle anyway: double purpose.

I could tell the grind was getting to her, though. Never a day off, unless all the female goats were dry, and she'd bred them sequentially so that never happened: good business. Sometimes she could get a friend from up the road to milk, feed, stoke the stove in the cabin, get away, but not often. And she did that mostly in summer when things wouldn't freeze, when she could get a quality break, or go sell her cheese at some farmers' market or festival.

No wonder she welcomed company. Customers dropped by regularly for the goat's milk and that great cheese, but most of them had to about-face and run tend their own places. Some of which weren't close. I'd slip off Saturday nights after the store closed, explaining that I was seriously land-hunting (true), spend the night with Crescent, albeit platonically—for now—and help goat-tend so we could grab a few hours on Sunday. And of course I'd bring provisions to share.

We slogged over barren draws together. No. Up on wind-scoured ridges. No. High up near-top mountains with surprise meadows. Maybe. But everything habitable had its price: folks who'd found it first weren't letting it go cheap. Crescent's acres looked better and better. *She* looked better and better.

~ * ~

Kay had some misgivings about her chosen career. It was, of course, all work, hard, exhausting work, bent over a microscope, cataloging samples, handling someone else's field work. But most of all, it shut out her sky. The store had too, but there'd always been the breaks, the goal of that degree, and the variety of college events, that mix. And of course, Sundays up the Blackfoot at the ranch.

She missed that most. So much so that she negotiated with her boss, who liked her unstinting work, to switch from straight salary to an hourly rate. She told him she needed more time for her studies, the result of which were, after all, benefitting the business. So, more of a project-based deal. Would he consider it?

"Kay, you're already one of my best people. And with that degree you're after to offer clients, we'll attract more and better. Yeah, I'll do it, just don't short me."

"You know I won't, boss. Have I ever?"

Her aim was to be able to make the almost six-hour drive home again when she found she just had to, or go stir-crazy, as well as racking up more hours on weekends when there was nothing else to do. Or when a deadline loomed. *Deadlines: hate 'em.* And of course she'd see Harlan surely, long as she called far enough ahead. Mistake not doing that Christmas. And Hall said he was off scouring the territory for that ideal piece of land.

Where had she heard that old saying that all it took was two people and a piece of ground? Maybe read it. *Yeah, that's how the pioneers did it: man and wife staked a claim, put up shelter, created a home. Built a life, really. Farm, ranch, kids, and all. Harlan and I could do that. I could match him in all of it; I know I could.* She let herself dream about that.

She hadn't been blind to the other graduate students, men at the college. They were almost all more focused, more mature than the undergrads she saw and remembered. Like her, they seemed to know where they were going and were working hard to get there. And some of them weren't the stereotype thick-glasses, balding specimens who'd never get hired without the advanced degrees. Some were even handsome, although most of those were married.

*But I'm not after a man. Hall still thinks Harlan and I are destined to be together: wrong. But I keep thinking we might be. He's not handsome, doesn't have girls following him around.*

*Probably didn't date much—still doesn't. Maybe he'd realize how little looks count if/when there's serious, bone-wearying work to be done together. I can't think he's shallow.*

Well, she'd stay the course, work, study, focus on reality, and not give in to these schoolgirl fantasies.

*But I'm still a schoolgirl.*

~ * ~

"Hello, Mr. McBryde. You remember I was by back in June. How y'doin'?"

"Oh yes, 'bout me maybe sellin' m'place here. Guess you heard th' Bujolds sold out, up th' river." The old man was forking hay for the horses in the big barn.

"Yes, that was us. Got a couple partners goin' in with me, work the place soon's the weather breaks."

"Gonna put in cattle?"

"Well, we've got several plans in the works, but sure, all that grass. Don't wanta go with alfalfa, though; try to avoid irrigation if we can. Plant graze, hay." *And not a whisper about what we've found there.*

"Well, good luck. But answer's th' same 'bout here: don't wanta sell. Kids maybe come on back, take it over."

"Not even for a really good price?"

"Don't reckon. Man's got a responsibility to his family, y'know: keep th' homeplace."

"You said before the boys were into careers off away. Your daughter still around?"

"Well, no. Got herself a good job in Idaho, in biology. Wanted her back, but she's gotta live her own life." McBryde moved slowly, but never wasted time. He was now heading for the corral this overcast, brisk February day, then to inspect and repair fences along the river. The latest hired hand had quit back in the fall, headed south to Texas, leaving him and his wife alone to keep the place up.

"Okay, then, just so you know we're serious. Wanta have enough land for our operations, and yours lays just right, good water and all."

"Bujolds dug out that good spring. Seems that'd be water aplenty." He opened the corral gate, stepped in, closed it.

"Hope so, but more can't hurt. Well, you think about it. Emergency, like medical thing comes up where you need the money, remember we're ready to buy."

"Will. Thanks, Mr. Calloway. You take care, now."

*Okay, wouldn't even talk about it. Guess Jack's right, have to push him a little. Samples tell us the ore gets better right on the line between this place and Bujolds'. Gotta have it.*

It had taken longer than expected for Calloway and his circle to acquire the thousand acres, move in, and set up a small sluice to begin washing out the gold there. The geologist had insisted on starting small, just in case their preliminary digs hadn't told them the whole story. Now though, on the eve of a new operating year, they'd get serious about the project. They'd bought a 955 Caterpillar track loader and dump truck, and built a larger sluice. More equipment was to come: once started, they aimed to move fast.

The problem now was enough water to operate the sluice effectively. They didn't own the land to the river, and besides, that would raise suspicions and involve local and state authorities. Samuels had hiked the McBryde property secretly several times over the winter, and assured his partners the two springs there would supply all the water they'd need.

"And there are old trout-farming ponds we can use for settling the muddy water afterwards. Let them fill in first that way, then have to plan on using our excavations, after we've dug out all the ore. That way, only clear water goes back into the river, help keep it all quiet, at least till we have to build bigger basins."

The group had also installed a locked gate at the farm road entrance to their property, a clear sign that visitors weren't welcome. Sooner or later word would get out of their operations, but they hoped that by then they'd each have made a fortune. They were aware a lengthy fight with environmentalists and government agencies would be long and costly; their plan was to dig quick and dirty, get their gold and disappear. Leaving, of course, a ravaged landscape, tipples, mud.

None of them cared.

~ * ~

March saw wind, rain, still a lot of freezing, but this time the spring promise seemed real. I was actually able to come close to finishing the terraced beds in time for Mrs. H to get hardy seeds, plantings in the ground, long as she covered them, coldest times. And we began talking about my replacement at the store.

"Part-time college kid, like Kay was, I guess," she mused. "You've made the operation more efficient, and I guess I can survive." She'd run an ad, ask around. In this popular place, with so many of us barely able to hold on, there'd be somebody.

And for me, more stonework. We'd gotten calls, some from folks who'd seen the work I'd done here, some word-of-mouth from Ridley and around. I'd finish at the ranch, then most of the summer was set. The university had another project, but to hell with them. Maybe when I was rich and famous...

Kay called, said she'd managed a couple days off work again at the college spring break, was coming over. I'd planned my usual Crescent Sunday, but no, I should be here. That great cap had warmed me all winter, and well... I'd been rude enough. And something in me wanted to compare the two women with a fresh eye.

Because I wasn't getting closer to Crescent. We were friends. She liked me okay, would go land-hunting with me when she could. Fed me, let me stay over. *In her back room, yeah.* Was evidently okay with the status quo. *Maybe thinks I'm just after her land.* Nah, we had too much going, were both too aware of how ugly that'd be. No, I wanted all of Crescent, and okay, the 20 acres would be icing.

So I'd stay, spend a few hours with Kay, check the Mustang out again. Renew the friendship, sure. If I couldn't give her my heart, I'd give her some time. Maybe we could even do something fun. Whatever. I was pretty sure she hadn't hooked up with anybody, much as I'd have liked to hear that.

Really.

So, despite the way the fates had worked to separate us, we did get a few good March days for her visit. Cool of course, but sun-washed, clear, streams running bank-full, early wild things venturing out. This could be okay. Despite the probable blizzard that'd follow.

"The prodigal comes home," she announced, stepping out of the car that morning, which shone in proud wax: *attitude. The bright lights of Moscow have paled, and Montana is the only cure?* Standing tall, she was... impressive, I guess. Had a pair of jeans on that fit like skin. Damn, she had a fine ass. *Now stop this!* Open leather jacket, just showing those breasts. Cowboy boots. Clothes actually sexy by what they didn't show. And her face lit up with a mile-wide smile you couldn't dampen with any criticism of that face.

You did zero in on the eyes; that deep, almost cobalt that dared you to look away. I'd remembered those eyes, and yeah, the rest of that lean body. Subconsciously, of course: Kay was no Crescent... and in spite of myself, a picture flashed, a canary and a hawk. *Where'd that come from?*

We got hugs, hers for me a little too long, too tight, too much body in it. Mrs. H was smiling. I was confused.

"Okay," Kay was saying, "I wanna go rock-hunting, Harlan. Say we can."

"Um. Okay, sure. Always need rocks. Not my idea of a vacation for you, though."

"It's mine. I have to go work out in the college gym to keep from going soft." Never would I think of Kay as soft: that picture of her horseback, going after a running steer... I found I'd had that in my head a lot. Odd.

"I'll make sandwiches," Mrs. H volunteered, and disappeared inside. Awkward moment.

"Got gloves? And I use a leather apron. Keeps the mud off and spares your gut a lotta scratches."

"Gloves, yeah. And I use a denim apron in the lab. That do? And got steel-toed boots from back doing construction on the ranch." Yeah, she'd told me she'd been her dad's right hand after the brothers had grown and fled.

"Sure. You're all set. Let me just put the plywood in, protect the truck bed." Did that. Loaded the thick plank for the big ones. I try never to pass up a good big one. Found myself blushing at a remembered crudism about 'good ole big 'uns an' big ole good 'uns', hoping Kay didn't catch it. She went in to help with lunch, picnic, whatever.

We rolled out, the Rover seemingly glad to have us, glad to head off on another adventure. *Only old coots think their trucks are human. Or crazies.* Kay read my thought.

"Rarin' to go, like a colt outta the barn," patting the spare dash. I glanced at her: nice profile really, that strong chin, good nose, unapologetic straight hair under the cowgirl hat. Shame it all just didn't add up right.

And who gave a damn anyway? We were off to score rocks, about as far from romance as you could get. Unless you were a stonemason. Then it was almost sensual. Don't expect anybody else to understand that.

But Kay did. Maybe she'd taken note of the stones I'd used, their size, shape, faces.

"Stop, Harlan! I want that one," pointing to one along the track I hadn't even spotted. Off my game. "See, it's flat, top and bottom, long. Maybe ugly back in the dirt, but hey, that opening in the planter retaining wall, huh? Or you can cut it."

Well, damn. She was right. We worked it loose from roots with the long digging bar I have, brushed dirt off. Fine rock. About 250 pounds, though. And as I was looking for the place to get the bar under to raise it, Kay stooped, got her fingers under it, then did what too many beginners don't do, she dropped that perfect butt two feet more, came up, and flipped that stone like a domino.

"Hey, wait! Wanta kill yourself?" She grinned. One strong woman. "No heroics, here. Let's get it over here where we can work it up the plank, okay? No tossing it in, Superwoman." I actually wanted to hug her. Girl'd make a damn fine stonemason. I said that before.

It became a scavenger hunt. We ranged uphill as often as possible, like the Incas: bring 'em down, not up. Made a game of spot-a-rock, with points for who was first, shaded by the quality of the thing. She'd been reading up on this. Had to've been, or memorizing my work.

We almost forgot lunch, close to filling the Rover in a couple hours. It was midafternoon, a short pre-spring day that'd end cold. She found a ledge above this singing little stream, a big shaft of sun coming down on it between the Ponderosas. Moss, lichens, a carpet. Broke out thick sandwiches, fruit, pieces of a chocolate cake Mrs. H had baked the night before. Lemonade, root beer from the ice chest. Feast.

And we did. You ever horse rocks around, you'll burn calories. Kay had a healthy appetite too, and we ate every crumb. This was really fun. I decided to get cute, wiped a smudge of chocolate off her cheek with a finger. She grabbed my wrist, licked the finger clean. We laughed like fools. Right at that moment, my whole world was Kay McBryde, scholar, horsewoman, rock hustler. Damn fine woman.

And looking better to me by the minute. Now howthehell had that happened?

I found that her brown hair blown across her mouth was entrancing. So were the tiny beads of perspiration now we were back to scrambling for just one more perfect stone, lifting it together, working our way to the truck. And one strand of that hair was finding itself across her wet forehead. We loaded the stone and I brushed it away, to that wide smile.

Then we splashed in the icy creek water, sloshing sweat and dirt, laughing, dripping, shaking ourselves like puppies, clothes clinging, molding our bodies. And hers...

She knew a low mountaintop not far away, and still laughing at nonsense, we drove up to it. Turnout, where we watched the sun sink, over the spiky evergreens, getting redder, bigger, casting long shadows to the end of the world as we sat on the tailgate, entranced.

It was surreal, the shaded rime of old sheltered snow, blue now in fading light, a fleece of cloud, shot through with pinks, purples, oranges, and that flaming red. Light show, over too soon. I don't think I'd breathed for a while. It was suddenly dark, with points of lights, far off and below, like tiny pinpricks in a black cape.

Kay's hand was somehow warm in mine. *I did that.* And before I could think it away, I leaned to her and kissed her, a long, deep kiss. How could I not? She responded, finally pulled back.

"Did you mean that?"

"I... I think so. I..."

And she slid closer, put her arms around me and kissed me again. With her whole body pressed hard against mine.

Now, I'd kissed girls before—not a lot of them, admittedly— but it was always a tentative kind of thing, lips touched briefly as a ritual at a goodnight, or a dutiful peck. But this with Kay was so much more. Not actually sexual, but a joining, of... well *souls,* is the only way I could describe it. Just a yielding, melting, incredibly intimate opening-up, and it wasn't just her. There in the dark I gave—couldn't help giving—all of myself to this woman.

The appeal, the vulnerability, the sweetness of her kiss almost overwhelmed me, lifted me—us—somewhere in the air, into a rare and beautiful realm, above this commonplace earth. It wasn't about our bodies, but it included that: my awareness of her fingers working in my hair, the exquisite feel of those breasts against me, my own fingers drawing another life, warm, eager, into mine.

The moment lingered, then started to pass. We drew back, my mind all confusion. How could this ordinary girl have that *power,* that other-worldly gift to unlock me—us—this way?

"Kay, I... uh..." *Words.*

No.

"Shh. Let this stay, the magic..." A husky whisper, now sexy beyond belief. This was hurtling toward flesh, our yearning bodies. No way could I fight this. Could she? Possibly?

A voice inside whispered. Hard to hear, with the singing in the air. But there. Stronger. *Not yet.* Not here. Not now.

We both slid off the tailgate at the same moment, stood apart, but with eyes like coals of fire in that starlight, seeing deep into each other, somehow generating our own sight, clear, penetrating.

I shuddered, turned, took steps toward the Rover's door. She moved as my exact opposite, my mirror, to her place. The throb of the diesel engine timed to the still-racing of my heart.

We drove home without a word, but with hands joined, shifting gears together. At Mrs. H's door we kissed quickly, chastely, and went to our respective rooms. Somehow it had gotten late, and the place was quiet.

I had to think. I knew she had to think—there just a thin wall away, lying there, soft. No, Kay couldn't be soft. Or was she, really? That picture had me aroused, and that made it hard to use my mind.

What did this mean? To us both? Love? How? Just the natural sharing of a moment, after our ideal day? Nothing I'd ever experienced or imagined matched our... call it spiritual, *joining*. Word kept coming up. Yeah, that was it: spiritual, not to be confused with animal, material, here. But flesh and bone. Connecting, and by a power a whole lot bigger than Kay McBryde and Harlan Kemp. Like another universe, where strange and beautiful things happened, if you let them. And by God, we'd let them, hadn't we?

The wonder of it suffused me, kept me awake. *What does she feel? This must be as new for her as it is for me. We're like little children discovering paradise.*

I tried to let reality in, the fact that we didn't really know each other, had just spent a few hours together, couldn't have anything special between us. But I found I didn't want to. Finally drifted tiredly into delicious sleep with one last thought: *Man who gets that woman gets all of her or nothing.*

# Nine

We were shy with each other next morning. Mrs. H knew immediately something had changed between us, but said nothing. We all jumped on breakfast, helping, sharing, laughing. Pancakes, sausage, eggs, homemade huckleberry jam, my favorite.

"So, what's next?" that lady asked brightly. "And before you protest, I can handle the store okay."

"Um, well," Kay said, "we're gonna unload the truck, maybe set that big stone..."

"And you're going to see your folks."

"Sure. And I thought maybe"—she looked at me—"Harlan might..."

"Yeah, I've had this image of you on a horse: indulge me." *Did I say that?* She almost clapped her hands. And I wondered just what I'd let myself in for.

So. Stone was a challenge, again, but it went up the plank and was just the right height, if a bit too short for the space. But that's what other rocks are for. We spent another half-hour filling a couple more spaces, and that planter retaining wall was finished.

Kay went inside to get Mrs. H, and I had a moment. Several times we'd brushed against each other, and it'd been electric. Here in broad daylight, too, mini-repeat of last night. *Whatthehell?*

The two women came out of the store, laughing, and I had to admire Kay's body again: sinuous, elegant. Suddenly wanted that against mine so much I caught my breath.

"I love, it, Harlan," my boss gushed. "Now Kay, before you have to go back, we'll shop for plantings, okay?"

"Deal. I know a little, but we'll discover more."

I felt proud of my—our—wall. Well, all of them. And building them had almost kept me sane over winter. *Yeah, until Kay came.* And I knew I'd have to wait till she left again to sort out my feelings. Maybe she would, too.

The ranch was less than 50 miles up Hwy. 200, past Ovando. Mostly flat acres beneath snowcaps, with the little hill where the house stood, and some of a mountain past where the north fork of the Blackfoot river came down. It had these two rushing creeks that got fed by big springs, which must mean the land tilted. I was shown a deep trout hole just down from the driveway bridge, with a small cabin on past. Bunkhouse?

And I realized, from the placement of the mountains, that this must be just downstream from where I'd camped on my way here last June. Yeah, I must've hiked across a corner of McBryde land to fish the river. And these creeks must come from snowmelt not that far away. Coincidence.

I met the parents, feeling like A: a specimen, and B: like I was here under false pretenses. Hey, a girl brought her *intended* home to meet the folks, and no way...

Dad Sam was about seven feet tall, late sixties, same angular features, eyes that bored into me like augers. Hand harder than mine. Mom, Emily, was pretty, round face, kind eyes. Boys probably inherited her looks. No justice.

"You ride?" was the inevitable question. And of course a no would damn me. Nothing for it; couldn't lie.

"Only work horses on the farm. Uncle insisted on keeping a team. Afraid I don't even know how to put a saddle on." Kay was no help, throwing me to the wolves.

"Well, that'll be first, then. Got time b'fore lunch; come down to th' paddock." We all went. *Oh yes, audience to see the greenhorn fall on his ass.* The women chattering, a glad background to my mortification.

Now, I'd been bitten by this dog before; friend once asked me to help with his cattle back home, had gleefully put me on a semi-wild horse that almost bucked me off and nearly ran away with me. I'd gotten him stopped finally, slid off, hauled that laughing-his-head-off fool off his mount, traded places. Would this grim father do that? And could I do a repeat? No, I was screwed.

Kay saved me. Called softly, and four of the horses came, eagerly.

"He'll ride Bruno." Flat statement. "You were gonna put him on Blaze, right, Dad?" She had him.

"Why no, girl. Wouldna done that. Yeah, Bruno's gentle, Harlan. You're cruel, daughter." Mock hurt-puppy look. Which on him made us all laugh. Quick lesson on saddling followed, as he and I prepared to ride. Kay abandoned me with a wave, grin.

Gray Bruno plodded along beside Sam, who looked welded to his sorrel gelding. I felt like a sack of potatoes. He showed me fields of alfalfa, stands of Ponderosa and Douglas Fir, meadows marshy from those big, blue-water springs of snowmelt. Irrigation equipment, necessary in this sandy ground that lets the water settle right out of it. Showed the remains of his own father's trout hatchery, square ponds that'd held different-size fish.

"He liked fish; I like cows. Since the big war, folks want beef, got jobs, money to pay for it. Hard work, but good business to be in. What kinda farm your uncle have?"

"Just truck farm. Corn, potatoes, few cows, hogs. He was about as self-sufficient as you can get. Mechanic, so sawmill, welding shop, woodworking setup, mechanics' tools. Little of everything."

"So, folks died; he raised you?"

"Dad died, Vietnam, early on. Mom remarried a desk job, so I left soon's I could."

"I see. And you're a stonemason. Don't see much of that around."

"I aim to change that. You've probably seen the walls I did for Mrs. Hall. Advertise my work, hope to build a following."

"Oh yeah. I don't get into town that much, but sure. Em'ly'n I've been sorta grounded this winter, no hired help. Whatta you do in winter?"

"Mostly worked in the store till this weather's near broken. Good days, I can work places; rare inside stuff like fireplaces till it warms up. Do need a second job as backup. Come fall, I'll be in the market for something else. Not wild about storekeeping, though I like Mrs. Hall."

"Hmm. So only a half-year job. Pay well?" Of course he was thinking his daughter would have that big degree, and hooking up with a guy just barely making a living? That had to be something to consider.

"Three to four times what I get doing carpentry. Done that, too."

"So, you could go south, work straight through..."

"Not for me. Less than a year here, but it's home. Find myself a piece of ground, a friend and I'll put up a timberframe cabin I can add to later. Picky though, passed up several just weren't right."

"You'll want water, and that'll push the price. And timber, for that house. Man startin' out nowadays got th' deck stacked 'gainst him. How much you lookin' for?"

"Oh, like to have some space 'tween me and the next man. Thought I might have a shot at twenty acres close to the Bitterroot, but that probably won't happen. *No, Crescent won't share that, or I'm getting it she won't. With me.*

"Well, I'm thinking I'll sell out, maybe next year, whole place. It's got to be too much for me. Boys didn't want to stay, and now Kay's going after that big degree, big job somewhere. Wife an' I maybe get a little place in town."

"Be a shame to let it go outta the family. But," I held up a hand, "you'd know best about that." I watched a brook trout jump for an early flying insect. Small fish, but beautiful. Man'd get a million or more for this place, easy. Paradise.

More general questions. As expected, I was getting the prospective son-in-law grilling, which was way off-base. Maybe the first candidate here? Didn't matter: I was just visiting, and I'd have to make sure Kay knew that. Just Western good manners to invite me, nothing more.

We rode near the property line upstream, and I could see the grove in the distance I'd camped in on the other property. I remembered those guys digging, and mentioned it to Sam.

"Weird, middle of the night like that. Place was for sale, so I'd sneaked in to camp, did a little fishing in the river on down next morning, must've been on your place. Did you know about that digging?"

"No, I didn't. Funny. And some feller, and I guess his backers, bought the place, been coming around to try to buy mine. Digging?"

"Yeah, small, deep holes, then they took soil samples, it looked like, filled them in. None of my business, of course, so I forgot about it till now. Oh, that looks like one covered up, here on your side."

It did. Loose earth mounded up a bit, about the size of those other holes. We rode closer, saw others.

"Well I'll be damned; somethin' goin' on here, for sure. Y'say soil samples?"

"Looked like it. But some of these are way over on your land, across the fence. And not something you had done?"

"No way." He thought a long minute, staring at the covered-up digging. "Well, I reckon maybe they wanted to know how good th' ground was, before they bought. But y'say th' holes were deep? Doesn't make sense." He shook his head, rode on. Then seemed to remember something.

"Now, my pa did tell me that way back, there was some talk of findin' trace of gold on up, closer to the mountains. Back in th' 1800s some of th' early folks s'posed to've dug a bit. But what happened, there was a big strike down at Bannack, went on for years. They even built a big courthouse, wanted to make that the state capitol. Guess nobody ever followed up around here.

"So maybe these fellers have got onto the rumor, have bought up the Bujold place there. But diggin' on my land? Never gave permission for that. Maybe think they're gonna strike it rich, got somebody backin' 'em." He shook his head. "Anything here, somebody'd found it a long time ago. Oh, there's trace on up th' river, but not enough to dig for."

"Well, it's your business, but it'd rile me some, anybody sneaking onto my place, at night, like I saw. Something not right about that."

"For sure. Well, I'll just hafta have a little talk with that Calloway feller next time I see him."

"Well, maybe that's why he wanted to buy you out? Actually found some gold?" Sounded right to me, but maybe I'm suspicious.

"Nothin' there, like I said, but yeah, that's likely what he's got in his mind. Guess treasure hunters all over want to get rich quick." We rode for the ranch house, Sam shaking his head at people's foolishness, I guess.

There we got fed nicely; they'd waited for us, and I caught Kay's eyes on me several times. *No, I didn't get the third degree; we talked land, jobs.* I did like the parents. Emily was all heart, like Mrs. H. She apologized through me for not getting by to see her over the winter, having been needed daily after the one ranch hand quit. I couldn't see her on a horse the way I had Kay, but of course, busy with stock penned, hay to scatter, feed, mucking out, when the crap wasn't frozen...

"Okay, Dad. I know you've probably turned Harlan against horses, so I want to drive up to the lake..."

"Oh, no," I objected, "We're gonna ride." Had to get that picture for real. "How far?"

"About five miles. We *could* get back before dark. You'd be saddle sore, though." Maybe, but this girl in her element: worth it. Then Emily, bless her, had an idea.

"You two go ahead. I'll bring your car, ride Blaze back, lead Bruno. Time then for chores. Okay, Sam?"

"Sure. You haven't been on a horse much lately. Missin' it, I know."

So. Off we went, down the highway shoulder a ways, then off on those straight, dirt roads between properties where we didn't have to dodge traffic.

And dammit, that girl surpassed my dream of her on this lean, eager black. Wished I had a camera. He was a stallion, maybe the ranch replacement for the one she'd had to sell? He was devoted to her, wanted to do whatever she had in mind; I could see that. So I was holding them back. Oughta let her run some.

"Need a minute; you go on ahead."

"Tinkle time?" Grin.

"You embarrass me."

"No I don't, everybody's gotta pee." I waved her on, turned into a field entrance. *Now go, girl.*

How did she read my mind that way? She touched Blaze's flanks and they shot away like an arrow, Kay bending low, hat clamped down, hair streaming from under it. I watched in awe. A quarter mile, the turn, they came back, hooves shaking the earth.

She drew up, flushed, radiant, and I couldn't possibly remember she wasn't pretty. She was beautiful. I rode close, reached, pulled her to me, kissed her. Almost chipped a tooth, with the horses moving. *Whoah, beasts.*

I slid down, pulled her free, that body like a coiled spring, somehow not heavy. I brushed that hair out of her eyes, gazed into them, then purposefully, gently, kissed her mouth, melted into her, felt her heart beat close to mine.

Then the level eyes, searching, questioning, but seeing, too. This time there was no denying the sexuality between us. Here, under the March sun, the sky everywhere, that seemed somehow to pulse with our hearts, our quickened breaths.

And somebody sure to come along the damn road. But I still held her close, knew she could feel me there, and I didn't care.

But then we stepped back, remounted, rode together, hands linked. Soon reached the climbing, switch-backed rise through timber that led to the snowmelt lake.

Cabins hiding in the trees, mostly silent this early in the year. Long stretches of just narrow road, with only us on it, dreamily moving without words, afraid to break the spell. This could go on forever.

I never thought of Crescent once.

The lake was a mountain jewel, still with some ice in the shallows, cold as the South Pole. I dipped a hand.

"Other rednecks and I'd try to go skinny-dipping by Easter, back home. No way, here."

"It's cold year 'round, but a couple of the girls and I've done that, around in that cove. You don't stay in long."

"Well, I used to go canoeing with this outdoor club, conservation people. We'd do an annual New Year's float on some river. Another nut and I'd dare each other, slip off, skinny-dip. Sometimes ice, like here. Fools. We were in and out like frogs, probably blue, but it was dark." She laughed at that picture. Loved that sound.

"Should I dare you?"

"You'd watch."

"Of course I would," she said with absolutely no shame.

"So I won't."

"Well, I'd guarantee that'd take care of that problem you keep having." *No* shame. I know I reddened.

"Hoping you wouldn't notice. Trying to be a gentleman here."

"Oh, hell, I'm a farm girl: seen every kind of stud there is. Glad I turn you on, though." Grin. Tease, surely. And that damn Puritanical inner voice of mine, too.

Then she bent, scooped up that liquid ice, drenched me. Almost paralyzed me, but I got in a good splash, too. Shrieking, laughing, shaking the water off. Two kids.

Of course, there were beds of pine needles where we sat, close, hugged to ward off the wet chill. And of course we kissed. Repeatedly. And of course my hands stroked a knee, then a thigh. Hell, I was/am human.

She caught my hand, raised it to her lips. Gave me that piercing gaze. It sort of said *reality*.

"Need another splash?"

"I think I can behave."

"I think I can too. But before we both need to cool it down..." And she slipped a hand inside my shirt front, ran fingers over my chest. Damn. We were on our backs, a dangerous position. Her perfect breasts, wet cloth clinging, up toward the sky.

"You're making this difficult."

"Be glad it's just my hand." *Now, what's that mean? Oh...* I felt I was about to burst. She drew it back, buttoned my shirt, then jumped up, ran, splashed water toward and on me again. I retaliated, and that did bring us back to the world.

Which very soon afterwards had her mother in it, the Mustang purring up. We untied the horses, rode up the short path to the parking turnaround.

"At least you didn't jump in," she observed wryly, appraising me.

"Voted not to, Mom." I saw Kay'd at least brushed the pine needles out of her hair; Emily would surely have read that wrong.

"Well, let me get on that beast. Like Sam said, I need my horse fix." She mounted Blaze easily, at maybe five-seven and a little bulky, still graceful. "See you at the corral, kids." She took Bruno's reins and followed us as we drove away.

"Okay, girl, we need to talk," I began.

"No, we don't. We need for me to go back to Moscow and for you to get to work, and for both of us to think hard about us for a while. Then, one way or the other, we need to see each other again..."

"Then talk. Okay, any more ground rules?"

"Nope. And letters are welcome, phone calls."

"How about I come see you? Be a few weeks before I can really hit the stonework." *No, that'd sure cancel out the breathing space, fool.*

"Maybe. I'll check my dance card."

"You *are* cruel. Should I check mine?"

"Up to you. Oh, and I guess now's the time to decide if we're going to play cute games, or be brutally honest, right?"

"Truthful. Okay, I won't try to sweep you off your feet till and if you're ready to be swept."

"And I won't tease you. Or have I already?"

"No, 'cause if/when that time comes, it'll be for real, and... well, forever." *Whatthehell am I saying?*

"Wow. What if I ravish your body?" That had to be a tease.

"Where do I surrender? No, I'm with you on this. Too important. Oh, and what's your take on the parents' evaluation?" I needed to know. Yeah, and I needed to change this direction, that problem again.

"They like you, so far. Not like I've dragged a lotta guys home, though..."

"Sure you have." Being nice: she probably hadn't. Ever? Well, I hadn't either. Lester the librarian would've cared less, but Mom? Her little boy? Another world. But Kay didn't act like a wallflower, knew who she was and proud of it. I admired that.

Well. Back at the ranch, I helped Sam feed, water, herd, separate critters. Kay'd gone in to cook. Emily got home, evidently having enjoyed the ride. Sure, and having made more time for Kay and me together. *These women.*

Dinner was great. The conversation sparkled, everything about me, and about Kay. The brothers in passing, mostly. Obvious Sam wasn't thrilled they'd run off to the bright lights and ice water. Obvious too, he wanted the best for his girl. What a pair they must've been, little girl and her dad. Best buddies.

No way could I picture her now, huddled over a microscope, peering at notes, samples. Hell, she belonged *here,* on that horse. And I made a bet to myself that she'd someday chuck it, PhD and all, and come back...*oh no, Sam'd said...* Well, to some ranch, somehow. People left the land, chased careers and dollars so they could eventually buy a place, land again. And here she'd had it all to begin with.

They invited me to stay, of course, and of course I did. Slept well, after a few minutes indulging a fantasy having to do with Kay's body and Crescent's face.

Rolled out early to help Sam again, who'd beaten me out of bed. So had Kay, who was forking hay already, laughing and talking with her father. Seemed I was a third wheel here, till I realized the horseshit had built up, was now mostly thawed. Okay, I grabbed a shovel, started to work.

"Hey, you don't hafta do that," Kay objected.

"Sure I do: burn off some of those calories from your great dinner last night." Sam just smiled. I shoveled manure for an hour, got to aching other places than my backside.

Emily called us to breakfast, steak and eggs, and biscuits a lot like mine: big. Yeah, beef, right off the hoof. And were *all* these women in my life good cooks? *Enjoy, dude.*

I borrowed a flyrod after satisfying myself I wasn't needed, and headed up the now-combined creeks to the forks. Sam had cautioned me against showing myself, with that crystal water. So I slipped up on one of the big springs, stayed low, flipped the first fly I came to in the borrowed vest. Jiggled it. Nothing. Tried again, and about 30 more times and three other flies. Trout not interested. Maybe saw the leader, line?

I tramped to a big creek hole where a stump and eroded bank caused a deep swirl. Got two strikes, but didn't land either fish. Concluded that trout, which I'd never fished for before except that time on the Bitterroot, were outta my bush league.

Kay had to leave, late afternoon, to get back to Idaho late next day. I reflected on how much I'd learned about this woman, all of which I liked. For one, Sam told me his girl was an instinctive shooter, could nail a distant target with a rifle from the hip. I'd heard of those, once knew an army vet like that, terrific hunter. And she could gut an elk without batting an eye, track wayward horses, rope steers. Damn. And educated too. Maybe too sharp a girl for me, but I wanted more of her.

Or was I just overwhelmed by this whole experience, this storybook ranch, her great parents, the complete package? Had to get some perspective, I guessed.

Emily hugged me, Sam gripped my hand again. We hit the road, me all warm inside, and surely Kay also. Fine people, kind who made you think the world wasn't rotten after all. *No, of course not, way things are working out for me.* But then I thought of Crescent. For an instant. And that night, I didn't dream of anything.

The store next morning was for the moment empty of customers, with Mrs. H busy back counting money after Kay's goodbye hug. And then we found ourselves in the storeroom, and we grabbed each other. Long kiss, and she gave me a little hip action, about drove me up the wall.

"That a promise?"

"Could be. Wasn't a tease. And okay, you'd better come see me." Another farewell kiss, and neither of us wanted to let go our hands. Then she was off, waving to us both. I realized I hadn't even cracked the hood on her car, and neither had she and Mrs. Hall bought plants.

# Ten

"How'd you like Kay's boy?" Emily McBryde asked her husband. "Think he's okay?"

"Seemed like it; not afraid to work. But y'know, Em, we talked about this a long time ago: had to admit she wasn't ever gonna attract men like a homecoming queen. Sorta made me think a fortune hunter type might just wanta marry her, get his hands on this ranch..."

"Oh, surely not. Harlan's not like that. Why, he doesn't know the first thing about..."

"Right. And no, I don't think he'd do a thing like that. But I sorta discouraged him a little, told him I was thinkin' of sellin' out."

"You didn't!"

"And I wouldn't. But sayin' he did have his eye on th' place— know he's lookin' for land—that'd put th' damper on that. And it didn't seem t'put him off any."

"I think he really likes Kay." End of discussion tone.

"Hope so. Plain she likes him. A lot."

"Well, we can't run our girl's life, Sam. Just have to wait and see how this turns out."

"Right. Oh, and we found where somebody's been diggin' holes in th' far field, our side th' line with Bujold. And Harlan, he'd camped on t'other side, back last year, saw guys diggin' there, middle of th' night. Weird, but must've been that Calloway's bunch, ones bought it after, y'know."

"Digging? What on earth for?"

"Harlan said looked like takin' soil samples. Now, I figger they've heard th' old rumors of gold, Em, gone an' bought th' Bujold place, and've sneaked over on us. Prob'ly why they're after us t'sell."

"If there was gold, somebody'd dug it all up a long time ago."

"Way I see it. Prob'ly just some pie-in-th'-sky bunch thinks they're gonna get rich quick. Always been folks like that; always will be."

~ * ~

The glow, the warmth from her visit stayed with Kay for days. She smiled a lot, which softened her features, and along with her innate kindness, this made those around her feel good. Her boss noticed, and promised himself he'd let her have a few days off more often. Of course, she'd worked a lot of overtime to finish the last project, had that time coming to her. But he liked to think of his employees as a tightly-knit team, dedicated, efficient, glad to be working together. And Kay McBryde personified that ideal. So anything extra he could do for them...

Kay now knew she and Harlan Kemp were indeed destined to be together, just as Hall had predicted. Just how and when that'd happen, remained to be seen. She'd take time when summer came, go see him again. And maybe he would come for a visit, before things got too busy for him. Meanwhile, she'd look for a letter from him, or a phone call. And of course she'd write him.

Wouldn't do to let what they'd shared get stale, or get covered over with work.

She started thinking about another gift she could get for him. Man didn't need anything, or maybe he needed everything, which made it hard. He'd thanked her again and again for the warm cap she'd sent, till it'd embarrassed her. She fingered the tiny carved horse on its thin leather string she wore around her neck, while peering through the microscope at river sediment.

This report had to be finished tonight, and the next project was already late. But the grind of work failed to intimidate her; she'd felt those strong arms around her—could still feel them— and the world was a good place. Even at eight o'clock, when she finally left the lab for the day.

Sediment. That got her thinking of the soil sampling somebody'd done back at the ranch. And the old rumors about gold. She knew enough geology to reason that whatever was in the mountain that rose from the ranch land had washed down, built up over eons. And okay, if there were even traces of gold in the fields, that'd indicate that the source was up the slope. *Couldn't have been much, though, or folks would've dug the place all up, long ago. Gold fever.*

But wouldn't it be something if, while her father and grandfather—and yes, she and the brothers too—had worked so hard to survive, there'd been gold right under their feet. She thought again ruefully of those student loans she'd sold her horse to pay off. Sending the three of them to college had been a strain on her parents, even though they'd each found part-time work.

And that got her to thinking of the future of the place. Brothers didn't seem to want it, which meant she'd have the chance to inherit it. Settling up somehow with Bob and Jeff, of course. Would Harlan live on a 500-acre ranch? Knew nothing about horses, very little about cattle, irrigation, haying on a big scale. And so far from probable stonework.

No, he'd want to be up some draw, with trees and maybe a spring, where he could build his own house, be closer to his work. Well, maybe a place big enough to keep a couple horses? Surely that...

*But get real here, girl: We've only just begun to know each other, learn a little of what we'll need to understand. We're both new at this; I can tell he's pretty green, too. So no silly fantasizing, McBryde.*

*Yet.*

~ * ~

Two days and two cold showers later, I'd figured out that Kay was either the wrong girl at the right time, the right girl after all, a temporary but powerful attraction, the first girl who'd responded to me—really—or none of the above. And now, before I made any serious commitments, I had to do some comparing.

Would/could I honestly be proud of Kay McBryde out in public like I knew I could with Crescent, away from magic nights and hidden glades? Would/could I trust myself to ignore other, more attractive women I'd surely meet? *Was* that vulnerability, that trust, that powerful child-woman magnetism, passion, as good as it could ever get? I was close to believing that. And no, I could never betray the love of a woman like that. I remembered a line from my favorite book, Benet's *John Brown's Body:* "If I kissed your lips, I would have to be yours forever." And I'd done just that. *Whoever gets her, gets...*

But Sunday I drove down to see Crescent. Predictably. She welcomed me with that brightness so a part of her. We did the chores together, comfortable now, complementing each other, fitting easily together. She fed me, something exotic, laughed with me, shared.

Was *this* love? This moving smoothly into each other's lives, getting familiar. By now it'd been what, six months? No, only a little over three. But surely, if this was meant to go anywhere... No real closeness, no sex, no...

So naturally I pushed it, end of that day. Had to. Fish or cut bait. Okay, we didn't hafta rush into heavy stuff, just get clear on this.

"Think we ought to talk, lady." Those eyes widened.

"Okay, let's. You first." She sat back, expectant, but maybe a little knowing, too.

"Well, you know I like you a lot. You've been great to me, and I know you can have your pick of any/all the men. I'd like to think you see me as special enough to let me in, so to speak, while shutting others out. Or have you? We're friends, Crescent, but I guess I'm saying that's not enough for me, now. I guess." I trailed off.

"Dear Harlan." She took my hands in her rough, reddened ones, gave me what had to be a sad smile. *Okay, here it comes.* "I like you too, and you know that. But I've been in love, see, really been in love. Glenn was everything I'd ever wanted, my knight little girls dream of. It's torn me to pieces, finally realizing that after all the excuses I made for him, all the determination to stand by my man, all the chances I gave him, he was just a piece of shit.

"I should have been over it by now. Hey, I'm thirty-two, not a kid anymore. But I've been to the mountain, I guess, as far as love goes. And you're just not the man I'll spend my life with, I'm afraid. I need friends, and you've been one—still are, I hope—to help me get through this life. And it's not all it's cracked up to be, this independence, this straight-arming the world. It's damn hard, and I know I could chuck it, stick my feet under some man's table, take the other road again.

"And maybe I will have to, someday. But for now, I'm aiming for all of it: the right man this time maybe, this great place, as much self-sufficiency as we can stand, in the twentieth century. I'm sorry I can't give you what you want, need. But I can't. And I know that maybe in time I'll see that you're the best thing that could happen for me. But you're young enough the world's still out there for you, the right girl's out there for you, so don't wait for me to come around, which right now I don't think will happen. Can you see that?"

"Guess I'll have to. And if I'm to be honest, I guess you've just been my ideal, maybe a little fantasy, the perfect woman, dropped out of the sky when I wasn't really even searching. And no way would I have guessed you were that much older, and wiser, than me." I sounded mature, reasonable, but really, I wanted to take this conflicted, actually hurting woman in my arms, protect her, be everything to her. And yeah, get into bed with her, feel that girl-body against me, get inside her, let her blow my mind...

She leaned to me, kissed me quickly, a goodbye, I knew, and tried to draw back. I got my arms around her, pulled her close. She hesitated a fraction, then came to me, yielding, kissed me deep this time, and I could feel her letting her body overcome her good sense, her resolve. We were both so needy, so lonely, so trembling with raw desire. I kissed her so much, so desperately, my hands working over that body, and she responded with so much passion, the world disappearing in a vortex of ecstasy, that there was no denying this.

"Yes," was all she said, and we were suddenly ripping each other's clothes off, somehow also moving toward her bedroom. Then we were naked, her perfect, tiny body there before me, there for me. She pulled me to her, and then we were on the bed, a union of flesh, a warm, smooth entry, her breasts hard against me, her arms, legs fiercely drawing me into her, molding us together.

I have no idea how long we lay together there. Minutes, hours? Then I was aware of her softly crying, the tears warm against my chest, then cooling. I stroked her hair, touched her face, clumsily, but with all the tenderness in me.

"This wasn't supposed to happen," she managed.

"No, it wasn't. But it needed to happen."

"Yes, I guess that's right, need." She pulled her face away, looked into my eyes. "And you know of course, that this is goodbye. It has to be."

And yes, I did know that. Despite my youth, my inexperience, I knew we both had reached an ending; the crossing of our paths had led—must lead—to separate ways. Both of us would treasure, remember. Suddenly I felt like a very old man, full of wisdom, long memories.

I drove away from Crescent, wondering if this had been a betrayal of Kay, of that magic we'd had between us, wondering if this... episode, meant anything, after all. Just animal lust? No, that *need* was real. Man and woman, elemental, the repeated, eternal coming together. And here, not a beginning for us, a sentence ended, a period. A meeting, a sharing, a parting.

*Life.*

~ * ~

Bruce Calloway drove up to the McBryde place, saw Sam at the big barn. He walked down, hailed him.

"Mr. McBryde, hello. Got some trouble at my ranch."

"Oh, hello, Calloway. What kinda trouble?" *Got troubles of my own: those cows...*

"Well, some crazy's killed three of our cows, cut their throats, just left 'em lying there. And I just heard on the radio that you've had the same thing happen here. Got any idea who's doing this? It's insane."

*Yeah, th' radio station would've got th' report from th' sheriff. So, some sick bastard's hit th' neighbors too.*

"No, and it's got me riled bad. Thought at first it must be somebody's got a grudge against me, but not if he's gone and done it to you too."

"Well, I've called the sheriff to look into this. No tracks, no sign. Whoever's doing this is slick, I'd say. Whattya think we can do about it?"

"I'm takin' on more hands, gonna keep a sharp eye out. You got help, don'tcha?"

"Just a couple guys. Can't patrol a thousand acres. Damn, this's crazy, man can't run a few cattle, try to get set up on his own place. We were just about to bring in a hundred more head of Black Angus, but now we've gotta rethink it. At least till they catch this guy, or this bunch—whatever it is. You heard of any more of this? Other neighbors?"

"Haven't. But these boys I'm gettin' all good shots, and we're gonna ride our fences close, take night shifts." *Won't hurt to let th' word out we're ready for anything.*

"Really? You'd just gun 'em down on sight?"

"Damn right. Whoever it is surely got guns, an' it'd be self-defense, way I see it. Sheriff agrees with me, too." McBryde's eyes were hard, his face grim, and in spite of himself, Calloway felt a chill. *This dude is old west; gonna be harder to get rid of him than we thought. Gotta let Jack know the next push'll have to be harder, McBryde on guard this way.*

"How many hands you getting?"

"Many's it takes. Couple of 'em's been in trouble, right rowdy, maybe a little quick on the trigger, but I've known 'em since they were kids, know I can depend on 'em. Puttin' up 'no trespassing' signs too, keep it legal, 'cordin' to th' sheriff. You oughta do that too, maybe go better if you hafta deal hard with this." As usual, the rancher was working while he talked. Calloway could see one ranch hand in the distance, and of course assumed there were more. And yes, that cowboy had a carbine with him.

"Well, I had another reason for coming by. You said you weren't interested in selling your place, but would you sell part of it? I'd like to build my house up on that mountain slope if you'd sell me just a few acres. Old house is in pretty bad shape."

Sam straightened, looked Calloway in the eye. It was all the man could do to keep the nerves from showing under that gaze.

"Don't reckon so. That slope's just where m'daughter's plannin' to build her own house, her and her man get married. Sorry." *Not true, or at least not yet, but wouldn't that be great? Dunno if Harlan's th' man, but Em'ly thinks so. Hafta learn about cows, ranchin'...*

As the gold-seeker drove away, he reflected on Sam's words. *No, your daughter's not gonna build on that mountainside, man, 'cause we're gonna take it all down.*

~ * ~

Well, what now? Did I rush into Kay's arms, after I'd ranked her second-best, or even not in the running? We'd had something with each other that now seemed a lot finer than my... *thing* with Crescent. Not to put that good woman down: it was just over. But Kay and I'd agreed... *yeah, that.*

Or maybe I needed away from women for a while, totally. I *did* have a trade to build, work to do, a place to find, buy, build on. So maybe just stay the course we'd agreed on. Think a lot, sweat out the few remaining weeks till real spring.

On that subject, it snowed two feet deep next day, a March blizzard that'd keep me inside with my groceries for probably two of those weeks. I read a lot. I sent Kay a note, feeling guilty about Crescent. No, about me. Kept that quiet. I would never burden her with my indiscretions, even if we did somehow become permanent.

Which wasn't as remote a possibility now. I'd found I never noticed what this girl looked like anymore. Too much to her, or maybe I was growing up. She was 24 now, me 25, and I guess getting perspective? Who knew.

I shoveled, scraped snow. Waited on customers, stocked shelves, ate Mrs. H's cooking. Resolved to buy a heavier truck to punish with rocks, save the Rover. That'd mean dollars I should be saving toward a piece of ground, but I should be able to haul two, three tons or more at a time if I got serious about work, and it was out there. And no way would I try to buy something new—be paying on it for years.

I bit the bullet, after figuring I'd spend the bucks anyway, small loads in the Rover, plus the danger of trashing it. *Yeah, break another axle, maybe springs.* So soon's most of the snow had been plowed off the roads, I went hunting. Vehicles gone to alternators instead of generators ten years before, and now electronic ignition, other gadgets. Wished for diesel, but that'd mean a big rig, too hard to load, too much investment.

I finally found a 1950 Dodge one-ton dually with a dump bed, in decent shape. It had the stock six-cylinder flathead engine, not the complicated V8; I could work on it okay. It had a little rust, needed tires, but I snared it for $350, and found not-too-used ones for $5 apiece, eight-ply. Seems the highway department replaced all theirs when some started going bad, and I picked and chose, along with the other penniless rednecks.

This truck bed was higher, but with the loading plank, I could handle it. Wouldn't be fast, but I was used to not-fast. And, of course, with that dump bed, I could unload it in seconds; that had decided me. Someday if I could afford it, I'd get a medium-size tractor with bucket, and a trailer to haul it on. Expenses, but necessary if I were to get into this stone-laying business seriously.

The snow eventually melted, and the Clark Fork ran bank-full, here below the mouth of the Blackfoot. Sound of rushing water, snowmelt, April mud, drippy days, but now believable spring.

I got a visit from Sam McBryde and Emily, on their way for supplies in Missoula. Mrs. H monopolized Emily, who'd actually hugged me. *Well, older women like me, anyway.*

"Had some trouble at the place, Harlan," Sam told me, his angular face grimmer than usual.

"How so?" No customers at the moment, and I was changing a tire in the parking lot, getting the Dodge ready for its first load.

"Some bastard killed five of my cows. Just cut their throats, left 'em lyin' there. Oughta hang him, I catch him."

"Wow, that's nasty! Any clues? Sheriff on it?" The image sickened me. *Yeah, string the weirdo up... this's Montana.*

"No tracks; too much grass. Deputy no help. Sheriff's 'n old friend, but he couldn't find out anything either. Then I heard th' neighbor got hit too, lost three. Thought I had myself an enemy at first, but now looks more like some cult thing. And I can't watch all the time, keep 'em in the barns. Got one new hand; tryin' to find a couple more. Know of anybody needs work?"

Well, the store *was* that Gossip-Central. I went over a few faces, names. Sam said they didn't have to be cowboys, that he just needed help. I asked Mrs. H what she thought of two or three I remembered.

"No, that Collier boy's bad to drink. Kenny Blair's okay, I guess. I'd shy away from Kip Kelly, too clumsy. Wreck your truck, fall over his own feet. And these drifters, you never know when they'll just disappear. I'm trying for another college kid here, but there'll never be another Kay. No offense, Harlan, but I'm losin' you, too."

"Okay, Susie," Sam said. "I'll look up Kenny. Know his dad, and I remember him too, on back. Had a boy came out, but he didn't want the job. One more, we can keep a closer eye out. Crazy people around, and I'm carryin' my saddle gun."

"Wish I could help, sir," I lamented. "Maybe, spell between rock jobs, I could come up, put in a few days?" Yeah, I'd do that, liked these people.

"'Preciate that. Jobs lookin' good for you, then?" He was eyeing my stonework, and nodding.

"Some. But there's always somebody wants to, or has to, put the work off a while. Biggest headache in any construction's lining up enough to keep busy."

"You heard from Kay?" Emily asked, maybe a bit pointedly.

"Did. Letter last week. Wanta go see her before it gets too busy, but it's a whole day there in my slow rig, and another back. Says she might get a few days maybe summer, soon's she finishes some project they're on."

"Yes, she told us that, last time we talked on the phone. Says she's doing a lot of overtime, and there's the coursework, too."

"We gotta get goin', folks," Sam urged. "Harlan, you just come on up, you get a chance. Put you to work. Hope it won't be vigilante stuff." He laughed, but there was a glint in the eyes as they left.

"That's so awful," Mrs. H lamented. "Who'd just slaughter cows? And do it to such good people?"

That angered me too. Guessed if I did get up to the ranch, I'd carry one of Sam's rifles with me all the time. Didn't think I'd have a problem blowing away a pervert slashing a heifer's throat.

~ * ~

"Think that'll send a message?" Calloway asked Samuels the geologist. "Or make McBryde just dig in deeper?"

"He loses enough, he'll deal. Thing is, to keep him from even suspecting us behind it. I've got the next strike all planned out. Now, look at this diagram I've drawn."

"What's it mean? I see a lotta contour lines."

"Right. Pretty obvious the ore's washed down off this mountain slope, like I told you, the part on McBryde's land. That means there's a source up there somewhere. I've slipped across a couple times, dug, and it's there, for sure. Now, it borders national forest land on up, but I believe we'll find it below that. Lotta solid rock farther up too, so this talus slope's where we need to set up. Why don't you offer to buy just that part?"

"Already did. Old guy says he won't sell even that part, but we've gotta have it. Any way to dig it on a small scale without him knowing?" Calloway was seeing dollars. Gold dollars.

"No, hafta get a loader in there. The 955 Cat's big enough to strip the overburden, get down to the vein. We need that land bad. And I think my next bit of persuasion will do it." He was keeping this plan to himself, because... well, it was maybe too drastic for the others to stomach. *Sorry about that.*

~ * ~

I got a cowboy hat in the mail. Not a cheap one, either. Kay'd somehow guessed the size right, like the cap, and hell, I imagined I did look good in it. Cowboy stonemason. Well, the Montana sun could burn you quick, I'd learned; dry air didn't warn you like it did back home. My boss for another week thought it was cute.

She'd found a kid named Drake, sophomore at the university, who'd be able to put in a few hours a day at the store, so I didn't feel bad about going south again. Rhys called from somewhere to say the mud at the ranch job was drying out, few more days and we could hit it again. Moira had already been planting stuff there, which would make my stonework look like we wanted it to.

That woman amazed me. She'd take the kids with her, give them their homeschool work while she planted, dug, seeded. Then she'd take a break, quiz them, spend time with them, then get them to help, keeping them involved, teaching them on several levels. Multitasking, I think they've started calling it. And of course, after navigating that non-road home, she'd have about twice the average housewife's work to do there. Helluva woman. The kind I wanted.

Speaking of, now I owed Kay a gift. Girl was just too nice to me. But I wasn't good at gifting; had no idea where to go with this. Didn't think I could ask Moira, since she'd pushed me toward Crescent. And Mrs. H was no help either. Hell, she'd probably suggest an engagement ring. And no, I wasn't ready for that one.

Yet?

Well, just to speculate, what'd that mean? Really. Girl was working at a real career a day's drive away, going after a PhD. How in hell could I ask her to chuck all that, come live with a struggling stonemason, never sure of the next job, living out of his truck? *Get real here, Kemp.*

Or could I just move to Idaho too, try to get set up there? Had less than a year invested here; could start over, I guessed. Kay'd told me there weren't any decent rocks around Moscow, though, some kinda prehistoric dust-blown round hills they grew grain on, didn't even have to plow, just disc. She already missed this place too, and like I'd figured, really did belong on that ranch.

*Hmm. Now, just suppose we did end up together. Sam, Emily, would want us—me—there on their place. Land thing solved: we could build somewhere on all those acres...but could I handle the 50 miles or more to where my work would surely be? Hafta stay over, maybe a week at a time. Don't like that idea.*

*And hell, I'm not gonna marry Kay for a piece of ground; that'd be chickenshit. No, just gotta let this whole thing work itself out, like we agreed. And oh yeah, Sam is thinking of selling. Bummer.*

But my real problem was that I'd been to the mountain, too. This unbelievable experience with Kay couldn't be infatuation— no surface attraction at all. No, that sharing, that... intimacy with her was real. And I wanted more of it. Crescent had been a complication that didn't really exist, and now the road was clear. Kay McBryde was the woman for me.

*Admit it, dude.*

I was lonely. And despite the negatives, I wanted that woman. Wanted a life with her, whatever that might mean. Moscow, the Bitterroot, Ovando. Kootenai Creek. Wherever, however.

"Mrs. Hall, would it be okay if I took off now? I think Drake's got the basics down." It was nearly eight in the morning, and we'd had the store open since six-thirty.

"Sure, Harlan, you know it is." Then she put a hand on my arm, laid those wise old eyes on me, looking right through me. "But are you sure, son? This what you really want?" And there wasn't a shred of doubt what 'this' meant. Damn, woman had some sort of ESP?

"Pretty sure, if she'll have me. And you've known it all along, haven't you?" I gave her a huge hug, turned, and began putting the basics into the Rover.

~ * ~

The drive west would be a challenge: go north forever to turn toward Idaho, then down to Moscow, or drive up to Lolo Hot Springs, over the Bitterroots and down the rivers. I didn't like major highways, so, since I'd never made the time to explore the mountains like I'd planned, I headed through Missoula down 93 to the turnoff on 12. Pretty along that creek, then I began the climb, which went on and on, gearing down on the curves, easing the Rover the way I always did, the country unfolding behind me.

Then, past the crest, I could coast, and I did, gaining time on the rare straight stretches, following the Lochsa River for miles and miles of evergreens, toward the Clearwater and eventually the Snake at Lewiston. More downhill first, though, more coasting, faster than the Rover'd ever gone, probably.

Long drive, and I had a lot of time to think. Was I doing the right thing? Following my heart instead of my head? Jumping into a life-commitment, a tying-down, the thing I'd wanted to avoid? Change everything, this would, and okay, I was 25, supposedly grown, making my own decisions, choices. Did I really want to team up with Kay—or anyone—and have to compromise everything I'd planned? Some soul-searching here, not like I hadn't been doing this a lot, last few days.

But then I remembered the actual magic I'd experienced with that girl, and I knew there'd never be another chance like this, never a more perfect woman to share with. Yeah, we'd be a team, facing this crazy world together. The thought warmed me all over, and I found myself pushing my mechanical steed faster.

I'd been lucky with my draft lottery number, although I had considered just joining the military to get that over with. But then

I'd reasoned that if my country really needed me, whatever government wheels would turn as necessary to include me. So, I'd opted for going west (young man). And really, thinking about that sweet woman, I was damn glad I had.

~ * ~

*Wonder what his reaction was, to the cowboy hat? Maybe thinking I'm worried about what's in his head, with that and the winter cap. But he'll like it; he'll wear it. I know so much of what's in Harlan's heart, now. Probably more than he knows, even. And now he's trying to think of something to send me. Not to worry, my man, all I want is that heart, 'cause you've got mine already. Wow, do I ever sound like a smitten schoolgirl! I said that before, didn't I?*

*Okay, prediction: he'll give up on gift ideas, he'll miss me a lot, he'll want more of that magic we experienced, and he'll make time before he gets busy with his rocks, to come see me, and we'll... well, I'm not sure just what we'll do, where we'll take this, next time. Just wait for it, girl.*

"Yes, sir, Dr. Blevins, I'll be finished with this specimen in a half hour. Yessir, I'll wait to go to lunch; I know how important this is." She hadn't brought her usual sandwich from home this day, having been in a rush to get to the lab, get this analysis for the fisheries people finished. There'd be time to grab something from town then, no hurry to hurl herself into the next behind-schedule project. And it was already three o'clock when she walked out the door to her car.

A red Land Rover was parked next to it. She did a double-take. *That's just like... no, it couldn't be.*

Then she was in my arms, eyes wide in still-disbelief, but gladness quickly taking over. I kissed that girl like I was drowning, and it didn't take her but a beat to respond. About crushed me to her, and we didn't need a single word. But I was thinking: *This woman is my gold. My Montana gold.*

We got lunch. She called in to work, told her boss she was taking the rest of the afternoon off. Then we drove her Mustang up to some high hill overlook she knew, parked, got out, climbed down to some big boulders, looked out over the countryside. Both of us knew why I was there, and after some serious hugging, I actually got down on one knee. *Do it right.* Which I did.

"Kay, will you..."

"Yes."

"When?"

"How's right now?"

"Umm. Gotta get a license, don't we?"

"Oh, that. Yeah, I guess. And I suppose we oughta call my folks, Hall, and your mom, shouldn't we?"

"Okay. And while we're thinking, we should make a couple plans, when, where, what we're gonna live on, where we're gonna live—stuff like that."

"We'll work all that out. First, you're gonna come to my house, where we'll maybe get to those plans..."

"No, first we go to a jewelry store and get you a ring. I thought about doing that first, but hey, it's gotta be your choice."

"I love you. Incidentally."

"Yeah, incidentally... I love you, too."

I wanted to take her right there on that flat rock, but disciplined the old organism. Just built the anticipation with more kisses, and an idea that we should do this right. It was gonna be for life, after all. A long look into her eyes told me she felt that way, too.

The ring was a white gold thing, with a subdued diamond, not devastatingly expensive. I put it on her finger with not a trace of regret, hesitation, misgiving. This was the woman destined to spend her life with me, wherever that led.

At her place, a tiny cottage up against some Douglas firs, we managed to keep our hands off each other long enough to start in on those plans.

"You've got this job, here. Now, I can come here, no problem, start looking for work, which is Possibility One. But you can guess that's not my first choice. Okay, your turn."

"All right, Two: I give notice, we go back to Missoula in a few days, get a place, where you've got stonework already, and I find a job. Next option?"

"We go back, move in with your folks or build ourselves a house there, and I work wherever I can, which might mean a long drive, or being away from you days at a time. That was supposed to be Option Three, but your dad says he might sell the place, and I ain't gonna be away from you. So..."

"What? He won't do that. Okay, we get married at the ranch, but we find a place temporarily, and I do stonework with you. Like that one?" Her smile made her beautiful. Not pretty, beautiful.

"You want to do that? Really?"

"Most fun I've ever had was hunting rocks with you, putting them in place. Yes."

"I like it. So yes." I took her strong hands, imagining working with her at my side, going home with her, keeping house in some cheap place till we could build our own.

Or whatever life threw at us.

# Eleven

Jack Samuels had harbored one goal in life from as far back as he could remember: make a lot of money. He'd disciplined himself enough to make good grades in school there in Texas, while also developing a sharp ability to fleece his classmates at poker. But occasionally he lost at gambling, and that was unacceptable. He honed his skills. But he realized this golden goose wasn't going to be permanent: couldn't victimize dumb teenagers forever.

He made himself curtail this activity, focused on schoolwork, won two scholarships to the University of Idaho, where he studied geology. It was hard, but with the looming, then actual controlling of oil prices by the Middle East, he saw a bright future ahead with somebody like Exxon, or Phillips, or Texaco. Plain to him that Americans weren't going to give up their wasteful consumption of gasoline and diesel, so exploration was in high order.

There was one problem. Too many of his exploits, winning money from dumb frat boys there, managed somehow to follow him after graduation. Seems a lot of those same frat boys had fathers in high places in industry, and well, the word made its way around: don't deal with Jack Samuels, the crook.

So, no future for him in Idaho, or even back home, then. Time to look around further out here, where unfortunately there were too many geology grads and too few jobs for them.

Finally taking a lowly assistant's job with a mapping crew out of Missoula, the determined young man kept his eye out for bigger and better action. And it had eventually come along, in the person of Bruce Calloway, who'd heard of Samuels from a friend of a friend, neither of whom was a paragon of virtue.

So, did the geologist know about mineral deposits?

"It's what I do. What kind of minerals?"

"Well, to get right to it, gold."

"Yeah, I know about trace quantity, concentration, economic aspects of recovery. So where we talking about?"

"We'll need to get to know more about you first. Got our eye on a piece of property with a history, but nobody's ever worked it. Rumors, of course, going way back, but the big strikes drew prospectors away before any serious panning or digging got going. Mainly the bonanzas in California. And you've maybe heard a man could make fifteen hundred a day down in Bannack, back in the mid-1800s."

"Never believed it, but they did move a lot of big machinery in there. Even piped water from like thirty miles, 'cause the creek there wasn't big enough for the sluicing. So your find—or is it that yet?—hasn't been proven at all?"

"Well, we've dug around, washed out some color, have a general idea there's more there, but we need a good geologist to confirm it, give us the direction, expertise necessary to go ahead."

"So you don't have the land, I take it?"

"Not yet, but it's for sale. A thousand acres of it."

"Wow. You've gotta have a lotta bucks for that kinda spread. What? Up in some remote mountains nobody can get to?"

"No, right on a state highway. What we wanta do is slip in there, dig some real test holes, wash out what we find, see if it's feasible. That's where we need you."

"And if it is? What kinda deal do I get?"

"Partners. There're three others besides me, a couple with those big bucks. We show the others the metal, we buy the land, get started."

"What about this new government agency, the EPA. They'll be all over you—us—soon's we start to dig, sluice. Sounds chancy."

"In the middle of a thousand acres, fenced, locked gates? This's still a free country, man's got a right to dig some holes on his own land."

"Umm. Well, I'd like to see this place, and yeah, do some exploratory digging. Keep it low-key, nobody'll know we're there. But just what do you expect from this, wildest guess?"

"From what I can gather, there's a vein somewhere on that property that should give us a lotta millions, way gold is going up in price."

Jack Samuels thought about this for maybe thirty seconds. *Sure would beat slappin' away rattlesnakes, climbin' over rocks, burned and thirsty out in the field.*

"Anything up front? Your money dudes willin' to finance the startup?"

"Some. I'd say we can offer you twice what you're making, to start. Soon's we get to the paying dirt, you're in for like I said, a fifth, after expenses."

"Sounds okay. But I gotta tell you, a shoestring operation like sluicing, which will keep us under the radar, will need a lotta water. What's there?"

"A drilled well for irrigation, supposed to be plenty for that, and a dug-out spring that looks good. But of course, this's springtime, so we don't know how good a source that'll be when things dry up."

"No. And there's the problem of runoff, muddy water that'll pollute whatever stream's close. EPA be all over us then."

"And you'll tell us how to handle that, won't you?" Calloway knew he had his man.

"Yeah, I will. So what else you need to know about me?"

That had been a year ago. Now, with a clear idea of where the group needed to go with their findings, they just had to have the McBryde place. That's where the source was, no doubt in both Calloway's and the geologist's minds. And they weren't going to be done out of it by simple legalities.

So it was during several days—nights, actually--of non-rain now, after McBryde's refusal to sell, that Samuels hid plastic jugs of gasoline and diesel fuel at strategic locations for a planned fire. He concentrated along the fence line between the Bujold place and McBryde's. There was dry grass here from the year before, albeit somewhat beaten down by weather. There were also young Ponderosas and Douglas firs scattered, and the occasional clump of mature trees, with mats of dry needles underneath.

Samuels worked to pile dry branches against trees to ensure a blaze big enough to ignite their limbs and generate enough heat for the fire to spread. He helped that along the last night of his preparations with trails of diesel fuel from brush-piled tree to tree, and noted approvingly the rising wind. The last of these locations was well onto McBryde land, in a dense grove of mature Douglas firs, near an outlying cattle shed. He'd observed ranch hands patrolling this border, but gambled against their being out at night. He was good at gambling.

The Company, as they liked to be called, hadn't hired a helper to do the real grunt work, fearing an information leak. So Samuels himself had cleared a firebreak with the Cat loader, to protect their property. Just a precaution, he'd convinced the others.

And just before three a.m., he poured a heavy trail of fuel along the weeds and debris bordering the ranch road clear up to the McBryde house and barns. They had no dog to give the alarm, and despite an imagined gunsight on him, the man finished: the stage was finally set.

He started the fire halfway along his path of destruction, seeing it race both ways toward the first of the brush piles. The gasoline burned quickly; the diesel slower but hotter. It'd been a tense operation, knowing the old man had armed his helpers, but it'd succeeded. *Burnout won't give us a bit of trouble when we start to work, but it should help ruin McBryde.* Calloway found out he'd been barely breaking even here: old truck, kids had to work their ways in college. *This should drive him out. Or there's always the next step if necessary, the big one...*

~ * ~

Kay, of course, wanted to call her folks right then, but for some reason, it'd gotten too late. We decided we'd call home in the morning, just before she went in to work and would give notice that she was leaving. Despite the excitement, we were both yawning.

So, we were pledged to each other for life, if not actually married yet. Did that make it okay to have sex? This *was* the enlightened Seventies; did that make it right? And I might well have been able to get her onboard: I sensed this. But okay, like I'd said, we had the rest of our lives for this, so why not, like I'd also told myself, do this right? I thought I could behave for a few more days.

So I slept in a tiny second bedroom a little roomier than a closet, head full of plans, sure I couldn't drop off. But the long day's drive, the excitement, the just-plain lateness of the hour conspired to put me out as soon as I hit the pillow. I had just this fleeting wonder how Kay was taking it, but grinned at that. I knew how she was.

So, unwelcome as morning was, we got moving, both of us creating breakfast. Then I called Mom first, knowing there was a—yes—three -hour difference in the time. Two from Missoula, I'd have to remember.

"Harlan, is this you?" Now how do women—mothers—know these things?

"Yes, Mom, it is. Got some news for you..."

"You've found the right girl, and you're getting married."

"Little bird tell you that? I'm amazed."

"No, but last time you called, you were getting along well as a stonemason, but had the winter ahead of you, when you wouldn't have work. So it was obvious you'd use that time, look around, find someone. What's she like?"

"Well, I actually met her last June. She's tall, sweet, cowgirl. Folks have a ranch. Working on an advanced degree in biology."

"Oh, nice. When's the date?"

"Soon, at the ranch, out of Missoula. She's in Moscow, Idaho now, but going back to home country. Names Kay McBryde, old Western family, two older brothers with kids."

"Oh, that's so wonderful, Harlan. How do I get out there to the wedding?"

"Um. Well, I think you have to change planes a couple times, or the railroad comes through Glacier Park, up north of us. Sure you wanta come this far?"

"Of course. Lester can't get off work, but I'll come. Always wanted to see what was out West. And I suppose you'll both stay there and you'll herd cows, right?"

"Hafta see about that. Really enjoying the stonework, and Kay wants to work with me. She's already helped me some."

"Really? Well, you write, send me all the details, because I know this long distance is adding up. Give Kay my love, son." And she hung up. *Okay, that's taken care of. Lester could care less, but the feeling's mutual.*

Kay dialed her folks to give them the news, but before she could, her mother's crying voice stopped her.

"Mom! What's wrong?"

"Oh, Kay honey, there's a fire, a big one. Must've started in the night. Burned over upriver, a whole grove of good trees, got one of the sheds, and looks like it's over on the Bujold place too. Sam's out with the volunteer fire boys fighting it now, just got it stopped before the house. They're pumping water out of the big spring. Oh, it's just awful! Thank God the cattle were up near the barn, and the horses. I'm looking out right now, and it looks like they're getting it out, but it's been bad."

"Wow, that's terrible! They don't know how it started? No, I guess not, this soon. Gosh, and I had good news for you, but it can wait. I'll call back tonight, okay?"

"No, it's not okay; we don't hear from you enough. What's going on?"

"Well, Harlan and I just got engaged, I'm leaving my job, and we're gonna get married there on the ranch. How's that?"

"Oh... Oh, that's wonderful, sweetie! Oh, I'm so glad! Wait'll Sam hears this. He likes Harlan, thinks they might work together some when he's between stone jobs. This's so great! Now you write me all the details, the when and all. I'm going out to take drinking water to the men, now. I'm so glad for you. 'Bye, now."

"Harlan, you heard? Big fire, burned one shed, but Dad and the firemen are fighting it now, think they can get it put out. Oh, that's so awful!"

"The livestock okay? Didn't get the barns or house, did it?" I was shocked, but there was some suspicion in it too. After that cattle killing, this was beginning to look like the beginnings of a range war, for sure.

"Mom says just the one shed, and a grove of trees. They'll still make lumber, beams, if we get the logs to the sawmill, but it'll be sooty, messy. You think this and the cows killed are connected, don't you?"

"Yeah, I do. But your dad saying he might sell the place, looks like now might be a good time…"

"Dad would never sell the ranch. Don't know why he told you that, but Mom did say in a letter they'd had somebody wanting to buy it. Same people bought the next place, the Bujold ranch. I went to school with their kids, but they've moved away."

"Well, we've talked about when to have the wedding, and I agree you should give notice, and finish that course first. I'll go on back, see if I can help your folks, at least till I can get started on the Sapphire ranch job. You come quick's you can, and we'll either find a place to live, or if your folks want us to stay with them a while, I guess we could do that." I was wondering what kind of a newly-married life we'd have right under their eyes. As usual, she caught it.

"We'll find a place. Spend a non-honeymoon getting settled, then maybe sometime in the future you can take me to Hawaii or someplace. Deal?"

"You got it. And I wanta show you off soon as I can. You'll love Rhys and Moira, and the Ridleys are great people. Yeah, if you can stick the stonework out, we can work twice as fast, take on more jobs, get serious about that place of our own."

I didn't want to leave Kay, but knowing it'd be for just a couple weeks, I managed it. Kissed her goodbye more times than I could count, then hit the road again. Long haul, but I should make it mid-afternoon or so. No, I'd go directly to the McBryde place, another hour or so, see what I could do to help. And maybe get a line on what was going on there? Maybe. Play detective. For sure join the cowboys with the rifles to keep watch.

The miles rolled away, albeit slowly, despite that coasting down from Lolo Pass. But my head was now really full of Kay, so I was at the ranch before I realized it.

"Volunteer boys are sure it was arson," a weary Sam McBryde told me, still wiping sweat and soot off him. "Diesel, gas poured all around, even here at the house, but we got it out before that could catch. Got to be the same crazy killed our cows. Seems the folks up next to us saw it early on, plowed a fire break with a track loader they've got, kept it away from their buildings."

"So they got hit, too. Well, I'm here if you need me, at least till Kay gets here. She wants the wedding as soon as possible."

"Oh, sure. 'Bout forgot. Congratulations. You're gettin' a mighty fine young lady, I guess you know."

"I do, yes, believe it. We'll look for a place to stay closer to my work, then keep on looking for land we can build on. I know she'd like to come back here, but you told me you're thinking of selling..."

"Well now, I might just reconsider that, Harlan. Somebody's out to hurt us, an' that just makes me more stubborn 'bout keepin' it. No, I'll talk it over with Em'ly, but I'd say you'n Kay'd be welcome anywhere here on th' place, if that'd suit you."

"Wow. I thought..."

"Don't think any more about it." He actually put a hand on my shoulder. "We'll talk more later. Now, you up for helpin' patrol with us? We don't aim for anything like this to happen again."

"I'm your boy. Put me on a slow horse and give me a rifle, and I'm on it." I was, too. Hey, sounded now like someday part of this'd be my place, too. *Wow!*

~ * ~

"Supposed to've burned the house and barns too, Bruce. Damn firefighters got there quick. And they got water outta that big spring, got ahead of the fire. Dunno how much damage..."

"You were going to torch the house? Maybe burn people up? That's heavy, Jack. Hey, we want McBryde out of here, but that'd be murder."

"Accidental forest fire, happens all the time. We'd have been in the clear, since it burned on our side, too. Still okay, but maybe we should talk about what's next, how far we'll go for this." It was a challenge. Samuels saw no reason to back off, but this timidity of Calloway's, which was probably shared by the other three, could derail the whole project.

"Well, let's see how this affects things, then talk with the others. Now, I'm not against some real pressure, but all the gold in the world won't help if we get slammed into jail. Or worse."

~ * ~

I drew the first night shift, joined by Kenny Blair, till midnight, when Sam and another hand I hadn't met would take over. Plan was to ride the perimeter in opposite directions, meet, then go ahead, covering each other's path. Over and over, and slowly, just in case some nut saw one of us pass and decided to come in just afterward. We'd check behind us often. Couldn't guarantee we'd catch an intruder, but we'd sure try.

I worried a little about just what I'd do if/when I did run onto a trespasser, and finally figured that'd depend on what he/they were doing. Setting another fire, I decided I'd shoot first. Just sneaking around, maybe not. But I'd sure as hell hold 'em at gunpoint till Kenny got there, then we'd herd them to the ranch house for the next step.

Didn't know how Kenny would react. Sam'd said he was a little impulsive, had been in a few fights on back. Likeable fellow, a cowboy to his bones. So with him out there too, maybe I wouldn't have to be the one making the big decision about any enemies.

And if the badasses opened fire first, it'd be every redneck for himself. I was a pretty good shot, and I was gonna be sure to see them before they saw me. It all still scared me, though, this New West shoot-'em-up scenario.

Kenny was a slow-talking guy, lean, slouched, who chewed on a straw constantly, his quick eyes belying the first impression of his not being quite bright. He'd had a couple years of college, was now just trying to figure out where to go with his life. Reminded me of what a young Sam McBryde might've been like. I watched him check out his 30-30 saddle gun with practiced fingers, in about five seconds. He worked the lever and a cartridge sailed out, which he caught. Yeah, looked like he knew the score, all right.

Okay, it was now good dark, with just a faint glow left in the west, and we started our circuits. Both of us carried long flashlights with fresh batteries. I was on Bruno, who probably wouldn't spook if a monster jumped up in front of him. And he knew the way: probably had walked this fence line a hundred times, reaching over for imagined better grass on the other side the way horses do.

My thoughts were of course filled with Kay, that wonderful woman who'd been right here under my eyes all the time I'd been in Montana, the one I'd have for my wife in just a couple, three weeks. And of course I realized this whole adventure with her had developed at supersonic speed, like one of those big passenger jet planes. So this wasn't the solo mountain man plan I'd been on, it was better. A whole lot better. *Enjoy it boy, just close your eyes and let it happen.*

But my eyes were searching every darker star-shadow under every tree, even as I planned, speculated, looked ahead to our time together. *Y'know, Kemp, you're a lucky redneck.*

Five hundred acres is less than a square mile, so it didn't take Kenny and me all that long to meet, nod, pass. We heard each other ahead of time, and nobody got trigger happy. I wondered what he'd been thinking, anticipating some further outrage by some insane marauder. Sam had described him as maybe a little quick to jump to conclusions. Probably a good trait when hunting the enemy. My thoughts returned to Kay's and my future.

*I wanta check out that upslope past where the river comes down from north, beginnings of that mountain we just passed. Some trees, south-facing, have a good view, be out of the wind in winter. And yeah, like Kay said, the burned trees can still make good beams for a timberframe house. Need a big truck to haul the logs...no, I can put a trailer together from junkyard axles, channel iron. Sam's surely got a welder; seems to be pretty well-equipped. Pull it with the Dodge okay.*

That got me thinking about equipment, machinery. Something Sam'd said...yeah, about the neighbors upriver having a 955 Cat track loader. Pretty good-sized rig for a ranch.

Wondered what they did up there, needed that big a machine. Of course anybody'd been able to buy a thousand-acre spread had bucks, so they'd probably gone for overkill. Dig a pond in a couple days with that thing.

Well, this had gotten boring, and it was just ten. Any fool who'd deliberately set this fire, which one had, wouldn't dare come right back the next night. Would he? Maybe, like they said on the detective TV shows and the crime novels, the killer—he was that, with the cows—always returned to the scene of the crime. Wouldn't be able to see much of the damage, but of course could tell easy the house and barns hadn't burned: see that from the highway.

I tried to work out who'd profit from harassing the McBrydes. *Follow the money.* Okay, Sam'd said he couldn't think of any enemies really, anybody'd maybe gotten the bad end of a trade, deal. And Emily was a sweet lady, probably never had a bad word spoken about her. So, no past grudge, that left the future, the money, if any. Kay had mentioned someone offering to buy Sam out, which was probably why he'd thought about it, said to me he might.

But neither he nor Kay seemed to believe that was now an option. So, inevitable conclusion: who'd start leaning on Sam, here? And just recently. What'd happened in the last few months to bring this on? Just a random crazy, some sort of animal-torture creep? And did he set the fire to burn up cattle, horses?

No, he/they'd sneaked up, poured fuel around the actual house, barns. Hadn't set that afire first, probably fearing getting caught, shot when it flared up. The obvious fire trail from the closest grove of trees meant the arsonist had surely hidden there to toss his match. It always amazed me what incredible damage just one stray bit of flame could do: cigarette butt, still-burning match, even a spark at the wrong time, wrong place.

I'd read about the Mann Gulch fire, when lightning had struck, the driest time of year, back in '49. Flames had caught up with the smoke jumpers, killed 13 of them. I shuddered. *Just kids, too.*

But this was deliberate. And the neighbors had been hit, too. Just lucky they'd had that Cat handy. I knew from just my few months here that the wind would've blown the fire that east direction faster, which was surely also why Sam's place hadn't burned worse. Fire volunteer guys maybe wouldn't have reached the Bujold place soon enough. Apparently just a couple guys there, not heavy into ranching yet. More so with cows getting slashed up.

So, somebody wanting to push both ranchers out? Make it so hard on them they'd sell? Be interesting to know who'd wanted to buy Sam out; maybe same people had hit the new owners next door.

My speculations got me nowhere, and neither did our night patrol. At midnight we rendezvoused with Sam and the other dude, who was named Willis Cartwright. He was a cheery, round little specimen, who looked like he couldn't mount a horse. Wrong: he sprang into that saddle like coiled wire. The two cowboys couldn't have looked more different, but both were probably born on horses.

Kenny headed home, just a couple miles up the highway at his folks' place, and I got some sleep in the little cabin down the creek. The McBydes kept it for people visiting, and for the occasional serious fisherman staying over. I remembered Kay'd said Sam charged a fee for them to pursue trout. Hoped they had better luck than I'd had so far.

Emily fed us all next morning, and shooed Sam off for at least a nap. Willis bunked down in the cabin, and I guessed I was the Lone Ranger here now. I was just a little saddle-sore, but wasn't gonna complain. Bruno, fed, watered, rubbed down the night before, was okay with carting me around some more, so we did.

Upriver, the mountain loomed beyond the bend, and I headed for it. Emily had found me a pair of binoculars one of the boys had left behind, and with them I could get a pretty good sweep of the whole place. And maybe pick out a possible homesite, sure. Also check out good scorched-tree material for that timberframe.

I envisioned Rhys Carter and me mortising, fitting, raising each bent, maybe with friends, family helping in a real house-raising. And of course Kay right in the middle of it: she wouldn't be content with just feeding the crew. No, be cutting, chiseling, pegging along with us, all the way. I could picture that. Gladdening everyone and everything around her as she worked. Damn, I could hardly wait.

*Okay, good spot here. Maybe too high for a well, so have to pump from one down below, to a big buried tank, gravity flow to the house, for when the power goes out. A retaining wall just down there, hold some fill so we don't fall outta the yard. Bring a road around through those trees, hide the house till the last turn. And of course a stone fireplace, chimney, which you'd see first thing, along with the raised stone foundation. Walk-out basement, maybe big woodstove down there, heat a lotta the house. Leave all these trees, hide the house among 'em.*

Then I realized Kay would have a lot to say about the house; *no need to speculate and plan, dude.* Hafta get used to being half of a team, that new role for the wannabe mountain man.

I found I could also see a lot of the Bujold place from here, so I spied on it a while. And there was that Cat at work, not far from the property line between us, scooping up soil, filling a dump truck, which the operator got off the Cat and into, and drove across fields toward a shallow draw. I guessed that was where there was a spring, maybe. *What, gonna build a house there? Barn?* No, the truck dumped its load against a pile of dirt, next to a strange-looking contraption.

I couldn't see well, so rode away from some screening trees, and up a little higher. That looked like some sorta flume, and I caught the glint of water. *Strange…*

Then it hit me: those dudes digging holes, last year. Must've found something, and maybe they were the ones who'd bought the place. Obvious now they were going after something, washing that dirt. But for what? Gravel, for their ranch road? Nah, too much work for just that, truck, loader. This looked like old pictures of prospecting, where the gold-fever men of the 1840's dug up and trashed some of the finest scenery in the West for nuggets.

Wow. Maybe gold here after all, like those old rumors. Something, for sure. Or silver? Like that Colorado place? Could be, I guessed.

But here? Nah, surely not, like Sam'd said, this place had been settled for at least 150 years. Somebody'd surely found whatever might be here. But I'd tell Sam, soon's he got some sleep. And maybe I oughta read up on deposits, sources. Be a helluva thing if my future in-laws were sitting on a vein of gold, wouldn't it? *Nah, nobody gets that lucky, even if it's worked out so well for me so far.*

But something was sure as hell going on with the neighbors. I could see the neat firebreak they'd plowed, which had stopped the spread not far from the boundary fence. Guessed it was lucky somebody'd noticed the fire early enough to get that done. Breeze would've probably blown it right to their ranch house, barns.

I resolved to show this house site to Kay just as soon as she got home, and to set aside whatever money I could toward getting that timber cut for our little haven. Pending the parents' approval, I didn't see why we couldn't get started right away, at least the planning, preliminary work.

I knew this place was too far from most of the stonework I'd find, and that was a problem; maybe we would have to find that cheap place for a while. Lot of driving otherwise, unless I/we could wrangle something a cut above the arrangement I'd had with the Ridleys. No way was I gonna stick my bride in some cave, even temporarily. *My bride: like the sound of that. Mine.* And I indulged in a prolonged fantasy about what life would be with that good woman, maybe a lot of it right on this spot.

Now, I admit there were still these flashes when I questioned my having jumped right into this union with Kay. Hadn't I resolved to put women aside till I was set? But again, Uncle John had imparted wisdom to me on back, saying there was never a right time to do something; you grabbed it first time around, 'cause it likely wouldn't ever get righter. His term, that. And every time a tiny doubt weaseled its way into my head, I'd remember that lean, sexy body next to mine, that yielding, passionate desire neither of us could resist much longer.

It was just as I was riding away from my chosen site I saw the evidence of more test holes. Not-too-carefully covered mounds, like those I'd seen before on the next property and those Sam and I'd spotted on his land. And dammit, these were freshly dug, not from last year.

Those bastards had prospected clear up here on the mountain slope! The realization hit me hard: guess I'd already taken possession of this spot in my mind.

I hadn't heard if Sam had spoken to the new owner of the Bujold place—he hadn't mentioned it—but he/I was sure as hell gonna do it now. My anger mounted as I discovered more evidence, a grid actually, covering a wide path down to the level of Sam's field.

Okay, after I told him about this, I'd get to the Missoula library, read up on mineral data, try to figure just what might be going on here. Well, I knew, really, guys looking for trace, maybe gold, and didn't stop with their property line. Just came on over, dug up the McBryde acres, no permission, and now wanted to buy them/us out.

So, must've found something good: no-brainer. Also not that illegal, just digging holes, except for the trespassing. And what did that have to do with the cattle killing, the fire?

Logically I'd have suspected those same neighbors, trying to intimidate Sam, get him to sell. But their cows had been slaughtered too, and their place burned. No, this was some other crazy. Maybe trying to force *both* owners off, like I'd wondered? *Possible.*

Back at the house later, I asked Sam about these new covered-up holes, told him what I'd seen. He said he'd gone up to ask about the others, but had found a new gate at the entrance to the Bujold place. Locked.

"Nobody around here puts a gate on his road, let alone locks it." He shook his gray head. "And y'say they're washin' out up there? Gold fever, reckon, heard th' old rumors."

"Buying a thousand acres, then wanting yours too, somebody's got major dollars."

"Yeah, some rich guy, wants to get richer. His business. Only thing bothers me's that comin' over, diggin' on me."

"Well, I think it's gonna get worse. All that sluicin' operation, the mud's gonna get into the river, sooner or later. I can see the EPA and every environmental organization shuttin' them down." I was seeing the North Fork in my mind, running muddy instead of the crystal flow I'd fished.

"Well, no creek on their land. And even with that spring an' well, it'd be a while before runoff'd reach the river."

"Would get to your creeks pretty soon, looks like." I wasn't into this hands-off stance. What'd happen to the trout fishing here? Somebody needed to let the right people in Helena know what was happening. Surely the trespassing diggers hadn't cleared their operation with the authorities, locked gate, midnight excavations, suspicious happenings.

So, was it up to old Kemp to blow the whistle on these guys? And how to go about it? Which bureau or commission or maze of offices did a man wade into with something like this?

I wanted Kay's help. This was her folks' ranch, hers and her brothers'. At the least, she should know about this crap. And surely she'd know more about the direction to go, people to see. I was the new kid on the block, the outsider.

Then a new thought struck: all I'd wanted was to be left alone to do my thing, build a craft, make a living, as far away as possible from the hassle of politics, business, The System. Maybe I oughta just leave this the hell alone. Maybe...

No. That mountain slope was gonna be ours, Kay's and mine. Hell, we might end up running this ranch, few years. Hafta make sure it'd still be here, for sure.

I wrote her a letter that night after supper, waiting for my twelve-till-eight shift this time. Told her all my thoughts about this, us, the future. Filled six pages. Damn, I missed that girl more'n I ever thought I could.

And she and I were already that team, would tackle whatever life threw at us together, stomp it into the ground. I wasn't overly religious, but I was pretty sure God had a hand in bringing us together. Hey, out of how many billion people on this planet, what were the odds? Didn't care: I was onboard, woulda been without Sam and Emily's blessing. Or the prospect of a piece of this land, not even asked for, just gifted.

# *Twelve*

"Water, Bruce. We've gotta have more water if we're gonna do more'n this piddlin' bit," Samuels told his partner.

"What about catching it in a pond, lettin' it settle, reusing it? We talked about that."

"Ground's too porous. Cost a fortune to line a pond of any size, and it'd silt up soon. No, if we're going to get in and out quick, we've gotta have a source. Need McBryde's big spring, his creeks. Go offer him more money."

"Yeah, intimidation's not workin'. Figured he'd be ready to retire. Most people, you make an offer, they get to thinking how they need that money, they come around. Been over six months though, all told. Yeah, up the ante, I guess."

So Calloway went to the ranch a few days later, found Sam and me at the corral. Little dude, eyes that never stayed still, or looked at yours for long.

Didn't like him.

"Hello, Mr. Calloway, y'heard anything more 'bout our crazy people?"

"Not a word, Sam. Checked with the sheriff this morning. See you've got those new hands. Seen anything yourself?"

"Well, this's Harlan Kemp, gonna marry my daughter, live here with us. Both of us got a question for you."

"Glad t'meetcha, Harlan," extending a soft hand. I nodded, drilled him with my eyes. He wasn't glad at all, and it showed. "What's th' question?"

"Well, seems somebody's been diggin' holes on our land" (*our* land: loved that) "an' didn't ask me first. Know anything 'bout that?"

"Oh, that'd be some men wanted to buy our place before us, probably. Soil testing, they told us. Must've got over the line by mistake or something. Couldn't get their money together, and we were able to buy it. Yes, back last summer, it was." *Slick.*

Sam looked at me. Both of us knew the digging we'd seen before was older, but what I'd found on the mountain sure wasn't. This was Sam's show though. *New kid...*

He chose to let it go.

"Well, what's on your mind, Mr. Calloway? Cows doin' okay?" He wasn't gonna mention the placer operation.

"Well enough. We're still holding off on more, though, till we're sure we won't lose them. Actually, I've come to increase our offer for your place, sir. Your water makes this a lot more valuable to us. Say fifty percent more. You see, with the herd we want to bring in, we'll need the water."

"That's a good offer. Really is. But like I said, even if my boys never come back here, Kay an' Harlan'll keep th' place, raise their fam'ly here. No, reckon it's still not for sale, sir." Both of us had been mending rails on the corral fence while we talked. I liked that about Sam.

"I'm disappointed. But it's your decision, of course; man's got his own priorities."

"Now, I *could* maybe work out somethin' like lettin' you pipe from my spring, enough for your big herd." Sam was shrewd, knew this wouldn't work for them.

"Oh. Well, that'd be nice, sure. But well, my partners really want to own their resources outright, I'm afraid. But I'll tell them of your offer, of course, and I thank you for it." There was confusion on the sharp little face. *Like a rat's.*

After he'd left, I couldn't help laughing.

"You called him on that one, Mr. McBryde."

"Hey, forget this Mr. stuff! I'm Sam, an' Em'ly's Em'ly, okay?"

"Well sure, if that's not too disrespectful..."

"It's not. Ain't gonna call you Mr. Kemp." Grin.

"Glad of that. So, what chance Calloway's behind the cows, the fire thing?"

"S'spected that of course, but him bein' hit too..."

"Cover story, my opinion. Only a coupla cows, not much burned. And what I've read about gold sign, that slope where we wanta build would be the source, if any. I think Calloway's dug there recently, found more trace, is determined to get it. My two cents." I spread my hands.

"You figure he'll do somethin' rash to get it?" His eyes were glints: *Western justice.*

"Maybe. Lotta money behind this. Now, I don't like trouble, but if somebody else starts it, I'm not one to roll over." Memory of a few fights I'd gotten into, growing up. I'd tried to be peace-loving, but there'd been times...

"Me neither. Guess it'll be after th' fight, then."

"Which we sure won't lose."

"By th' way, Kay's always liked that spot, too. Now, sayin' there *is* some gold there, would you wanta dig it out?"

"No way, muddy up your creeks, the river, cut all the trees, ruin the site? For probably nothing? Not on your life, and I bet Kay'd agree."

"Already has. We called her last night while you were ridin' with Kenny."

"Wow. Y'know, Sam, I could get to likin' you."

"Hope so... you're stuck with us." That granite-cracking grin again. And he actually put a hand on my shoulder, squeezed.

~ * ~

Kay got permission to take her final exam early, claiming a family emergency. *Yeah, like getting married.* She packed up the Mustang, said goodbye to her employer, who hated this.

"Gonna have to hire two more people to replace you, Kay. Sure you can't talk that man into moving here?"

"Afraid I'd have to talk myself into it, sir."

She decided to take the south route home, down to Lewiston, up the Clearwater, the Lochsa, and over Lolo Pass, the way Harlan had gone. It was a favorite drive, mostly the Montana part, and the mountains, the clear streams, the views flooded her with love of this country. And the anticipation built in her too, with each mile. It was May—green, beautiful May.

There was so much to learn about Harlan, so much to discover together. And it didn't matter whether they'd have to live in a hovel to be near his/their work; it'd all be worth every gritty bit of it.

And that about her favorite spot on the ranch. Trust him to find it, too. The prospect of eventually building their home there, raising their children there, made her warm inside.

Harlan had spent the last week down on the Sapphire ranch job with Rhys and Moira. This was Thursday, and he'd be home the next night. *Home: great place.* And yes, the wedding was now just over a week away.

The curves of the creek road down from Lolo Pass unfolded, the car coasting in top gear. The thought occurred to her that the Sapphire place wasn't that far from Lolo. She'd just go see him on the job, surprise him. Wanted to meet his friends, anyway.

He'd written that he was camping on this ranch in his tent, after one night with the Carters. Maybe she'd stay over... *No, we agreed we'd wait. Just drop in, see them.*

There was only a farm gate at the ranch road, and Kay drove through, closing it, following the main track on a guess. There were Herefords grazing the new grass, and a fenced field with horses. Eventually she reached a side drive, up which an open timberframe shelter stood.

She could see Harlan's red Land Rover at a small grove, and a curving stone wall. A Jeep was also parked near, and sawhorses held beams, with a bearded man at work with mallet and chisel. As she shut off the engine, she could hear the regular thumping.

"Hi, I'm Kay. I see Harlan's truck. He around?"

The big man's face split in a huge grin as he came toward her. At the same time a pretty woman emerged from the shrubbery, trowel in hand, also smiling. *Rhys and Moira, surely.*

"Hey, girl," the man greeted, and Kay thought of a friendly grizzly. "He's at th' quarry, gettin' a load of rocks. Should be back. Welcome, lady." Both of them took turns hugging her, and Moira held both her hands, looked into her eyes.

"We're so glad to meet you, Kay. Harlan's been going around like half a pair of scissors way too long. Let's sit here on his wall, catch up."

They did that, neither of this couple in a hurry to get back to work, apparently. Kay learned all about the Carter kids, their place up in the sky where a friend was with them, and this job so far.

"You're a cowgirl," Moira observed. "Gonna teach Harlan to ride, cut hay, herd cows?"

"Whatever he's up for. Know he wants to keep on slamming rocks, and I like that too. See where the work is, where we need to be. Then later, maybe..."

"You're up the Blackfoot, right?" Rhys asked.

"North Fork, out of Ovando. We're already planning to build there, on my favorite spot. Timberframe, Rhys, so we'll need you."

"Can't wait. Harlan says you lost a lotta trees in that fire. Ponderosas, Doug firs. Get 'em soon, they'll be okay. Sawmill close?"

"On up 200, toward Lincoln. Harlan's collected pieces to build a trailer to haul logs, beams behind his dump truck. Think that'll work?"

"For sure. He's good at improvising, saving bucks. And the frame'll go up cheap, but finishing will take time, cost, unless you go primitive."

"For a while, maybe. But we'll be close to my folks, cabin there."

"Gonna have time for a honeymoon?" Moira smiled.

"Later. I'm chucking a non-career in biology to work with my man for now, period. See how things happen."

"You can keep on at UM part time, get that grad work. Be handy later. I never thought I'd need my degree in horticulture, but here I am, planting, loving it, getting paid."

"Maybe. And Missoula's probably where the stonework will be, all right. See how that works out."

I spotted the Mustang first, grinding along in the Dodge with a load of that ledge quarry stone. *Okay! My woman's here.* I jumped out, took four long strides and had her in my arms. All of us were laughing, and we were getting in words between kisses.

Finally we broke apart, and I took Kay around to see the project. Flagstone paths among Moira's shrubs, pools with waterfalls fed by water piped from a well. Recirculating pumps kept the water from going to waste, quiet little things hidden under ledges. Electric lines buried outta sight. I was proud of my/our work.

"Okay, Moira, you've gotta come landscape our place when we build it: I can't grow good weeds."

"Girl, Harlan says you can do anything; don't disappoint us."

"He's biased, Guess I've got him fooled. For now, anyway."

"Blinded by love? No way."

It was fun. Best friends, co-workers, and my bride-to-be. Didn't get any better'n this.

"Say," Moira invited, "just another day to go this week. Why don't you come stay with us tonight, Kay? Let the old bear sleep with the owls..."

"Hey, don't I get to see my favorite kids?" I was mock indignant.

"Not this time. We're gonna keep you two separate long's we can. Torture." She laughed, and Kay just turned up her palms, said sure, nobody expecting her till later.

Well. Temptation removed, in the kindest possible meanness. I pretended to sulk, but couldn't bring it off. At least no one'd mentioned Crescent.

And Kay helped me extend that wall into the next little pool area, and we got one stone seat set. She had a good eye for stone, I'd observed before, and the muscle to carry it out. I couldn't have been happier.

So, day's end, she got what she needed out of the car, piled into the Jeep with the friends and headed off up the mountain. I fired up the Coleman, hoping this'd be one of the last bachelor meals. And lonely campouts.

Later, coyotes howled, owls talked to each other, and I eased off into sleep, thinking how God or something had taken care of me. *Always seems to happen; guess clean living's really not the answer.*

~ * ~

"Young guy's making this harder," Samuels told the group in the old ranch house. The other four had come to see progress, confer, plan a strategy to oust McBryde, get at that gold-bearing mountain slope.

"Take 'em both out," Stooped, hawklike Charlie Benson stated flatly. "We've given 'em the chance, more than one. And we already put too much money into this to let it fail. One, two cowboys can't be allowed to stop us." Benson was the group's lawyer, with the track record of handling acquisitions, mergers, whatever made the most money the quickest for his clients. And himself.

"What, like a hunting accident?" from Hubert Hedges, a Chicago-based developer with one continuous, black eyebrow scowl. "So then the widow takes our offer?"

"Nah, no hunting season on," Samuels pointed out. "But we've established that some lunatic's on the loose, and this can just be the next unfortunate incident."

"We'll be the likeliest suspect," Calloway said. Despite his dedication to this venture, serving as point man, he didn't actually like the idea—or the risk—of killing.

The fifth man, venture capitalist Eli Cabot, remained silent. The assurances, the soil test results, the plans for this project weren't working out. The gold was there: the samples proved that. The necessary additional equipment, machinery, labor were ready, on hold. A swarm of earthmovers could strip that mountain slope in days, enough water, enough hands wash out the gold before the ponderous wheels of the regulating agencies would/could act to shut them down. Or maybe they'd hit the source itself, a rich vein of solid gold.

And with the shielding of their corporate structure, each of them could disappear with his share like shadows, leaving it all like a bad dream for the environmentalists, the government agencies, the lawyers to try to unravel. After the fact.

That had been the plan. But now an old-timer and yes, a younger version, it seemed, were getting in the way. People who got in Eli Cabot's way always got hurt.

"One more outrage, that hits us too, will drive McBryde out, like Charlie said. Phantom crazy hits them, and us, disappears. All we need is the event."

A lengthy discussion followed, with wild and wilder suggestions. Finally, Calloway thought he had it.

"Poison the water. We lose a few cows; they lose a lot. Little creek feeds their pasture. We dump enough chemicals in, they die. We feed some to a couple of ours, they die. Simple." He looked around in triumph.

"Gotta plant something solid to point away," Hedges insisted. "Last thing we need's some hick sheriff poking around."

"So how about this, then," the resourceful Samuels offered. "Stolen van abandoned far along 200 with poison residue in it. No fingerprints."

"In Lincoln, maybe?" Calloway.

"Sure, that's far enough. And maybe a few more cows mutilated, more confusion. That oughta do it."

"Where do we get the poison?" Cabot asked the obvious.

"Enough weed-control stuff'll do it," Benson the lawyer said. "Everybody buys that. Get it from several sources, nobody suspects. But away from here, no ID later."

"Okay, agreed," Calloway said. "So who'll do the actual deed?" He knew: Samuels was no longer needed. He'd done what'd been necessary, so let him run the risk. So far nobody could connect him with the group, as planned; he'd stayed completely out of sight.

Risk, because they all knew McBryde was having his place patrolled. And despite Samuels' knowing the land, he could get caught. And yeah, be the crazy, even. And be unable to finger the rest of them, with another contingency in place, long-range rifle shots out of nowhere. That'd be Hedges' responsibility, and he had the connections.

~ * ~

The weekend with Kay was great. We rode to the mountain slope, staked out a house, lay side by side on pine needles, planning, kissing, coming dangerously close to ripping each other's clothes off. *What'd it matter, this close?* my devil voice whispered in my ear.

It mattered. Other, insistent voice: *Do this right. Sure she's a virgin; save this for wedding night. And if she's not, well, neither am I.*

Invitations sent before, ceremony now just a few days away. Not that many guests anyway. Emily and Kay rushing around, getting ready. I'd work down on the Sapphire place through Thursday, come on back. Had bought a decent suit, even a tie. Shoes, these slick black boots with a heel, make me look taller than her. Not that it mattered: look up to this woman if necessary.

So it happened that it was my fiancée who offered to fill in for me, riding lookout twelve-to-daylight Wednesday night. Sam'd said no, things quiet lately, no need. And if something *did* happen...

"Hey, I know every inch of this place, Dad. And you know I'm a better shot than anybody else here. Besides, you've got these walkie-talkie things now, so I'll check in often. *And* I'll hang back, wait for you if I see anything. Promise."

Emily didn't like it. Sam didn't either. But like he'd said, it'd been quiet...

"Go with Willis then, and watch each other's backs. I'll take the early shift by myself. Kenny's due back from Great Falls tomorrow, so..."

"Nothing's gonna happen, Dad. And if it does, you know I can handle it. Hey, this is our *home* that's at stake."

I'd have forbidden it, if I'd known. No way was I gonna let Kay face a lunatic, if one really was out there. I'd have thrown her over my shoulder and locked her in her room before I'd allow that.

But I didn't know.

Couldn't know.

I was worn out from a day of setting those great big blocks of quartzite, prying them into their tight fits, my hands working by themselves while my mind was on Kay. The Carters loved her, especially the kids. The Ridleys would love her, next time we worked on that ongoing job together. I loved her. Everybody loved her.

So I slept, there under those huge stars. And didn't know the love of my life was riding into danger up on the fork of the Blackfoot. No clue, no premonition.

*Damn.*

~ * ~

Jack Samuels began carrying the bags of poison onto the McBryde spread just after full dark. He'd watched the old man riding away to begin a perimeter circuit of the ranch, and verified he was alone this time. Easy to evade him, so the geologist made several trips the half-mile to a spot on the little creek that flowed past the barns. The cattle and horses were quiet, and Samuels reasoned they'd probably not drink till daylight.

He planned to get set up where he was hiding the bags, wait as long as possible before dumping their contents into the stream, avoid dilution. *Yeah, be outta here before any light, when whoever spells McBryde might see me.*

It happened this way: Kay and Willis took over at twelve, when all was quiet. They had begun the usual periphery circuit, but now on a hunch, were riding parallel, he still on the fence line, she inside, in case someone had gotten in already: her idea. They'd checked in on the half-hour, the walkie-talkies crackling noisily. So they agreed to muffle them under their jackets, keep them low.

Both had powerful flashlights. Both carried lever-action, chambered rifles. Both were alert, even as dawn neared.

But it looked as if this would be just another normal night, another watchful effort to prevent the kind of craziness that'd come into their world like a disease. Both riders looked forward to daylight and the reassurance of one more night's safety.

It was Kay who saw the dim figure setting a bag of some substance down next to the little creek. She halted Blaze, tied him well back, crept forward, rifle at the ready, flashlight off but aimed ahead. The figure was opening the bag. *He'll hear me if I call Willis. By himself, looks like. Poisoning our water. And the cattle will head right for the creek, come daylight. Can't just let this happen, let this crazy do this, can't wait a second longer... This has gotta stop, and right here's where I stop it.*

But could she? Actually draw down on this human being, even though he was plainly the enemy? You just didn't kill a man and toss it off like a normal event. Maybe he'd give up, not push it. She hoped that'd be the case. Threaten him, march him to the ranch house for her father to deal with...

Samuels felt the exultation of having pulled this off: he was opening the first bag after watching the cowboy ride the distant boundary in the dim starlight. He'd heard and seen two riders earlier, but now there appeared to be only one, and the telltale sounds of their communications system were silent.

Kay was within a dozen yards of the man, having slipped between creekside bushes like a wraith. Now she stilled the adrenaline rush inside her, steadied her hands. *Like a rattlesnake he is, nothing more.* She stood, rifle at her hip, clicked on the blinding light.

"*Drop the sack!* Step back, hands in the air or I'll blow you all to hell!" *That was _my_ voice. I'm bad!*

Jack Samuels froze, dropped the half-empty bag. *I'm caught, dammit. Thought they'd ride just the perimeter. But wait, it's a woman. The daughter, just a kid. She won't shoot.* He slipped a hand behind him, where his .357 Magnum was shoved into his belt.

"I said *in the air!* Her command cut like a lash. He hesitated, weighed this. Exposure. The entire operation blown. *And I'm the one they've caught. The others'll disappear: no help. And hell, she doesn't even have that rifle up...*

He decided. And dropped instantly to a crouch, whipped the gun around, got his other hand on it, bringing it to bear on that intense light. *No, that'll be in her left hand, gun in...*

The sounds double-boomed across the fields, echoed back from the mountain, died away.

The shock had been like an internal explosion, the slug tearing through center mass tissue, exiting in a ragged cavity of flesh. Samuels' face registered surprise for an instant, there in that bath of white light. He crumpled, the gun still gripped, smoking. Kay stood rigid for long minutes, the rifle still at her hip.

Willis galloped up, his flashlight bobbing, his round face alarmed.

"What? Who?" He hauled in the reins, saw the shape across the stream, blood running into the water.

"Don't touch a thing, Willis! Dad'll hear the shots, be here. He got his gun out, was fast. I was faster." She was oddly calm. Looked okay.

"Sure as hell were." He could see the gripped pistol. "Damn, did he shoot you, Kay?"

"Not quite. Dumping poison into our stream. The crazy guy."

It was soon that Sam raced up, his own light adding to the glare. Kay still hadn't moved. Neither had Willis.

"You okay, girl? He got off a shot." He was off his horse, had her tightly in his arms. Then he stepped over the narrow stream, looked closely.

"I'm okay. You see what he was doing. Surprised him, but he went for it against my light. Dumb."

"An' final, looks like. Willis, you ride now, call th' sheriff. We'll stay here, not touch a thing. Git!"

Willis rode.

The rest was a blur for Kay. The only clear thought was: *This's gonna mess up our wedding.* That she'd killed a man was a shock, but she knew it was that or be killed. And yes, now the lunatic was gone. The threat. *So maybe now...* A wave of nausea rolled over her, but she fought it down, gripping Blaze's saddle for support. The stallion nuzzled her.

Emily called the Sapphire ranch early that morning, and the foreman came and told me. I threw stuff into the Rover, gunned out of there before Rhys and Moira arrived. Pushed the truck the miles to Missoula, then up the Blackfoot to Ovando, two hours total. Emily'd assured me Kay was safe, but I knew she'd be in pieces. Killing a man'd surely do that to you.

Sheriff's car there, and he was still taking notes. The body'd been removed long before, the other lawmen gone.

"How is she?" I asked Emily, rushing into the house.

"Shaky, but she's not hurt, thank God. She's in there."

I knelt by her bed, took her hand. She was staring at the ceiling. Delayed reaction?

"Kay."

"Harlan. I killed a man."

"No, you killed a snake. Before he could kill you."

"Yeah, I know. A snake. Crazy snake." She turned a tear-streaked face to me. "Hold me, Harlan."

I did. For what seemed hours. Vowed never to let this precious child of God go. Ever.

# Thirteen

We went ahead with the wedding. I'd thought we should maybe wait, but Kay was okay with it. Like blowing a badass away wasn't enough to torpedo her/our plans. Sam had insisted on the sheriff's men knowing for sure it'd been self-defense: fingerprints, the still-gripped gun, fired once. All of it.

Case closed.

So we repeated our vows there among the pines at the ranch house. Me in a fog, supported by this strong woman's hands in mine, love flowing between us. Then with the longest of kisses and some more words from the minister, we were man and wife. Lots of hugging, back-slapping, laughter.

My mom was indeed there, beaming, so glad for her new daughter. She looked older, but the joy in her face belied that. And Kay's brothers and their wives, kids everywhere. Rhys and Moira's two ran, screamed, laughed with them. I felt like I had a real family for the first time. Warm.

And damn if that girl didn't insist we camp out on the very site we'd chosen for our house. Home, she'd said. Tent decorated with flowers. Food, drink, water and 'no trespassing' signs up.

"We'll look for you in about a week," Emily had joked.

"Or longer," from one of the grinning brothers. They were so alike, so images of their mother, I had trouble telling them apart.

"I see any of the rest of you near that hill, you're history," Sam warned. "Hell, they might just build that house up there b'fore they come down."

It was late now, the revelers departed or being directed to sleeping places. We rode in twilight, on Blaze and Bruno across, up through the gate, hobbled them. It seemed there was nobody else here in this world but us.

I swung Kay up in my arms, crouched down somehow, and deposited her inside the tent, both of us laughing like fools. I took time to position the two rifles and flashlights near the opening. Then yeah, we got outta those clothes.

And it wasn't just those fingers on my chest now: hard nipples, and just for starters.

I woke up around three a.m., slipped out, not waking Kay. The chill air seemed to magnify the stars. Stood there filled with more happiness than I could ever have imagined. I had a woman of my own, and what a woman! We had our life ahead of us, and we were welded together to take it head-on. And yeah, even if it meant blasting homicidal weirdos when necessary, we were up for it. A team, a single/dual force out to live every moment to its fullest. *Watch out, world.*

Back inside, I snuggled up to that warm body, got a sleepy kiss. Damn, I'd died and gone to heaven.

~ * ~

"Well, that plan went all to hell," Bruce Calloway said to Charlie Benson, the only other one of the group there. He'd called the lawyer right after the sheriff had come, asking questions. And now they needed another plan, quick.

"Sheriff know Samuels was one of us? Any connection at all?" *Damage control.*

"No, we managed to keep him outta sight. Wasn't even here over most of the winter, and always went to Lincoln for supplies. I'm sure everybody thinks he was the lunatic, cow-slasher, arsonist, water poisoner. We're in the clear."

"But no closer to the gold. Maybe time to cut our losses?"

"I've talked to the others on the phone. They won't back down. Wanta go ahead and take McBryde and the boy out, some way. Hedges, mostly."

"Do I have to remind you we all agreed we'd be in the law's crosshairs if that happened? I know I suggested it, and it's still probably the only way, but it's gotta be clean.

"And thinking about it more, there's no guarantee the women will sell, even after. Could hold out long enough for the EPA, others to come after us."

"Maybe. Samuels did mention maybe tunneling under, but no way could we keep that quiet."

"Okay, our geologist's gone. But what'd he say we could expect from mining just our side of the line?"

"Peanuts, essentially. Too much effort for too little gold. He maybe strung us at first, but told us all along we had to have that mountain slope, sure the source is under it."

"So we either get that land, or we eat a thousand acres, the equipment, and go home losers."

"We could raise cattle, I guess, but I don't know anything about that. You?"

"Not worth my time. Wanta run a dude ranch? Turn the place into a resort? That's legal."

"Joking, of course. Well, I guess we have to take one more meeting with the others, see where to go. And I gotta tell you, Benson, I'm getting cold feet about the idea of killing those guys."

"You've always been chicken, Calloway."

~ * ~

We spent a lot of time in each other's arms. We slipped down, skinny-dipped in the icy river at night. We climbed the mountain, beyond the ranch boundary. We even rode the miles to the lake and swam briefly (very) in that cove Kay knew. Hell, we just honeymooned. For days.

From our home-to-be, we saw the digging, sluicing next door had stopped. Ore played out? No, if anything, it would be richer on this way. Well, not our business. We *did* have other priorities.

Finally we packed up, rode back to the world, which seemed to be still there. Got hugged a lot, got my back slapped some more.

I'd had the foresight to ask the absentee Sapphire ranch owners if we could rent space in a guest cabin above the river on their place. When they heard it was for my new bride and me, they'd said sure, and forget about any rent money. Nice people.

So we picked up that job, working alongside Rhys and Moira, till well into summer. There were plans for more work, mostly for Moira: more plantings, landscaping. Rhys was off to another job upriver in Stevensville, and our stonework also came to a halt pending further ideas from the owners.

I have never seen a woman more radiant than Kay, those weeks working beside me. We'd be at opposite ends of a long stone, carrying it to its place, catch each other's eyes, stop, lean forward for a quick, glad kiss. And nights listening to the Bitterroot far below us were as close to heaven as you get in this life.

And omigod, the joy that filled us with our bodies, the tender touching, exploring with fingers, lips. And the dizzying heights of our joining. And our lives molded together into one, out before us into the faces of the years. No wonder we sang. No wonder we laughed.

Work nearer home in Missoula, we stayed with Mrs. H, to her delight. These were short jobs, a patio here, a pool and waterfall there, with Moira's plantings. We were able to save an inside fireplace and chimney for late fall, when the outside projects had to go on hold or were finished. Busy time in all, but of course my favorite summer. Kay's, too.

Weekends, we'd managed to cut the fire-scarred trees at the ranch, haul them to the sawmill on my trailer, getting soot all over us. Then bring the beams back, stack some of them at the foot of the slope below where we'd build. We wanted the foundation finished before winter, when we'd be able, with Rhys's help, to put at least the first bents for the timberframe together.

Not enough time. But we did get some corner piers up, enough to support sills and whatever else we could manage. And by cold weather we'd be in residence here on the ranch, to help Sam with the cattle. Sounded like it'd all work out, but if it didn't, there was next year.

~ * ~

With Calloway's reluctance to carry the Bujold ranch actions to the group's logical deadly next step, their meeting hadn't produced a solution. And when he contacted the others later to tell them he'd learned the McBryde daughter and her new husband were starting to build on the very spot they'd coveted, needed, the others agreed it was time to back off.

"For my part," Calloway'd said, "I don't want any part of that woman. Jack Samuels was badass, and he was quick, but she blew him away."

Their land went up for sale, at a significantly higher price, with the step of converting the diggings into a leaking, not-very-successful pond. Eventually it was indeed bought by yet another group of investors Calloway knew, to be turned into yes, a dude ranch. With riding trails, some show cattle, seasoned cowboys to service the city slickers.

The McBryde place seemed secure. And whether or not there was gold under the Kemp house site, it remained secure, too.

~ * ~

But the thing with the gold just wouldn't go away. For water, first for our foundation mortared stonework and later, we had a well drilled at the base of the slope. Like I'd figured, it made more sense to pump uphill to a buried holding tank and gravity pressure than to drill way down up there and maybe not get water at all.

So the driller got all excited when he spotted tiny specks of glitter in the tailings. I saw him sneak a few handfuls of the spoil and figured I'd better head this off.

"Yeah, last folks up next to us got all worked up, thought they were sittin' on a bonanza. Dug, sluiced, put a lot into it, but gave up on it. Anything real here, it'd been mined a hundred years ago."

"Oh," he said sheepishly, "I just thought..." He dumped the sample.

We got good water, got the power line extended, got on with beginning construction. Every weekend and days between paying jobs. With Kay at my side, we were doing okay dollar-wise, and could see maybe a roof at least, by next summer.

And Rhys, bless him, wanted to trade out work on the timberframe for retaining walls on their steep place. Seemed Moira was determined to terrace more garden space up there, grow vegetables, get even more self-sufficient. Well, if anybody could do that, this lady could/would.

So, we'd each learn the other's craft more, have fun doing it, and both save bucks. Of course, by now Kay and Moira were best friends, even 70 miles apart. That distance had come to mean less and less to me. We used the Mustang to commute, the Dodge for heavy work, and I could let the slow Rover rest.

Except that Kay loved driving it, up crazy non-roads, to hidden little pieces of paradise above the snow line, in ravines, up lost creeks. And of course we could bring back any unsuspecting trophy stones we found.

Which went into our dream house, which we played hooky often to work on.

We got to know the Kenners, the dude ranch couple who were actually to live on that place year-round. Roy was a sure-enough cowboy and Leslie was an outdoor girl like Kay. They had two kids, five and eight, both boys, Cal and Hugh, respectively. Hugh was pretty sure he was a grown-up already.

Most of this summer they'd spend getting glorified bunkhouse space ready, upgrading buildings, buying horses, repairing fences. The place was a flurry of activity, with hired help hammering, laying out forest trails, making this a true-as-possible ranching experience for the paying folks to come.

Kay and Leslie got the chance to girl-talk when we were in residence, and she even baby-sat for them some to let them get off that hectic place. *Good, that'll give her experience with kids when ours come.* Of course, she and Moira had probably shared that lore *ad nauseam* already. And yeah, Kay'd put in her time watching neighbor kids, growing up.

I guessed we were now Young Marrieds, a term I'd never imagined for myself, and had a sorta disdain for, like a lotta clueless guys. Wasn't bad. And maybe soon, parents of our own little monsters.

We'd decided to wait a couple years before kids, since it'd be half a lifetime before we'd have just each other again. Emily kept hinting, and so did Mrs. H, but Kay'd just smile and say we weren't in a hurry for that.

~ * ~

That summer ended. We had work lined up for next year, but with the exception of that one inside job, we were free for the duration. By end of September, we'd completed two terraced spaces for Moira. And the piers for our house.

And had a stack of timbers ready for mortises and tenons, most of them now in one of Sam's barns, where Rhys and I could work in foul weather. Of course, Kay wanted in on this too, a way also to fight winter cabin fever.

The plan was to follow Rhys's practice of laying out each bent, fitting joints, knee braces, all the pieces together individually inside, without having to raise the bent. Even the post mortises were pre-fitted to the sills, with post and sill laid on their sides. We cut Roman numerals into sets of beams to keep everything straight, since #2 post wouldn't necessarily fit #3 girt. Hand work, all of it, and true to a long heritage of such construction.

Roy Kenner liked to forge his own horseshoes, and had learned a lot more about blacksmithing. Sam, Rhys and I visited him one Sunday afternoon and he showed us hinges, latches, tools and knives he'd made. Sam commissioned him on the spot for chain hooks, gate latches, kitchen pot rack for Emily, and a hunting knife. I wanted all the hardware in our house to be forged, and got him to promise me, soon's the weather got too bad for anything else.

The three of us youngish guys got along well, and we found time, despite Rhys's aforementioned distance, to work together that winter. So much so that Roy and Leslie invited the Carters to come down off the mountain and spend the season with them on the ranch. They made it a live-in proposition to their ranch owners, pointing out Rhys's expertise in construction. Everybody won.

"I am so glad we don't have to fight that road this year," Moira confided to Kay. "And so's Rhys. He spends half the winter digging us out, clearing our way down."

I often reflected that life just didn't get any better than this, even with the wind that scoured the ranch, the chill getting way down there. This location got a lot more snow than Missoula, down in its sort of bowl. But we dressed for it, in however many layers it required, and of course the rest of them were used to it.

And after helping with ranch chores, there were the bones of the house, waiting for us inside, with a big woodstove we'd bought, churning out heat. Roy saw what we were doing, and hammered out mortising and corner chisels for us. Nice to use handmade tools.

By Christmas we had half the bents ready for raising, but decided to finish the others, raise them all at once in the spring. I was antsy about getting the house up, but managed to keep sane those days it was hard just getting out to the barn from the little cabin.

Kay loved this work. She was neater than me, slower but more precise. Rhys was proud of his protégé, and of course so was I. Timberframe is a lot like furniture-making: you have to figure ahead a lot to make it all come out right. My MO was always to leave extra lengths to allow correcting after I'd screwed up. Good thing, too.

We spent a lot of time planning interior spaces. Kay naturally wanted the dream kitchen, and as much of that view as possible from there. I left most of this up to her; I'd live in anything.

We'd also carefully laid out the road up to the site, both to reduce the slope and to come upon the house as a surprise. You'd see the big stone chimney and the raised foundation stone as you cleared the trees, with the long open porch across the south side.

I like dormer windows, so we lighted the half-story above with five of them, all facing south. Passive solar, with the back wall against the bulk of the mountain, blocking most of the winter wind.

For the present, we'd use the ranch road across the wooden creek bridge, then across the fields past where the river came down from the north before our mountain. I'd build an arched stone bridge someday, and route us along the creek before turning up the slope, to make the approach more of an experience in anticipation. We were having fun with all this.

# *Fourteen*

Crescent could not believe this. Glenn Ormond, her ex-husband, had actually written her. She had no phone—didn't want one—but here that creep, that closed door to her past, had broken into her years-long isolation, with a letter. For days she didn't open it, just let it stay there on a shelf with some of her pottery, wood carvings, and the tiny hummingbird she no longer wore. Harlan Kemp was a memory too now, and so was Glenn, his a bad one.

But she couldn't help her mind going over the good times, those first months. Yeah, when she'd been sure Glenn and she were fated to be together always.

Finally, in that nostalgic state, she tore the envelope open, read:

"Crescent, my love, it's been too long. I was rotten to you, and it's made my life rotten. Everything's empty now, and I've realized long ago I've never stopped loving you. I've got to see you, talk to you, even if there's no chance we could get back together.

"I'll keep trying, because you're the only hope I have for any kind of a life. Think it over please, and try to forgive me. I'll do anything to win you back. I've found out you're not dating, and that tells me you might still care a little, and that we can get back what I threw away.

"Please, please. Glenn."

She held the paper for long minutes, there in the failing winter light, letting the outrage, the anger consume her. *How dare that piece of shit ask me to forgive? Try to drag me back into that hell. Regain my trust so he can destroy me again. No! A thousand times no. I've got a life now, you conniving bastard, and I won't let you wreck it again.* She crumpled the letter, opened the woodstove door, threw it in.

A life. Yes, a life of independence, choices, all of it on her terms. And her cheating husband wanted back in it. No way would she open that door again. Surely some other gullible woman had finally thrown him out, and he was crying in his beer. Let him.

"I've got a *life!*" she shouted. And she realized that the scars of that other life could be torn open again, fresh wounds inflicted.

*No!*

Okay, so it was a lonely life; that was her choice. And that life didn't need a man in it. Certainly not that man, by any wild imagining.

Men. Always after her. Now, the guys at the farm markets, dropouts, the studs, the married men out for a stray piece to brag about. All so sure she was desperate to share her bed, her body. All seeing her as an object, a *thing.*

Except Harlan. Damn, he'd been decent. Never pushy, always there to help. And she'd returned the favor, feeding him, going land-hunting, laughing with him. Like a brother, really. Sure, he'd wanted more, wanted her. But not as a trophy, a conquest. And he'd understood, that last night together. Like a real man should, not the boy she'd thought him.

Moira had told her Harlan had married. So as she'd told him, the right girl had appeared, the girl he needed. So soon. No, Moira said they'd known each other almost a year. *All the time he was here.* She guessed he was one of those people who hadn't seen what was right there in front of them.

*Like Me? Could Harlan and I have made it work? We were easy with each other, comfortable...*

*But he understood. The road not taken, and now he's taken his. Maybe I was a fool. I think he loved me, but apparently not enough. Wonder what his Kay is like? And I guess, with loser Glenn's letter, I'm a little envious.*

*No, I wish them well; I'm just lonely.*

Leslie Kenner admired our stonework, and went to work on the dude ranch owners to have us do some more nice work there. Of course, she'd already gotten them onboard with some really good landscaping by Moira, with our accent boulders, seats, steps, paths.

There was to be this big outdoor patio with stone barbecue, separate stone wide firepit with raised stone seating along the rim. And they eventually even went for an archway entrance to a small stone amphitheater for gatherings, music, whatever.

Now this'd be great, right next door, come spring. These owners had big bucks too, and knew they'd have to spend a lot on a first-class operation to compete with other such layouts.

They'd already been advertising for their summer opening, and we'd be working around their clients. I wasn't thrilled at that prospect, but figured Kay could handle the PR and tact necessary to keep them outta our hair. Back in Missouri, I'd had onlookers plague me with dumb questions: "Are the rocks heavy?" *Betcher ass.* "You can't really *like* to work this hard, can you?" *Beats starvin'*. And of course Kay would catch it—"How does a *woman* do this work?" *Same's a man, dumbass.*

She insisted we could stand it.

Maybe so.

Meanwhile, there was the rest of winter to get through. Breaking ice in the livestock watering tanks. Forking hay, feeding, tending young calves. Shoveling, scooping snow. Cutting the scorched tree tops for firewood, left from our logging. Kenny had stayed on, so it wasn't that hard.

And that one inside fireplace in Missoula. We'd overseen the digging and pouring of the reinforced concrete footing for it, and the carpenters had left us the hole in the subfloor to come up through. There was a lot of wheelbarrow work, bringing in stone, sand, cement, working in the confines of the roughed-in structure. At least it was closed in, with the heat on.

We'd go back upriver to the ranch weekends (it took three for that job) and build on our house when we could, so we got through it. And the owners of this new house loved its raised hearth, arched fireplace opening, warming oven with Roy's forged iron door, hinges. Hand-hewn mantel beam of imported, bold-grain ash. Roy's andirons and poker, fire shovel. Sorta a preview of what ours would be. We topped the chimney out in a couple days of freak good weather in early March. Flashed it, capped it, then got outta there, final check in hand.

Rhys was all eagerness to get back to their mountaintop. He'd picked up on stonework quickly, working with us on those retaining walls, and with Kay and me still on the dude ranch job, he could handle the Sapphire ranch ongoing work. He'd done a lot of carpentry for his hosts here over the winter and was square with them. They packed up our favorite kids and left, end of March.

So we finished the pre-fitting of beams, purlins, knee braces ourselves, and would gather the Carters, Kenners, Sam, Kenny and whoever else we could find for our house-raising, by May we hoped.

Every half-decent day, we'd slip up to the mountain to fill in stone between the piers, locking it into steps we'd left in the foundation. Had to wrap it in insulating blankets to keep it from freezing, but we made progress. We'd scrape the snow off our site with Sam's tractor, get a load of rocks anywhere we could, set whatever stone we could. Then it'd usually snow again, or sleet, and we'd have to stay in, just get out to tend the stock.

Sam and I fixed things in his shop, welded broken things, replaced worn things. He could do about anything, the way a rancher or farmer must, and I learned a lot from him that winter. We liked each other, could work hours with no talking, and were mutually respectful. That he was more than 40 years older didn't matter: we were family. More so even than my time back with Uncle John.

Kay couldn't keep up with her classroom graduate studies with our moving around to jobs, or now too far from the university. But she did get a couple of directed study courses, which meant she just had to check in with her professors periodically. She wasn't gonna waste that degree or her biology knowledge. And who knew where we'd be or what doing, in a few years? Be prepared: I might suddenly find myself under a big rock.

*Bite your tongue, Kemp.*

~ * ~

The dude ranch owners had hired a local lawyer to handle the details of their operation. They'd wanted a no-nonsense type, and had been directed to a one-man office with a reputation for smoothing the way for various development efforts. His name was Charlie Benson, and it turned out he already knew the 1,000-acre Ovando property well.

*Ironic: I'm right back next to that gold. Maybe that's supposed to come around for me again.* Benson knew from past experience that ventures like the dude ranch often failed, and he thought it prudent to get part of this for himself, the land part.

The shell corporation he'd been part of with Calloway and the others hadn't revealed his ID, so no one was the wiser.

*Bide my time. If this goes south, I can maybe grab the pieces, no partners, no weak links. The Kemp kid's building on that slope, but maybe he'll go broke, too.*

Benson was sure, now almost a year later, that the McBryde family had put the vandalism, the violence behind them, wouldn't be on their guard. No more digging was necessary, no intrusions. The dude operation seemed like a good neighbor: *keep it that way.* He could come off as everybody's friend, as long as he had to.

~ * ~

I liked the ranch owners next door: all four were under forty, had made their bucks in the corporate world. Wanted the outdoors. Guess everybody's got that cowboy mystique back somewhere inside him. They'd be in and out all season, with their cute wives and cuter kids.

Long's they stayed outta our way, I was fine with that. *Cool with that—term's coming back around.*

And they did. These weren't dabblers, they all pitched in on the work when they were here, determined to make this a success. These people knew how to hit it, how to make sound decisions, how to demand quality work from everybody—cowboys, construction workers, the Kenners, us. Good to work for. All in all, about as close to independence as we were gonna get. At least for now.

The weather finally broke for good, and the Kemps got all over that stonework. I especially liked the archway, solid on its footings, deep, thick enough to withstand an earthquake. Lichened stones we'd scrounged from a big landowner down a back road not too far away. Kay was good at spotting the tapered ones for the actual arch, and even scored the keystone. It was a 300-pounder we used a hand winch and tall tripod to raise and set.

I'd rented scaffolding and a small backhoe for this work, but looked ahead to the time we'd save money by getting our own equipment. *After* we'd finished our house, not before.

The house raising did happen in May, under clear skies on a Saturday.

Emily, Leslie, Moira, and Kay cooked for an army, and eight of us assembled the numbered pieces. We heaved the first bent up by hand till the cable from the Rover winch could take over, raised it vertical, where we caught it with a check rope and it thumped into the sill mortises. We set the bottom knee braces, pegged them, and the bent stood tall and true. Cheers, applause.

The others followed suit, with the joining plates pegged in, along with a pair of roof purlins each to hold it all in place. Lunch followed, with a load of calories, range beef, potato salad, veggies, beans, ham, biscuits, gravy, pie. The rest of us watched Rhys inhale a big part of it.

We got the last bent in place before dark, and Cale Carter scampered up to nail the traditional pine bough at the peak. More cheers. Started to look like a house.

The Carters stayed over at the dude ranch to do some more work there, and the others left, with our promise to return the favors. Kay had lifted, hauled, pegged with the best of us, and we were both exhausted, staggering into the home ranch cabin. I patted her perfect derriere there in bed, about all I could manage.

"Boy, are you safe from me tonight."

"But are *you* safe from *me* tonight?" Wicked laugh.

Loved this woman.

~ * ~

It seemed like a coincidence, seeing him there. But Crescent knew Glenn had planned it. In another letter, he'd written he was moving back to Stevensville. He'd bought, no doubt with his family's money, the old clinic there, planning to turn it into a small, upscale hotel. He'd be the manager. *Another venture:*

*dad's propping him up again. Well, if he can stay sober, maybe it'll work this time.*

She'd gone to one of the first of the season's farm markets in Florence with her goat cheese, her booth decorated with early flowers, her brown curls cascading over a newly-sewn, colorful dress. New season, new prospects, all out there before her.

And there he was, the same silly grin she'd first noticed in college. *Handsome devil, still. And devil's the operative word here.*

"Hey, girl, how y'doin'? He was standing back with two customers ahead of him.

"Busy," was all she replied. *Yeah, busy. With my life, you toad. Disappear.*

He didn't, wouldn't. And now no one else was near, as he edged up to her booth.

"Goodbye, Glenn. You're not welcome here." This despite a distinct flutter somewhere inside that she tried to smother with anger. He still could do that to her, damn him.

And he knew it. Knew too, that if he could just stay, see her enough, she'd cave. He saw her reddened, chapped hands, the tiredness now starting to etch lines at the corners of her eyes, the worry there. *She needs me. Always has. And I need her. The others... well, they were just others. All over, now. I can be her man again, take care of her. Fool to leave... no, she threw me out, over that little affair. Hey, this is the enlightened Seventies, woman: open marriage and all. Live with it.*

~ * ~

We reached a stopping place at the dude ranch mid-June, but needed money for the permanent roof on our house and the rough-in plumbing and electric wiring, the expensive stuff. So we'd taken the Ridleys up on a month's work on their creek place.

They'd added a wing out over the edge of the drop to the water, and wanted the temporary posts replaced with stone.

Straight work, and the footers were already in. Easy enough job, but endless corner rocks.

And the minute Nancy met Kay, she insisted we stay in the garage apartment for the duration. No charge. Wow. So we set up, hauled stone, got on it. Hard.

So hard that at one week's end, we nixed racing back home to work on our place. Elected to unwind; maybe go fishing, swimming. Be human.

Nancy was going to the Stevensville farm market early Saturday, and talked Kay into joining her. I said okay, we'd go exploring later, had the Rover. I thought briefly of Crescent, but knew she went to the Florence venue, well on toward Missoula. Or maybe that small one wasn't making her any money. No problem anyway—Crescent would be cool. And sure, so would I.

We followed Nancy across the river and to the market. Should be everything there by now, first veggies, eggs, smoked meat, honey, jams, bread, and sure, cheese. Crescent wasn't the only cheesemaker around.

~ * ~

*It's been a whole month,* Crescent thought. *Damn guy can't get it through his head it's over. Been over. Well, maybe he'll go look for me in Florence, not figure I'd be here right under his nose. Today, at least.*

*And if he shows here, this's the day. I didn't go through all that hell getting rid of him, busting my ass to get set up alone, to have him waltz back in, mess my mind again. He's going, if I hafta get the sheriff after him.*

So of course before long, I spot the little sprite with the long curly hair, and despite my resolve, something skips inside. *No, Kemp, you got it all, now. So, do I go right up, introduce Kay, get it over with? Dunno what Moira's maybe told her, but that lady's solid. So whatthehell.*

Nancy had stopped at a yarn stall, with its rich colors and a spinning wheel going. I took Kay's elbow and started toward my...

friend, I guess. Got jostled by some dude who smelled like a brewery, lurching the same way. He got ahead of us, leaned on Crescent's counter, no customers at the moment.

"Hey, babe. Nothin's happ'nin' here. Let's pack this shit up an' get outta this dead scene."

I have never seen disgust so plain on anyone's face as appeared on Crescent's normally joyful one. *Now whatthehell?*

"I'll make it plain, Glenn. I don't wanta see you. Ever again. Not here, not at Florence, nowhere. Now…"

"Aw, you know y'don' mean that, sweetheart. Why, I know y'been thinkin' it over, want me back…"

*Glenn. The ex. This drunk? Looks like an overage frat boy.*

"Just *go*, Glenn! Leave me alone, or I'll get a restraining order. *Go!*" She was highly pissed.

"Won' go, 'cause I'm not givin' up on us…" He started to push inside, reached for her.

*Okay, do I step in, or… She's a grown woman, not my business. We can just…* My bride stepped forward to block him. They were the same height, but she made him look small.

"What part of 'no' don't you get, guy? Lady's made herself clear. Now why don't you just disappear?" The jerk turned, focused.

"An' whothehell're you, you ugly bitch?"

I had Kay out of the way in one move, clamped a hand like a vise on Glenn's shoulder, digging fingers hard into that soft place on top, spun him. *Bitch? Ugly <u>bitch?</u>* And my right fist freight-trained into that leering face with all the anger I'd ever felt. All the force. And more. *My* woman? *Ugly bitch?*

His head snapped back. Blood flew. Somebody was screaming, maybe Crescent. People were turning, gasping, I guess. All I could see was what was left of that face, above the body that was starting to crumple. I hit him again on the way down, and felt his jaw break. He was on the ground. I was aiming a giant kick when I felt Kay's hand grip my shoulder. Not gently.

"Harlan." It was quiet, but it got through. She pulled me back, got her eyes on mine, gave a quick shake of the head. I stepped back. And then, damn if tiny Crescent didn't come outta that booth, take one giant step and land a boot to the side of that bastard's head. That was hard too, made a sorta smashing sound.

Three men rushed over. I held up a hand.

"Guy insulted my wife." My adrenaline was screaming.

"And she's a friend of mine," Crescent said.

"Yeah, girl, we heard. This's the dude's been bothering you?" They knew her, of course. "Had it comin'." The speaker was a big leatherworker, from two booths down. Then to me, "We're your witnesses, guy: all cool. Somebody go call the cops, okay?"

He and the others dragged that piece of shit away. Things quieted.

"Harlan, thanks. And you'd be Kay. I'm Crescent, friend of Moira's." The girl hugged my wife, maybe a foot shorter, but with warmth. "I've seen Harlan around, slammin' rocks. That was my ex, who's crazy."

"Moira's mentioned you, and her kids adore you. So glad to meet you." Kay held her away, with a smile that lit up the whole market.

"Me too. Thought you were gonna deck that slob yourself, there. You're a helluva woman."

"At least kick him in the balls." *Did sweet Kay just say that?* "You okay now?"

"Not till I pile cheese on you. Where you workin', Harlan?"

"Up Kootenai again. Kay's right there bustin' it with me. Best stonemason I could want."

"What a team: rocks don't stand a chance. Gonna stick around? We could do lunch." I could tell she'd really like that, but no...

"Guess not," I said. "If the fuzz don't need me, I don't need them. We'd best be splittin'."

"Oh, you'll just be the anonymous stranger, saw his duty an' hedunnit." That silvery laugh.

"Well, hope you'll be okay, now. Think he'll hold a grudge?"

"Maybe, but soon's the sheriff's boys get here, I'm onto a restraining order. Problem is, his daddy's bought him the old clinic here, to turn it into a hotel, like this place needs a boutique hotel. So he's around."

As we were leaving, I asked the leatherworker if any of the others could keep an eye on Crescent, some way. Thought of that slob getting after her again, this time with a grudge, bothered me.

"We live on her road," he told me. "Crescent's our favorite people. Yeah, dude'll hafta go through Maggie'n me, an' that ain't gonna happen. By th' way, I'm Eric. This's m'wife Maggie." We shook all around. Maggie was bigger than Eric, a red-faced, smiling mountain of woman.

"Guess they'll take care of her," Kay observed as we hunted up Nancy to say goodbye. I also remembered the shotgun Crescent kept for coyotes. And Glenn, yeah, a coyote. Mangy.

"You know, she called me a friend even before she met me. That was sweet."

"That girl doesn't have enemies, Kay, except for the ex."

We drove up to the forest stream where I'd camped, collected stones before. It was a beautiful day, light breeze in the tops of the evergreens, deep blue sky above. There's a silence in that kind of forest I'd never experienced, a kind of suspenseful, sweet aloneness, among those tall, really elegant trees.

Kay'd grown up with that open but tree-shadowing, that deep peace, but I could tell she didn't take it for granted. Her face was in a sort of worshipful repose, and there was no way I couldn't stop the Rover, reach, pull her to me, kiss those eyes, lips.

And we gathered a few more corner stones, splashed in the water, laughed a lot. Renewed our game of find-the-rock, an ongoing competition whenever we were out in the woods, which was often.

We'd snared fresh bread, ham, jam at the market, and with Crescent's delightful cheese, we munched. Don't know why, but I loved watching that girl eat (weird?), but she just ate cute.

And briefly looking back on that first time I'd seen them together, Kay hadn't come off in any way second-rate to Crescent. The hawk and the canary? I had the hawk, and I was proud.

"Bastard called you ugly. Kay, you're *not* pretty, you're beautiful." I gave her a bearhug and a jam-flavored kiss. And well, things got a little outta hand there all by ourselves on the pine needles, and that woman got all over me. Somehow I fought it, for maybe half a second, there with nobody else around for maybe ten miles. Or maybe fifteen, twenty, yeah.

Some kind of flowering tree was above us, and the petals decorated our lovemaking. They drifted down, white like snowflakes. Beautiful.

"Hey, right/wrong time of the month; wanta get me pregnant?"

"Do you?" I paused. Not easy, just then.

"Yeah, I do. Stop and I'll kill you."

That experience topped all the others, we later agreed. We about tore up the ground, almost fell in the stream.

And yeah, we did get ourselves pregnant.

~ * ~

The house got closed in. I knew inside finishing would go on for weeks, even if we could spend all our time on it. And we had paying jobs out there; the Sapphire ranch owners wanted more pools, waterfalls, and Rhys said he wasn't ready for that level of stonework. Besides, he was busy with another timberframe. Okay then, back to that guest cabin for most of the rest of the good weather.

"We'll finish our place this winter, girl. Have it all done before the baby comes, okay?"

"Sure. A year's not too long for a dream house. And we won't owe a cent on it, no mortgage, no payments. Independence, Harlan. How about that?" I loved it, but I wanted to tease her.

"Oh, I was gonna borrow on the house to buy a Mercedes."

"Over my starting-to-bulge body." Speaking of that, Kay was radiant now, healthy, no morning sickness, strong. Make a damn fine mother.

"Oh, I'm gonna breast-feed, so don't get into an old-fashioned snit. The inside's for the baby; the outside's for you, you cannibal." Biggest smile in Montana. And sure, why would I object? I did know guys who said they didn't want their wives used as cows, but that was bullshit. Kay even got to La Leche League meetings Saturdays when we were in Missoula.

*Outside's for me, yeah.*

# *Fifteen*

Charlie Benson's fixation about that gold under the Kemp place became an obsession. He knew he couldn't get his hands on it by direct force—tried that—so he'd have to use a more subtle approach. And reflecting on his earlier perception that the dude venture might fail, since almost nine out of ten new businesses did, he planned to help that failure along.

So, as the group's lawyer, he began advising them about such things as the local attitude toward outside ventures, the old-timers' aversion to change in general.

"I think this is the best idea that's come along, and I want to help make it succeed, but we have to tread carefully, not make any enemies," he cautioned the owners at a planning session.

"Surely nobody can object to a ranch, here in ranch country," Sheila Blevins, one of them, had reasoned. "Not like we're gonna put in something gross like a chemical plant or strip mine."

*If you only knew.*

"Of course not, but I've worked with enough developments around here to know the folks have odd ideas, carryovers from the pioneer days. Just saying we need to be aware of this and act accordingly."

"Well, we have Roy and Leslie," Adam Stone pointed out, "locals in every way, as sort of ambassadors. People around here like them, and that's part of why we hired them. But we hear you, Charlie, and yes, we'll tread lightly here."

*Young upstarts. Didn't give any of them the right to call me by my first name. We're not equals, despite your money.* His pasted-on smile belied his inner thoughts. Benson was good at that.

"Well, I've become friends with Kay Kemp and her mom," Ava Stein said, "and they don't seem to fit any stereotype of stuck-in-a-rut resentful rednecks. Seem pretty open to our plans. And Kay's husband, the stonemason's, sorta quiet, but not the least resentful."

"Good people, all right, and we can hope they're in the majority. But those folks had some trouble on back too, for some reason. Okay, let's go over this EPA thing again, people. Legally, everything we're doing here is on solid ground, so..."

Stone thought about this. *Guy's maybe seeing hurdles where there aren't any. We're not anybody's enemy. And we're not going into this with our eyes closed, but maybe it's better to be aware of potential concerns. He's obviously deep in this with us, that about taking the small share instead of legal fees.*

George White had made his money in insurance, and felt he was a good judge of character. This Benson plainly knew his law, and was just aggressive enough to get them what they needed. And yeah, all of them were from somewhere else, didn't know the local customs well. He gave his wife Kathy a nod across the table. *Seems like we've got the right guy.*

Benson knew every business needed at least a couple years to turn the corner, make a profit, and some needed far more. His plan was to undermine this operation, then as it began to lose money, he'd offer to bolster it, keep it going, by generously putting his own money into it. While of course requiring as collateral a bigger share of the ownership of the land, a perfectly reasonable arrangement.

If he could make that happen, he'd eventually own enough of the dude ranch property after the dust settled, to be in a position to go to work on young Kemp. And start building his own estate, which would eventually include the bonanza site.

The parents would die in a few years, and there'd surely be ways to drive the stonemason off his holding. Or worse. Patience was the MO, and Charlie Benson was no impatient youngster, with the eventual reward of that certain fortune under Kemp's new house.

~ * ~

When a couple's expecting their first child, it sorta changes things, priorities. But we were gonna finish our house in time for the newcomer, so it'd all fit. And while I'd lose my prime stonemason at least for a while, I was happy as a fool.

Okay, I did reflect again for about ten seconds, that this new stage of life I was now a part of, didn't jibe with my planned independence, my recluse/mountain man image. And to hell with all that anyway. Kay and I could go anywhere and do anything we wanted; choice was ours. And we couldn't want anything better than this, so no running after adolescent pipe dreams. Our kid would grow up here on the family ranch, make his/her own choices in this big country. Thought of that made my heart swell.

And hey, now I had my mountain woman at my side. Well, my big sky woman.

It wasn't all roses: couple of people I'd worked for wanted to chisel me on payments, using such excuses as challenging my measurements of face square footage, or conveniently forgetting they'd ordered extra work. Part of the construction business, I know, but galled me anyway. Sometimes I'd negotiate a little, trying to be fair (okay, I could make a mistake too) but usually I toughed it out, got my bucks outta them.

Change orders helped: get the owner to sign any additions/changes they'd ordered. Also, Kay would insist the chiselers watch as we measured, see just what they'd gotten for their bucks. She had more patience than I'd ever get. I just wanted to punch the cheapskates out. Somehow, that woman of mine never made folks mad. She just had a way of bringing them along. Hell, she'd sure done that with me.

Thank God.

So things rocked along okay, with the house getting closer to a reality, work ahead of us, and big plans for our child-to-be. Of course, I worried about Kay horsing rocks around, in her 'delicate' condition. She told me her doc said get lots of exercise, so just shut up, sweetheart, and hand me that hammer and chisel.

~ * ~

Crescent's ex Glenn never knew who'd broken his jaw that time—happened too quick—but he'd asked around everywhere, suspecting it'd been somebody she'd slept with. He was insanely jealous, although his own string of affairs stretched off toward infinity. He'd tried to go see her, but had been stopped by big Eric and bigger Maggie, who'd made a habit of parking their truck to block the road to Crescent's end-of-the-lane farm.

They'd made it clear their friend didn't want him anywhere near her, and with the court order in effect, Glenn had backed off. He guessed he'd just crapped in his own nest one time too often.

But he wanted to know who that guy was who'd cold-cocked him for no reason. He'd had to take care of other guys on back who'd crossed him, and he'd do it this time, too. If the dude hadn't been with Crescent, he was surely with that tall, ugly woman who'd started it, and surely somebody'd know her. But nobody did. Or nobody was telling, more like it. Glenn found he wasn't particularly liked here in hospitable Stevensville.

Every time he asked about his attacker, he emphasized that he must've been a huge guy, a description that helped his ego. He hadn't actually seen anything but a big fist coming at his face, so he couldn't give much of a description. The few people who'd been at the market agreed that just some stranger had popped him, and some of them remembered his insulting the tall woman.

"Maybe you oughta watch that mouth of yours, guy," was big Eric's advice.

"Well, I was maybe a little drunk, all right, but..."

"End of conversation. Now turn that car around, and if we see it here again, one of us is gonna fill it fulla holes." Eric had taken the precaution of having his hunting rifle with him when he'd gone out to halt this pest. And made sure that truck was in the middle of the narrow road.

"Okay, okay. You don't hafta get all hot about it..."

"Yeah, I do." And he racked a cartridge into the chamber. Glenn fled.

He was already sick of this place, but the hotel project tied him to it. His father had told him this financing was the last he'd ever get, and he'd better make the place a success. So he'd hired a lot of people to refurbish the old clinic, spent many thousands on it, and it was now open for business. He'd seen to it the hotel was on all the regional Chambers of Commerce fliers, as *the* small but elegant place to stay in the Bitterroot Valley.

With the non-result that a very few bored rich people began to show up, drawn by the spectacular scenery, and their natural aversion to cheap motels. Resorts were just beginning to flourish in the area, from the Lolo Hot Springs one to a couple outside Missoula.

Glenn liked these scarce people, whom he considered his peers, and spent a lot of time with them, hoping they'd recommend his hotel. He advised them of the best fishing guides, hunting experts, places to buy gear, fine restaurants, of which there weren't many. Except, of course, his own dining offerings.

His father had insisted that if this hotel thing were to work, the boy would have to go first-class in everything. So he'd found a really good local cook, hired the cute red-headed waitress away from the local ice cream place to begin with, and started advertising his small, intimate dining room.

But again, the place couldn't seem to build a reputation. That he wasn't yet making money at this concerned him more than his father, who was, after all, a practical businessman. But as time passed, Glenn did discover that it wasn't the worst place to be after all, as long as he could continue being supported. And of course back in his mind, he just knew Crescent would someday tire of the goats and that rough life, and come around.

So it was that a prominent attorney and his wife from Missoula came one weekend late in the summer, the only time in many months the man had grudgingly taken off work to spend time with his wife. And they loved the place. Charlie Benson and his Melissa hadn't been out together in forever, she'd complained, and she'd heard of this new place.

Glenn picked up on the lawyer's aura of power right from the first. This dude would be a good guy to get to know. As hotelier and maitre d', he naturally made sure the couple was well attended to, and was able to start a conversation with Melissa, who was easier to approach. More so since Glenn, despite his worn-frat-boy air and now-crooked nose, was still a handsome man.

"This place is so sweet," she'd gushed to him as he'd personally seated them in the cozy dining room. "Charlie thinks there's definitely a need for upscale accommodations, don't you, dear?"

"I guess. Yeah, that dude ranch is aiming high, too. Just don't know if there's enough buying power here to support it, or this, frankly. You heard of it, Glenn?" Benson wasn't going to address this fellow as any sort of equal. And he'd already forgotten his last name.

"No, I haven't. Where is it, sir?"

"Out of Ovando, on Hwy. 200. I'm representing them. Group of owners are going all the way, but I don't know, with winter drying things up and all." Benson wasn't usually this forthcoming, but he'd sized up this man immediately, and was working on his own plan for him. There was a certain recklessness about him, which might be useful, a don't-give-a-shit attitude showing through this ingratiating facade. Might come in handy, somehow.

*This place will fail, and the dude venture will, too. Somebody else is financing this, and I'd bet when it closes, I can buy this boy cheap. They don't often come like Jack Samuels, ready to act, cross lines, but I'll need somebody like that. Get to know him better easy, the way Melissa's eyeing him, find out what kind of man he is.*

So the Bensons suggested Glenn have a drink with them after things quieted down for the evening. That didn't take long, as Charlie suspected. And he also noted that this Glenn drank freely, which loosened his tongue. The result was his confirming Benson's initial impression that here was a chronic failure, probably with no prospects beyond this doomed venture. He'd never liked failures, but they were easier to manipulate.

Inwardly, the lawyer speculated on which venture would go under first, the dude ranch or this too-expensive non-watering-hole. *No bet: those kids at the ranch are smart, patient. But they'll also know when to quit, when to fold up and leave, like Calloway's bunch.* So he should start building up some tight help he could depend on, with the eventual goal of getting his hands on that place, plus the McBryde land, or at least the stonemason's part of it.

He told his host more of that operation, including the landscaping and even the stonework being done there. By this unlikely couple, who just happened to live next door.

"Woman's a horse, works right alongside her husband. Had to shoot a lunatic on back, was poisoning their water. Word was, he drew down on her, but she blasted him all to hell. Whattya think of that kind of action?" A probe.

"Well, I'm in favor of direct force when it's called for. In fact, I got blindsided by some jerk back in the spring, didn't even see him, got my jaw busted. I ever find him, I'll more than even the score."

"Don't say. Some short-fuse cowboy, maybe?" Benson didn't care, but he needed to hear more about this prospective muscle.

"Yeah, right here in town, farmers' market. Some big ugly woman stuck her nose into my business, and I was about to tell her to butt out when the guy attacked me. Thought at first it was somebody my ex-wife knew, but turned out it wasn't. Just some drunk, I guess. Maybe with that woman." He'd been sure he'd recognize her if he ever saw her again, and sure, if the guy was with her, he might find him. Hadn't worked out, though.

"Well, if you ever need legal help with that kind of thing, or with this place, here's my card. Hope it's a success. Like Melissa said, country needs some class." *Give it a year, tops.*

Benson got a little more from this man as the evening wore on, enough to strengthen his perception that here was at least a potential errand boy/fall guy/muscle for the group he planned to organize. He didn't believe half the versions he was hearing of Glenn's past, but the signs were there, chronic misdirection, trying to prove to his father/financier that he could cut it, which he plainly couldn't.

*From small beginnings... I'll need all the help I can buy when it comes time to take young Kemp down. And I remember how that wimp Calloway was afraid of the girl, too. Well, she won't know what hit her either, when that time comes.*

*And it will come.*

~ * ~

The Sapphire ranch job started up again, with more designs from the owners for their planned outdoor venue. The wife had visions of weddings out among the waterfalls and plantings, with the timberframe shelters there handy. And maybe nature study events for schoolchildren, a retreat for artists. Outdoor concerts? She aimed to make this a jewel, a destination. Suited Kay and me; we had their cabin, the job we enjoyed, and sometimes Rhys and Moira working alongside us. It was now fall, but we'd get in some good work before the weather got bad, when we'd pack up and head for the McBryde/Kemp place.

Kay was showing now, but she was energetic as ever. She'd insisted I accompany her to childbirth classes, and hey, I wanted to share this experience with her as much as I could. I was surprised to see so many husbands there, but times they were a-changing, all right. Kay'd wanted a midwife and home delivery, but I was firm about her having the kid in the hospital. Doctor had told us that if there *were* an emergency, even across the street was too far. And while he'd told us only one in a hundred or so births was a problem, I wasn't about to let that one be us.

Of course we'd heard all the old wives' tales, again and again, soon's women and some men had learned we were expecting. Best be safe, I'd insisted. I wasn't gonna take any chances with this terrific woman I'd found, nor with the baby, either.

And I finally did get her to slow down a little with the stonework. And she let me know that little was all I was gonna get; she felt fine and she'd continue to pull her weight, Harlan, so don't do the mother-hen thing. With a smile and a kiss to show she knew I was just watching out for her.

So, this late in the season, Moira was busy planting, and she often brought the kids with her. And between other jobs, Rhys would come too, bringing baby Cormac, to help. We made a tight little group, Kay showing Cale and Siobhan the fundamentals of laying stone. And when I had a really big one, Rhys would help, too. We picnicked, laughed a lot, drew closer to this great family.

"Oh, meant to tell you, Harlan," Moira remembered. "That jerk, Crescent's ex, has opened the hotel in Stevensville, and it's fancy. High-priced, of course, and I doubt if it'll make it, lost in nowheresville." She was just making conversation; I couldn't care less about loser Glenn.

"Oh, how is Crescent?" my bride asked. We hadn't seen her since the farm market episode, but I knew Kay'd liked her. Hell, like I'd told her, everybody liked Crescent.

"Milkin' goats, makin' cheese, like always. Girl works hard, hardly ever goes anywhere. We've expected her to give up and move back to town somewhere all along, but she's sticking it out. And apparently that loser Glenn is leaving her alone, thank God."

"That's good. I like her, just from that short time. Has she hooked up with anybody else?" Just normal girl-talk, but I'd put that whole...what? Indiscretion? out of my mind, and wanted it to stay there. But as I'd seen before, that woman could be cool, no recriminations, no awkwardness. She'd plainly liked Kay too, so maybe she could be in this friendship circle with us. Maybe.

"No, guys hit on her all the time, but whoever gets her will be somebody special, and I'd say the odds here in Florence are way down there. But who knows? May happen." And nobody looked at me.

So it was decided between the women that we all oughta just go visit the sprite cheese genius. I kept telling myself I was cool with that: girl alone like that needed friends, and we *were* friends. I did try hard to forget our impassioned lovemaking that fated night, that perfect little body pressed to mine... Yeah, that night I realized I already had found the love of my life. *Just like we said: need. And that was yesterday, and yesterday's gone.* But of course I'm an animal, like every other man, with flaws.

Predictably too, that talk led to the "why not right now?" question, so we quit early and all trooped over to see Crescent. Where the kids petted the goats, we all helped milk them, then the women went into her little kitchen with things they'd picked up at a grocery store more or less on the way. And we'd stopped at Eric and Maggie's, who just came along also. Big party, so if our girl was getting lonely, we'd fix that.

It started getting crowded inside, so we guys went out and split firewood by the barn light. Eric had brought beer, so we hit a few. I'd seen too many drunk rednecks back in Missouri ever to wanta indulge much, but I had my usual one, sipping it till it got warm.

We talked. About ex Glenn and his pink elephant in Stevensville, about stones and beams and leather, the state of the country, which we all agreed was going to hell in a handbasket. Guy stuff, like the world over. It was a Wednesday night, but no one cared much about whether tomorrow was a workday or not.

We ate. My lord, did we eat! Those four women all knew how to prepare a feast, and the bunch of us put away enough for a small army. I was glad I wasn't eating my own non-cooking anymore.

The kids were learning to play musical instruments, which they just happened to have along. So they and Rhys got all over the fiddle, guitar and banjo, and none of us could keep our feet still. We spilled out into the yard, stomping to some really fine Bluegrass music. Moira and Kay sang, and I realized my bride had a great voice. Knew that, but here it sounded so fine. I can't carry a tune at all, but I've always liked to dance. Back at the college, which was Presbyterian, not Baptist, there'd been lots of dancing, though the chaplain there discouraged the dry-rub stuff.

The kids got sleepy, and Crescent insisted on tucking them in there in the little bedroom I'd slept in, and we grown folks partied on. She didn't want any of us to leave, so we didn't, for a long time. Finally, Maggie invited Rhys and Moira to stay with them and not fight that non-road home. Kay and I were close, in the ranch cabin, so sometime late we said our goodbyes.

"I like that lady a lot," Kay told me. "She's about as independent as anyone can get."

"Yeah, but it's pretty obvious she gets lonely. Moira tells me she hardly ever dates. Burned too badly by slob Glenn, I guess. But I liked everybody tonight. Are you civilizing me?"

"Trying to. You're not a hermit, but you do get lost in your work." Kiss, snuggle, as I eased the Mustang up the bumpy road to the cabin. I remembered Uncle John saying a man's work became his recreation as he got older. Okay, I wasn't old, but there was something to that.

We went to bed with that glow still enveloping us, from friends, music, good food, sharing. And those kids, including little Cormac, who were icing on the cake. Both of us were thinking how great it was gonna be for us to have our own.

Next morning we slept in, had careful sex, much later had breakfast, finally got off to work. I was so damn happy nothing short of Armageddon could've spoiled my mood. We just had it *all,* right in our callused hands. Which we found ourselves holding whenever they weren't slamming rocks. Rhys just grinned at our displays of affection, and so did little Siobhan. Cale pretended not to see.

~ * ~

There was some small talk around that we got wind of, mentioning the possibility of gold to be discovered up the north fork of the Blackfoot. Guess maybe that well driller, or whoever'd been behind the digging next door, had gotten it going. Anyway, we'd get a question now and then, when people learned where we lived. Sam told us he'd been through that a generation ago. The curious.

I filed this away, having more important things to attend to: family, house, work, and the approaching winter. That part didn't bother me much, since we had our plans set: work indoors to finish the place, help Sam with the livestock, get ready for the baby, who'd come in March. Good time to be born, with the best of the year ahead of him/her.

So we completed another phase of the Sapphire ranch job, some more on the Ridleys' place, and a couple other smaller jobs, before winter and the necessary shutting-down. We'd laid in a supply of good stones to work on the retaining walls up on the slope to our house, which we could add to anytime there wasn't snow or ice to contend with. Shouldn't go stir-crazy.

And my now-beautiful wife got bigger. Healthy, energetic, like carrying our child was just as natural as breathing. Her mom and I worried some, but finally just threw up our hands and let her make all the decisions. Her body, her experience, her choices. And on reflection, when had she blown it, really? By contrast, whatthehell did I know about babies?

*Yeah, that.*

The money situation was okay. I'd held off buying that tractor with the loader bucket we needed, keeping our priorities straight. Old Dodge would last a few more years, and if I rebuilt the engine, replaced parts, it could go on indefinitely, like the Rover and Kay's Mustang. We weren't into the throwaway thing.

But as winter came on, the dude ranch folks had to admit this first year of their venture hadn't done well. They'd advertised a lot, knowing you hafta put most of your energy/dollars into that for a new business to succeed, but not that many city dudes had responded. Sort of a disappointment, but these sharp people knew also that no new venture turned the corner the first year. More like five years, and while they hoped it wouldn't be that long, they were in for the haul.

They did cut back on some more planned goodies that'd have meant work for the Kemps, but assured us these plans were just temporarily on the shelf. Little oases of big stones, greenery, waterfalls, places to go unwind.

In due time. Their optimism was infectious, at least among us friends. And even if nobody much had shown up this first season, they all enjoyed the place themselves: their own paradise.

# Sixteen

The winter wasn't as bad as the ones before, or maybe I'd just adapted. Actually got to enjoy working with the livestock, getting outside on bitter days. You dressed for it, you rolled with it, you crystallized plans for the spring.

Which included the arrival of our firstborn, in the small hours of a March pre-dawn. Kay told me about the first contraction after lunch in our nearly-completed kitchen, and her water broke shortly after. We hustled over to Emily first thing, who took over. Kay already had her necessities packed, and we loaded up. But not before Sam insisted he and I have a shot of bourbon, to fortify me, he said.

So, fifty-odd miles to Missoula, and not much change in the frequency of the contractions. Normal, Emily assured us, and Kay knew this from the childbirth classes. She mostly just wanted her mom around for the big event, I guess in case I freaked out as things got hectic.

Not to worry. I was gonna be there in the delivery room, mopping my bride's brow, timing the contractions, whispering encouragement to her. Emily understood this, and had told me she'd stay in the background.

Damn, I liked that woman.

But of course that day dragged on into night, and we knew first babies took their time coming into the world. The nurses' shift changed sometime before midnight, and some older good old girls came on, who'd seen it all. Efficient, a little surprised to see me there, but okay with it.

I got scrubbed and gowned around one, and things started to move faster. A lot faster after a bit. These stoic women had been chatting, waiting, going in and out, checking, on some schedule born of routine. Then one of them went for the doctor, told us it'd be real soon. I sure hoped so; Kay had been able to keep her cool for most of it, but now the contractions racked her. She'd bite down on the washcloth I gave her, hands gripping mine hard till they passed.

"Don't push yet, honey," the nurse in charge warned her. "Just a couple more, then give it hell." *Yeah, give it hell. The love of my life's already going through hell, lady.*

This doctor materialized, checked once, joked he was gonna play center field and catch, and told Kay to push. She pushed, groaned, was told to go ahead and yell, which she also did. I felt about as necessary as tits on a boar hog, but she'd told me she didn't think she could do this without me. Well...

All at once there was this bluish little shape in the doctor's hands, that moved of itself, and there was a sudden commotion of his and the nurse's movements. She wrapped the now-squalling kid and laid it on Kay's chest, where it—he—quieted at the sound and feel of his mother's breathing, voice. I was aware of a lot of laughing, back-slapping, congratulations, and Emily was there, beaming. I kissed Kay, whose eyes were moist and full of gratitude for my having done absolutely nothing.

She'd never looked more beautiful.

I took a few pictures of mom and son, then was ushered out to let Kay rest. Emily hugged me, suggested we get a bite somewhere, early breakfast at a truckstop. I was in a sorta daze, but then realized I—we—had ourselves a man-child.

"Wow!" I kept saying. "Wow." I was about the proudest papa in the whole damn world, and Emily maybe the proudest grandmother. Yeah, despite having been there before, with the sons' kids.

Sam came later that day, beamed at his daughter and grandson, then spirited Emily off home. Cows, horses to be tended, and Kenny the one remaining cowhand off for the weekend.

Couple days later, we headed for home, our son Cody getting used to this new world he'd been shoved out into, and reasonably happy about it. Kay kept being amazed and overjoyed at the miracle of it all, and we were both up in the clouds somewhere. I pictured an all-too-soon cowboy riding our range, living the modern-day stereotype, 'with the whole wide sky above (him)', to quote Benet. I still did read a lot.

So now a father, and finishing up details in our house, waiting for the weather to decide what it was gonna do so I could slam stones. It'd be a solo thing now, at least for a while, even though Kay was anxious to get back outside. Said she could carry the kid in a pack and keep up with me any day. Spunky girl, but I wasn't gonna let that happen till I knew she and Cody were a bunch more independent.

That again.

The dude ranch folks were still holding off, not spending any more money than they had to until things got better, or worse. I had a few small jobs, which was okay, since there could be whole weather weeks when I'd hafta pull off. And I stockpiled stone, throwing in some nice rocks from along the river for variety.

And I'll confess, since I'd spotted a little color when putting in the retaining walls, I was curious about the gold rumor. Not that we were about to dig our place up or anything that stupid, but since there was talk again about it, a little of it got back to us. Ran into the well driller in Missoula one day, and he joked about it.

"Been diggin' any up there? I know you said wasn't a thing worth it, but I just figgered..."

"Nah. Wife's folks been there a long time, and they know there's nothin' but a few specks. And been working on the new dude ranch some, and they've found out it's all just talk." I wanted this over with. Guys be sneaking up on us armed with shovels if the rumor persisted.

~ * ~

*Well, another season, and we'll just see how the dude ranch thing works out. They're not going ahead with more construction, landscaping, so I know they're hedging their bets.* Charlie Benson knew these entrepreneurs didn't get rich being stupid, but he also knew some of this venture had a bit of cowboy fantasy in it. *Get that knocked out of them, another bad year.* But as soon as he saw signs of discouragement, he'd show his support, his faith in the project. That offer to buy into it more, talk it up, keep them thinking he was onboard.

And when, not if, it tanked, he'd be right there, long face and all, to take it all off their hands. He knew they all had other investments, other prospects back where they'd come from, and sure, they'd want to pursue those, not ride this horse into ruin.

He'd kept hands-off watch on Glenn Ormond, the ne'er-do-well hotelier in Stevensville, who'd had no one stay there all through the winter, and almost no locals patronize his dining room, even when he'd discounted prices for the season. His aiming high depended on visiting tourists with money, and they stayed away till spring, apparently. His financier father had known that, and advised the boy to stick with it, at least through the coming summer, preferably even for a couple more years, again, reasonable for a new business to turn the corner.

But Glenn was impatient, as Benson knew he would be... wanted instant gratification, like too many of the new generation. So yeah, keep his eye on this potential tool. Charlie liked to think of his cohorts as tools, and himself as the master craftsman. Or maybe the puppeteer, pulling the strings.

He was also planning to cultivate others for his proposed team. He'd eventually turn the dude operation into a real ranch again, and he was already choosing the people he'd need. Glenn would be worthless at that work, and maybe not up for rough stuff either, though Benson was certain he'd seen that potential in the man. There was the broken nose, for one thing, and some other really shady bits he'd picked up with some digging.

*So wait, but be prepared.* Someday Charlie Benson would own a gold mine. Yeah, and maybe even retire to that great house he could glimpse through the trees on the slope he coveted.

~ * ~

The new season came, and it was a delight for Kay. Cody wasn't even crawling yet, just being cute, and Emily warned her this inertia was the last time she'd know for certain where her son was at any given time. Her man was an absolute fool for the boy, and hadn't been too much of a bear, forced inside most of the winter. Prospects for work were good again, and the little family was now securely in their own dream house. Harlan had made their furniture throughout the winter, and Rhys Carter had also created a few pieces for them.

She was making plans to take the baby with them on stone jobs, having spent about as much time indoors as she could stand, now that May was here. Lisa Kenner and she had visited as often as possible, and a few old classmates from the university had also ignored the bad weather to come. Too, Kay and Harlan had insisted that the Carters spend two weeks with them during the worst of the winter, and somehow nobody had felt crowded.

Moira's good humor and her own smoothed any and all friction before it developed, and little Cormac had been just about the focus of everything.

Well, almost.

The plan now was to refit the Land Rover with its camper cap, in which would go Cody's playpen, toys and everything necessary to tend to him. Kay wanted him to get used to being there when Mom and Dad were working, and to get to be a part of that early on. Any subsequent children would follow that regimen too, she informed her husband.

"Kids need to contribute, feel they're a necessary part of the whole family/work operation," she told him. He seemed okay with that, having deferred to her on almost everything having to do with their offspring.

"Yeah, have this'n slamming rocks soon's he can lift one. So he'll probably grow up to hate the whole idea: maybe become a hairdresser or ballet dancer."

"And what's so terrible about either?"

"Just putting you on, girl. Whatever this little chunk wants to be, he'll manage it. Our job's to raise him, then turn him loose on the world, isn't it?"

"Mom's always said she couldn't believe how fast the time went with us, all right. Underfoot, little monsters always into everything, then suddenly out the door. So should we have a whole tribe, so they'll be around longer?" She asked that with a broad smile, and he wasn't sure if she meant it. Maybe she did.

Kay often looked back on growing up the left-out loner, everywhere but here on the ranch. She and Sam had always been close, and the brothers learned to respect her as soon as she got big enough to demand it. She still remembered how astonished they both were when she shot up past them, and how, determined to outdo them, she'd done it. Kicked their butts when they'd needed it, too. It was at school, and out away from the ranch, that she'd had it driven home: tall plain girls weren't cool.

She had played basketball, and well. The competitive spirit she'd honed with her brothers served her well on the court, and there at least, she felt anybody's equal. That the other girls, the cute ones, excluded her afterwards, had only added to her insecurity.

So now, with a good man, a son, close friends, a house to die for, and her parents near, Kay McBryde Kemp felt a lot like a queen. *Yeah, queen of the whole damn world, all you who gave me a hard time. Wouldn't trade with any of you.*

Predictably, her having killed a man still weighed on her, despite its necessity. You just didn't end a human life without paying an emotional price. She often questioned whether she'd done the right thing—maybe should've slipped away to bring reinforcements. But then the little creek would have been full of poison, killed fish, killed the family's livestock, flowed into the river to continue killing.

No, every time remorse slipped up on her, she quelled it. You killed the snake that was about to strike you. And yes, he'd gotten off that hurried shot, meant to kill her. *So put that away. Again.*

Harlan was even learning a lot more about ranching, to Sam's guarded delight. She didn't think he'd ever become a fulltime cowboy, but nobody was demanding that, least of all her. Maybe when time for raising children would let her, she'd take over that part of their lives, along with whatever little cowgirls and horse wranglers they produced.

For now, Kay couldn't imagine being happier.

~ * ~

He'd parked his car well back from Eric and Maggie's place, and slipped wide of their cabin. There was still barely enough light for him to see his way, as long as he didn't hurry. The leatherworker had a big dog, but he was downwind, and the stalker knew the ground well enough to stay beyond detection. He hadn't drunk enough to make any mistakes this time, and he was determined to get what he was after.

Crescent was just finishing with the goats, putting the fresh milk away in the concrete block building when she heard a noise at the door she'd just closed behind her. She froze. *That was somebody. And I'm alone in here, with no...*

She lunged for the light switch, flipped it off just as the door burst open. She dropped to the floor, began easing away as the intruder adjusted his vision to the suddenly dark interior.

And she remembered that every woman she'd known who'd been attacked, was small, like her. *Cowardly bastards don't wanta get hurt. Weapon. Need a weapon, and the damn shotgun's in the house.*

She forced a mental picture of just where everything was in here, what she might grab, use to fight her way out and to the house. Or at least to safety outside somewhere. Fight or hide, the choices. *Dear God, don't let him have a flashlight.*

He didn't. Glenn was half-drunk, hadn't planned his attack well. He groped along a wall toward where he'd glimpsed Crescent before it all went dark, trying to remember where the light switch was. She wasn't there. He cursed, stumbled over a pail of goat's milk, fell heavily. Then heard her running around him toward the door.

He reached out blindly, caught her ankle. She went down with a scream and he scrambled to pin her under him. Before he could reach her, she lashed out with her other foot, caught him in the groin, and it was his turn to scream.

She was free, lunging for the door again. This time she made it outside, raced for the house, hearing him scrambling behind her, spouting obscenities.

Inside, she grabbed the shotgun by feel, aimed it at the open door.

*"You take one step in here, I'll blow you away!"* She realized her voice was frantic, tried to steady her shaking. She didn't know for sure who the intruder was, but suspected it was her ex-husband. *Glenn, and he's drunk. But can I kill him, really? Have to.*

"You won't shoot me, Crescent; you know you can't. Jus' let me in, hear me out. We c'n make this work, if you'll jus' give me a chance..."

"Gave you a thousand chances, you bastard! It's *over*, Glenn, been over. Now *leave,* or I damn sure *will* kill you! Think about it: you've violated the restraining order, sneaked out here, broken into my place, attacked me. No way in hell could I have known it was you in the dark, just defended myself against a strange madman. And imagine my surprise to turn on a light and learn it was you! You see, Glenn, I can't lose." She remembered now to cock the shotgun. *Damn, not thinking straight.*

That sound froze him, in the very act of stepping across the threshold, despite her warning. And some of what she'd said penetrated the blur, the rage inside him. Could she actually pull that trigger? *Nah, we've had too much between us... she's bluffing. Scared to death. I can take that gun away from her, give her some real loving. Gotta get that hot little body again...*

He stepped inside, reaching.

Flame leaped from the muzzle of the shotgun, a deafening roar almost split his head, and he felt himself falling, as his left leg disintegrated. Too late, he realized she could see him, outlined against what was left of the darkened sky.

Glenn was on the floor, howling, clutching his shattered leg with both hands as the lights came on. Somehow he was aware of the sound of another shell being racked into the chamber of the gun. And when he opened his eyes, it was to see the muzzle inches from his face. It looked like a manhole, and the sight shocked him into momentary silence.

"Oh, my God, it's *you,* Glenn. Now why didn't you identify yourself? Might've saved your leg, or even your worthless life." She was so calm now, so completely in charge. And with all that blood, she was aware that this piece of shit would bleed out very soon, despite his clamped hands on what was left of his leg.

And she didn't care. She stepped back, out of reach if he went for the shotgun, held it on him as his screams resumed, his thrashing knocking over furniture. *All I have to do is wait. Not like shooting him was premeditated or anything. Just defending my life. Oh, maybe I should rig some kinda tourniquet, look like I was trying to save him.*

*Just not yet.*

Eric had been taking an armload of cookstove wood into his house when he heard the distant shot. He raced inside, grabbed his rifle.

"That was at Crescent's place. I'm going!"

"I'll come too." Maggie grabbed a jacket, ran out to their truck. Eric spun the wheels in a 180 turn, spitting gravel as the headlights swept the darkness. The quarter mile flashed past with the vehicle yawing, tires grabbing the road.

Sliding to a stop, they could see Crescent's lighted door open, and a thrashing shape on the floor. Eric was out, rifle gripped. The sound of a badly wounded animal shattered the air.

"Crescent! You okay, girl?" *No, you fool, she's not okay. Somebody's broken in...*

"Yeah, Eric, I'm okay. Had to shoot a crazy man in the dark, and turns out it's Glenn. Trying to get a tourniquet on his leg, but he won't hold still." He could see she had a towel twisted tight, and the man's leg blown almost completely off, his hands clutching it. The shotgun leaned against a table behind her.

"Here, I'll hold him. Maggie, get his arms, let Crescent put that around, stop the blood." Which was at the moment spurting out past Glenn's ineffectual fingers. A pool of it surrounded him. *Damn, gotta be about to bleed out. He may not make it.*

"What happened?" Maggie asked, pinning both the man's arms beneath her considerable weight. "He jump you?" Glenn had stopped moving as Crescent tightened the towel around his leg, passed out from blood loss, shock.

"Just putting the milk inside, almost dark. Heard somebody at the door behind me, killed the light, tried to get away, but he grabbed me. Kicked him in the balls and got to the house. Kept the light off, and he came storming in. Didn't wanta kill him, but didn't know who it was, or if he was alone. And damn if it wasn't this shithead."

"Bastard must've sneaked around our place," Eric muttered, his eyes on the now-chalky face. "Oughta just let him die."

"Believe me, I thought about that, but can't do that, buddy, open up a can of worms. Doubt if they can save that leg, though, too much missing. No, he'll be a cripple for the rest of his nasty life, but I don't want any of us to be murderers."

"But he won't leave you alone after this, girl," Maggie pointed out. "Hold a grudge big time, now."

"Maybe, and guess I shoulda gone for his head, but I didn't. No, just hafta hope this's the end of it. Damn, this is a mess."

"Not your fault, any of it," Eric assured her. "Just wish we'd been able to stop him, stomp his ass good. But he'd of found a way anyway I guess, sooner or later." He shook his shaggy head.

"Yeah, I guess. So let's get him to a hospital, if one of you can help me. Maybe he'll die on the way." Crescent wouldn't have mourned that outcome. *If they'd been just a few minutes later...*

*But no, I'm not a killer.*

She thought of Kay Kemp, outshooting that crazy at their ranch. Woman was tough, but that'd been clearly self-defense. Well, so would this have been; no telling what Glenn would've done to her, drunk, angry. *Well, whatever else, now he'll be a one-legged loser. And I hope this'll make him afraid of me. Because if there is a next time, I won't hesitate.*

~ * ~

We all heard about the shooting from Moira, and well, we said good for Crescent. More Montana justice. She didn't get charged with anything, although Glenn loudly insisted they'd been having a peaceful conversation when she'd snapped and gone for the gun. Nobody believed him, least of all the sheriff. And with the violated restraining order, even his hitherto-indulgent father refused to back him in a lawsuit.

He did pay for extensive rebuilding of the left leg, which required several surgeries, bone grafts and a stainless steel plate. Eventually Glenn would be able to walk again, after a lot of months and a lot of therapy. He'd have a limp, which he guessed he could deal with. *Better'n just one leg. But that little bitch: she actually shot me, after all we'd shared together. Crazy for sure.*

So, now the struggling hotel venture was headed for the rocks, with nobody at the helm. None of us cared... too busy living our lives. And if anybody'd asked us, we'd have said "Glenn who?"

~ * ~

The dude ranch owners, probably owing to their careful preparations and intensive advertising the year before, were seeing a welcome surge in bookings this new season. They decided to go ahead with other projects for us after all, not liking having to quit halfway on plans. I liked them a lot.

And there were other jobs to keep me busy. Well, not just me: Kay insisted on taking Cody with us on jobs, just as I'd predicted, and she soon was putting in almost full days slamming stones. Take a little time to feed the kid, change him, give him toys, and she'd be back at work. When he cried, I'd take a break and carry him around a bit, toss him up in the air, which he loved, and work some of his energy off before putting him down again. Taking turns that way, we almost handled the situation okay. Close enough, anyway. Kay started calling our business 'Kemp and Son.'

"No, it's 'Kemp and Family' or 'The Kemps'." That started a round of inventive names, which included 'The Kemps Rock', 'Stoned Kemps' (no), 'Rock Out with the Kemps' and a lot more nonsense. I'd put 'Kemp Stonework' on my business cards and on the sides of the trucks early on, so we just went with that.

Some narrow-minded folks had objected to our charging just as much for Kay's work as mine, until they saw how good she was.

Now with Cody along, there were raised eyebrows, but since we charged exclusively by the face foot, there was no basis for complaint. Also, having the kid along melted some hearts. Of course he *was* the best-looking baby anybody'd ever seen.

~ * ~

As expected, the Stevensville hotel venture failed, and sooner than Charlie Benson had predicted. With what Glenn's father saw as the last straw, his son having attacked Crescent, the old man wrote his son completely off. After all, George Ormond had seen the girl as perhaps the saving influence on irresponsible Glenn, and well, everybody liked her.

*Just blew it one time too many. Going after that tiny girl— just too rotten, too... animal. I could take his acting out in college, high spirits like most boys. Drunk too often, though. Wrecked that sportscar I bought him. And that other thing... Guess I indulged him too much.*

"But George, he's still our son," Ruth Ormond almost wailed.

"And Crescent was our daughter—close as one, anyway. No, dear, he's on his own now, sink or swim. And if he shows up here, I swear I'll knock his teeth in. He's a bully, Ruth, along with being a drunk and a failure. Embarrassment to the family." For George, CEO of Ormond Industrials, the subject of the former heir-apparent was closed. Forever.

But of course Ruth had hovered by her son's hospital bed, listened to his side of the story. But knew in her heart he was lying. She'd loved little Crescent, the daughter she'd never had. And the mental image of her son, big, strong, and yes, undisciplined, attacking her, forcing her, beating her? wouldn't go away.

For his part, Glenn, finally almost literally back on his feet, blamed everyone and everything but himself for his fall, as he always had. *I've never had a fair chance. Always people against me.* And now it appeared he had not a friend in the world. No kind word, no hand extended in help, no support. *That bitch! And*

*I wanted her back. To hell with her! To hell with Ormond Industrials. To hell with a father won't stand up for his son. Old fool will die alone, end of his line, and I don't give a damn.*

*And I thought Mom'd come through for me, again. But she's even thrown me under the bus, looks like. To hell with her, too. I can make it on my own, don't need anybody's help. Start over...*

But where and how could a failed, aging, immature boy with no prospects, no money, crippled, hope to begin again? The whole world looked to him like closed doors, barred against him, every possibility a dead end, a brick wall. Long way from his so-well-planned role as the promising son and heir of the successful owner of a big industrial complex.

Glenn Ormond locked the door of the empty hotel he owed so much money on, got in his rattly car—he'd kept the heap, pouring any money into that white elephant—and drove north aimlessly. Cursing his fate, his ex-wife, the whole damn world, and everyone in it.

So, what to do? He'd counted his money, enough for maybe a week on the road, gas, food. Have to sleep in the car? No, he'd never get that desperate. Rob a store first, if it came to that: he did carry a gun now. He turned that possibility over in his mind: *masked raider, like something outta an adventure novel. A Robin Hood, only I'd keep the money.* The image had an appeal to it. Get back at the rotten system that'd kept him down, thwarted every plan he'd had.

*No, get my ass thrown in jail, really bottom out. There's gotta be somebody I can turn to, somebody'll put me up for a while.* He thought of the women he'd been with. There was that girl in Great Falls... No, she'd gone back to her husband. That waitress in Kalispell, lived in that trailer... No, she'd never take him back: he'd taken that money that time. Okay, what about that country singer, lived with her group, had tried to get him to join them. *Oh, no, they all got busted for drugs. Dunno where she'd be now, anyway...*

"Dammit! There's nobody!" he screamed at the highway before him. It didn't help. *So, do I just blow my brains out, kiss off this sorry life? Crescent would laugh: bitch. Dad could care less. Mom'd cry, but not for long. Damn them all!"* He fingered the gun for a moment, then laid it aside again. Realized he'd been swerving across the centerline, even too near the ditch. *Gotta get a grip here; can't let this keep me down. There'll be a way, there always is. Glenn Ormond doesn't go under, no matter who or how many try to shut me out.*

Reaching Missoula, he drove aimlessly around, trying desperately for a way out. Any way out. Up one street, down another, as if keeping moving might just open some door for him. And he envisioned people inside those doors: secure people, families, all knowing there'd be a paycheck at the end of the week, food on the table. Warm, cozy places full of love, sharing. Some version of the American Dream, even in those little houses he was shut out of. Right then he wanted inside a house like that, more than anything he'd ever wanted.

*Dumb, dumb. Whatthehell am I doing? Waiting for some magic fairy to come make it all okay? Get a grip, Ormond!* He looked for a driveway to turn around in. *Like going the other way's gonna open it all up for me? I'm goin' crazy, crazy's that bitch Crescent...*

Then he saw it: that lawyer's sign, discreetly attached to a restored cottage office, with trees around it. *That lawyer. Said he could handle any problems with the damn hotel. Well, it was all problems. His wife liked me. Wonder if he even remembers me, though. Not that long ago, but...*

*Oh hell, give it a shot.*

# Seventeen

My fourth summer in Montana, and I had a wife, a child, a great house, a good business, good friends. And I even found a farm tractor with a loader bucket like Mrs. H's to handle rocks with. We could tumble them into it, raise the load and slip it into the Dodge. Big ones we pried onto the bucket, raised them level and slid them in, to keep the scarring down, to dump them carefully at the site. Could move the tractor on the trailer too, to wherever it wouldn't turn over on a slope.

Kay had driven tractors all her life, and could ease a load sidehill, keeping the bucket an inch from the ground in case the rig started to tip, better'n me. And that woman almost caressed each stone like it was another kid.

I couldn't imagine a better wife.

Mom came out that summer to spoil her grandson, and I thought she'd about decided to dump Lester and stay. Contrary to the prevailing idea that mothers-in-law are a pain, she and Kay developed not only a mutual respect, but a binding love. The two of them hatched all kinds of plots about shopping, picnicking, outings, surprising me in delightful ways. Sorta did want her to stay. But she was a loyal woman, and finally we saw her off at the Missoula airport. Made us promise to go to Missouri that winter, which we'd try to do. Hey, you only get one mother. And Kay'd probably see to it that we'd actually go.

~ * ~

Fall came again, and I got to play daddy a lot, despite helping Sam with the stock, fence upkeep, and the world of other ranch chores that never get done. No building at home now, so it did get boring, though.

So just on a hunch, one late October day the sun warmed things a bit, I decided to do something foolish. The gold rumors still lurked way back in my mind, even with my full life. Not that I'd go after that lode, even if it was there. Just curious.

I got this flat pan, went to the nearest part of one of the little creeks, scooped some gravel. I'd read about panning back when I'd hit the library that time, and knew the basics. So, me in the old prospector's role, a century and a half later. Big hat, shovel, crouched down looking for color.

And sure enough, after a half-hour, a coupla glints. Tiny glints. Be dust, was all. Take forever to amount to anything. Waste of time. But then I remembered the well driller, and even a few specks when we'd dug and backfilled the retaining walls up below the house. We'd laughed at our 'strike' and (almost) forgotten about it.

*But just suppose I do dig down below frostline now, while I can. Could hit it more later, no matter how frozen it gets on top, find whatever's there.*

Sam'd think I was crazy. So would Kay. Well, I *was* a little crazy, I guessed. Had everything a man could want, wish for, and go dig for gold? Why? Well, like I said, just curious.

*Oh, maybe if I found even a nugget or two, I could make Kay some jewelry? She likes those little figures I carve. I could cast something, the way Uncle John did with brass. Sand mold, yeah.*

No way did my bride want jewelry; she'd told me that. But she *had* treasured those wood carvings. Wore them on thin chains or leather strings, proud of them.

That was my excuse. Surprise her, not let her know what I was planning till I could put a finished one around that graceful neck. Yeah.

I started a hole about three feet in diameter, hidden in a copse of willows not far up the slope, likeliest place below what should be the source. *If any,* I kept reminding myself. Got about three feet down before I figured I'd better get home, avoid questions. Took some colored creek pebbles for Cody to play with.

Kay liked them too, but reminded me they'd end up in the boy's mouth as quick as he could grab them. *Oh.* But she put them in a glass jar on a shelf to admire. *Okay, got away with it that time.*

Later I found some free time, slipped down to my project, dug another three feet, tossed dead leaves and grass over the dirt pile, and laid old barnboards over the hole. Scattered dirt on them, then more leaves and grass.

My secret.

~ * ~

"You aimed too high, Glenn, with not enough of a buying public. Now, I admire you for the way you did the place first-class, showed real taste. But maybe ten, fifteen years too soon.

"So, what's next for you? What else have you done, can go back to?"

"That's the problem, sir. Crescent and I wanted off the grid on back, took any jobs we could find, to buy that place out of Florence, get into the cheese business. Like too many back-to-the-earth kids, I guess. Thought we could take on the world, and

206

found out we couldn't." He spread his hands. *No need to tell him Dad financed us.*

"And she was able to buy you out? My wife knows about her cheese: good stuff. Has even met her."

"I had a lot to do with the whole operation, built it up with her, saw that it made money, then she threw me out." Bitterly.

"Well, I'm afraid I'd have to say you deserved it, from what little I know of your colorful past, Glenn."

"How do you... What 'past'?" *This old bastard's after me too.*

"Small town. Word gets around. Couple of women you banged, one of the husbands is a client of mine." *Now squirm, you incompetent playboy. But I've got my hook in you now.*

"Oh. Well...look, I used to drink too much, I admit. But when I got onto the hotel project, I cleaned up my act. Don't get into that crazy stuff anymore. Well, Dad made that a condition, when he backed me that time."

*Yeah, sure. We saw you putting it away, boy. And that's something you'd have to get under control if we even talk about you working for me.*

But Charlie Benson had seen the flash of anger in this man's eyes before he could shift back to the repentance mode. *He might do, manage him right.* He remembered his first impression, back at the hotel, how Glenn had reminded him of Jack the geologist. *Have to prove himself, but maybe...*

So Benson hired Glenn Ormond to run errands for the law office, plus a little simple investigating, do odd jobs around the Benson house, help out, be there when needed. He'd known the man would be insulted at such gofer work, but had told him if he went straight, there'd be bigger and better things ahead.

"Now, I think it'd be wise for you to get yourself another name, since there'll be others who'll know some things, make it harder on you. Pick one."

*Another name? Wow, this dude's big time all right. Okay, always liked the name Brent. Brent... Breckinridge. Got class.*

"Okay, I like Brent Breckinridge. How do I get new ID?"

"Leave that to me. And here's a little something to help you find a place to live. Be here at nine tomorrow."

"You got it. And thanks, sir." He left, about a foot off the ground. *Damn, I'm in! Just when I thought there wasn't any hope, I'm scoring.*

Benson watched him go, thinking this might turn out to be a mistake, but he was sure he could bring this loser along, make him useful.

*Boy's good-looking. Probably get tangled up with women left and right, which could be trouble. May have to watch Melissa around him, too. Nah, he'll have himself enough diversions to keep him busy.*

~ * ~

The almost sudden success of the dude ranch came as a surprise to the lawyer. Those people had done their research well, had the money to do it right, had advertised, delivered a good product. Smart, all of them. *Yeah, what brains and money can do for you.*

So over the winter, Charlie had abandoned his plan to buy into the venture and come up with a way to get at the McBryde place later. He'd gone back to his original scheme to see to it that land ended up on the market, within reach.

By eliminating both rancher McBryde and the stonemason.

Glenn Ormond would be the instrument. Benson had let him observe some of his more direct methods in dealing with the opposition, and told him he needed a strong hand for some of the situations that arose.

"You need a leg-breaker." A statement.

"Sometimes. Can you handle that?"

"Try me."

So the lawyer had sent him on a few collection forays and he had done well. One of them was for child support payments to a young divorcee client. Her ex-husband had fallen behind, and while it was not Benson's place to collect, she'd asked him to, and he'd built much of his reputation by going the extra mile for those who hired him. Besides, Lisa was a shapely, outgoing blonde, and he'd speculated she might repay his generosity with her own favors.

Glenn hadn't relished this assignment, but he was anxious to impress his employer. *This's my last chance, can't blow it, or I'm gonna find myself out on the street again.*

"McGilvray's a truck driver," he was told. "Gets paid Fridays. You catch him before he can spend it, bring back this amount due." *And we'll see just how tough you are, boy.*

Well, the truck driver was a big man, and Ormond felt a twinge of fear when he saw him coming out of the company's office with his paycheck. So he didn't accost the man right then, but followed him, staying two cars back, a few blocks to a bank that was open late. *So I'm playing private eye, and why not? This's exciting, if I can pull it off.* He got a mental picture of himself as a Humphrey Bogart tough guy, smooth, dangerous.

McGilvray emerged a scant five minutes later, counting his money as Glenn had hoped he would. And as the big man opened his car door, he felt the sudden pressure of the gun to his side and a hard shove.

"Slide over, shithead, or you're dead meat."

"Whothehell'er you?" But he slid over, eyes wide on the gun as Glenn got in after him.

"I'm the guy who's gonna make sure you pay Lisa her child support. This figure right here." He showed an official-looking paper.

"You can't force me..."

"Yeah, I can. Legally. And if you even think about making a move, I can shoot you down and walk away—self-defense." He cocked the gun. "So pay up, before I shoot you anyway, just for the hell of it." Glenn felt a surge of confidence, power. *The bigger they come, the harder they fall.*

And McGilvray, after looking wildly around for any help, any witnesses, knew he was caught.

"And I better not hafta come for you next time, or I *will* kill you." He took the money.

At the office, Glenn laid the cash on Charlie Benson's desk.

"Have any trouble?"

"No, he cooperated, after I got serious with him."

"How serious? You have to bend him a little? He's a hardcase."

"I was harder." He flipped back his open sportscoat to show the automatic shoved in his belt. Charlie's eyes narrowed.

"You tell him you work for me?"

"No, 'cause you said not to. No connection."

"Okay. And you just got a raise."

~ * ~

I panned samples of the dirt I'd dug from my secret prospecting hole. Only tiny specks of color, like in the creek gravel. So any real gold would be deeper. This was a talus slope, dirt washed off the mountain forever, and no telling how deep I'd have to go to the source.

And hell, the well driller hadn't hit it, further down, deep as he'd gone, so what made me think... *You're a fool, Kemp, and this's a fool's errand. Fool's gold, that's all this is.*

I filled the damn hole in, gave this up. Could've been doing something productive instead. *Fool.* I went over to Sam's horse barn and used the same shovel to muck out stalls.

~ * ~

Rhys and Moira visited that winter for a week, and brought disturbing news. Cale was almost fifteen, Siobhan twelve, and they'd decided it was time to put them into public school.

"Socialization," they told us. "Can't keep them hidden any longer, if they're to cope with this crazy world."

Baby Cormac was now three, and it seemed wouldn't get to grow up there in the sky after all. Bummer.

"Where'll you live?" The obvious question.

"We've listed the place, but don't expect anyone even to look at it till spring. Hoping to sell, buy something easier to get to by fall. If we don't, we'll hafta rent."

*Ouch,* there went a homesteader's ideal. But just that non-road made their place 'too fur an' too snaky,' to quote Uncle John. So, coop that great family up in some cramped house on a postage stamp lot in town? Surely not.

But I'd spent the better part of a year searching for a piece of land with no luck, so they'd face the same frustrations, I knew. We tried to help, contacting everybody we knew who might know of a place not too awful, but with no results. Well, it'd be all those months more, so maybe...

Rhys had been a ranger for the National Forest Service when he met Moira, a service brat who'd lived all over the world. As young marrieds, their mountain top adventure had seemed the dream so many of us cherished. They'd built their house, workshop, created that oasis among the Ponderosas and firs with their own hands.

And now they, and those shy, wild children, would be forced to leave it all. Probably to some rich Chicago or LA sportsman, a trophy hunter, as some plaything to take his buddies to. Helluva thing.

This made Kay and me realize again just how lucky we were. If I'd found the wilderness I'd searched for, hidden ourselves away, we'd have to give it up too, with all we'd put into it, now we were a family. Couldn't keep Cody running wild like a young colt, when the bright lights would call to him.

And we planned to have at least one more.

"At least," Kay smiled.

Wow.

~ * ~

Charlie Benson's plan to remove the two obstacles to his getting his future gold mine needed one thing: a man with a sniper rifle. A man who could hit from so far away there'd be no way to find him.

Glenn Ormond wasn't that man.

Yet.

There were hunting outfitters and gun dealers locally—too close--but Benson had a friend in Idaho, a big-game hunter, recommend and buy for him the modified Mauser Karabiner 98k with the top-of-the-line scope.

"Helluva gun, Charlie. Finally gettin' off yer ass an' goin' huntin'? 'Bout time, but season's over."

"Well, Calvin, I've got to learn to hit with the thing first. Send me a dozen boxes of ammo with it. By fall, I'll outshoot you."

"That'll be the day. We'll go up to Canada, do it right, okay? Look forward to it."

The question was, would Glenn kill a man outright? *Will if I handle it right, make him an offer he can't refuse.* But well, that was really just the first question. The other three were: One, could he learn to shoot? *Anyone can learn, given time. And if he can't, I can.* Two, do it soon, plain murder, or Three, wait till fall, make it a hunting accident?

Or both?

He'd have to wait a respectable interval after blatant killings to approach the two widows. Make absolutely certain there could be no connection to him. Which in any case meant he'd have to dispose of Glenn Ormond later.

Hardly a problem.

Waiting till hunting season, nine months away, would be better, obviously. Stray shots, excited hunter spraying the forest after an elk or deer, both men hit. Make a shorter period of grieving more likely, and less investigation by the authorities, too.

Or that *both,* but not that way... take out the old man now maybe, direct any resulting suspicion away somehow. Old enemy? Everybody had them. Another crazy on the loose? *No, too obvious.* But the stonemason later, as that hunting accident. Totally unrelated, months apart.

Or another option: *Glenn could even mug the rancher in town, robbery gone bad. Hit him too hard. Or hell, even at home. Little disguise, it could almost be done in daylight…*

But the only part of the McBryde land Benson wanted was the gold-bearing hill. If he could just take the stonemason out, it'd all be simpler; one killing would be easier to handle than two. And be a lot cheaper to buy the girl out than the whole 500-acre spread.

But the lawyer then checked courthouse records, and learned the McBrydes hadn't deeded the mountain slope to the kids yet. *Old man's sharp: won't take the chance the boy might end up with it all if the marriage goes bad.*

The choices weighed on Benson as the weeks passed, but he made good use of the time. He took Glenn out to a remote area he knew, where they both practiced with the Mauser. The gun was a marvel of craftsmanship, and both scored well.

"So we're goin' hunting?"

"We are. I've got enemies, Glenn, and I've been threatened a number of times. Wouldn't doubt that McGilvray, drunk, would come after me. You know I carry a pistol. And I can and have, taken care of myself. But there's such a thing as a pre-emptive strike. Sometimes you can't wait for the other guy to hit you first. Like a rattlesnake: don't wait till you're bitten to blow it away."

*So I'm gonna be a hit man? No, more of a bodyguard. Yeah, I can live with that. And tell the whole goddam system to go screw itself. Glenn Ormond's back on top, shit-heads.*

~ * ~

Crescent's arms burned from shoveling the snow from the path to the barn and the cheese house. It'd taken an hour of intense effort, and the girl's breath was coming in gasps.

*I'm getting too old for this. Too damn much to handle alone. Should've teamed up with Harlan when I had the chance. No, he'd already met Kay. Didn't know it, but was on the right road before he'd met me. Not that I couldn't've roped him in...*

*But even that bastard Glenn worked hard, helped get this going, when he wasn't in bed with some other woman. No, I don't need his muscle, but I need somebody's...*

The sound of Eric's tractor grew louder as he plowed the lane to her house. And there came Maggie, walking behind as the blade pushed the drifts off to one side. *Oh, good... company. About to go stir-crazy, drown in self-pity here. What great neighbors I've got.*

Maggie was carrying a big Corningware dish, her red face in a broad smile. She set it on the little porch, engulfed Crescent in a bear hug as Eric shut down the tractor.

"Venison stew, girl. Know you've gotta be bluesin', stuck here at th' end of th' world. You okay?" Eying the shovel, her glistening face.

"Oh, yeah. Just feelin' the aches more. Middle age creepin' up on me, I guess. C'mon in, botha you." She tiptoed, gave Eric a quick hug. He swung her off her feet, set her on the porch.

"Well, little 'un, we're tired of yellin' at just each other, so we'll swap off with you, okay?"

"You got it, hoss." They all scraped the snow off their boots, went inside where the woodstove had the little house cheery. Apple cider bubbled, the smell of cinnamon scenting the air.

"Wow, that's enough to feed all of Florence. Thanks, you sweethearts; get it heated up, here." She poured cider for them. They sat, beaming. "So, what's happening out in the world? Not that I really care." *Well, maybe I do, a little.*

"Same old. Just Maggie an' me an' th' dog an' th' leather. Oh, Rhys and Moira decided to come down off th' mountain, put th' kids in school. They're up to see Harlan an' Kay, now. Start lookin' for a place."

"No! Oh, that's bad. Gosh, all those years, all that labor, heart, in that great place. Oh, I hope they stay close."

"Hope so too, but it'll depend on what they can find. Place won't sell for much, so hard to get to." Eric shrugged.

"But I can't see them in any town," Maggie worried. "Can you? I mean, those kids are like mountain goats—be a shame to fence 'em in."

"Well, Moira works harder'n me to hold it all together. I'm more and more wondering how much longer I can do the goat thing by myself. Need another pair of hands. Even thought about hirin' somebody."

"Gotta getcherself another guy, honey, like I been tellin' you all along. Don't hafta pay him, just feed him an' keep him happy in bed." Maggie grinned at her husband.

"Trouble, all of 'em. You two are lucky. I had the world's worst loser. Don't wanta go there again."

"Speakin' of, Eric saw a 'for sale' sign on th' hotel. Guess hotshot's gone, finally."

"Yeah, you made it plain he'd wore out his welcome, girl."

"Shoulda just let him die, but I'm fool enough to've let that bother me."

"Bound to be a good man out there. How likely was it I'd run into Eric? Outta all the rednecks on the planet?"

"Rednecks? Woman, you lucky I took you in. You'd still be slingin' hash for tips, I didn't take pity on you."

"Bullshit. I coulda found me a banker, or maybe even a doctor, who'd appreciate a good woman." She poked Eric in the ribs. "Just damn glad I didn't."

"You two. Behave now, or I'll hafta spank you both, send you to bed with no supper. By the way, Maggie, this stew's the best." They were at her little table, digging into it and her freshly-baked dark bread.

"Only reason I keep her around, she feeds me good."

"Like a stray dog, yeah."

"You sayin' I'm a dog in bed, woman?" Around a mouthful.

"Hey, let's not go there, okay?" Their friend held up a hand. "I'm the one's gotta sleep alone."

"No reason for that," Maggie insisted. "Hey, you remember Eric's buddy, Josh? He's…"

"No way. You saw how he dumped that Lucy. Guy's a predator."

"Yeah, I guess so. Well, we've tried to match-make you for years, now. Picky."

"And gonna stay that way. Any man I'd have has gotta be a god, and not afraid to work, get goatshit on his boots."

"Too bad Harlan's not got a brother. Thought you two'd hit it off, back then. But he'n Kay are the team, now."

"He was too young, but I did like him okay. Like 'em both, a lot. And that little Cody? To die for."

But after her friends had left, Crescent, though warmed by their visit, lapsed into a funk. Not the first time, either. She remembered Cody's delight when she'd held him. *He could've been mine… ours.* The empty house seemed emptier.

*Okay, girl, guess it's really time to go see what's out there, dust off the old skills. Biological clock's ticking.*

~ * ~

Glenn stood after the last echoing shot, cradled the rifle. He'd come alone this time to practice, although he and the lawyer had enjoyed competing as they'd both improved. He walked with his limp to the Jeep he'd bought, drove over the rough ground toward the distant target. Almost a half mile. *If I've scored this one, I'm ready for anything Benson needs done.*

He hadn't. One round had just nicked the edge of the foot-wide circle, and the others had missed. Then he remembered. *Windage. Damn breeze was enough, at that distance. Keep forgetting that.* He saw where the other shots had gouged the ground in the dirt bank, just downwind from the one almost-hit.

He drove back, repositioned himself with the rifle on its tripod. How far to shift, then? Just a little wind, but it was steady. *Okay, try it by degrees.*

This time he aimed an estimated three inches left, upwind, steadied, let out a half-breath, squeezed the trigger. Felt the fine weapon buck, like something alive in his hands. Then he chambered another round, put the crosshairs another equal space to the left, fired again. Then clear off the target, another round. Then on a hunch, two more like it.

He knew he'd hit close. He'd been rock-steady, caressing the trigger, the target clean in that bright scope, the elevation right. Hellyes, he'd hit.

And he had. First shot solidly into the white circle. Second one well toward the center. And the three-shot pattern clustered just to the left of the bull's-eye, not an inch apart. *Damn, I'm good. I've got this cold. Stronger breeze, I can compensate. Ready to go hunting, Benson.*

On the way back to the lawyer's office, Glenn also realized that he'd been distracted those times with the man along. Today's solitude was the answer: *focus. And don't forget that windage.*

Back at the law office, he stripped, cleaned and oiled the Mauser meticulously, per the game-hunter's instructions to his boss. *Part of the job, keeping this thing in top condition. It's going to make part of my living.*

After a client left, Glenn knocked, entered, laid the target on Benson's desk.

"Seven hundred fifty yards. Last three tight, just off center, you can see. Wind gusted a little, first shots. I think I'm ready."

"Yeah, I think you are. But now the hard part: you'll have to scout the real target, wait for your chance. Might take days. You'll have to be patient. Think you can handle that?"

"Know I can. What... who's the target?"

"Man's cost me a whole lot of cash. I'm the one should hold a grudge, but he's sitting on my money, wants me out of the way.

Old rancher, that's all you need to know for now. I think, soon as the weather breaks, he'll come after me. It goes back years, but he won't let it go." The lie rolled smoothly off the lawyer's tongue, the result of half a lifetime of practice.

"And if you can't see taking him out, I won't hold that against you. I'll just do it myself. But..." he eyed his employee shrewdly, "I do know about that boy you killed, back in college."

That was a shock. *How could this lawyer know...?* Well, he did, however he'd found out. *Okay, out in the open, now.*

"Never proved. I was acquitted."

"I know. I know a lot about you, Glenn. That's why I hired you. But there's more: I can pay you a big bonus if you pull this off clean."

How big?

"Well up into five figures. Say twenty Gs."

"Wow. That's a chunk."

"And there'll be a second act, later. Another twenty."

*Forty damn thousand. That's a stake, all right. Dunno what the second one's about, but that much money...* He thought fleetingly of that Italian kid with the big mouth, and the odd way the tire iron had left the deep crease in his skull. He'd made it look like a robbery, but they'd questioned him intensely anyway. No evidence, though. None. No fingerprints, good alibi... He'd never told Crescent. Or anybody.

"I'm your man."

# Eighteen

We were all cabin-fevered, just itching to get out and get to work. Mud, refreezing, freak late snow. Working hard to be nice to each other, both at our house and at Sam's. Oh, we liked each other okay, and recognized what was really eating us, and nobody got mad, really. But dammit, it was just *time*.

So Sam and I saddled up one morning we just couldn't stay inside any longer, and rode the fence lines. Ostensibly to see what if any damage the winter had done, like trees blown over on them, or just decayed posts finally giving up; wood lasts only so long, and even metal posts rust out.

It was chilly, and overcast, with a gusty wind trying to dry things out a little. Bruno was glad to be out, and Sam's sorrel was downright antsy. I expected my father-in-law to break him into a run, first open field we came to. Didn't.

Every spring things were a little different, in that constant change that is the only dependable aspect of life on this planet.

The little creeks were bank-full, swirling around the little pines and cedars that grew right to their edges and held clumps of soil. Snow had drifted down off the mountain slope to push and lean a section of fence, which we'd have to rebuild.

The sleeping, dormant grass was just waiting to burst forth and reclaim the dead landscape, any day now. Migrating birds would be back soon to take up their routines and remind us of how much life there was here, how the ecosystem functioned, restore our faith in this rebirth.

Sometimes Sam and I would talk a lot; sometimes, like I said, we didn't say anything to each other for hours at a time. Comfortable with that, both of us. I reflected again on how lucky I'd been to marry into this great family. Even the brothers were okay when they visited with their wives, kids. Not a hard bunch to get along with.

I've said it before, but all in all, I couldn't want a better situation, big sky and all. And to hell with all that mountain man lonely existence I'd planned.

~ * ~

"They'll be out by now, Glenn. That place gets a lotta wind, chill way down, so it'd have been a waste of time to try to get the old guy outside before this. What you'll have to do is hunt up a spot well back across the highway, with a clear view of whatever part of the ranch you can get good sight lines to. Stay hidden, which will take some doing. I'm guessing he'll be riding the whole place now, after whatever damage the winter's done. Then you'll just have to wait, maybe days, for your shot."

"And you don't want me to take out the young guy at all?"

"No, two deaths would be a massacre, and the pressure would be intense. Stray shot, even with no hunting season on, will pass without too much scrutiny. If the stonemason gets to be trouble too, we'll get him in the fall, when there'll be trigger-happy hunters out." Benson had given up on the idea of having Ormond jump McBryde maybe in town... too risky. And no way could he afford to have his man caught, with the real possibility that he'd finger his boss under pressure. And for now, the story of the fictitious money didn't include the son-in-law.

And if this plan went all to hell and he had to eliminate his hired gun, well, accidents happened to everybody, and this guy just seemed to attract them.

"Cold and wet, but I can handle it. I'll hide my Jeep somewhere, hike across those old fields you mentioned far enough there'll be no connection, get set up. Check back in tonight, then." He geared up with a thermos of coffee, sandwiches, a tarp for the wet ground, binoculars and the rifle with its tripod. Benson watched him go with a tingle at what was surely about to happen.

*I'll get that gold. Let things settle down after McBryde till fall, and if I haven't been able to buy them out by then, that boy will meet with an unfortunate accident. And the two women will have no choice but to sell. Or at least the girl will. She's young, will want another life, and I'd bet away from there; surely she'll need the bucks from the sale of her place, at least. And I doubt the mother would deny her title to that piece of land.*

Charlie Benson knew this scheme was a gamble: it might turn sour after all. But he was so obsessed with the idea of all that gold under the Kemp place, it clouded his thinking. Gold fever? It'd affected hordes of men over the ages, and yes, maybe he had a little of that.

*So what? So damn what?*

~ * ~

Glenn scouted up and down the highway for access into the fields across from the McBryde ranch. Finally, on past a quarter mile, he saw the roadside ditch was shallow enough, and he just drove his Jeep across into a brush-grown expanse that led into distant trees. No houses were visible just there.

He concealed the vehicle well back in those bordering trees and worked his way toward his target, staying away from the highway until he could see part of the McBryde property. *Need a little elevation, but cover too.* He finally located a spot, although the ranch house wasn't visible from there.

*Best I can do: see part of the cattle pens, and the old man'll be there sooner or later. And if he rides the highway fence line, he'll be the ideal target.* He spread the tarp on the thawing ground, set the rifle on its tripod, lay behind it. Adjusting the scope for the estimated distance, he put the cross-hairs on the corral fence, got as comfortable as possible, tightened the hood of his coat against the damp breeze.

The camo should make him nearly invisible against the broken landscape, and Glenn didn't expect any company, raw day like this. It would be as Benson said, a wait and watch situation.

And for twenty grand, he could do that.

~ * ~

As Sam and I had ridden near the front fence, I'd seen the black Jeep cruise past twice, and thought that a little odd. Just somebody looking for a farm road probably, and it disappeared up Hwy. 200 toward Lincoln. Traffic was picking up on this road, as more people built houses along it, more commuted to jobs in that village or even to Missoula. Like I'd observed, distances weren't such a big deal out here.

It was chilly, but we were glad to be out, the horses were glad, and it wasn't hard to imagine this whole world was about to break free of winter's last gasp. Steam rose from the damp ground as the sun hit it, and my mind was full of upcoming projects. *Got that retaining wall beyond Ovando first, soon's the ground's completely thawed. Hafta wait a couple weeks for the contractor to pour the footing for that chimney in Missoula. Kay will wanta be in on that, so we'll stay with Mrs. H...*

I smiled at the picture of that good woman spoiling Cody, and welcoming us like family. Of course, I'd realized on back how much she'd had to do with bringing Kay and me together, and I was grateful. Women sure had a way of getting things done, and not necessarily out in the open. Man was blind to think he was always in charge.

There were new calves, most of which had been born in the pens or the big barn, and they were out with their mamas now, frisking in the sun. Man could get to liking this ranching, watching them. Kay had told me she used to make pets of every one, and when she was little, she'd cry when they got too big and were sold.

We completed our circuit at the back side of the property along the river at mid-morning, and headed back to the ranch house. Kay had taken the baby to spend time with Emily, and we'd stay, have lunch. We unsaddled, turned the horses loose, went into the barn.

And Glenn Ormond lost sight of the two men before he could draw a bead on the older one. One moment he was standing clear, lifting the saddle from the sorrel, and the next he'd turned, stepped beyond a young, bushed-out fir tree this side of the corral. *Damn, almost got lucky, first thing.*

But the man didn't reappear. The other cowboy was stocky, youngish in the scope's vision field, just an ordinary guy he'd never seen before. *Cowhand, or the son-in-law?* Didn't matter. But the picture Benson had shown him of the rancher matched the tall one exactly.

So, a day of waiting for his next chance loomed ahead, and no help for it. Glenn had never hunted, but had been told the sport was nine-tenths just this, plus luck. *Okay, I'm waiting. So send me the luck.*

It didn't come. Not that long day, or the next or the next, when a storm rolled in and he had to leave his lair before noon. He wasn't a patient man, but this job needed patience. And what was the alternative? *Being out of a job, that's what.* And although he *could* always just pack this in and hit the road to somewhere else, he knew he'd probably starve. No, he was in this, for better or worse, and the thought of that 20—no, 40—thousand kept him at it.

~ * ~

Another bright day, and this time Sam and I had tools to replace a post on beyond the corral that one of his former hands had broken when he'd backed his truck into it. The two posts on either side had held the wire fence, but it was sagging, and Sam expected spirited Blaze to jump it.

"He wants to run, and if he smells a mare in heat a mile away, he'll be gone," he explained to me. So head that calamity off right now. Fool horse could get hit on the highway. Yeah, I'd read *The Brave Cowboy* by then, and couldn't get the picture of that maimed horse out of my head.

We were riding around the corral to strike the fence through some pines, Sam ahead a few lengths, when he came out into the open, in clear sight of the highway ahead. And he turned in the saddle to say something to me.

Glenn had caught sight of the two men beyond the corral as they rode, and he followed them with the rifle. The old man was in the lead, and after disappearing among the trees, he emerged in the clear, coming right at the highway.

He acquired the man's center mass in the scope, tried to steady his hands. But this was no stationary target, this was a living human being, and a shaking began. *Whatthehell, buck fever? Get a grip on this, man! This's your chance.*

In that space of time, the rancher rode behind some sparsely-spaced trees, and Glenn got his nerves under control. *Deep breaths, steady those hands. He'll come into view again.*

Sam McBryde did emerge in the open, and despite being on the verge of shakiness again, Glenn Ormond centered the cross-hairs on his side as he moved across, squeezed the trigger.

I couldn't quite make out what Sam was saying to me when he turned, and I was touching Bruno's flanks to catch up, when I saw him jerk, then pitch off his horse. A distant echo of gunfire came, and I was instinctively off and crouching in a run the few steps to him. He was face-down, and I saw a red stain spreading from a hole high in his back.

Glenn, actually smiling, folded up the tripod, gathered his belongings, and slipped away across the brush-grown field, almost a half mile distant. Since he hadn't seen the other cowboy after his shot, he was sure he'd run away. *Got the old guy clean.*

It hadn't been like killing a man at all, just a target, one that happened to be alive.

Then not.

~ * ~

"Stay down, Harlan," Sam was conscious, and appeared more angry than hurt. "Bastard'll get you too. Don't think it's... deep. Must've... been a long way..." Then he did pass out: *shock.* I opened his coat, shirt, in a sort of daze and yeah, my own shock, and anger. Got the bleeding stopped by wadding a handkerchief and stuffing it in. No exit wound. *Yeah, bullet almost spent? Got here way before th' sound. Okay, drag you behind these bushes, then get you across your horse.*

Sam was tall, and yeah, heavy enough, but you can do more than you think when your adrenaline's screaming. I got him up, tied down, checked to make sure the bleeding was contained, led his horse to deeper cover. Mounted Bruno and we got outta there for the house, staying hidden behind willows, trees, brush. Which took a little longer, but kept us out of range, I hoped.

And my mind was racing, every step. *No accident, and somebody who knows how to shoot. Well, no shortage of hunters around here. Okay, get Sam taken care of, then I'm digging into this for sure.*

And I realized that with Sam shot, these past months, years of peace had just been shattered, and surely this was just the beginning of something sinister, violent, that'd tear its way into our lives. This was a whole ratcheting-up of the harassment from before.

Or not.

I managed to ride up to the ranch house from behind, out of sight of the highway and that shooter, who had to be still watching, ready to fire again. Couldn't keep my mind off this, though.

So, what did we know? *Been years since that other shit, but something's the same. Different people with the same scheme? Or same people? First thing's to find out who was behind that weird stuff on back. I'm thinking the guy Kay hadda blast was maybe just hired help, for starters. Okay, here's the house: get him to a doctor, quick...*

Kay saw us first, came running out the back door.

"Call an ambulance, girl. Your dad's been shot, but I don't think he'll die."

"No," came from Sam, who'd regained consciousness. "Call Doc Caperton, honey. He c'n take th' bullet out here." He was trying to get out of my grip, to stand. I wasn't letting him.

"Dad, you're going to the hospital..."

"No, listen a second. I been goin' over this. An' I want whoever's done this t'think I'm dead..."

"What? Crazy talk. I'm..." Just then Emily ran out, and I heard Cody cry inside the house.

"Wait, Kay," I held up a hand. I was getting this. "He's right. Shooter'll watch: if an ambulance comes, he'll think Sam may be okay. We bring the doc here, it'll be like just a neighbor, or if he's recognized, it'll be him pronouncing him dead, see..."

"And we got a better chance to flush th' bastard out," Sam managed. He was in a lot of pain. We got him into the house, where Emily got his coat, shirt off, cleaned the wound. Kay brought painkillers. They really wanted him out of there, and in a hospital, quick.

Cameron Caperton, the white-haired doctor, came, asked Kay to stay, attend him. She never flinched, brought hot water, cloths, alcohol. He injected a local anesthetic, waited, then went to work with probe, forceps. Sam hadn't wanted Emily getting hysterical around him. Tough guy.

"Not deep, Sam, good news. There, it's out." He examined it: not flattened much at all. "Either a low-power load or a long way away. Any idea which?"

"Long way, Cam. I was lookin'... right across th' highway at him just b'fore I... turned, an' nothin' there. We're talkin' scoped rifle here, an' a good... shooter. A pro, maybe. So somebody's got it in for me." The pain was still bad.

"Looks like it. You see anything, Harlan?"

"No, I was behind. But Sam and I have a favor to ask, Doc."

"What's that?"

"Well, we know you have to report gunshot wounds, but we think we'll stand a better chance of finding out who's behind this—motive, I guess—if the shooter thinks he's dead. I'm even thinking maybe putting an obituary in the paper. I've got an idea what may be behind this, but we wanta know *who*. And he/they oughta make their move if Sam was the... well, no longer the obstacle, I guess."

Doc Caperton wasn't slow. Not slow at all.

"You're askin' me to fake his death." He thought a moment, looking at Sam. "Okay, say I report the gunshot wound, but fudge a little, say the patient died."

"You'd do that for us?"

"Do it for Sam, yeah. We go back a long way. And hey, everybody's gonna die, someday, just a little mix-up on the date, right?" A twinkle: I liked this old guy a lot. And Kay had even suggested having him deliver our next baby, at home. Well...

After Caperton had left, we called the sheriff, Blake Ingraham, another old friend of Sam's, hiding him away in the back bedroom, which would be his forced convalescent center. He'd have to stay quiet, but the doctor had given him a strong sedative, and he'd rest.

"Doc's been here, took care of the body and everything," I told the lawman, who was there in a surprisingly short time, clearly angry. "Some bastard shot Sam right out of the saddle, on past the corrals. Here's the rifle bullet Caperton took out." He examined it. No doubt it was a rifle round.

"Accident? No hunting season on."

"No way. I was right behind him, looking right at the highway, where the shot came from. Didn't see a thing, so must've been a long way off. Hadda be a scoped rifle, for sure."

"Yeah, maybe even a sniper gun, that far. Okay, deputy an' I'll go across, see if we can find any sign. Come show me where it happened, an' we c'n get a line on his position." He gave Emily and Kay his heartfelt condolences; he too had known Sam a long time. Made me feel a little chickenshit about this deception, actually.

"We'll find him, Em. Wherever he is, we'll get him." She managed a tear-streaked thanks. We went down to the barn, got horses, and the three of us rode our earlier path. Once there, I showed them exactly where Sam was, how he'd turned to say something to me, got hit in the back. And I admit I was keeping behind brush all the time we were there; this had me spooked.

"Doc Caperton says it might've been a stray shot, but it did the damage, anyway." I was bitter—no act required—that whoever had done this was still out there somewhere, ready to take whatever next step he—they—planned. The sheriff took notes, measured some spaces, examined our tracks. Apparently didn't suspect me at all, since not a close-range shot, and I was obviously right there.

On the ride back, he reminded me of the trouble those years back.

"That'uz just a crazy Kay had to shoot, Harlan, but this looks premeditated. Not a chance in a million somebody'd use a long-range gun out shootin' targets, or even poachin' a deer, with th' highway there. Unless he was crazy, too. An' I don't believe in coincidences. Johnny'n I'll scout out that grown-up field of Blackburn's across, see what we can find. You let us know if you see or hear anything.

"An' Harlan, you keep an eye out. You been in this family long enough, whoever's got it in for Sam may be after you, too. Dunno what for, but you take care, y'hear?" I said yeah, I'd do just that.

~ * ~

"Y'think we really oughta put that obituary in th' paper?" Sam asked, after the sheriff had left and he'd had time to rest. "Folks all over be comin', bringin' food, wanta go to th' funeral."

"Well, I thought like you said, we oughta make it clear to everybody that you're dead..."

"We could tell folks who call that we had a private burial right here, Dad, like we did for Granpa, the old cemetery. Maybe a short memorial service at the church?"

"Hate t'fool folks like that, but it's dead certain th' feller will come at me, an' maybe all of us, again, if he knows. Well, we got a day or so to decide b'fore we call it in to th' paper.

"What we need t'do is sit an' figure what's goin' on, an' all of us gotta put our brains on it. We can't do much of anything till we know more." He was all over this; little thing like getting shot wasn't gonna slow Sam McBryde down.

So we did. But when nobody else ventured much of an explanation, I laid out my suspicions.

"Well, I've been pushing this around in my head ever since that first craziness, folks. And I don't think that lunatic you had to defend yourself against, Kay, was the whole story. First of all, what'd one young guy have to gain by poisoning our water, burning us out, killing our cows?

"I think he was expendable, a hired gun. And I think whoever was behind that mess is either behind this, or somebody else has the same agenda."

"But what agenda?" from Kay.

"I think it's the gold rumors. We're sure the people who bought the dude ranch place before dug soil samples. Probably had a geologist hired, reason they gambled on that big, expensive place. They never put but a few cows on it, spent their time digging, sluicing the ground. Must've found enough to get worked up over."

"And they wanted this place, bad," Sam put in. "Where'd you say they were digging, washing out, on their place that time?"

"Right up next to your line. Right where the fire burned that time. Right closest to where they must've figured the source was. And that's another thing—I think they set that fire to burn you out, get you to sell. And looking back on it, I think they were also the ones killed your cows, and tried to poison your water. And then for some reason, just gave up and sold out."

"Well," Emily pointed out, "they sold out after Kay had to shoot that guy."

"Who like I said, was probably one of them, not some random crazy. That'd be the connection, his getting shot the reason they figured things had gotten too hot. He tried hard to kill you, Kay, which means he had a lot to hide, going up against a blinding flashlight and a rifle like that.

"So somebody from that bunch, or somebody else who's convinced there's a bonanza under probably our house slope, is obsessed enough to kill for it. Now, the well driller only brought up a few specks, so I agree with you, Sam, there's nothing under there. But I'm no geologist. I did find from research on back, that a talus slope like that was where the old prospectors dug, figuring the source had gotten covered up by the soil washing down off the mountain. If they did have a geologist, I think he'd have told them that'd be the logical source.

"We know that Calloway guy was lying when he told us his people hadn't dug on our land... it was too fresh. What we don't know is how high a concentration of sign they found, with all their digging. But it must've been strong enough to encourage them. And I'm thinking this is the only motive for any of this, and that yesterday's shooting is part of it, if maybe not the same people. Hey, anybody who'd buy a thousand acres, get machinery in, offer to buy more, is serious enough to kill, I'm afraid." I spread my hands.

Sam's mind was working.

"So whoever this is, he's gonna kill me, an' maybe even you, an' make th' girls an offer they can't refuse? That it, you think?"

"Yeah, I do. And I also think maybe somebody is gonna contact Emily before long, with an offer. Now, I've also been thinking about this: we never got around to deeding any of the land to Kay and me, and that's okay—not necessary. But that might keep us alive, since I can't sell it, and neither can Kay. Any fool can look up the courthouse records, see you all still own it outright.

"But that'd change, if you did sign part of it over to us, so I'm against that, keep us safer, for the time being. But sooner or later, I think I'll be the same obstacle they see you as, Sam. So I wanta see who shows up, and jump on that with both feet."

"This is terrible!" Emily cried. "We're not safe here on our own place?"

"Apparently not, as long as somebody thinks his version of paradise is waiting there right under us. And maybe there is some gold down there somewhere, but you and I talked about that back when I first showed my ugly face, Sam, and I told you I wanted it to stay right there. Still do: no illusions of becoming a rich playboy. I just wanta slam rocks, go on lovin' your daughter, raising Cody, and maybe herd a few cows with you when you get back on your feet.

"But we're in a bind here, and I think we have to do something about it. I know it'd be embarrassing later when folks find you're alive, but that's a lot better'n being dead, don't you think? Which is what the bad guys want. And maybe not just you.

I don't wanta take the chance Kay and Cody, and yeah, you, Emily, could be part of the extermination plan too."

"Oh, that's so horrible, Harlan," Emily was envisioning that. "We can't let anything like that happen; we have to do *something*." She was actually wringing her hands.

"While we're speculating," Kay began, "I know it's beyond possible, but could there be any connection between the dude ranch owners and this whole thing? I hate to think it, but we're talking the safety of our family here..."

"Surely not. They've been great to us, upfront with it all, not like that Calloway guy from before. Still, we don't know much about their backgrounds. I guess I'd have to say we can't rule anybody out, till we know."

We left it there: hide and watch.

And yeah, we did put that obit in the paper, after the supposed private burial. Bait that hook, and see what greedy fish came out from under its rock and took it.

Or tried to.

# Nineteen

"Clean shot, boss. I blew that old bastard right out of the saddle. Around six hundred yards, clear view, not enough wind just then to matter. He didn't get up, and nobody came for him. No ambulance, nothing. He's outta your hair."

"Good job. But now don't get your nose outta joint, Glenn. I want to wait a coupla days. Even if it doesn't make the news, there'll be his obituary in the paper, and there won't be any doubt. So you're sure nobody saw you? Or your Jeep?"

"No problem. I didn't even use a farm road, went right across this grown-up old field, hid th' Jeep in th' trees. Moved away from my position after, watched till the sheriff came. He and a coupla deputies checked out the kill site, then went back, prob'ly came across to hunt for trace after I left. All clean." He didn't mention the one solitary car that'd slowed, maybe turned in at the McBryde driveway as he was moving away, nothing official about it.

"Well, sounds right. Now, I'll have a follow-up for you later, but nothing rough. I want that ranch, but I don't want to be the one making the offer. You can be my buyer for that when the time comes. Okay?"

"Sure, I can do businessman." *Hell, I could prob'ly even do lawyer, if I had to.*

~ * ~

It wasn't easy, keeping Sam out of sight that way. He was very soon up and rarin' to get outside, and we all had to remind him this wouldn't work if just one person spotted him. Kenny was back for the summer, and somehow Emily kept him out of the house and in the dark. Like everybody, he was really sorry to hear about Sam, wanted to help in any way. I liked Kenny okay, and yeah, I guess I understood why he got itchy feet now and then. I'd found my place, and maybe someday he'd find his. Probably right back where he'd been raised.

I'd resolved to stick close for a few weeks, this crisis being a lot more important than rockwork. Perfectly reasonable for me to be around to help, and also when and if a prospective buyer appeared. And I'd even urge Emily to sell, if the offer turned out to be anything sane. We had it all worked out.

Kay even told me she'd go out and get on the next stone job, and I could stay home and take care of Cody. But no, I wasn't gonna let my bride do that. Wanted her here too, kind of circling the wagons.

The brothers could've been a problem, but Emily swore them to secrecy, and Sam told them if word got out, he'd cowhide both of them. They were hundreds of miles away, anyway. We all felt bad about the sham memorial service at the little community church, which they dutifully came to, but again felt we had to play this out. Or face a repeat, surely more deadly next time. Easier to ask forgiveness than permission, or in this case than risk letting any slips happen.

It was just two weeks later this dude drove up in a black Jeep, which I sort of thought I might've seen before—*well, lotsa Jeeps around*. Guy in a suit, I could see from a distance, there from the barn. I started for the house, then stopped in my tracks.

*That bastard is Crescent's ex-husband, broken nose and all. Now whatthehell is this...*

Kay wasn't there, and maybe I'd have to let Emily handle this alone. No, I was sure the shithead hadn't had a good look at me that time I cold-cocked him. And if he did? Just hafta let that happen. So I resolved to tough this out, be there for that woman, dealing with this snake. Whatever this could mean.

"Help you?" I called out before he could reach the house, limping a little. And me brazenly striding right up to him, cool. If he recognized me, well, like I said, let him deal with that.

"Oh, I was hoping to catch Mrs. McBryde at home. I'm Brent Breckinridge." He offered a hand, not a sign of recognition.

"Harlan Kemp. I'm her son-in-law. What's on your mind, Brent?" Like I said, I was cool.

"Um, well, I represent a very famous man—you'd know his name at once. He's looking for a ranch to buy. Is Mrs. McBryde here? I'd like to talk directly to her."

"Yeah, she's here somewhere. And sure, she's the owner, so c'mon in." I let him go first, not wanting him behind me. That good an actor?

Emily sat us both down, brought coffee. She didn't know this guy, but did know he was probably in on whatever bad stuff was happening. She too, was cool.

"I was explaining to your son-in-law, Mrs. McBryde, that my employer, who's quite well-known, is searching for his dream ranch, and wants to settle near here. He's a lot like Ted Turner, some movie stars and some other notables who've found places not far from here.

"And I'm sad to hear that you've recently lost your husband, ma'am, and I hope I'm not intruding on your privacy, coming here like this, but I wanted to offer my condolences, and meet you personally." He was *so* solicitous, so sincere.

So full of bullshit.

"Thanks, Mr. Breckinridge. It was a shock—apparently a stray shot by some irresponsible gun handler who should've known better, but I'll have to learn to cope with it. However, this place has actually been in my husband's family for several generations, since the first settlers here. I hadn't thought of selling..." My cue.

"But Emily, you can't run this place by yourself. And you know I've got the stone business. Maybe you should give this some thought." I spread my hands. Was I an actor?

"Well, I guess I hadn't thought that far ahead, dear. But you've got your new place on up the slope. Surely you and Kay don't want to leave, so soon?"

"You're the important one, though. And I'm finding it a hard thing to have to drive to Missoula or down on the Bitterroot every day for work. The only real reason we built here was that you and Sam let us have the land free."

"Well, you know we wanted us all to stay together..." She appeared a little confused.

"And we have been. But that's all changed now. You know your sons won't ever come back, and Kay'll go wherever I go. I'm not saying this is something you should do, but maybe think about it: a possibility."

"That's all I'm asking, Mrs. McBryde. This is one of several places my boss is looking at, but I should tell you, price is not an object with him. When he finds the right place, he'll pay whatever's necessary for it." *Not quite true, but this'll get her to thinking, all right: money talks.*

"Well...I'd want to talk it over with my sons, and with my daughter too, of course. But I do appreciate your employer's interest in the land, Mr. Breckinridge; he obviously knows something about this place—lots of people do, really, come fishing here. Let me think about this new idea, sir, and yes, you call me in a week or two, would you? Then perhaps we can talk further."

"Certainly. And again, I'm sorry for your loss."

*That worn-out bromide. I may gag. Or I may lose it and smash this dude's face. Again... No, Kemp, that'd be counter-productive.*

Breckinridge, aka Glenn Ormond, took his leave, not quite hiding the smirk on his face. He'd go back to whoever was behind this and give a positive report, and the game would be afoot, as Sherlock Holmes used to say. Well, Arthur Conan Doyle... fiction, after all.

So should I follow this guy? Wasn't good at that, and would probably botch it. Sam had said we could call in some help, probably his buddy the sheriff, so let him pick it up, I guessed. I watched the black Jeep head back toward Missoula, writing down the license number.

We reported to Sam, who'd only seen Slick leaving. Hadn't been able to hear the proposition.

"I think he's part of it, Sam," I told him, and Emily agreed. "Emily played him like a trout, and he bought it. She just might think of selling to the nice man. So we'll hear back I'm sure, maybe get closer to who's behind this. I can't see this dude with his Jeep being a major player, probably just a gofer, front man in a suit. In fact, he's actually the ex-husband of a friend of ours, just gone broke trying to run a hotel down in Stevensville. Real loser." I didn't add that I'd altered Glenn's face at an earlier non-meeting.

"Okay, let's get Graham Ingraham on this, now. He c'n locate the guy through that license number you got—good thinkin'—and sniff around him, find who he works for. You ask him t'keep it quiet till we uncover more, and he'll do it, old times' sake. I'm sure he's got his suspicions, too." That event perked Sam up. Progress made his immobility bearable. Just.

~ * ~

"She'll sell, boss; I just know it. You told me their kids had to borrow, work through college, and there's nothing high-dollar out there. I'd say she's starting to wonder what she'll have to live on now, and any offer will look good to her real soon."

"Think the daughter and her husband will get stubborn?"

"About that. Guy was there, urged her to think about selling. Said he was hating to have to drive so far for his stonework every day. Only built there because the land was free."

"And it's not in his name, either. Oh, he did work for the dude ranch next door, but they're surely through with that by now. Yeah, that boy might just disappear on his own. You didn't mention any figure, of course."

"No way. Didn't wanta give them the idea you were made of money. I'd say, play your cards right, you can get the place cheap, before somebody else gets onto it. Those Hollywood types buying up places and all. They see those creeks and that river frontage, they'll be on it."

"Yeah, there's that. Okay, sounds like you've laid the groundwork, Glenn, and oh, here's that check for the twenty grand. Old man's in the ground and it looks like the door's open, and thanks."

*Yeah, I did this. And if that rock guy does get ideas, we've already planned how to take care of him, hunting season. Get to use my new skill with that rifle, find the right place and time.*

~ * ~

With Sam playing hermit, I got to be a cowboy a lot that spring, riding with Kenny and Kay after Black Angus cows, wrestling steers, squirting medicine down their throats, shoveling manure. Yeah, all that romantic Old West stuff they put in movies.

Sam did get out after dark, and in the daytime when Kenny was off and he could stay way back from the highway, out of sight. Man would've gone batty if he'd had to stay inside all the time. So he was able to keep running the place okay, although he grumped a lot. I did insist he keep back in cover those times, since the guy who'd shot him had surely used a rifle scope, and it wouldn't do to let him spot him again, if he happened to be looking, say through a telescope.

Alive.

But he didn't like it one bit. He kept trying on ideas that'd let him get on with his life. Even some sort of disguise.

"Doubt if you'd fool Kenny. And any day now, whoever's out there will follow up on the land offer. We'll insist on meeting the real buyer, not just his hired help, and that'll bring this crap to a head."

"Still won't be any proof he was the one shot me. I guess we'll just have to see how serious he or they are, how hard they push."

And if wife-beating Glenn Ormond pushed very hard, I had my own plans for him, and I was sure Kay would hold my coat when that happened. Maybe take her turn.

But well, things don't always go according to plan, I'd already learned. And I couldn't have known that very loser would amuse himself by setting up a watch on us at the ranch as we went about our work.

~ * ~

Glenn, in thinking back on it, began to fear his discussion with the McBryde woman and her son-in-law had gone too easily. *She was okay, but something about that guy wasn't right. You don't just build a nice house, get set up the way he has, then want out, more so when it didn't cost you much. Like he was pushing her to sell for his own reasons.*

*He didn't say it, but I'd bet he'll urge her to sign over that part of the land his house's on, real soon. That way, he can stay as long as he wants, let it get worth more before he does sell. I don't know what the boss has in mind, but I'd say he wants that house. Old ranch house isn't much, but from what I can see, the new place is pretty impressive, all that stonework, that view.*

Glenn laid aside the binoculars to rest his eyes. He could glimpse part of the mountain slope and a bit of the Kemp house through the trees, but not much. He'd driven here up the North Fork to scout more of the spread Benson wanted, partly out of curiosity. He was scheduled to call the woman in maybe two days, to talk price. He'd no doubt she'd sell, had convinced himself he could persuade her.

Unless that stonemason really did have something else in mind. *And the boss said we might have to deal with him later. So what's he know that I don't? Expects some resistance there, obviously. Which doesn't square with his talk. Doesn't square at all, Ormond, so we need to find out more.*

He saw, from his distant vantage point, a bright red vehicle moving between the trees, coming down from the Kemp place. Through the binoculars, it looked like one of those British Jeeps, only this one was a truck. It disappeared among trees several times, but came on toward the ranch house. He couldn't see the driver: could be anyone.

But when the door opened at the McBryde yard, the woman who got out and lifted a baby from its car seat seemed familiar. *That'll be the daughter. Damn, she's tall. Can't see her face, that cowboy hat. So, just taking the kid to grandma, I guess. Wonder where her husband is? He and another dude were just down at the corral, but gone somewhere, now.*

Glenn had stayed hidden for nearly two hours, and he was aching. He decided to leave, having learned exactly nothing. Well, he'd insist on seeing more of the place next time, check it out good, if only to be able to tell Benson everything that was there. The lawyer had told him he hadn't ever been there, so give him a situation report.

He was about to rise, hike back over the fields to his Jeep, when the tall woman came out the front door of the house alone, walked toward the corral. He trained the binoculars on her face, now visible with the sun full on her.

*Holy shit! That's the ugly bitch got me beat up, couple years back. Isn't it? Gotta be... not two tree-tall women look like that in the world. So that's the stonemason's wife, for sure. Okay, does that mean he was the one blindsided me? Has to be, the guy those others lied about not knowing.*

*Oh, you're gonna catch hell, rock guy. Boss says you could be trouble, and you're already in trouble with me. You're history, you bastard. Bust my jaw, get the cops on me... I can't get near that bitch blew my leg away, but I can reach you.*

*And I will.*

On the highway back to Missoula, Glenn formulated his plan for revenge. He did have to admit he wasn't completely sure the husband had been his attacker. Hell, woman might've not even been with him, that far back. But with that about maybe trouble from him, wouldn't hurt to go ahead and take him out, neutralize that problem ahead of time.

*So, even if Benson says he doesn't need the guy out of the way, I can make him a problem. Say he's changed his mind, wants to keep that place of his. Like I thought, it's probably the part the boss wants, so that'd be the first step. Yeah, and tell him I've learned the McBryde woman plans to deed that part away, that'll push this.*

*Damn, Ormond, you're a genius.*

# *Twenty*

The phone call came. Could Mr. Breckinridge come visit again, perhaps tour the ranch in order to give his employer a better picture of the place? Emily said sure, come on out, but please bring the man who was to make the offer with you. At this Ormond demurred, insisting his boss was much too busy to attend to this himself. He'd come, yes, if and when a better idea was reached of the place, with a figure he was willing to offer.

"Dodge," I told Sam and the others. "The head guy will stay anonymous as long as he can, because he'll know we're sure he's the one behind shooting you. So we're no nearer finding out than we were before. Unless we can stall long enough he'll have to come out of the woodwork."

"I can just say I won't consider selling to him till we know who we're dealing with," Emily declared.

"And maybe hint you're talking to somebody else?" Kay suggested.

"Well, I got a peek at that boy was here," Sam said, "and if I ever saw a crook, he's it. Maybe he's even th' one winged me."

I thought about that. Could easily be, if Glenn the Loser knew how to shoot. Simple enough to find that out, since we had a friend who'd know.

"We'll ask Crescent about that," Kay decided, before I could put my thought into words. Woman was psychic, had to be. "Been a while since we've seen her, and she doesn't have a phone. Wanta go visit, Harlan?"

Well sure, why not? Go on up and see the Carters too, while we were at it. Hadn't heard how their property search was going, or whether anybody'd been up there to shower them with dollars for that great place they had. Of course they'd have found a way to let us know, but something could be in the works.

So we trucked on down to Florence, hunted up our goat girl. She about melted at sight of Cody, who I'll admit had gotten the best of Kay's and my genes, apparently... good-looking kid. And he loved this little grownup who must've appeared about half our size. Had learned a few words, and she knew somehow just the right language to draw him out. Damn shame she couldn't find herself a real man, start a family of her own.

At least she hadn't been bothered by her slimy ex, who must've finally gotten the hint. Shot-away leg should do that for anybody.

But no, the Glenn hadn't been a hunter, never owned a rifle. She did let us know she'd taken an automatic off him after she'd shot him. I wondered that she'd been faster when it counted, but supposed the bastard had been so cocksure he could charm her he hadn't resorted to going for it.

Admittedly, that had been many months ago, which didn't rule out his being Sam's shooter, but it lengthened the odds. No, the big bad guy who'd wanted him taken out could've easily hired a gun. Surely enough green stuff could get you an assassin here in the still-wild west. Or anywhere.

We helped Crescent with the goats, so she could take off and go with us up to see the Carters. And those two tough outdoor girls actually rode back in the camper on the Rover, leaving me with Cody in his baby seat up front. I could hear them going at it, girl-talking up a storm back there, all the way up the mountain. Tried to avoid the biggest boulders so I wouldn't toss them around too much.

Rhys was off on a job somewhere, but Moira welcomed us like she hadn't seen us in years. Those kids mobbed us. And that good woman appropriated Cody, Crescent shifted her attention to little Cormac (gotta spoil everybody). Cale had to show me the hunting knife he'd forged, all by himself. Kid was becoming a good craftsman. Siobhan shyly showed off a jacket she and her mom had sewn from soft deerskin. What a trio they were, kids the way they oughta be.

When Rhys got home, we had an even better time of it, with his good humor, music, and my chance to talk with him about my/our problems. I hadn't let him in on Sam's non-death, sticking to our closed circle re the facts. But I wanted his take on the situation as we saw it. We walked down to the workshop; no need to get the others riled over this.

"Somebody wants the ranch in the worst way, guy, and I think that's why they gunned Sam down."

"Damn bad, that. Got any idea who?"

"Well, the last bunch who owned the dude ranch property had dug test holes all over, even on our side of the line. Had a sluice operation going, but wanted the McBryde place, surely figuring a mother lode of gold is under it. They gave up, after what I believe were efforts to force Sam to sell. I told you about the burning, the attempt to poison the water, the cattle killing. I never bought it about it being just the one crazy Kay had to shoot. Anyway, I think maybe the same people, or another bunch with the same idea, want that land. At least our part of it, the talus slope."

"And you think they shot Sam to get Emily to sell? That wouldn't get them your part of it."

"We've never taken title to ours, and the courthouse records show this. Legally, Emily sells, we're out. And that's okay, for now. I'm thinking as soon as she gives us title to our part, the bad guys will come directly after Kay and me. We built right over where I'm sure they think the source is."

"Wow, heavy stuff. So somebody sees the possibility of striking it rich as worth killing for. That's scary, dude." He was shaking his head.

"That's the way I see it. Sam's getting hit wasn't an accident—long shot with a sniper rifle cartridge, the sheriff told us."

"Okay, so has anybody showed up to try to buy Emily out?" Logical question.

"Yep, and guess who: Crescent's ex, Glenn the loser, posing as front man for some super-rich guy wanting a Montana ranch. He didn't recognize me, since all he saw that time was my fist, but he slipped in like an oily rag, gave Emily the whole bullshit package. Sorry about her loss, worried she couldn't live on the place anymore, painted his supposed boss as the perfect solution to her problems."

"Sleazy bastard. Crescent shoulda let him die, but she couldn't live with that. So, hotel failed, along with everything else that loser has touched, and now he's in it with the get-rich-quick richie—or bunch of them—who'll kill again to get the place. Emily too, or you and Kay, even. Hey, what's a couple more bodies to that sort?" He was clenching and unclenching his fists, a lot like I'd been doing, in frustration and anger.

"Bad thing is we have no idea who's behind him, but this has already escalated beyond that burning, poisoning stuff, to shooting Sam. They're deadly serious, whoever they are. Now, what I'd love to hear from you is, how do we flush the real nasties out of hiding? Glenn won't tell us who he's representing."

"Maybe don't consider any offer till you know who?"

"That's the best we could come up with. He's supposed to come next week to scope the place out more, report back, before any actual offer. Now, the sheriff's tracked his license number, knows who he is, but nothing more. I thought about trying to follow him, but I'm no detective: blow it big time. And so far, he's done nothing wrong. This time."

"Suppose he was the shooter? Sounds like his kinda deal."

"Crescent says he's never had a rifle, didn't know how to shoot. But that was before. And I guess the head badass could hire a hit, kind of money he/they're willing to spend. Hey, buying Emily out ain't gonna be cheap."

"No. Hey, just supposin' there *is* gold under your house, bro. You gonna dig it?"

"Not a chance. Well driller came up with just a faint trace, right where it oughta be. Got all excited over a speck of color, but it's just not there. Oh, you might tear down the whole mountain and find something, but nobody's ever tried, and the rumors have been around a hundred and fifty years. No, we're satisfied keepin' our place just like it is. With the help you and a bunch of others have given us, we're sittin' stupid happy, wouldn't do anything to spoil it. No illusions of grandeur."

"So I wonder what makes the greedy shitheads believe there's a bonanza under there?"

"I figure the other people maybe hired a geologist: those test holes, taking samples. From what I've read up on, the stuff washes down off slopes like ours, gets buried under talus, soil buildup. The holes on our side must've told him a higher concentration was just ahead. Only thing I can imagine."

"But to kill for what might not even be there? That's diseased, man."

"Yeah, such a long shot, taking out the owner, gambling his widow will sell, figuring Kay and I, and even the brothers, will let it all go. Then the expense of digging for it. Somebody's obsessed."

"Okay. Don't know what I can do to help, Harlan, but I want to. I'm afraid these sickos will get impatient and start a war, take you all out. Now, the dude ranch folks have contacted me, want more construction, like they talked about before. I can put off stuff down here for later, come up, help you keep an eye out." He was planning. "Maybe take the family up again, if we can stay with them...

"No need for that. Plenty room with us, and Kay'd insist."

"Maybe. So we at least patrol, search out likely sight lines, places where a shooter like the one got Sam, could set up. Your house is hidden in the trees up there, but you'd be visible all sorts of places on the ranch. Now, it'd be stupid as hell to take you all out just after Sam, but we're talking crazy people."

I was feeling the bond of friendship big time the more Rhys talked, but I really didn't want him taking a risk for us. But again, the more we discussed this, the more I got the idea that maybe my/our time was getting short. *Gotta head this off, and the more help I can get, the better.*

"You sure you wanta get involved in something this weird could get you killed, buddy?"

"Listen, if some crazy came after us here, you'd be here like the Lone Ranger, now wouldn't you?" He clapped me on the back.

"Well, sure, but..."

"So, that's your answer. And Moira'd kick my butt if we left you all open like that. What are best friends for?" He meant every word of this. Good feeling.

"Just talk it over with her first, promise me. You got more family at stake than we do."

"Dunno about that, got the feelin' you'n Kay are gonna populate that place with little cowboys and cowgirls right regular." Another backslap.

So it was that just before slick Glenn's next visit, the Carters were in residence. And talking more about it, Rhys insisted Kay and I stay out of sight, let him go with Emily to show the place.

Just maybe, he said, that jackass might recognize Kay and put two and two together, hold a grudge. Hadn't thought of that. I *said* I needed his head on all this.

"Let me get my take on his scam. He knows me, but as a friend of the family, nothin' suspicious about me helpin' Emily out that way. I don't want the bastard pullin' a gun on you. And here's another thought: what's to've kept him from checking the place out with maybe binoculars already, seen you and Kay, figured out who you are? We can't give this piece of shit any slack."

*Wow.*

"And if he even looks at Emily sideways, I'll break his head." That sort of decided me he was right. Good guy to have on our side.

So just before the appointed time that day, the Kemps visited the dude ranch owners to go over the proposed next phase of construction. Those waterfalls, hidden glades, stonework in general. Both of us were worried about Ormond being right in our house, but knew Rhys could handle it. He'd even maybe drop it that we were anxious to move down to the Bitterroot valley, encourage Emily to consider offers. And Moira and family were in residence, too. He did know them from before, but that should be no problem with the work Rhys was to do at the dude ranch.

And this time, I'd called Sheriff Ingraham and asked him to have a deputy follow the black Jeep when it left, see if it could lead us to pay dirt.

"Know it's a lot to ask, sir, but we're sure this guy's part of Sam's shooting, showing up so soon this way, wanting to buy Emily out."

"I'll go myself, then. I want this guy as much as you all do, partner. Give me the when, and I'm there." *Partner? Well, this is Montana.*

Then we drove into Lincoln to buy groceries, make time for the ranch tour. Which of course wouldn't include the back room in Sam's house he hid in. Our dream house would naturally be the residence any future owner would want.

It was almost dark when we got back to the ranch, to pick Emily up and gather at our place. She and Rhys were both grinning.

"What an acting job, folks," Rhys declared. "Emily had that dude right in the palm of her hand. You oughta be in th' movies, lady."

"He was like a hooked trout, believing he'd talked me into it," she told us. "We made it easy for him, but not too easy. I absolutely insisted we meet the buyer himself before I'd hear any offer. And he drooled over this house, kids. Moira helped explain why you'd leave it."

"Yeah, told him we're best friends, Kay, and that I'd talked you into coming down to the Bitterroot to live, for all the right reasons."

"My acting troupe," I applauded. "Now maybe we'll hafta consider that." Wink at Kay. "So, did he promise the big dog, the mangy one?"

"He did, since I insisted. But that won't get us any proof that he's the one who had Sam shot, Harlan." The worry lines in her face were deeper, I noticed. This was wearing on my favorite mother-in-law.

"No, but Rhys and I've been scheming. We know you've been wanting to deed this place to us, record it. If you're okay with that, let's do it, and let Breckinridge/Ormond know you've changed your mind, will only sell your part. That'll flush the evil one out, to come after us." I held up a hand. "Now, we want Kay and Cody to go stay with Moira while we men clean this mess up. Kenny can help. And I'm sure Sheriff Ingraham will too, since I explained what we're up against. He knows Sam wasn't shot by accident."

"That's too dangerous," both Kay and Moira said, almost in unison. I went on.

"Not really. Rhys is not a target; neither's Kenny. And get this... I'm gonna disguise myself, get a long-hair wig in Missoula, wear sunglasses, be just a hired ranch hand. Come and go just fine, and be seen as little as possible." Chuckles at that picture.

"Okay," my bride said dubiously, "then what? The bad guy won't see the real you, so what happens next?"

"Well, the sheriff told us he'd found where Sam's shooter was positioned. Now, if he's sure that spot works, we think he'll go back there, use it again. We'll keep watch from beyond it, one or more of us, and if he comes, sets up, we take him." I spread my hands. Sounded okay to me.

"Let the sheriff take him," she stated. "Not either of you." Moira and Emily nodded.

"Best case, yeah," Rhys agreed. "But we don't know when he'll hit. Ingraham told Harlan the guy apparently spent several days watching, till he could get his shot. We have no idea of the timing this round, and we don't think even a deputy will be assigned to the job for long, without a direct threat.

"Now, he could very well pick another spot, so we have to patrol every possibility, staying beyond even sniper range. If one of us spots him, there'll be time for us to contact the sheriff, while he's waiting to spot Harlan."

"Okay." She thought about that. "But if there's no activity here with all of us gone, he'll surely guess we're onto him some way, won't he? I mean, deserted ranch, why'd he wait? Come back another day and find the same? I'd be suspicious." *Damn, logic rearing its ugly head. This woman of mine is just too sharp. Okay then, I'll try the old line.*

"Anybody's got a better idea, I wanta hear it. Can't accept the status quo." Which started a lot of speculation, most of it wild. I had to point out again that we had to catch the would-be assassin in the act of aiming his rifle at the ranch for any accusations to stick. And if he had a good lawyer... But then Moira had a different idea.

"Why not publish an article that you've already dug for gold here, and there's nothing? You said your well driller found only specks. It'd make a good feature story, with the old rumors finally laid to rest. You proved there was no gold, so built this house on the likeliest spot. Just remove the incentive, and get on with your lives?"

Yeah, I'd forgotten she was a writer. But...

"Problem with that is, it leaves Sam's shooter still out there, unpunished, for starters." I guess I was into revenge.

No, justice.

"And I don't think that kind of diseased mind would believe us," Kay pointed out. "Maybe he'd even fly over or slip in here, see no evidence of a dig. The people who had the dude ranch before tore the place up, with sluicing and all. Wouldn't we have done some of that?"

The phone rang, and Kay got it.

"This's Blake Ingraham, Kay. Tried the ranch house, but no answer. Emily with you all? Or Harlan'll do."

"She's somewhere around here, Sheriff. Here's Harlan." She handed the phone to me, mouthed 'sheriff'.

"Mr. Ingraham. Got anything for us, I hope?"

"Not a lot, Harlan. Just that we did follow th' Jeep into Missoula. Guy drove right to this lawyer's office, Charlie Benson. Now, I did a little checkin', and he's the attorney for the dude ranch folks, and also was for the people who owned the Bujold place before. Handled the filings, stuff for both groups."

"So could he be behind this?"

"Doubt it. He's well-known around, and is prob'ly representing the folks wanta buy Emily out. Dunno if we're any closer to an answer."

"Maybe not. But I didn't tell you before—this Breckinridge's real name is Glenn Ormond, ex-husband of a friend of ours down outta Florence. She had a restraining order on him, but he slipped in, attacked her and she hadda blow his leg half away. Mean dude. Went broke with that hotel in Stevensville, couldn't be rich enough to try to buy this place. So whoever's behind this stuff's got some shady characters in it. Gotta be connected."

"I heard about that. Girl makes goat cheese, yeah. Got 'n odd name..."

"Crescent. Best friends with Kay. Everybody likes her, but the ex is trash. What kinda reputation does this lawyer have?"

"Oh, 'bout like all of 'em. Pushy, but handles a lotta big deals. Could be this Ormond's his errand boy, all right. But nothin' real here, yet."

"Guess not. Well, thanks, Sheriff. But oh, I gotta tell you, Emily's deeding our part of the place to us, and I think my hill is what the buyer really wants. You know the old gold rumors, and that the last owners next to us dug and sluiced a lot. From what I know of geology, this slope would be the logical source. Now, my well driller came up with nothing, and Sam told me the old timers had tried, too. Just nothing here. But those test holes, samples I told you about? Maybe somebody's got it in his head there's a bonanza here. Whattya think?"

"Enough to shoot a man over? Hafta be crazy, but from what you said about this Ormond, maybe we *are* dealin' with another nut here, like that last one." A pause. "But that'd put you'n Kay in his cross-hairs, Harlan, soon's he finds out about th' deed transfer, which'll be in the paper. Don't like that much."

"Well, we're tired of somebody gunning for us, Sheriff. Figure to bring this to a head if we can."

"Now don't you go playin' cop on me, Harlan. Get y'self shot, too."

"I'll be careful, I promise you. Anything we find out, we'll call you first."

"See that you do. An' if I have to, I'll have Kay hog-tie you, boy, keep you home an' outta trouble."

"She'd do it, too. Well, thanks again, sir. Be in touch." I hung up.

"Well?" from Rhys. I filled them in, but we agreed this news didn't help us much. For my part, I wanted to know more about this lawyer. *Ask the dude ranch owners about him.*

~ * ~

Sam McBryde had more of this hiding out than he could stand. Like the rest of the family, he'd felt bad about fooling people, but had gone along with it, since it'd been his idea. But it now looked like we weren't getting anywhere, after I told him what little we'd found out. I'd driven Emily home, and the three of us were having a late-night hashing-over of the facts, such as they were.

"Gotta change tactics, son, this ain't workin'."

"Okay, but where do we go next? I'll ask around about this lawyer, but don't really think that'll help."

"Well, first thing, I gotta get outta this room. I'm well now, an' got cabin fever bad. Sneakin' around at night's not cuttin' it. Thought it'd be over b'now."

"You wanta go ahead and let everybody know you're alive?" I could tell he'd thought about that, but there had to be another way.

"Maybe not, since we went to all this trouble to set this up. But if we do try to catch th' shooter, I'm one more out there lookin' for him. An' I won't be nice about it when we find him."

"I promised the sheriff—and Kay too—we'd turn it over to him if we do." I didn't like where this was going.

"Well, I didn't, Harlan. An' I'm th' one got shot. If I get him, to keep him from shootin' you, or Kay, that's legal, in anybody's book."

Well, I liked the prospect of his helping search, but not that of his being seen alive, blow this all away. Then I thought of my proposed disguise.

"You wanta disguise yourself, like I'm gonna do, not be identifiable, go on out there right in their faces?" That kinda appealed to me: fool the bastards.

"You're jokin'." And Emily looked astonished too. Maybe trying to picture her husband as somebody else.

"No, not at all. We could go anywhere, be seen by anybody, at a distance, just a coupla long-haired hippie cowboys. Maybe ride different horses, just be two hired ranch hands Emily needs here to run the place, with me off doing stonework. Besides, with everybody knowing you're dead, been dead, you couldn't *possibly* be you."

~ * ~

Charlie Benson had installed a second telephone line, given Glenn Ormond the number, to receive calls he didn't want connected to him or his law office. It rang next morning as the two were discussing details of the ranch tour. Benson nodded for his employee to pick up.

"Breckinridge." He was all business, and the lawyer again felt he'd made the right choice in hiring him. *Boy can play any role, and that's what I've needed.*

"Mr. Breckinridge," the woman began in an apologetic tone, "this is Emily McBryde. I'm afraid I've had to change my mind about selling the whole ranch."

"You have? What's happened?" Ormond felt a chill.

"Yes, I'm at the courthouse now, recording the transfer of twenty acres to my daughter and her husband, where they've built their house. I just couldn't let them sell, knowing it was just to make the rest of the place more valuable. They've put so much into it, you know."

"But your son-in-law said he wanted to relocate, and Mr. Carter reinforced that when we talked..."

"I know, and they both mean well. But the rest of the ranch is still for sale, if your employer is still interested. And I wanted you to know as soon as I decided, so you both would, well, know all the facts."

Ormond didn't know what to do with this bombshell. His first reaction was to try to talk her into keeping their prospective deal, but then he realized this could actually make things simpler for him. *In fact, it couldn't have worked out better.*

"Well, I'm sorry, ma'am, but I do understand. We'll think about the new prospect, and be back in touch very soon. Goodbye, now."

"Whatthehell was that about?"

"Old woman's decided to cut off twenty acres with the daughter's house, wants to sell just her part. Complete switch from yesterday." He spread his hands, but he was thinking this out.

"Damn! Just since you were there. What do you suppose happened? Just got cold feet?"

"What I think happened is that damn stonemason's queered our deal. I didn't like that guy the minute I met him. Got some kinda agenda of his own, I'm sure." He paused, as if a new idea had come. "But boss, this just means..."

"I know what it means. It means that meddlesome bastard's history. I don't give a damn about the rest of the ranch, Glenn, I want that mountainside and that house." His eyes glittered. "And we're gonna get it."

# Twenty-one

It had taken some persuading of wives, but the vigilante band was now prepped and on the job. Rhys, Kenny, and I—now one of two supposedly hippie ranch hands (Sam was still staying out of sight) —rode out together the next morning. Sam had gone out before daylight to circle in the opposite direction from ours, and I'd stayed mostly out of sight the day before. If he saw us, he'd ride off, not get close.

The girls had left the day before for Florence, taking Emily with them. I didn't want anybody exposed to the crazy I was sure would be out there.

All I'd told Kenny was that whoever had shot Sam was out gunning for me now, and we were gonna ambush the bastard. He laughed when he realized this new hand was me.

"Damn, Harlan, you sure fooled me. Figured you'd hired one of those beatnik fellers. Ears gave you away, though, soon's I got close. I was gonna ask you to slip me some dope."

"Not funny, Kenny."

"Jokin', of course. But that oughta make you 'bout as anonymous as a cow pie."

"You sure know how to make a guy feel important, cowboy. Now, we split up, get beyond sniper range, which is over a half mile out, and circle, spacing our paths apart, and looking sharp. We should find some sort of vehicle hidden somewhere, and a spot close, with good sight lines. I'm guessing probably that half mile max, with the way the land lays, but that'll depend on what he can see. He'll stay as far back as he can, give him time to get away after he shoots me."

"But he won't see you anywhere."

"Right, so he'll hunker down, wait. That's what the sheriff said he did last time, from signs he found, maybe several days. But it's important we catch him all set up, hang back till we're sure."

"Then what? We blast his ass? After what he did to Sam..."

"Whoever spots him has to find the rest of us. Shooter won't leave, maybe till dark, and we'll have time to call Sheriff Ingraham. He doesn't want us to take the law into our own hands, but he won't hunt for somebody might be just my imagination."

"What if he spots th' one found him? Draws down on him?"

"Then he gets his sorry ass blown all to hell," Rhys put it simply. "Self defense." *Yeah, if Sam finds him first.*

"You think this's the day?" Kenny was onboard with the plan. 'Nuff said.

"Maybe. He might've even been out yesterday, after Emily told the guy who was here she was signing over our place to us. I'm pretty sure he wants my hill, as well as me."

"Who's this guy, anyway? Slick-lookin' dude, Miss Emily said."

"Badass, but he's just hired help. If I thought he was the sniper, it'd make this simpler, but his ex says he can't hit the side of the barn."

"So we're figurin' maybe a pro."

"And dangerous as hell. Can't be too careful. They usually work alone, from what little I know, but we oughta be on the lookout for backup."

"Well," Kenny spat out a straw he'd been chewing, "I'd say let's git this roundup movin'."

Did I say I liked this guy?

We'd been riding out, and now planned our routes, at varying distances from the ranch. We agreed to meet at noon, come back in. That way, even with no activity at the place, it'd look normal again for at least an hour, while we made ourselves visible. Then we'd ride out one at a time, in different directions, just ranch business, but resume the hunt.

I really didn't think it would come to that. For some reason, I had the real conviction that we'd find our man this morning. I remembered from a psychology course in college that an obsession bred impatience, and I felt our stalker would get right to it. After all, he knew he'd maybe have several days' wait for his shot, so he'd want to get started.

~ * ~

Kay hadn't liked this plan from the first. She'd argued against it, with Moira's help, but neither of them, nor Emily, had come up with anything better. And when Harlan had put on the wig and re-entered the room, it was as a stranger. Cale and Siobhan had stared wide-eyed at this apparition, and weren't even sure after he'd spoken to them. The younger ones had cried.

So okay, they'd try this for a day or two, but no longer. Her mentioning that the empty ranch would be a giveaway had merit, so if no results, they'd have to plan something else. She plainly didn't want her husband going around with a target on his back, now that they'd set things in motion. But of course, she and Emily were in danger too. They were dealing with a maniac, after all.

Or were they overreacting, really? How much of this was paranoia? *Well, none of it, with Dad getting shot. No, this is deadly serious, and we have to do something, deal with it now, the way I had to before. Violence, killing: not supposed to happen in our civilized world.*

The women could talk of little else, there in the sky over Florence, tucked away into the Carters' hideaway. Emily was awestruck at the place, but played grandmother as if she were at home. Even with the tension that was heavy among the grownups.

"Two days," Kay insisted. "Then we change tactics. So let's put our minds on this, and see if we level heads can come up with a better way."

"To counteract the men's charging in, locked and loaded?" Moira asked.

"At least that. Maybe there's something we've overlooked, and we can get some perspective on our own." Emily was reading a storybook to the little boys. Kay focused on the distant white-capped mountains, trying to clear her head for this dilemma.

~ * ~

Sam McBryde kept his sharp eyes out not only for the suspected shooter, but for the others also. He knew this territory's every square foot, and he had some ideas where the assassin might hide. He rode purposefully, from one of these sites to the next, calculating distances, sight lines, putting himself into this man's boots, seeing through his eyes.

The others had concentrated on the rising ground beyond the highway, since that was where that other shot had come from. And on the north side beyond the river, the mountain rolled back in a hump, giving no clear visuals of the ranch unless far down, on the property itself. *Not far enough back for him to get away clean, though. An' no good spot on Bujold, either. But if th' bastard does set up close, takes everybody out, he'll have plenty time to leave, after.*

But there was a little gently rising land across the river, before it came down from the north, which could possibly afford a spot visually above the low willows and evergreens along the creeks. He rode for it, after boldly crossing the highway bridge in his disguise. No one took notice of this shaggy cowboy, hat pulled low, going about his business. He chuckled at this.

Then, ranging upriver toward the mountains, he could indeed see parts of his ranch. Not far ahead was a sort of den among rocks and bushes he'd often used as a hunting blind, a natural hiding place. He reasoned the stalker would have searched carefully for another vantage spot, different from before, but as near ideal as possible. *Sniper'll be a patient devil, take all th' time he needs, an' I'm bettin' he's there, if anywhere.*

Sam carried his scoped bolt-action 30-06 hunting rifle instead of the shorter saddle guns the others had, the 30-30s. If he found the shooter, he wanted to stay well back. *Play th' man's own game.*

~ * ~

I'd let Kenny check out the former sniper's nest across the highway, while I rode further out, with Rhys somewhere between us. We'd started our circuit at the highway beyond the dude ranch, knowing there were no good sight lines on that property. And with the tourist season starting, only a complete fool would try to set up there.

Bruno was content to amble along, giving me time to check out any and all dips in the ground, elevations behind which a man could set up. The grass was well up now, but not tall enough to hide a crouched man. The occasional stunted cedar or young pine could conceal one, so I approached each of these with the carbine out front, ready.

There was a lot of territory this far out from the ranch, and I zig-zagged, covering as much ground as I could. Maybe after lunch we'd shift our paths to take in the spaces between. I wondered just where Sam was now, with his lifetime knowledge of the place. *Probably got his likely spots picked out. Just hope he doesn't get trigger-happy if he finds the bastard first.* No, not Sam, coolest head in Montana.

~ * ~

Kenny Blair was past thirty, the typical ranch hand of the region. He'd been hot-headed as a teenager, had drunk his share of beer and been in more than his share of fights. His father, who owned a farm east toward Lincoln, had tried to work the wildness out of this son, with the long hours and toil a place like theirs required. But the boy just dug in, tackled any chore like it was something to be beaten down, and to be finished fast and hard. Which always gave him time to sneak off for some adventure with the other young bloods out for fun.

When he'd dropped out of college, Kenny had picked up odd jobs around the territory, traveled some, come home to work the farm, tried to plan a life. Hadn't happened. He liked Sam McBryde, had been a little in awe of tall Kay, but had been intrigued by that nasty cattle-killing, burning-out situation, and had actually enjoyed being part of the vigilante effort to take out the weirdos doing it.

He'd toned down his act a lot, having come very close to getting on Sheriff Ingraham's shit-list more than once on back. And he liked Harlan Kemp a lot. Guy busted ass, knew where he was going, and by damn, had got there, too. Kenny could sense the tough stonemason had surely been in his own scrapes back in Missouri growing up.

*Don't drink much, but hell, neither do I, anymore. 'Bout as good a buddy's I've ever had, come down to it. Take on th' cows, shitty weather, hard work good's any of us born to it. Man'll do to tie to.*

The former sniper's hidey hole, in a sort of depression a half-mile from the ranch, hadn't been used again, he saw. But there were others, nearer, further out, and bushy cedars come back after bush-hogging, any of which could hide a man. He walked his horse slowly, slipping up on any suspected concealment, vowing not to be detected. He was good at this, having perennially hunted stray cows that often lay in the shade, almost invisible.

~ * ~

Rhys Carter was enjoying this. Out in this still mostly-empty land, big stretches of which contained a few cows, some overgrown fields, pine groves that talked in the wind. He and Moira'd have to find themselves a piece of this, come down off the mountain, give the kids a life. *Just not too damn civilized. Don't wanta make pussies outta them. Nah, no danger of that. Cale's always gonna be a mountain man.*

*Harlan's sure done okay for himself. Got a good woman, fine house, good livin'. Like fallin' into a bed of sweet hay. Worked his ass off for it, though. Know he had a thing for Crescent, but couldn't want a finer girl than Kay. And givin' them a hand in this mess is nothin' but bein' a friend. Do th' same for us, sure.*

He noted a copse of trees, rode wide to come up on it from beyond. Cows had gathered here for shade already, but no good view of the ranch. Or from a depression further along, which did have sight lines. No beaten-down grass where a man would set up. He rode on, watchful, trying to imagine himself a shooter, now the hunter he'd always been, the stalker. *Be noon b'fore long. Guess I'll head closer, meet th' others.*

~ * ~

Sam rode higher, further out and up from the suspected hunting blind. Then he dismounted, tied his sorrel beyond hearing if the animal snorted. He started his approach, keeping low, threading a winding course that provided what cover there was. With the rocky ground, nobody mowed this slope, and the grass would soon be high. As it was, he could lie prone, work his way slowly forward, and stay hidden.

He smelled the man first: cigarette smoke. He eased sideways, up a low incline he knew would let him see into the den. *Come at it just opp'site th' way I hunted outta there.* He moved inches at a time, silently, patiently, the elk hunter slipping up on his prey.

And it was there. Within a hundred yards, a man with a tripod-set rifle, aimed at the ranch. Leaning lazily against a boulder, telltale tobacco smoke curling up, a pack nearby.

Sam settled himself, rifle extended, his scope cross-haired on the man's center mass. *Now I gotta make th' choice: take him out like th' snake he is, or slip away, bring Ingraham in, do it 'cordin' to th' law. Or...*

He knew, seeing no activity at the ranch, the man might well pack up, come back later. He'd found the ideal spot for his killing, could take out Harlan... *an' yes, by God, Kay too when she comes back!* Anytime he chose.

Anger coursed through the rancher. He had no doubt this was the man who'd shot him, would surely kill his daughter, in whatever craziness these fools were into. He weighed the situation carefully, chewed on it for long minutes. *Man looks like he's set for th' day, could stick, give me time. Or not. If he's a pro, he'll be patient, even not seein' th' boys on th' place...*

Just then, the shooter shifted his position, turning his profile, in the circle of Sam's scope. *By God, I know that bastard! That's th' one's been after buyin' th' place.* He remembered peeking out the darkened window as Glenn Ormond, aka Brent Breckinridge, left the ranch house.

And that realization decided Sam McBryde.

He steadied his rifle, then called out, *"Hey!"* The man jumped, an automatic appeared in his hand as he stood, searching for the source of the sound. Sam reacquired his target, squeezed the trigger.

Watched the man lurch, fall, knocking over his rifle.

Sam ejected the spent shell, retrieved it, waited a full minute. He knew the man was dead, but stood slowly, ready for a second shot if necessary. The shape didn't move.

Nor did it respond when Sam nudged it with his boot, rifle trained. The exit hole was a mass of torn flesh, blood saturating the ground.

Glenn Ormond, perpetual loser, killer, misfit, former playboy, rich man's failure son, wife abuser, philanderer, had reached his inevitable end.

Sam carefully picked up the fallen pistol, fired it into the ground well upslope, wiped it clean, then pressed it repeatedly into the man's hand for his fingerprints. He righted the tripod, and leaving no fingerprints of his own, aimed the Mauser again at the ranch far below. Then he surveyed the scene carefully, noting none of his footprints on the crushed grass. He picked his way toward his horse, mounted, rode away.

~ * ~

I heard the distant thunder of the rifle shot as I rode toward the ranch, and stopped to listen. Then the second shot, sharp too, but not from a rifle, and I knew that either Sam or the sniper was dead. I rode hard for the highway, then across, past the ranch house, splashed across the shallows of the river, through the screen of trees, onto the rising ground ahead.

Sam was riding toward me, his whiskered face further shielded by his low hat. I reined in, relief like a blessing inside me. We met, his face grim, and I turned Bruno and followed him to the house. Wordlessly, he dismounted, handed me the sorrel's reins, disappeared inside.

I led the horse to the barn, unsaddled him, turned him out. He headed away, so nobody would see his legs wet from the river. *Hafta explain that for my horse too.* Not two minutes before the others arrived.

"Heard a couple shots," Kenny reported, gazing across the river.

"I did too, and headed across, but then thought I'd better wait for you. Don't think there's any place that way's got a sight of much of the ranch, though. I've ridden all of that with Kay, last year or two. But I think maybe we oughta go see about that." I remounted.

"Yeah," Rhys agreed. "Sounded like a big gun, th' first one did. Maybe a sniper rifle? You point out th' way, Harlan, then we'll split up, come at it from beyond, okay?"

"Sounds right. Then whatever, we'll come on back, get fed. The women've left us chow." We headed out toward the river, the others hoping to head off the shooter, or find him still there.

I knew better.

And a half hour later, we found Glenn Ormond, in a little hidden spot I'd never seen before. Saw the rifle first, on its tripod, extended right toward the ranch house in the distance. Well, we found what was left of him. Ants and flies already there.

"Now whatthehell, Harlan? We were all across th' highway." Rhys was puzzled. Kenny chewed his ubiquitous straw, scanned the horizon.

"Well, I'd have said the sheriff, since he could guess our plan, but he's not here. Got any ideas, Kenny?" *Hafta play this out, keep Sam hidden till we can find out who's behind this. And it looks like that lawyer will be the next step.*

"Naw, but looks like somebody's done our job for us, wouldn'tcha say?"

"Dunno what to say, but guess we'll call Ingraham, let him figure it out. Does look like this scumbag had enemies. Besides us."

So we called it in, got lunch, waited for the lawmen. But before they could get there, I lost the wig, sunglasses and the torn jacket I'd been wearing. No use muddying the water.

"Heard two shots from across the river, and things being a little nervous here, we rode out. Found that guy was here, th' one tryin' to buy us out, with a sniper rifle. I'll show you." We saddled horses for the sheriff and his deputy, whose name I couldn't remember. *Billy Paul something…*

"'Course y'didn't touch anything, Harlan." Not a question.

"No, none of us did. Hit from the front, though, lotta blood. We guessed the rifle shot, probably clear through. Pistol there, which must've been the other shot, but you'll figure that out."

The scene was as we'd left it, except more flies. I'd set my Christian charity aside, had been thinking how this loser deserved this, but also that now we couldn't sweat any information outta him. I'd like to've thought he'd drawn down on Sam, got off a shot before he blasted him, but that couldn't have been the way of it, with the rifle firing first. Maybe Rhys and Kenny wouldn't remember the sequence; I sure wasn't gonna mention it.

And that might become an issue, after Sam surfaced again, but that was sometime in the future, and I wasn't about to worry over that. I couldn't help thinking, though, that Ormond's shadow boss could just send another gun after us, so how'd this help? Didn't know but what I'd have done the same as Sam, if I'd been the one to find this guy with his lethal weapon pointed. For now, though, one fewer would-be killer in the world, and how bad could that be?

Rhys left for home to send our folks back. Couldn't expect them to stay hidden forever, though we'd all still have to stay outta sight. The sheriff was puzzled, naturally, but he'd just hafta stay that way. With us across the highway, which we'd all sworn to, it looked like Ormond just had other enemies.

Oh, and eventually Ingraham, who'd actually found the rifle bullet where it'd hit the ground, with little velocity left, had done whatever they do to determine caliber. Said it was a 30-06 apparently, and he knew by then the three of us carried 30-30s. I was impressed that they could tell that from a smashed piece of lead.

Anyway, Sam was in the clear, until whenever he could be resurrected, and probably then, too. Not so me, or Kay, since we were still the obstacles to the big bad wolf's getting our place. I couldn't imagine the degree of obsession, obviously about the nonexistent gold, that drove whatever diseased mind or minds out there somewhere.

~ * ~

With what we'd discovered, Sheriff Ingraham called on lawyer Benson, with almost an accusation. This was before anyone else knew of Ormond's death.

"We know the sniper worked for you, Mr. Benson. He claimed to be representing a potential buyer for the McBryde property, and on the surface, that would appear to be you."

"No. I represent a man who wants the place, but I'm just his lawyer. And I have no earthly idea why Breckinridge would have a sniper rifle aimed at the McBryde place. Didn't even know he knew how to shoot. Must've been some sort of private grudge or something."

"You know, of course, that Sam McBryde was shot and killed a few months ago. And now we know it was by a bullet from that same rifle. And I grew up with Sam McBryde, a man without an enemy in the world, until now. Neither has Harlan Kemp.

"And we've found out a lot about this shooter; real name was Glenn Ormond. Shady guy, wife beater, habitual drunk, may even killed another student in college. He went broke a year or two ago over that hotel venture in Stevensville. And I think you knew his background when you hired him. *And* that's a very, very expensive sniper rifle. Somebody bought Ormond that gun, used him as an assassin."

"I knew nothing of the man; just hired him to do collections, run errands. My wife and I met him at that hotel, and when I heard he'd lost it, I reached out to him. Apparently a mistake on my part." Benson was cool. *Nothing to connect me with the McBryde place. Nothing at all. Ingraham's just fishing.*

"Well sir, this whole thing has grown to big proportions. Three killings connected to the McBryde ranch all told, coinciding with offers to buy the place. We're gonna dig deep here, just so you know. You've got a reputation for hard dealing, and some of this is the work of a hard man."

"Are you accusing me?"

"Take it any way you want to. Have a good day." The sheriff left.

*So, Ormond botched it this time. Somebody was watching for just what we planned, somehow got the drop on him. Ingraham didn't say just how he died, but it'll come out. Just hope he couldn't say anything to anybody before...*

*Have to rethink this whole thing. Brick wall with the Calloway deal before, and everybody bailed on it. This is a lot more serious, and most people would say I should back off, forget it.*

*But I don't back off. Not now, not ever. This has gotten personal now—old fool rancher gone, and now a hick stone guy's all that stands between that gold and me. I could hire another hit man, but that doesn't seem to be the way. They'll be on the lookout for that too, along with the sheriff.*

*No, I'll work on this, let things cool down a little. Won't do to rush into something, now Ingraham's suspicious. Too bad: I thought we had it taken care of before, but that dumb kid must've thought he'd handle it himself, maybe ingratiate himself with me? Strange.*

*And Kemp told Ormond before, he wanted to move south; wonder what changed his mind? The McBryde widow did deed the 20 acres to him and the daughter, recorded it. Trying to keep them there? But she seemed ready to sell, if I'm to believe Ormond. Something wrong, here, and it's in my way...*

# Twenty-two

Crescent took the news of Glenn's death with no outward reaction when Rhys told her. So the man who'd taken her youth, destroyed her illusions, betrayed her, stalked her, was no more. *Should I be elated? Feel remorse? Relief? Yeah, relief, that's more like it... no more wondering, fearing he'll materialize at my door again, deluded, dissipated, just plain crazy.*

"Well, thanks for stopping by, guy. How's my favorite family?"

"Okay enough, I guess. Kay and her mom have been with us last couple days, sorta hidin' out while I was helpin' Harlan patrol his place. Seems Glenn was set up in a sniper's nest, rifle aimed at the ranch. Dunno 'bout you, but I'm glad th' bastard's dead."

"No! What the hell! He was gonna shoot who? Harlan, Kay? That's insane! Omigod, I knew he was crazy, but... Oh, he might've remembered Kay putting him down that time at the market. And maybe he found out Harlan was the one knocked his lights out that time. Damn!"

"Harlan doesn't think that was it; very expensive gun, an' he was workin' for a lawyer in Missoula, th' sheriff learned. Dunno that guy, but he—we—think somebody else's behind this, Kay's dad gettin' shot, and all th' trouble her folks went through, back a couple, three years."

"Kay told me some of that... fire, cattle killed. But I don't think Glenn was even back here then. So with him gone, the threat's still out there? Wow, this is scary."

"Yeah, scary. My lady's pissed, didn't want Kay an' Emily goin' back home, but y'can't hide forever, I guess. Well, I'm headed for the big ranch. Harlan's turned some of the stonework there over to me, wants to stay home, keep watch, run their place till this settles down."

"You tell Moira I'll come up, soon's I get a break. Maggie said she'd help, give me maybe half a day. Thanks for the news, Rhys. You tell her and Eric?"

"Did. Both of 'em wanta go up, kick some major ass. So do I, but we don't know where to start." He drove away.

*Glenn dead. And in the act of shooting my friends, for sure. Coward, slimy bastard, killer. Wonder if he was the one who shot Kay's dad? Wouldn't put it past him, hired gun. Must've really hit bottom after I crippled him, gone completely off.*

*Omigod, he could've come here, in his twisted mind taken me out for revenge.* She shuddered, imagining a long-range rifle he'd learned to shoot, trained on her from somewhere beyond sight.

*Okay, put that aside for now. Absorb the fact that he's dead, then try to help some way.*

*So. I've been contemplating the rest of a life for myself, and now that evil door's slammed shut. Can go forward with whatever's ahead, a clean, blank page. But to what? Goats, cheese, the so-called good life, independence. Not what I'd envisioned it, and I'm seeing others giving up, going back to the false security of towns, apartments, warmth without endless firewood, drudgery.*

*And there'd be that drudgery in spades, with that surrender. No, I've got it all here, as near as we get in this life. I've got my craft, good neighbors, friends, and still good years ahead of me.*

*And I'm lonely as hell. The few guys I've started noticing are all losers, or married. Guess I could toss my principles, shack with the first one's not repulsive, become the local easy piece. Sorta pass myself around, become a dirty joke.*

*Get a grip on it, girl! You've been horny before, and it hasn't killed you yet. You're not a rag here, or a doormat. You're in charge still, and by damn, you'll stay that way!*

She slammed the door of the cheese shed, harder than she'd intended. *Okay, enough self-centeredness. How can I help Kay and Harlan?*

~ * ~

The Ormond shooting wouldn't leave the sheriff's mind. Hidden place, but somebody else'd found it, somebody who'd shot the man. *Or did somebody trail him? Or even go there with him? Maybe some friend of the McBrydes, knew somehow th' sniper was there? But who? Boys across th' highway, carryin' 30-30s. Sam and I used to ride that slope, back when we were kids, but I never knew of that little blind.*

*Blind. Okay, some hunter then, had maybe used that spot? Sam had a lotta friends, but unless one knew this piece of trash was maybe the one had shot him, I can't see any of them doing this. Or maybe it had nothin' to do with Sam or the place. Don't think Harlan has enemies, though, and sure not Kay or Emily. Two of 'em never stepped on any toes. Unless of course, that lawyer's behind all this.*

*And Sam's gone, so was Ormond after Emily? Or maybe Harlan and Kay? Damn, that's low-down. Harlan thinks the old gold rumors are behind this, but he knows—hell, we all do—there's nothing there.*

*Lawyer won't tell me who's after the land. Damn attorney/client privilege, but maybe th' murder investigation can trump that. Or not. Any way you look at it, th' world's better off with that Ormond gone.*

It appeared the McBrydes or the Kemps had a friend somewhere, and one who didn't screw around when it came to protecting them.

Ingraham now knew the dead sniper was also Sam's shooter, but that didn't help the still-dangerous situation any. And he saw no way to head off another attempt on the family, short of their leaving the country. Which, he was certain now, was the whole purpose of the harassment those years ago, and now. Somebody wanted them all gone, it looked like, and the prospective buyer had to be behind that. Twisted way of doing business, but maybe this was some crazy, with too much money and an obsession.

*Gettin' too old for this kinda weird stuff, I guess.*

~ * ~

Charlie Benson stared at the gold samples he'd kept from geologist Jack Samuels' digging, sluicing out. The labeled vials showed clearly the progression from the center of the dude ranch, a few specks, to heavier concentrations as the digging had approached the McBryde place. And there were even samples taken from downriver past that ranch, showing almost no color.

And while the soil Samuels had taken from the slope where Kemp had later built his house were also weak, Benson remembered the geologist had said the rich vein would be quite deep. Yes, requiring a quick and dirty dig, before any environmental agency even knew they were there. No problem, he'd insisted, for several big machines working at once to strip that slope in just a few days.

The geologist had been excited about the evidence, which had explained his willingness to be point man on the harassment to drive old McBryde out. And now that excitement was kindled again as the lawyer contemplated his next move. *No way am I giving this up. I've read enough about gold deposits myself to bolster Samuels' findings, and I know it's there. Deep. And those people don't even know it. Their well driller didn't find it, but Ormond said the well was clear down near the creek, water pumped up to the house, missed the vein entirely.*

*It's there, right under that house. Which, from what I hear, I want to live in.*

*And I know how I'll go about it this time: non-intrusive shaft, like in the old days, only camouflaged, and down as deep as necessary; dispose of the dirt there on the place, spread it a little at a time, plant grass over it. That way I can take all the time I'll need, and nobody'll know a thing about it. All I'll need is a few grunts, maybe Mexicans, cheap, and since I'll own the place, I can dig wherever and whatever I want.*

*So it's back to the original plan. May even have to take out the old lady as well as the kids. Won't sell, it's obvious, or maybe she will, just her part, but that won't get the site. Better hold off for a while though, with that hick sheriff on my case. But stonemason, you're history, just as soon as everybody's guard's down and I find the way.*

*And I will.*

Benson's wife Melissa slipped back from the crack in the door she'd watched him through. *Those damn gold samples. He doesn't think I know about them, but that must be what's got him so obsessed. He told me about the former owners of the dude ranch, how they were convinced there was a bonanza there. Guess that geologist they hired, the one who went crazy, must've found enough to've gotten all this started.*

*I just wish Charlie would agree to go for counseling with me. I've tried to bring it up, hinted at it, but he won't even hear me. I hope he doesn't get into something crazy over whatever it is. Nah, he's sharp, so I guess I'll just have to grin and bear it.*

*For a while, anyway.*

~ * ~

Kenny'd been getting a little antsy, there on the ranch, and seemed like he wanted to move on. Done that before, I learned, and this time it'd make things easier, let Sam outta the house more. I talked to him about it, and he said he kinda was ready to see more of whatever was out there. And he'd probably come on back from wherever, after he'd seen that whatever.

Sam was okay with that when I told him, and Kenny rode off into the sunset, at least for now. Sam had gotten used to the disguise, so now rode with me right out there before God and everybody, almost like old times. A lot less grumpy too, not that he'd been all that bad, at least not with me.

Along with Kay and Emily when they could, we played cowboy, and I put the stonework on the shelf till we could clear this mess up. Ormond's demise hadn't changed the equation, and it became clear I was gonna be the target now.

So we'd decided I'd go ahead and become the second hired hippie on a horse full time and let any watcher think the real me was gone on stone jobs. I did worry about Kay, and well, Emily too, if that obsessed nasty tried to take us all out.

"Be after the fight," my bride declared, and all three of them carried firepower too. Wouldn't be much protection against another sniper, though.

The sheriff helped, got the word out about the sniper, and that his men would keep patrolling the area for a possible repeat. Didn't know how much that'd help, but we appreciated it.

Bottom line was, though, if the bad guy(s) tried hard enough, we were all dead meat.

Enough to really piss me off.

~ * ~

Admittedly, I really wanted to take the lawyer Benson out, a pre-emptive strike, since I was sure he was the one behind Ormond and Sam's shooter, too. But the sheriff stopped by, told

Emily he'd almost accused the man, but hadn't made any real progress.

"He claims he's just representing the buyer, Em, and swears he doesn't know a thing about any shootings, or what Ormond might've been up to. I don't believe any of that, but the lawyer/client privilege is solid, with just our suspicions, so I'll need more to go on. And I dunno how I'll get it, unless some way we can catch him actually trying somethin'."

"And that means we have to wait for just that? Let him come after us, maybe kill one of us, before you can put him away? Something wrong with that, Blake."

"I know it. But I gotta go by th' book. Where's Harlan?"

"Out with the stock. Kenny's left, out seein' the world, though I expect him back soon's he runs out of money. It's just Harlan, Kay and me now, with this old ranch hand we've hired. And Harlan's not taking any stone jobs till this is all settled. One way or another."

"You'll make a cowboy outta him yet. Well, I'm diggin', an' will keep at it. But all of you, keep your eyes out. Man can hire another hit man, though that'd be pretty obvious, and we're watching for that. I'll see if the county lawyer knows if there's any way to force Benson to disclose his client, if there really is one." The sheriff drove away.

Emily filled us in on this conversation, which didn't get us any further along. The pressure Ingraham was putting on Benson might cause him to hold off, but on the off-chance he really wasn't the bad guy, the real one could hit us any time. Like I said, that really had me biting twenty-penny nails.

Nobody'd followed up on the offer to buy the place, surely because it no longer included our part. I was suspicious about Ormond's being the front man, since as the supposed buyer's representative, Benson shoulda been the one to make the offer, handle the deal. Why'd he sent Slick, anyway? The answer had to be that the lawyer was the real would-be buyer, our enemy, and he was still out there, free to do whatever his evil mind conjured up. And it was crystal clear to me that now he'd kill me, or both Kay and me, to get our hill, with its supposed bonanza under it.

Maybe I was just the suspicious type.

I'd thought about pushing this, going right after Benson in an Old West shootout, end it all. But I'd hafta make it self-defense first of all, and not get myself killed. Tall order, unless I could someway force him to pull a gun on me first. Risky, and did I really wanta kill anybody? Well, Kay had been forced to, and I guessed I was man enough to defend myself, too. So, I could...

*But whoa.* What if Benson really *wasn't* behind all this? What if I sort of sold my soul to the devil, and got the wrong man? I'd have to get some kinda admission out of him, and the only way to do that would be to let him know absolutely I wasn't gonna live to tell it. Sorta the last thing I'd ever hear.

Worse than risky.

But this needed resolving. I hadn't come west, worked my young butt off to get established (okay, I'd had a lotta help) to be in some greedy bastard's cross-hairs, have to look over my shoulder forever. And the woman I loved, and the son I loved, were both in danger, too.

This realization worked on me. While I rode with Sam, two shaggy dudes herding cows. While I played daddy to Cody. While I played lover to Kay. No, that wasn't playing: woman sent me up to the moon and beyond. But it got so there wasn't an hour I didn't beat myself up trying to figure a way outta this one.

I was waiting for the other shoe to drop, the bad dude to take the next step. Which I/we would then have to react to. Didn't like that much, be at a disadvantage from the get-go. Have to trust to luck, God, or just be faster and better. Wasn't that fast, and maybe not that good either.

So I'd had it with waiting, and that left only one option: go after the enemy. I was sure enough the enemy was Charlie Benson, the lawyer. Everything pointed to him. No other suspect had shown. Glenn Ormond had worked for him, no doubt at all shot Sam, had been stalking me, and Kay too.

So again, go after Benson, plain and simple. Take the initiative, hit the snake before he could bite. Again. Just go out there and do it, that pre-emptive strike, not wait to be killed. Maybe stretching the self-defense thing, but I determined to make it happen, and that cleared the air some.

I had a solid purpose now. Maybe not the best strategy, but I couldn't live with this uncertainty, this outright danger, any longer. I knew Sam couldn't, either. He was sick of this hiding, not being able to have a life, not sure when the next hit would come. I could tell he was about to do something rash, too.

But just how I'd take the guy out, I didn't know. Just that I had to do it, to protect my family, my own life. I reflected that Kay'd had to shoot the first one, then Sam had wiped Ormond out. So it was my turn now, to step up, do my part, be *the man.*

And I guessed it would be plain murder, really. Not my thing. And there was the real probability that I'd get caught, and that wasn't a nice prospect either.

So, have to do it in a way that it *would* be self-defense. That old-fashioned shoot-out? How'd I set that up? I'd hoped the enemy would come to us, like Ormond had, like the water-poisoner had, but it hadn't happened. And I was afraid Benson, or whoever, could/would just hire another gun, try again. He was o for two so far, but thought he was 50/50.

If I could somehow get him to come after me/us alone, take it into his own hands this time, maybe... But that'd mean I'd have to be able to anticipate him, stalk the stalker, and that was too long a chance. No, have to keep this in my hands, force it, make it happen.

Which again meant I had to go to the enemy. And he was no doubt planning his next move too, a carefully thought out one, alerted by Sheriff Ingraham's pushing him, almost accusing him. The lawman was an ally, but that wouldn't help in a clear case of cold killing.

My conscience kept intruding, telling me I couldn't do this, couldn't kill, couldn't descend to the level of my enemies. But my loyalty, my love, my total commitment to protecting my family overcame my scruples.

And how could I live if I waited too long, and the bastard killed my wife? No doubt he knew who she was; she wasn't disguised. And he couldn't take this place with her still in the picture, even if that's what he was hoping for.

That decided me absolutely: I *had* to kill Charlie Benson.

And not tell a soul. Kay would talk me out of it. So would Sam. And of course I couldn't go to Ingraham. I'd have to be the Lone Ranger on this, and never let Benson or anyone else know where it came from. My secret, which I'd carry to the grave.

First step would be to scout out the territory—find his office, his home, plan an ambush. Maybe rifle shot from a safe distance, quick getaway. Use another vehicle, abandon it very soon afterwards. Leave no fingerprints, no trail.

Think like an assassin.

Hell, I was just a stonemason, green kid, against an enemy who'd already shown he could hit us from anywhere. What made me think I could pull this off? Like some Western movie hero.

*Hah.*

But I did start practicing my shooting. I aimed to get to be a sniper, if that proved to be the way to go. I wasn't a bad shot, but I wanted to be deadly, from way out where I could disappear quickly. If I planned to sell my soul, and I guess I did, I wanted to be able to live to enjoy whatever kinda life that'd leave me.

First thing would be a good rifle. Regrettably, Ormond's Mauser had been impounded, locked up by the county. Sam had his 30-06, and there were four 30-30 lever actions at the ranch, but nothing really long range. And I realized I'd have to go to a distant town or otherwise cover my tracks buying the thing. I had no idea I was planning exactly what Benson/Ormond had done before; it just seemed logical.

So, how did I keep this evil plan from my bride? She'd never consent to outright murder, even the pre-emptive kind. We'd discussed just this possibility endlessly, always agreeing that self-defense would be the only possible justification for killing our enemies. But just maybe I could get Benson or whoever, to threaten me/us. Didn't wanta take that chance, though, hence my current resolve.

Because it was now the end of my dithering: I was going to kill Charlie Benson, before he could kill us. Man was deranged, obsessed, deadly, and I was now just a half-inch from blowing him all to hell.

~ * ~

I'd gotten a good look at the Mauser sniper rifle Ormond had been about to use on me/us, and when I got a chance to read up on its specs at the library, it seemed the ideal gun for my plan. Problem was, it was way out of my price range. Ditto any others I researched. And I couldn't justify any major purchase to Kay, or hope to keep it secret. Too bad I couldn't borrow that gun from the sheriff's office.

So again, new tack. I'd have to use the firepower we had, or maybe buy a small handgun, get up close to this enemy. Could maybe do that. I'd been thinking there should be a way to lure Benson away from home and office, which I now knew were one and the same. If I could somehow pose, or get somebody else to pose, as someone who could help him get our land, that should do it. Then just put holes in him.

Okay then, make it look like a robbery. Take stuff, bury it? Trying to think like a criminal.

"No." Kay looked me in the eye.

"No what?"

"No whatever you're planning on doing that'll get you killed. I know you're thinking hard about ending this... stalemate, but I don't want you risking your life. Got that?" She wasn't kidding.

And okay, I guessed I did, really. Well, at least as far as she'd know. I loved my lady, loved this whole life I'd found, and I still wasn't gonna let it get blown all to hell. So, maybe back to the drawing board?

~ * ~

Charlie Benson's wife Melissa made an appointment with a psychologist recommended by a friend. Her husband had shut her out of his life almost completely, the past months, and he wouldn't talk to her about whatever the problem was.

"He's off in a world of his own," she told the shrink. "He's even let his practice slide, misses appointments, resents my trying to help. And no, he won't hear of any sort of counseling. I'm at my wits' end, and I'm worried about him."

"Well, I can't do anything if he won't come in and talk about the situation, ma'am. But maybe if you can be more specific about his behavior, I might be able to direct you somewhat in dealing with it." He spread his hands.

"All right, then. I guess it's gotten worse since Glenn Ormond, his... assistant, I guess you'd call him, got killed a few weeks ago. You may have heard about that—some sort of shootout up on the North Fork of the Blackfoot. We'd met Glenn at a hotel he'd opened down in Stevensville, which later went bankrupt. Charlie liked him, so he hired him to handle errands, collections when deadbeats wouldn't pay child support, things like that."

"I did hear something about that. And your husband's behavior has what, gotten erratic since then?"

"I'd say more erratic. He's been shutting himself away more for years. That dinner out, down in Stevensville almost three years ago, was the last time we've gone anywhere together. I thought I'd just be patient, wait out whatever it was that was bothering him, but it's worse than ever now."

"I see. Do you know of any outside interest he's developed? Does he spend time away from home? Do you suspect another... attachment?"

"Oh, no. No, Charlie's never even looked at another woman, if that's what you're suggesting. And except for spending time with Glenn out hunting, target shooting, he hasn't ever shown any interests except his law practice. Very focused, until recently, like I said."

"So he isn't really an outdoorsman? You said they'd go out shooting..."

"And I thought that was strange, for him. I do know he bought a really expensive rifle some months ago. He didn't tell me about that, but I ran across the receipt, and actually saw the gun once when I was cleaning the office."

"So. And now his well... hunting buddy ...is gone too, and he's not going out on his own?"

"No, and something else odd too: the gun's apparently gone, now."

"Well, there's no season on just now, so I guess that's to be expected."

"Well, I catch him just staring into space, there in his office. Something's on his mind; I just know it. I've even suspected he might've learned he has maybe cancer, or heart disease or something he doesn't want to tell me about." She wrung her hands in frustration.

"Now that's a possibility. But surely you'd know if he'd been to a doctor. Unless he's hiding that from you." The psychologist actually steepled his fingers.

"I just don't know. But I did hear a little of a conversation he had with the sheriff a few days ago. I wasn't eavesdropping, but that man has a big voice, and I heard him say something about knowing Glenn worked for us, and he seemed to be accusing Charlie of something."

"Could you hear what that might have been?"

"No. I've never dug into Charlie's cases much, since we've always had a part-time secretary. So I didn't pay much attention, except that Sheriff Graham seemed ...insistent, I guess you'd say."

"That seems strange, but probably not. And surely he'd come to Ormond's employer, about that case. Well, all I can say is, you try to be there for your husband, maybe start becoming more involved in his work, let him know how valuable you are to him."

"But he shuts me out. It's almost as if he's well, *obsessed* with something. Or maybe I'm blowing this out of proportion." She seemed confused.

"Oh, I'm sure you're not doing that. You wouldn't have come to me if it hadn't become very important to you. So just keep trying to get closer to him, as I'm sure you've been doing. And I'm always here if you need me." The psychologist showed his new client out.

*Same old story: man gets so buried in his work, it leaves the wife out, and she resents it. Only this woman seems genuinely concerned for her husband. Odd that she got the impression the sheriff was pushing Benson; could he be a suspect in something? Did he and this Ormond quarrel over something? Western shootout? Surely not, this is Jimmy Carter America, and we don't do things like that anymore.*

*Do we?*

~ * ~

Obsession was exactly what this gold thing was for Charlie Benson. He was only dimly aware that he was letting his practice slip all around him. He'd depended on Ormond to handle more of the little stuff, and now it didn't seem important anyway. Well, he *had* just made work for the man, grooming him for the assassination job.

And he'd delivered: shot old McBryde right out of the saddle, literally. And it hadn't been his fault the widow had deeded away the very site with the gold under it. So yes, Ormond had taken the matter into his own hands, obviously planning to take Kemp out, and maybe his wife too, pave the way for the lawyer to realize his goal.

But now he was dead, somehow. He wondered: had Kemp been able to stalk the stalker? Or was a friend of McBryde's watching the place? Too many questions. And sitting here, staring at those vials of gold dust, wasn't getting him any closer to that treasure.

Finally, Benson realized he must have more information. He'd trusted Ormond to check out the site, handle the contacts, keep him out of the picture. But now Ingraham was on this, and anything further along couldn't be allowed to lead back to him. No more weak links. And he'd stopped looking for others to bring into the tight circle he'd planned before, with Ormond's being able to handle more than one role.

So now he'd simply have to see for himself what the situation was, and yes, it would be the soul of simplicity! He was the lawyer for the dude ranch, had supported them completely, and why couldn't he visit the place, ride around on it, enjoy himself there? And slip across to get a closer look at the stonemason's place, that house he'd heard so much about, even glimpsed through the trees that surrounded it on that slope.

*My damn slope. My damn goldmine. Even my damn house, too.*

*Mine.*

# Twenty-three

Kay argued with me to let her go next door and get on with the dude ranch stonework. But I knew she'd be just as vulnerable there as here at home. Another sniper with her in his scope sight? No. And there was the very remote possibility that one or more of the owners might just be in on some of our problem. Not that I believed that.

"You know I'm going stir-crazy here, Harlan." A statement. *Yeah, all of us, girl.*

"You think I'm not? You've suspected me of just going out and blasting that lawyer all to hell, and sure, I'm goin' crazy, trying to break out of this. So yeah, I'm stuck here too, not being able to get my hands on rocks, among other things."

"You get to ride with Dad, run the ranch with him, be on the lookout for us. And is that all bad?"

"Well, no, but being under the gun twenty-four/seven is bad, and not knowing from one minute to the next if I'm gonna lose you and everything, including my own life, is hell."

"That's what I'm saying about me. Nothing at all wrong with playing wife and mother here, but not having choices is putting a strain on all of us. I feel the walls closing in." She put her hands out, as if pushing them back.

We were at home on that Sunday afternoon, playing with Cody in our own space, about as fine a situation as I could imagine. Except for that big black shadow over us we didn't seem able to escape. And of course, I was still working on details of how I'd eliminate Charlie Benson.

"Okay, we'll both go over, see Roy and Leslie tonight, when nobody can see us, okay? At least get outta this house, visit some." Lisa'd been over, but I'd been out ranching with Sam, so missed her. And while I knew a little time with them wouldn't lift the cloud pressing down on us, I felt the need to *do somethin', even if it's wrong.*

Kay was okay with that, so after calling them, we later packed Cody up and drove the Mustang out and up the highway to the dude ranch. By then, the boys were in bed, so we talked.

"Place is hummin'," Roy told us. "Owners want that extra stonework, but they're willing to wait till you can get to it. Ever'thing okay at the place?"

"Having to cowboy more'n I bargained for, but yeah, we're on top of it. So this place is turning the corner, is it?"

"Close. They figure by next season it'll show a profit. Their lawyer called, wants to come out, spend some R and R time, but go over business too. Seems gung-ho, wants th' place to succeed much as the owners."

"So your job's secure. That's great," Kay said. "We'd hate it if the venture failed and you had to move away." Leslie was holding Cody, who was about to drowse off. They'd been girl-talking, but I'd noticed my bride catching that about the lawyer. "You know this lawyer? We've seen him here, but don't know anything about him."

"Just seen him around, time to time," she said. "Kinda intense, but that seems to be how most of them are. He's never really gone over the place much, wants to do that this time. Roy'll have to find him a gentle horse, since he told the bosses he never rides." She set Cody in his car seat, gave him a kiss.

I got the picture of Benson, our arch-enemy, poking around this ranch, and next thought was, just like those gold-seekers, he just might stray over onto our place. With a gun? Nah, that'd be too obvious. Like me, he'd hafta make any attack look like self-defense. Wouldn't he?

But well, could that possibly give me an opportunity? If he rode out alone, no matter on what business/pretense, could I somehow confront him, anger him maybe, get him to make the first move? My mind was on fire.

"Penny." my wife poked me in the ribs.

"Oh, just thinking about those rocks. Missing slammin' 'em around." To Roy, "Gonna try to maybe get another hand, with Kenny gone, get back to what I'm better at. Kay's trying hard to make a rancher outta me, but it's not takin', so far. Figure she can boss the cows while I'm doin' my thing."

"Saw that old dude you hired and another guy out with th' cows. Who's th' other one?"

"Friend of his, helpin' out a little. Can't put in much time, though." Again I marveled that even these neighbors didn't have a clue to Sam's and my identities... just two rough-looking cowboys out there punchin' cattle, anonymous.

"When's that lawyer coming?" Kay asked it like an afterthought. "Hope you won't have to ignore paying customers to babysit him, Roy."

"Tomorrow, when all the owners will be here. No, I get it he just wants me to saddle a mount for him, let him wander around after their business meeting. Don't think he'll get lost, with the trails and all. Other dudes be here too, in case he falls off his horse."

We left for home, both with spirits maybe lifted a bit, but my head was going way over the speed limit. *This could work, if I can set it up right. Be rid of that bastard once and for all, and not a trace to link it to me.*

"I know what you're thinking, Harlan," Kay put a hand on my arm. "You're afraid that lawyer has more on his mind than looking over the dude ranch, right?"

"Sure, and you are too. We'll have to keep our eyes open while he's here, make sure he doesn't do anything rash. Bet you dollars to... rocks he'll have a gun on him."

"Maybe. Pretty ballsy, though, coming after us in daylight when everybody knows he's here. Or he might have some secret plan, which scares me. Suppose he'd come with hidden reinforcements?"

"Ouch, hadn't thought of that. Y'know, girl, you always do th' heavy thinkin' for me, and I'm glad." I leaned, kissed her, trying to keep my eyes on the road. *Reinforcements, like another sniper, or just muscle. Too easy to come across the fence on foot, catch us off guard. Oh hell, he wouldn't even hafta be there: have an alibi, back at the ranch when it happens. Something like a home robbery gone bad, drifters maybe seeing our nice house up there, deciding to raid it. Well, you slimy paper-shuffler, we'll be ready for you.*

~ * ~

*Just an exploratory thing,* Charlie Benson told himself. He knew the odds of being able to confront the stonemason were nonexistent, but he had his automatic along anyway, tucked into his belt at his back, under his summer sports jacket. He aimed to be the picture of a laid-back man on a holiday at the dude ranch, just unwinding.

So he'd get a better look at that house up the slope, scout out approaches, get the lay of the place as Ormond had, before perfecting a plan. That way, there'd be no room for error: *Devil in the details.*

He drove in, took his briefcase into the now-spacious ranch house living room, where one of the owners, George White, was greeting a group of four customers. Seeing Benson, he turned them over to Leslie Kenner, who herded them to their rooms.

"Charlie," he greeted. *Damn, will they ever stop calling me by my first name?*

"George. Everybody here?" *Better be, or I'm wasting my time: need all their signatures on this.*

"Sure. Couple of us flew in to Missoula yesterday, rest just came in now. Kathy's got 'em gathered in the office. C'mon back." He led the way to the paneled room that Rhys Carter had built onto the main house since the last time Benson had been there. He took note of the fine handiwork, and remembered that Ormond had told him this craftsman had also done finish work on the Kemp house. *Place'll be a damn palace, if it's anything like this.*

He greeted the others—the Blevinses, Stones, Steins, and settled at the long conference table he knew Carter had also crafted. It was of several woods pieced tightly together, a blend he'd never seen. *People spending money like water here, and the damn place is humming. Well, I don't care now, new plan, and this'll actually help, all the activity right next door.*

But it wouldn't hurt to try to get more information about his prey. Benson handled the details of the owners' changing the dude ranch operation from a partnership to a limited liability corporation routinely, almost on autopilot, while he planned some time with the horse wrangler, Roy Kenner. He'd seen the man talking with the stonemason and his wife on former visits to the ranch, and surmised they were close.

Accordingly, all the paperwork done, forms signed, changes in the works, the lawyer sought Kenner out. He'd just turned a group of trail riders over to an assistant, a bright girl from Lincoln who helped when the dude volume got high.

"Got a gentle horse for me, Roy? *I think his name's Roy.*

"Sure do, sir. Saved one for you. This's Dolly, and she'll do anything you want, except run. She's a bit old, but really a favorite. Just likes to mosey along, give you time to see the place." He led the aging mare from her stall in the big barn.

"Good, don't wanta fall off or get swatted by a low limb." He watched Kenner saddle the horse, noting the man's efficiency, his closeness with even this plodding animal. *Prob'ly one of the reasons the place is doing so well; these people know how to hire the right workers.* He viewed the well-built outbuildings that mountain man from Florence had created, finished, restored. And the neat stone walls, flagstone paths, that arch with its climbing vines Kemp had done. *Sort of a shame that bastard's got to go, I guess, but well, that's life, rock guy. Win some, lose some, and I don't lose. Ever.*

"Sure do like this stonework, Roy. That mason still around?"

"Yes and no, sir. Since his father-in-law got shot back a while, he's stayed close, running the ranch with his wife, Kay. We're waiting till both of them can get back here, go ahead with more work the owners want. They won't settle for anybody else, now they've seen what those two can do."

"So he's a cowboy now. Big place to run, for just the two of them."

"Well, they've got one hand too, and sometimes another one, live on up 200 somewhere."

"Oh, then. Well, this is good work, all right. Okay, I want to sort of explore today, I guess you'd call it, so where should I start?" *I know damn well where to start: as close as I can get to Kemp.*

"Pick a trail. Here's the map we've marked. Last bunch is headed up toward the lake, since we've got permission to ride that land. If you wanta be alone, nobody's gone toward the McBryde place. We're working on getting the widow's okay to ride part of that, but she's not making major decisions just now. Almost sold out, I hear."

So, having played the dumb tourist, Benson rode the somnolent horse toward the rising mountain on which the Kemp house stood, in its grove of evergreens. It wasn't far beyond the property line fence, which actually cornered up against a steep rise. There was a gate on the faint trail leading up to national forest land that'd possibly let him get a view of the coveted ground.

*That must've been where Ormond set up, had sight lines to part of the ranch. But no, I believe the report said it was across the river. Well, check it out, anyway. Probably the best way to slip up on Kemp's house, from behind it.*

But as the would-be assassin Glenn Ormond had found, the rolling-back configuration of the mountain hid the new house from above at any distance. Benson, seeing this, crystallized his decision to confront Kemp on the man's own place. Just cross the fence anywhere, stalk him, kill him. Then if the wife didn't leave, he'd kill her too. That simple.

The lawyer didn't examine his motives closely, or try to determine just where or when he'd crossed the line of human decency in his obsession. He simply wanted that land, that house, and that gold, and that had become his objective, no matter the obstacles. Benson had no religion, no fear of punishment, believing that only the strongest survived, dominated, ruled. And he was thoroughly convinced that he was superior to any simple working man, especially one who wasn't even exploiting his own resources, taking advantage of the material bonanza right there under his feet.

*Some of us are just winners, Kemp, and you're not one of us. Some way you took out my man, your wife took out our geologist, so we evened the score somewhat with McBryde, and you're next. Nobody messes with Charlie Benson.* The mare Dolly plodded on as the man built this image of himself as the dominant force there, comparing himself to a mountain lion or a grizzly bear, master of any and all obstacles to his rule.

~ * ~

Sam and I had agreed to keep riding the property line in case our enemy planned to invade us. We did this at odd times, both still disguised, even knowing a determined adversary could/would scout us out, hit us when he knew we weren't on guard. Guess it just made us feel better, doing that 'something' even if it was wrong.

So it just happened I was the one who spotted the rider up past our property corner with the dude ranch, an ambling horse and unhurried rider, apparently just sightseeing. He was alone, which wasn't the way the operation worked, but okay, maybe it was one of the owners, just exploring.

I had the binoculars, so I trained them on the profile of the horseman, who didn't appear to be much of one, actually. His horse wasn't dynamic, either. The image came into focus, and I almost dropped the field glasses.

Charlie Benson, the very evil target I'd determined to eliminate. Charlie Benson, whom I'd seen a couple times at the ranch, now out riding our fence line, obviously scoping out our place. Charlie Benson, who I'd convinced myself was behind all our troubles, dangers. *Charlie Benson...*

And without realizing it, I found myself slipping closer, planning on taking him out with the 30-30 I carried. One well-placed shot, and it'd all be over. *Kill the snake before he can kill you.* I'd actually turned Bruno that way, begun a slow stalk.

But just how would I handle that outright murder? And what'd be my defense? The old prospect of spending my life in jail surfaced, away from Kay and Cody, away from... my *life*. Yeah, my conscience wasn't gonna let me do the obvious, the animal solution, the needed action, even to preserve my/our safety.

But I wasn't about to let this man just amble along, doing whatever he was doing, without learning more. I dismounted, tied my horse, slipped through the trees, the clumps of cedar, bushes, to follow from cover, see what I could.

*Could he actually climb the fence, come after us on his own, right out in the open, in daylight? When we'd least expect him. And oh crap, is he actually alone?* I peered around, fearing his out-in-the-open progress might be a diversion, a ploy to let hired guns storm my refuge undetected. *Expect the unexpected, Kemp.* My skin crawled at the idea.

I froze, but eyes ranging, binoculars focused on shadowed spots, so alert my heart pounded in my ears. Then I found myself behind a big Ponderosa, the carbine out front, actually trained on the now-receding figure sloppily staying on top of the horse. *No, Kemp, keep watching for others.*

I backed carefully, casting my eyes everywhere, hoping nobody'd gotten past me. Reached Bruno, rode quickly back to Sam's house.

"Damn lawyer Benson's riding our fence line, Sam. Wanted to shoot him outta his saddle, but no legal way to do that. What's your take on it?"

"Um. Well, no law 'gainst th' dude ranch folks' lawyer ridin' their trails, but y'say it was along our fence? That's gotta mean something."

"Like he's figuring on how he's gonna come after us. And I got the idea he mightn't be alone, might just be out in the open, a diversion so some goons could slip in here, broad daylight." I still hadn't shaken that creepy feeling, maybe of evil eyes on me.

"And the hell of it is, Harlan, we still don't know for sure he's behind all this. Evidence sure points thataway, but what if we do somethin' rash, and turns out we were wrong?"

"We're not wrong. Not a shred of any of this points to anybody else. Oh, I know we'd hafta catch him red-handed, makin' a move against us, but I can't wait for that. I'm sure you know what I mean." Image of him drawing down on that bastard Ormond. Sam'd made his decision then, and I'd have to do that too, when the time/place came.

"Here's another thought, Harlan. S'pose he's there on the Bujold place as 'n alibi, if he does have bad boys comin' our way." He was hurrying to the stables, me right behind him. He threw a saddle on the sorrel, caught up his 30-06, and we galloped for my house on the hill.

"What's the rush, guys?" Kay greeted as we hauled rein at the porch. "Bear after you?" She had Cody in her arms, and the relief I felt struck me dumb.

"Just makin' sure, girl," Sam assured her as we both caught our breath. "Harlan saw that slimy lawyer ridin' our fence, and we got to thinkin'."

"Really? Roy said he was due at the ranch today. Think he was after us somehow?" She put our son down for a nap, got us some iced tea. Worry lines in that face I couldn't live without.

I'd completely forgotten Benson was to be at a meeting there, and sure, Roy had said he wanted to ride. If you could call that riding. Danger might be the horse'd die under him. Had I almost gone over the edge? Almost allowed myself to shoot a maybe unarmed, innocent man? Right then I doubted there were lawyers like that.

"Just got spooked, hon," I explained. "Seeing him checking us out like that, maybe I jumped to the wrong conclusion. But I suspect anything that guy does, until and unless we find out he's not the bogeyman. We were both afraid he might've hired another gun to sneak up on us. And I shoulda come here first, I realize."

"'S okay, I keep my rifle at the door, out of Cody's reach. Nobody's gonna surprise me in daylight. But we need to find a way to end this."

"Not 'we' girl. You've done your part, and so've you, Sam. I'm the man on this one, only I need your ideas. And yeah, we're both tired of this ragged hippie routine.

"It lets you both get outta the house, and so far, it's worked, hasn't it?"

"Maybe, but the frustration level's going up a mile a minute. Gotta do something about this, like you said. Longer we wait, the worse it'll get. And maybe our enemy's counting on that, drive us out in the open where he can get at us easier."

"And maybe let himself be seen, provoke you more? I'm sure you thought seriously about blowing him away."

"Still thinking about doing just that. Except I don't wanta spend my life in jail, or worse. Afraid it's sort of a Hamlet thing. I know I need to take him out, but my conscience, or maybe that thing about jail, keeps me dithering."

"I'm glad. Don't want you shot, or put away. And there's gotta be a way out from under this cloud, if we could just find it." Worry lines again. Didn't like that...girl was too young for this much crap. Hell, we both were.

~ * ~

Charlie Benson had in fact clearly seen the disreputable-looking rider briefly, slipping through the trees at the property fence line. *Damn guy's guarding the place, for sure, but I got a right to be here. Just hope the bastard doesn't take a shot at me. So Kemp's hired a couple of pissed-off guys just looking for a chance to take decent people down, looks like. Well, you losers can just go back to your slums; we don't want your kind here.*

*Ah hell, doesn't matter who you are, you can't protect that man once my plan gets solidified. And I won't have a thieving one of you on that place when I own it. So go on back, tell Kemp you saw me riding the fence line, get him to wondering what I'm up to. I have no doubt now that he thinks I'm the man behind all this, and it's open warfare from now on.*

During this ride, Charlie Benson finally figured the way to remove that stonemason. It was classically simple, and not the violent way he'd envisioned from the beginning—just call him, agree on a time he could go and meet him face to face. Sounded at first like a suicide mission, but it wouldn't be. No, the lawyer would simply be upfront about wanting to buy the property, exercise his right to visit the place, make an honest offer. Of course, Kemp could refuse to see him, and might, if indeed he knew who his real enemy was.

But he couldn't know, not really. Since neither he nor the sheriff had come after him, Benson knew they had nothing but their suspicions. Which he'd allay, with this frontal action. He'd be the perfect, sincere, prospective buyer, telling Kemp the man he'd represented had backed off, and now he himself was interested, from what he'd learned about that terrific house on the mountain. Which information, after all, included the mason's telling Ormond he'd planned on moving closer to his work.

Benson turned this brash plan over in his legal mind many times, searching for flaws, red flags, any possible slip-ups. He couldn't find any, because well, there weren't any. And yes, he'd thought of the ideal way to forestall any rash action the boy might try. *Damn, Benson, should have thought of this before... mend some fences at home and set this up at the same time.*

If old man McBryde were still alive, he probably wouldn't try this at all. Crusty cowboy probably would've shot him on sight. Hell, that old man had probably thought this was still the Wild West. *Well, maybe it is, really.*

But now the kid was alone in this, and even though he held title to that part of the land, Benson was sure he'd give it up. Money was no object, with that bonanza under it.

And if he wouldn't, then Plan B would kick in.

~ * ~

Sheriff Blake Ingraham was also concerned the stonemason might take matters into his own hands, despite the real fact that he'd be in over his head. He could imagine the strain the young man was under, living day to day with the fear of another assassination attempt. *Guess I might let m'self get pushed into doin' something stupid, I was in his position. Man isn't s'posed t'hafta be on guard every minute of th' day like this.*

But he knew there was nothing he could do to stop Kemp from acting, if the situation got out of hand. It'd be a case of his having to defend himself and the family, surely, and so far the enemy, whoever he really was, had all the advantage. Kemp wasn't a killer, or even an experienced shooter, far as the sheriff knew. *Sure to get himself killed. But if he's right, Kay and Emily are targets too. Damn, wish I could head this off some way.*

The thought of that girl he'd known since she was a baby being gunned down, along with Emily, about the two finest women there were, angered him, frustrated him, almost drove him toward some outside-the-law action. If only there were some way to justify that.

So once again the lawman went over everything he knew, what he suspected, what the facts were. Maybe he'd missed something, all those other times he'd racked his brain over this.

One thing was sure: Blake Ingraham wasn't going to stand by and let these good people get hit again. Every time he thought of Sam's getting shot, the rage inside him threatened to boil over.

# Twenty-four

The call came, and it about knocked me flat. Here my archenemy actually wanted to come on my turf and confront me? Not gonna happen. But could he be legitimate? Not my enemy at all?

Of course I wouldn't consider selling our place, for any amount, and I was sure he knew this. But well, I *had* encouraged Emily to sell, saying I wanted to move, when Ormond had come that time...

Oh, hell, this hadda be some sort of scheme of Benson's, some frontal approach, cover-his-ass thing while he attacked maybe from behind. Confusing.

But on the phone he'd expressed sympathy for Emily's loss of Sam, insisted he'd known nothing of Ormond's planned assault, been the soul of oily lawyer-speak reason. Which made me suspect his motives more. And, fool that I was, I'd said okay, come on out, wanting so badly to end this, one way or another.

Kay and I mauled this around, trying to figure it. And we needed help, so we went to the ranch house to let Sam and Emily know the score.

"He's trying to pull something," Sam said flatly. "I'd have said no to you lettin' him come out, except I've about had it with this thing draggin' on: ready t'end it, one way or another." We all agreed with that, but couldn't find a way to take the next step.

"One thing for sure," Sam declared after we'd talked a while. "I'm gonna be in the next room with a loaded gun when you talk to that snake." I knew he meant it. Kay'd probably be right in there with him, too.

"So, you hear him out then, Harlan," my bride proposed, "see what this's about. Give him the benefit of the doubt, up to a point. It's just possible he's not the enemy, even though we all are sure he is. Maybe play along with him, say yeah, you'd consider selling, your work being so far away. Get him to name a price, even. Although, if he *is* behind all this nastiness, I'm afraid he'll have backup, or some other scheme. He'll try to get this place cheap, but don't let him think he can."

"Okay, so where'll that get us?"

"At least we'll get up close to him, get a better idea what kind of man he is. I don't buy for a minute he didn't know what Ormond was up to, and I'm worried, letting him in the door. But we have to do something to force this to a head."

"You know," mild-mannered Emily spoke up. "Why can't one of us just blow that bastard away, set it up like he attacked us? I mean, he's tried to kill Sam, probably was behind that meanness on back, sent his goon to shoot us down. I've had it with being nice." I did a double-take. Was this my gentle mother-in-law? *Well, her daughter wiped that other crazy out, no regrets; maybe she didn't get all her toughness from her dad.*

"Mom! You can't mean that! That's murder!"

"Yeah, it is. And it's only a miracle Sam wasn't murdered, and that you and Harlan weren't, and maybe me, too. No, I'm tired of this. Got a better idea?" That sweet face was grim. Sam looked about to hug her. So'd I.

"I'm thinking Sheriff Ingraham should be here," Kay suggested. "He could just have dropped in, friend of the family. That should keep Benson from doing anything drastic, don't you think?"

"Sure, best idea yet," I agreed. "But of course the guy won't do or say anything out of line with him here, so how'll that get us any closer to wrapping this all up?"

"I'm just thinking Benson won't be able to pull the wool over Graham's eyes, the way he might think he could yours—ours. Hey, we're just two green kids, right? No idea what this place is worth, no business background, easy prey for a slick lawyer. But not with the sheriff here."

"Are we that dumb?" I couldn't keep a grin off my face.

"He probably thinks so. Seriously, he may believe, with Dad supposedly gone, and that idea you planted with Ormond, that we might sell, that we'll go for anything. We know Ingraham's leaned on him hard, and just maybe when Benson sees we've got him, the law on our side, he'll back off." She spread her hands.

"I think he's obsessed, sure there's pure gold under us, and it's gone to his head. No, I'll never believe we're safe here as long as that shyster is on the loose. Call me paranoid."

"Try this," Sam ventured. "Get him outside to look the place over, and he maybe falls off his horse. Or loses his footing on this slope. Or falls in the big spring, drowns..."

"Or we just shoot him and all swear he drew first," Emily offered. "Or he gets hit by a stray shot from somebody shooting at tin cans. Or a ricochet."

"Okay, okay," I held up a hand. "This isn't getting us anywhere, because it just won't work. Nothing I'd like better than to blow this creep away, but let's be realistic. We can't just wipe him out. More so since there's this tiny doubt that he's the real enemy. So let's keep thinking till Friday, two days off, and maybe it'll come to one of us. Okay?"

They said they guessed that'd have to do.

~ * ~

"You keep shooting yourself in the foot," Benson had told the truck driver Tim McGilvray. The man had gotten himself in deep trouble this time, drunk, assaulting his ex-wife. And since the lawyer needed a replacement for Ormond, he'd decided to bail the man out of jail, made him an offer he couldn't refuse.

"You're that damn lawyer got after me about support payments," he'd accused, seeing Benson at the jail. "What th' hell you doin' here?"

"I'm your ticket out of here, Tim. Yeah, I got you to do what was right, and you damn well know it. But now I'm doing you a favor, and we're going to work together, or I'll see to it you spend a big part of your life in here."

*Damn smooth-talking lawyer. Like to smash his face in.* But the very real prospect of more time—a lot more time—in this place edged out the anger, distrust. A little. He'd already gotten into two fights with other inmates, and those dudes had friends in here. And knives. Maybe time to take whatever deal he could get.

"You c'n get me outta here? Really? Hey, I was just drunk, hadda go see Lisa..."

"I know all that. And I've talked to her; she's willing to drop all charges."

"No!"

*Oh, yes, for the right amount of cash, she's forgotten all about it.*

"Yes. That is, if you're open to working with me on a few jobs. Remember that guy I sent to collect for her that time?"

"Sure do. Dude put a gun to my head. I coulda taken him, wasn't for that."

"Okay, he's gone, and I need somebody better than he was. I need you, McGilvray, and I'll pay you more than your miserable trucking job." That set him back for a long space.

"Okay, why? Why'd you spring me, offer me a job? You prob'ly hate my guts."

"It's all business with me, Tim. I had to lean on you, but you did what was right with Lisa in the end, and I'm willing to forget that, give you another chance. Now, if you need time to think about it, I can come back tomorrow." He stood, turned to go.

"Hey, wait a minnit…" *Oboy, I stay in here another day, those bastards put a shiv in my ribs.* "Just tell me a little about what I'd hafta do, okay? I'm listenin'."

"All right, nothing illegal." He sat again. "You got priors, and you'd be no good to me if you got out of line, so I'll keep it above board. Collections, which you know about, some surveillance—spying—on cheating husbands, that sort of thing. You handle it okay, I'll have more responsibility for you. Ormond, that last guy, could be places I couldn't, handle some pretty important stuff for me. You could work up to that." *Like hell you could; you're a redneck through and through, but that's okay.*

"Now I know you're a tough guy, and maybe sometimes you'll have to be that way a little, but you'll have to toe the line if this is going to work. And you have to know, I'm talking to several other people on this, so I don't want to waste time if you're not on board." He stood again.

"I'm on board."

~ * ~

"Em, like I said, I'm not lettin' that boy go up against that crooked lawyer tomorrow by himself," Sam told her. "No matter how he decides to handle this, I'm gonna be backup."

"I think all of us should be. Kay and I'll be there, and you can stay hidden, but not let them out of your sight. That sound right?"

"Yeah, I guess so. But say the guy wants to look the place over, which he will, how do we handle that?"

"You'll just stay out of sight. You're supposed to be dead, remember? But you'll be able to watch. Hey, I've been thinking about this, hon, and I'm sure we can handle one shyster, all of us, right?" She gave him a kiss.

"Okay, we'll set it up that way, then. I'll ride over, tell the others." He headed for the corral.

*And Blake Ingraham is definitely going to be in on this, Sam. I know who shot that sniper, and it'll be our secret, but I don't want you doing it again, push your luck too far...*

So she made the call, told the sheriff about Benson's plan to come with an offer for the kids' place. Only she didn't tell Sam or Harlan, or even Kay. Emily was too afraid one or more of them would get hurt. Old story that motherhood is incurable, and she wasn't gonna let that happen.

"What can you do to help, Blake? I'm afraid for the kids."

"Wow. So he's comin' right up, face to face. Yeah, I don't like th' sound of that at all, Em. Okay, I can be there, so he won't try anything drastic, but that'll just mean he'll put it off, do whatever he's got planned later." He was turning this over in his mind. *An' could we be wrong about Benson? Wouldn't put a thing past a slick one like him, but just maybe...*

"I know," she went on, "but at least it'll keep them—us—safe for now. That's as far ahead as I can see. S...the kids and I'll just have to see what's next." *Almost let it slip about Sam.*

"Well, I'll come on out, keep him in my sights. Like to see that grandson, anyway." *Yeah, and I think maybe I've got th' way to force that slick lawyer out in th' open, I handle it right.*

~ * ~

So Charlie Benson had taken Tim McGilvray on, at first just giving him the grunt assignments, as he had before with Glenn Ormond. This lout was an investment, a tool to be manipulated, used. And he wouldn't even have to get into trouble, if it all went the way he'd planned it.

So the lawyer had paid his new helper well, seemed to depend on him more, groomed him for the one important task he'd ask—no, require—him to do when the time came.

And now it was time.

~ * ~

Ingraham's plan was to call Emily before the Benson meeting to tell her he couldn't be there after all. Something'd come up he couldn't miss. Then he'd make his move, get this over with. He hoped.

And if that fool tried anything inside their house, Ingraham was absolutely sure Kay McBryde would blow a hole in him, maybe from behind a door. And well, he'd just mention that idea when he called, so she'd be sure to be on guard. Either way, they'd have him cold if he moved first, or if he didn't, no harm done.

*But have to let him think he can get away with taking Harlan out, once they're away from the house, looking the place over. Don't know how he could think he'd get away with anything, but probably claim self-defense or something: set it up to look like that. Know Harlan will have a gun, and of course Benson will, too.*

*I'll just make sure the right man goes down.*

"So that's all you have to do, Tim, just pop off a few wild shots, as soon as we get well out of sight of the house. I'll have my gun on Kemp as soon as you fire, and you just get the hell out of there, fast as you can."

"That's weird, boss. Just whatthehell's this all about?"

"You don't have to know. But okay, this guy's determined to ruin me, and I'm not going to let that happen. So whatever happens to him, it won't be by the gun you use, and mine'll disappear afterwards anyway. You won't even have been there, so both of us will be in the clear. Just some crazy out there, like once before, who'll have tried to kill us both. This Kemp's mixed up with some vicious people who've already tried to take him out, so it'll just be that they succeeded."

"Then what happens?"

"Then you keep working for me, and you also cash this check for ten grand, a bonus. How's that sound?" Benson handed him the check.

"Wow! Sounding better all the time. So I won't even hafta hit the guy, then?"

"No, just make it look like a shooter's after us both. And if something should go crazy and it doesn't come off, neither of us has done anything wrong. You're gone, and I was a target, just like him. I'll tell you when and where."

It'd been several weeks since McGilvray had come to work with Benson. Weeks of those relatively easy tasks, and the pay was good. Good enough that when the lawyer'd insisted he keep paying Lisa's child support, there was plenty left over. The ex-trucker had to admit his new boss was a straight shooter, treated people right.

And if this Kemp dude was after his boss, sure he'd help. No skin off his nose what Benson did to the guy, and it sounded like he was maybe gonna take him out. That was a little heavy, but it'd mean the bucks would keep coming.

And ten big ones, wow! Get himself some new wheels with that. Yeah, and maybe a new woman, too. *To hell with you, Lisa.*

~ * ~

I can't say I wasn't nervous, with the prospect of the man who was almost surely my biggest enemy—well, really my only one—about to face me. I was sure he had some sinister plan, sort of a fallback if I refused to sell, and that was scary.

But I'd play along with him, Kay and I'd agreed, pretend that yeah, Emily'd decided to stay on at the rest of the ranch, but I really needed to be closer to my work, so what'd you have in mind, Mr. Benson? *You snake.*

We'd set it all up—Kay's Mustang was in one of the ranch barns, along with the Rover, so she'd be gone, but not really. We'd agreed with Ingraham that my lady would have her eye on us through a crack in a door, gun in hand, in case the nasty tried anything. Cody was safely at Emily's.

And if, as was likely, Benson wanted a tour of the place, I'd have my gun on me, and I'd been practicing enough that I felt sure I could be fast enough, if it came to that. He'd probably have one too, but I'd see to it he was in front of me all the way.

And I was really hoping he *would* make a bad move. Of course I'd also thought of just blowing him away, making it look like that old self-defense plan, but then I'd have to live with that. Not saying I wouldn't decide to go that route, though.

There was another possibility I had to figure. Damn guy could have backup out in the bushes somewhere, and that could get hairy. Decoy me out, shoot me down. Only Kay hadn't been about to let me go alone; she'd insisted on shadowing us, with that trusty 30-30 she was so good with. Repeat of her MO with the water poisoner that time.

*And,* Sam'd determined that he'd be out there too, cocked and primed, and having scoured the surroundings minutes beforehand. So our boy Benson would have three guns on him from the minute we stepped off my high porch, and at least two of them were in the hands of the two people who knew every inch of this place, every vantage point a backup shooter would choose. *You won't have a chance, Benson.*

The drill was, if Sam did find a sniper, he was to take him alive this time, so the sheriff could sweat him for whoever'd hired him. I had no doubt at all my father-in-law could handle this, even if he had to wing his target. *Blow the damn rifle outta his hands, maybe with part of an arm with it.*

All this had an air of unreality about it, like a bad Western, but we were cornered up against the canyon wall, and the bad guys were coming for us. And the posse wasn't gonna show up just in time, like in the movies. *We* were the cavalry here, and if it took some Montana justice to right this grade B script, the Kemp/McBryde trio were just the folks in the white hats to do it.

So it was hide and watch, with my father-in-law still with the wig, sunglasses, set to ride the logical perimeter as soon as Benson arrived. I was to stall the guy so Sam could do a complete circuit of the likely places backup would be. And if there were more than one, Sam could handle that: keep moving around his route with his gun in the first one's back. And if he/they got cute, he had no qualms about blowing assassins away. Done that before.

My nerves were on high, and so were Kay's as the time neared. Two p.m. was our high noon. I had my gun shoved into my belt in back under my un-tucked shirt, and I wasn't gonna let Benson be anywhere but in front. Kay had her rifle, and I wouldn't have wanted to be in that woman's sights. Hey, she didn't even hafta use sights: instinctive shooter. We kissed a last time as the clock's big hand almost touched twelve.

He was right on time. His yellow Mercedes slipped up the drive slowly as he gazed around, taking in our little domain. Then he stopped, got out, stretched, and damned if he didn't go around, open the passenger door.

And gallantly help his wife out.

~ * ~

"I know I've been neglecting you, Melissa," Benson had told her. "Fact is, I've been working on a surprise for you—well, for both of us, really." He looked, she thought, as smug as a cat with canary feathers scattered around.

"What kind of surprise?" *Can this be real?*

"Well, I've been thinking of making a major change, hon. This place has never been what I've wanted for us. And working with those people at the dude ranch, I've seen the next place, just up the mountain slope before the river comes down from north, and I've learned it might be for sale. But it's complicated, and I've wanted to keep the deal quiet until I was sure we could get it.

"It's twenty acres, and Brent told me the house is a real treasure, built in part by that talented carpenter who lives down near Florence, with stonework by the owner, who did such a great job at the ranch. Terrific view, close to the river." He was using his hands to illustrate.

"Wait a minute. You're thinking of buying that place? Moving up to Ovando?"

"Yes, and I'm sure you'll love it, once you see that house. I can work from there, with this new computer stuff, and the place is a paradise. It's a chance that won't come again."

"But just leave here? We don't know anybody way out there, and Ovando? There's nothing there, Charlie."

"Not far up 200 to Lincoln, and it's less than an hour to here. I want to cut down on my practice anyway, and I see this as the ideal opportunity."

"This is too much to take in, all of a sudden..." *Has he gone crazy? Has all this secretive stuff got him warped?*

"Well, let's go up, let you see the place. No need to make any decision yet, but I know you'll agree. You see, this stonemason's too far from his work, and these friends of theirs want them to go down to the Bitterroot Valley, build there, Brent found out. It'd be a win-win for all of us."

"Well, I suppose it won't hurt to go see the place. What's the house like?"

"Unbelievable, from what I hear, and have been able to see from the ranch. Heavy beamwork, big stone fireplace, raised stone foundation, and the ranch hand Roy said the interior is amazing. State of the art kitchen, layout. The perfect place for us to live, and for me to retire to. And I'm sure we can get it cheap, since the owners are anxious to move."

*And no way will that guy try anything out of line with you there, dear: you're my life insurance.*

~ * ~

So all our preparations for a shootout went out the window as the couple mounted the steps to the porch. Kay came out, greeted them as if they were *sooo* welcome, like we'd been honored by their visit. I've said my wife could charm anyone, and she did. I was shaken, but managed to be civil, held the door for them. Like I said, I'd keep this shyster in front of me all the way. Sam slipped out the back door, to get on with our plan anyway, since he didn't trust this dude any more than I did.

Benson's wife, who we learned was Melissa, was overwhelmed by our house. She couldn't stop staring at Kay's kitchen, the view out the south-facing windows, the interior stonework, the woodwork, mostly Rhys's. Benson too, was taking it in, and almost salivating. Well, why not? We'd put heart and soul in this place, and it was fine.

"This is magnificent," Melissa gushed. Her enthusiasm masked the harried look I'd noticed when they'd entered. Kay gave her one of her best smiles, played the game, showed her around. Yeah, like her husband wasn't the rattlesnake we all believed him to be. They went into Cody's room, the nursery.

I'd been looking for a bulge in Benson's light sports coat, and I'd seen it; he had a gun. But so did I. I played nice, didn't think he'd start anything with his wife and Kay there.

"Mr. Benson, glad to meet you. The folks at the dude ranch think a lot of you and the way you're handling their business." I could do bullshit too.

"Glad to meet you too, Harlan. Seen a lot of your work next door, but hadn't the time to meet you. Glad you're bringing good stonework to Montana." *Okay, standard lawyer-speak, calling me by my first name. Sure, just buddies.*

"Thanks. Hope you like the place. Kay will talk your wife's ear off about the house, and of course our kid, who's at his grandmother's now. Have a seat here. Hot outside; like a beer? Or ice tea, maybe?"

"I'm okay, thanks. Incredible house, and I couldn't get a sense of it from what my crazy former employee told me. Very impressive." He was still taking in the beamwork, the view through the south-facing glass, the big fireplace.

I sat where I'd planned, off his left side, so he had to turn his head a bit, and I took the chance he was right-handed, since most people are. I hoped I looked cool, although my heart was thumping. The thought of Kay just out of sight, showing off the rest of the house, calmed me though, and I waited for him to make his pitch.

He didn't hurry, devouring our house. Clearly wanted this place for his very own. Then he got to it.

"I rode close enough to see this house a few days ago, Harlan, and with what I'd learned, I decided I just had to try to buy you out. Breckenridge's report had me interested, and when the prospective buyer I was representing backed out, the idea grew. It's everything I've wanted in a place to retire.

"Now, you've apparently considered selling, being this far from most of your work. And since Mrs. McBryde has deeded it to you and your wife, we'll be prepared to make you a generous offer, if the land is as good as the house." He sat back, assuming that vague opening statement would make me jump on the sale? Didn't know; wasn't up on what a slick lawyer's MO was.

"That's what I told Mr. Breckenridge, yes. And we'd thought your buyer's interest was legitimate, until your employee showed up with a sniper rifle, aimed right at us. The sheriff tells us you've denied any connection with that." *Get it out there, first thing.*

That didn't faze him one bit.

"Yes, apparently the man I tried to help get back on his feet had an unsavory past. I have no idea why he'd do what he did, other than that he must've indeed been crazy. I did find out later that he'd killed another student in college, and seems to've gotten away with it. Then of course he attacked his ex-wife, and learned that was a major mistake. But that should have nothing to do with our discussing a sale."

"I suppose you're right, although my father-in-law's death shook us up a lot. Along with trouble we had here before. Well," I stood, "I suppose you and your wife will surely want to have a look around the place." I reached for my hat.

"We'd like that, certainly, but not today, I'm afraid ...short of time. We'll talk about this, and if she's on board, we'll come back in a few days for a complete tour, if that's satisfactory."

Just then Kay ushered wife Melissa back from the kitchen, and the woman was plainly in love with the house. *Yep, just two nice people paying a visit. Only one's a liar, a creep, and for all purposes, a killer.*

"I've told Harlan we'll have to come back when we have more time, dear, see the whole place. You like the house?"

"I love the house. It's such a shame you have to leave it, Kay, after all you've put into it. But I realize, with your work, this is too far from everything. Yes, Charlie, we'll have to weigh all the factors before we decide." She got her purse. As I showed them out the door, Benson's gaze swept the land.

"Twenty acres, right? Just the size place I want." He let Melissa precede him down the steps and to their car. "We'll be in touch." The wife waved as they left.

*Well, whatthehell?* Here the enemy had come right in, sat right down, tried to act civil. *But he had that gun on him. Guess though, unless he'd have shot both of us, and maybe even his wife too, he wasn't up for violence this time.*

"Okay, Harlan, have we been wrong about this guy? Wife's surely not in on anything sinister."

"I'm not fooled. I think today was just to feel us out, get us off our guard. Now he's been here, seen the lay of the land, and he'll put some kind of evil plan into action. I was ready to take him on a sightseeing tour, be ready for action of my own, but you saw that wasn't on the agenda."

"Or just not this time? You could be right: reconnoitering, planning. You really think they'll make us an offer? Or try to wipe us out?"

"Probably both. If we did decide to sell, there's no need for him to get nasty, even though it'd cost him. Guy like that's probably got plenty green stuff. I'd say he'll try the legal route first, then if we don't budge, it'll be all-out war."

"Which we were ready for, anyway. Okay, let's keep our defenses up, hope for the best. Well, I'll go get Cody, if I can pry him away from Mom." She headed for her horse, to connect with Sam, and I took the gun out of my belt, where I'd been careful not to let it show.

So, more hide and wait. And, of course, that nagging little doubt that Benson was the real bad guy. He'd done all he could to dispel that, of course, the real reason for this visit.

And I'd bet dimes to donuts he'd come alone next time. Or even arrange for my demise in the meantime. *Never, never underestimate the enemy.*

# Twenty-five

We were, of course, on the proverbial pins and needles for the next few days. Sam and I did ratchet up the scouting thing, making that our top priority, one of us always out there searching for any kind of assault.

Nothing.

Then we got the expected phone call: could the Bensons come back out, with more time to go over the entire place? Kay took the call, assured them we'd be there, and of course, come on out. *Yeah, get this over with.*

I didn't know this, but Emily had again called the sheriff, to tell him the Bensons were coming back, and she'd let him know just when. She hadn't been fooled at all by the nice people's visit, and of course Sam hadn't, either.

For his part, Ingraham had watched through binoculars the arrival and departure of the lawyer and his wife, and he too, was a bit perplexed at the seeming normality of it all. And he weighed the necessity of being there next time …couldn't waste another half-day on this if nothing was going to go bad.

*And I'm sure that's just what that lawyer wants me—all of us—to do, let our guard down so he can pull whatever he's got up his slimy sleeve. So yeah, I won't just let this go. Better to try to head it off than have to pick up the pieces afterward.*

~ * ~

So, a repeat of our whole MO, with Sam set to scout the perimeter, Kay to be backup, Cody with Emily at their place, and me all nerves, but armed, readier than ever to end this, one way or the other.

The yellow Mercedes cruised up to the house, and sure enough, Benson was alone this time. He got out, came up the steps, and I met him. Invited him in again, same drill, with my sharpshooter wife just out of sight, and Sam on his way to grab any Benson backup.

"Sorry Kay's not here, sir, and I see your wife's not, either. So I guess you and I are it, this time." *Yeah, right here on the main street in Dodge City, ready to shoot it out, Deadeye.*

"Melissa got a call from her sister, and had to go to the hospital to see her; some recurring spells she has. I'm covered up in work any other time, so decided to grab this window, come on out myself. At least I'll get to see the rest of the place. She's not really that interested in the land, but I like the idea of having a buffer against any future development."

"Oh, I'm sorry to hear that. Hope it's not serious. Okay, let's do it." I stood, put on my hat, feeling the pressure of the gun in the belt at my back.

He stood too, and I motioned him to precede me out the door. He did, again gazing the entire sweep of the land, all of which, of course, wasn't ours.

"We'll walk it then, since it's not that far. Let's go down this trail to the little creek." I let him go ahead, sure that just as soon as she could, Kay would slip around from behind the house and have us in her sights. But I tried to defuse the situation anyway, nothing to lose.

"Now, I have to tell you, sir, I was told about the possibility of a gold deposit here, just along this slope. I didn't have a lot of time for it, but I did try to follow up some trace our well driller found. Dug holes myself in the places my wife's geology studies told us were the most likely, as I could." I wanted to discourage this guy if possible, make him maybe back off?

"Oh? And did you find anything?" Casual, like this was the first he'd heard of any gold rumors.

"Just the same tiny specks the driller found. We followed up with a professional geologist before we started our house, and he assured us there's nothing here. That, of course, squares with the fact that nobody's prospected here for the hundred and fifty years the place has been settled."

*You're lying, Kemp, trying to throw me off. Don't know why you haven't really gone after the gold, or maybe you're just waiting to save up enough for that. Building this house must've set you back a lot.*

I took him past where I'd dug my silly pit, which still showed a mound of disturbed soil. Fudged some about the depth I'd gone to. He didn't seem interested. I glanced back up the slope, out of sight of the house now. *I could drop you like a sack of rocks right here, Benson, make it look like self-defense, like I've been fantasizing. So just you make a move, and I'll do it.*

But he didn't. Kept up a stream of legitimate questions about the place: how good the well was, whether I had cattle on it, how bad the drive up the mountain was in winter, stuff like that. I didn't hurry, knowing Sam was doing his thing out there in the woods and brush, also stopping often to let Kay get set up as she could.

Then I noticed a subtle change in Benson's attitude. He was looking around more, seemed tense, belying his smooth talk. Almost as if he expected something to happen. *So this is it, shithead? This where you're gonna try to take me out? Or set an ambush?* The hair on the back of my neck rose; I could imagine some shooter sighting in on me. I started to move out of a line of fire, hand on my gun. Problem was, I didn't know where that line was.

Then from off to one side where a space between trees had let underbrush thicken up, a big man lurched toward us, his hands in the air. And Sam McBryde showed tall behind him, with a rifle jammed into his back. I registered Benson's startled reaction.

"Who're you?" he managed, and I caught a quick shake of his head: he'd signaled this guy, obviously the backup shooter. *So he's gonna play the surprised innocent here.*

"Well, I'm Sam McBryde," my father-in-law drawled, pulling off the shaggy wig, "th' man your sniper didn't kill. And this clumsy bastard's just told me you hired him to help you kill Harlan." It was then I noticed blood dripping from more than one wound to the dude's head. Sam'd pistol-whipped him. *Nothin' subtle about him.*

"I don't know what you're talking about," Benson managed, but I'd seen his eyes go wide at realizing who Sam was. But he still tried to pull it off, despite his hands shaking. "I'm making a legitimate offer for this place..."

"Save it, lawyer." It was my turn to get tough. "We know you hired Ormond to shoot Sam, and to try to take me out, too. You're obsessed with the idea there's a fortune in gold here, and it's made you crazy. And I'm betting you were in on the cattle-mutilation and fire and poisoning before. So get your hands in the air, and I'll just relieve you of your gun, now."

"You've got nothing solid on me, none of you. And whatever you've beaten out of that man I've never even seen before, won't get you anywhere." He drew himself up, defiant, and I confess, I hesitated.

Then damned if he didn't go for it. Sam was behind the big guy, and Benson dropped, whipped out his gun before I could even think, let alone get my own out. *Oh, shit, I've blown it; I'm gonna die...* it was gonna be me, then Sam, and he might be quick enough.

*"Drop it, Benson!"* from my woman, stepping from cover, her saddle gun leveled at her hip. "We've had it with your stalking, and it ends *now!*" And then things started happening at warp speed.

I hadn't drawn my gun yet. Sam was still behind the big guy, who looked like he'd bolt any second. Kay was now the immediate threat, but she was a woman, and that deadly attitude that a woman wasn't tough enough to pull a trigger, must've been in Benson's mind. Along with the split second he figured he'd have before she could actually fire.

Because he dodged sideways, whirled, and his gun went from me toward Kay in a blur as he got both hands on it. But instinctively I'd already launched, a giant step, and I was in the air. Benson saw this, and the gun jerked back toward me. Then my right fist snapped his head sideways with all the momentum and force and anger I had, built up over the weeks, months of being in his sights. There was a cracking sound, and he collapsed, with my 200 pounds landing, crushing him. I rolled aside as Kay covered him, and the big dude froze again as Sam jammed the rifle harder into his back.

Benson thrashed some, then stopped moving. Benson wasn't ever gonna move again, head at that crazy angle. His neck was broken; he was dead.

*Omigod, now I've done it. Who's gonna believe our story; how'll we...*

"It's okay, Harlan," as Blake Ingraham stepped from behind Kay. "I saw all of it. And you just saved your wife's life, from that bastard. And you, Sam, you just startled me outta next year's growth, cowboy." He stepped, cuffed the big guy, then I covered the dude as the sheriff bear-hugged his old buddy. Sam just grinned. Then Ingraham took over his prisoner. I turned to Kay.

"You okay, girl?" I saw she'd gone a little white. Nerves, sure. I went to her.

"Yeah, I guess," Kay assured us. "Just a little leftover morning sickness. Meant to tell you, Harlan."

And her smile broke all over Montana.

# *Epilogue*

Seems a long time ago now, all that: green kid going out west to seek his fortune. I'd sworn to stay independent, straight-arm the whole damn world, and fell right into a bed of roses. A few thorns in there, sure, but more than worth it, way things worked out.

Little update. We're still working the ranch, the kids are long gone out into the world, and we've got grandkids. Except for Cody, who's glad he came back from roaming around after college. We're a helluva team, he and Kay hittin' the saddles right along with me.

Rhys and Moira found that piece of ground out of Florence, built a log cabin/timberframe with some help from us. Then when their kids left, they actually sold out, moved back up on top of that mountain, growing old but not really, treasuring each day up there in the sky.

Oh, and Kay did her matchmaking thing, with this far-fetched idea of pairing Kenny up with Crescent. I told her no way: he was too young for her, and he'd go roaming around the country, wasn't ready to settle down. And no way was he sharp enough for that little spritely piece of dynamite.

Wrong. He settled in on that jewel of ground with her, then they managed to buy more land off one of the big ranches, put in cattle. Happiest cowboy I ever knew, and papa to three great kids. We were all tickled to death for that girl, too—finally had herself a life. And maybe the best-loved grandma around.

Well, one of them.

Funny though: we three were all in Missoula one day, meeting up after separate errands. Ran into this guy who'd just moved there from back east, and he got all excited when he learned where we live.

"Hey," he said, eyes wide, "I hear there's a gold bonanza right about where you are, up the North Fork. You gonna dig it?"

"Already did. That's what's paying for my car collection." I pointed to my gleaming red Land Rover, Cody's BMW Z3 and Kay's sassy Mustang.

## *Meet Charles McRaven*

Charles McRaven is a former journalism professor, restoration contractor, stonemason, blacksmith, timberframer, cabin builder and minister. He and his wife Linda live in the Shenandoah Valley of Virginia.

# *Books From The Pen of*
# *Charles McRaven*

**2020**

**<u>*A Piece of Ground*</u>** - The story of a troubled pioneer veteran seeking land, a livelihood and peace.

**2021**

**<u>Troublesome Creek</u>** - Pioneer pursues lost love into Kentucky Territory wilderness, defends missionaries and remote villagers against ruthless marauders.

**<u>*A Piece of Stone*</u>** - Crusty, aging craftsman Liam McLeod drops out, retreats to a wilderness remnant to find peace. His odyssey parallels an unlikely faith journey, with pain, doubts.

**<u>*Sagebrush Treasure*</u>** - A troubled cowhand finds a home with independent ranch sisters, and must use his deadly skill to defend it and them from a scheming enemy.

**<u>*Pricking of My Thumbs*</u>** - Wesley Whitestone, gifted woman carpenter, quick with a sexist put-down or a literary quip, suddenly finds she must escape from a tangle of violence.

***<u>Tranquilla, Book 1 – Pioneers</u>*** - The story of a gifted, outstanding woman who had it all, lost much of it to prejudice and war, but defied, survived and prospered.

***<u>Tranquilla, Book 2 – No Peace</u>*** - Tranquilla's life was anything but tranquil. She was a plantation chatelaine unlike any other, living the tumultuous years before, during and after the Civil War.

***<u>Tranquilla Book 3 – Horizons</u>*** - Follow this remarkable woman's continuing journey through the ending of war, and into the bleak future it left her.

***<u>Border Crossing</u>*** - Prescient girl carpenter is 'directed' to south Texas, to follow where this leads, gets drawn into human trafficking web. Forms unlikely partnership with undercover agent.

## *Dear reader,*

I hope you've enjoyed reading another of my adventure stories..

Your opinion is valuable to other
readers like you,
who may be looking for books like mine.

Please consider taking a few minutes to post a review,
however brief,
on the site where you purchased this book
or on the Wings ePress web page.

You may also want to visit my author page
at the Wings' website where you can find the titles and brief
descriptions of the other books I've written.

Thank you!

Charles McRaven